WAVE OF LIGHT
DARK WORLD TRILOGY
BOOK THREE

AMARAH CALDERINI

This is a work of fiction. All of the characters, organizations, places, and events portrayed in this novel are either the products of the author's imagination or used fictitiously.

WAVE OF LIGHT
Copyright © 2023 by Amarah Calderini

All rights reserved.
No part of this book may be reproduced in any form or by any electronic or mechanical means, including information storage and retrieval systems, without written permission from the author, except for the use of brief quotations in a book review.

Cover Artwork and Design: Sarah Hansen of Okay Creations
Interior Formatting: Tiarra Blandin
Editorial: Tiarra Blandin of Allotrope Editorial

To Jas—my home.

*And to anyone still looking for theirs.
I see you. You've found it here.*

PROLOGUE

"You must keep up Aurelius."

Iara's hair streams after her like a ribbon of spun gold, and her fine dress is bunched around the tops of her thighs as she races across the cliff top. The world is different in this memory, older and lighter, but the crash of the sea is the same. And so is the way her laughter sounds like summer grass drenched in sunlight; the way it effervesces in my chest, somewhere near my heart.

"Surely you've grown faster since we were children with those long legs of yours," she says, throwing a pointed look over her shoulder. My face grows hot. "Unless you haven't quite figured out what to do with them yet?"

Now, I laugh too, and use my long stride to easily pull up beside her. Iara has always been faster than me, and though I now tower over her, it has simply become habit to let her lead, the shape of her a beacon to follow.

She turns her head and her brown eyes glow with mischief, the color of warmed cocoa. Too late, I realize her intent.

"Iara, you can't mean to—"

But my words are lost in the morning air as she leaps from the cliff with a squeal of delight, skirts swirling around her like an ethereal cloud. My heart hurtles into my throat, and I mutter a fervent curse, because wherever Iara goes, I must go, as well.

It has long since stopped being a decision and become more of an inevitability. We've been inseparable since we were children, never one far from the other. And at some point, Iara's presence changed my very shape: my hand always stretched for hers, my laugh responding to her voice, my heart a malleable thing that only felt solid when she was near. But just as she had embedded herself into my very bones, so had a burgeoning fear.

Fear that Iara, who has always shone so brilliantly and traveled so fearlessly, would someday go where I cannot follow. That someday she would be gone, and I would be left misshapen and alone.

So, without hesitation, I leap over the sea cliff and sprawl out into the open air. My stomach lunges up into my ribs, and my feet flail in a moment of panic before I hit the water far less gracefully than she does.

As a water-wielder, she never has to worry about drowning, but as my clothes begin to log down, their heavy fabric pulling me toward the inky depths, my own panic surges. I, as a powerless, unremarkable man, am entirely capable of drowning.

I splash wildly, struggling to keep my head above the crashing waves. Iara surfaces a few feet from me, bobbing calmly and blinking at me through sodden lashes. With a flick of her hand, the waves circle around me, lifting me up and carrying me to the rocky shore. I sputter and spit, my mouth gritty with sea salt and sand as I shake my head, attempting to clear my eyes of water. Iara climbs out after me, hair now plastered down her back in streaming yellow ropes.

I have seen Iara every day since I was five years old, and still, her beauty is one of surprise. Much like the sea itself, it rises up to ensnare me every time it catches me unaware. It does so now, feeling like a punch to the chest, as I take in the cling of her dress and the rosy flush staining her cheeks.

She smiles and the punch becomes an explosion, one that threatens to shatter my ribs.

"Don't be so fearful, Aurelius. The world is ours for the taking."

CHAPTER
ONE

Mirren

I wake with a jolt, my heartbeat frantic against my ribs. Sweat plasters thick tendrils of hair to my forehead, and I swipe at them wildly in an attempt to soothe the rising panic in my chest.

It was only a dream.

And yet, I can still feel the edges of it even in waking, somehow trapped beneath a blinding fog of feelings the dream conjured. In the weeks since magic returned, my dreams have become increasingly vivid, as if the old gods themselves reach through death to haunt me with images of a past I have no claim to. It's become more difficult to pull myself from them, to find my way back to reality.

I breathe deeply, the air of the quarterage as sterile as always, willing the dream to fade until all that remains are a few wisps of memory.

A seaside cliff. Golden hair. And a hungering *want* that felt endless.

Fisting my fingers into the sheets beside me, my heart wrenches as I discover they are long cold.

Anrai has been plagued by dreams as well, but they're of a different sort. Nightmares of blood and burning, of the destruction wreaked at his own hand, drive him from bed every morning long before dawn. And that's if he can sleep at all.

Rolling from bed, I wrap his cloak around my shoulders and shove my feet haphazardly into my boots without bothering to tie them. I ease the bedroom door open carefully. The sun has only just begun to peek over the horizon, and it wouldn't be kind to wake Max and Cal at this hour. In the weeks we've been camped in Similis, our days have been filled from the moment we wake until night falls. Helping Sectors dig their belongings out of piles of rubble. Organizing aid for those in need. Training the willing Community members to protect themselves now that their Covinus has left them to the whims of the Dark World.

The work never seems to end, especially since the Community labor force has been cut in half. There are still those who cower in the Covinus building and refuse to adapt to life without the Boundary. After endless discussions and mindless hours of negotiations, little progress has been made, even as they watch their fellow Community members suffer without the medical care locked inside the building.

I pad down the hallway and through the front door. The streets are quiet, the silence eerily pervasive. Though its people have always been muted, Similis itself was never so still. There was always the buzz of the lights, the metallic whir of our factories, the rumble of Covinus vehicles. But since the collapse of the Boundary, and with it, the outage of everything electric, the city has existed in a thick hush.

I wander slowly through our Sector and into the fields beyond without meeting a single person. Even without the

Covinus to enforce the Keys, the Similians follow the familiar patterns of their previous lives. Curfew and work schedules are still adhered to, and laughter is still exceedingly rare within the confines of the city. Patterns wound into their souls since birth are not so easily unraveled.

Their ability to work together in spite of everything will serve them well in the coming months. The air is cold, biting at my nose and bare legs, a sign that winter's first snow will arrive within the month. In my life before Ferusa, I was always oddly comforted by the ice season. Snow was the only beauty I was ever able to witness, and I looked forward to the way it transformed everything that was normally sterile and uniform, into a soft, sparkling place of magic.

But I'd had the privilege of heat then. Of machines to harvest our crops and produce our clothes.

Now, the ice season is edged with desperation for many.

When I reach the edge of the agricultural field, my breath hitches sharply. What remains of the Boundary towers above me in the misty night air, and out of habit, I embrace myself for the horrible feel of it, like it will pull me beneath its desiccated thrall at any moment. But there is no feeling, no sound, nothing other than the puff of steam escaping my lips with each of my breaths.

Even the stone itself now appears ordinary, like it was only the magic imbuing it that caused its once odd appearance. The rubble is piled higher than the Covinus building, and even weeks later, the destruction still manages to steal my breath. The first few times I gazed at it left me feeling absurdly unmoored, proof of time's ability to ravage even in the most infinite of things.

I slip through a small opening between two particularly large chunks of rock, the tunnel compact and cleverly hidden to any who are ignorant of its existence, and out the other side. The Nemoran rises up before me, the damp smell of leaves permeating the chilled air.

Anrai is only a few strides inside the trees.

Though I can't see his face from this distance, I know him by the elegant grace of his movements as he works through his training exercises. Despite the cold, he's shed his shirt, leaving his arms and chest bared to the elements. His muscles extend and ripple with a mesmerizing grace, his abdomen contracting and bending with fluid power. Though he hasn't regained all the bulk he lost during his recovery, his newfound thinness only serves to accentuate every hard ridge of him.

He hears me long before I arrive, turning to meet my gaze with a grin already tugging at his mouth. "You're supposed to be asleep," he says, pulling me into his arms with an ease I'll never get accustomed to. Like I was born to fit in the space inside them. His warmth sinks beneath my skin, and his scent of a campfire in the first snow envelopes me. As I breathe him in, the last of the dream's disquiet evaporates into the early morning air.

"I needed you." My voice is muffled against his chest, my nose pressed into his sternum as he dips his hands inside my cloak and runs them up the length of my bare arms. Shivers erupt in the wake of his touch, and I burrow deeper into him.

"Ah, Lemming," he whispers, taking my chin between his fingers, and tilting it upward until I meet his gaze. Glacial blue, even in the dark of the Nemoran, and glittering with the promise of flame. "I always need you."

Anrai brushes his lips against mine, gently at first, as if we have all the time in the world. As if the beasts of the forest don't howl around us—as if the beasts of the world don't rage on all sides. I whimper needily, and he smiles against my mouth before moving deeper, sweeping his tongue deliciously along the edge of mine.

That's all it takes to ignite the fire that burns inside me at all hours, the flame of his soul and mine, entwined. I grip his bare shoulders, his skin searing hot beneath my fingertips as I tug him closer. He responds in kind, his long fingers coming around my waist, his chest moving with ragged breaths. The rapid rhythm of his heartbeat thrums beneath his scar, and I wonder if I'll ever tire of the heady power that fills me every time Anrai is under my thrall.

Before I can consider it further, he pulls back with a groan. His breaths are almost pained as he rests his forehead against mine, lashes a dark sweep against his cheek as he struggles to gather himself. At my questioning look, he mutters, "This may be my wholesome soul talking, but we can't do this in present company."

I rear back in alarm, my eyes whirling to the forest.

But everything appears still. All I detect is the presence of the trees, their unnatural weight pressing into me and tugging at my power.

A smile that settles somewhere between amusement and annoyance twitches at the corner of Anrai's mouth. A mouth I want to take beneath mine once more, until we are only skin against skin, and neither of us can remember the haunt of dreams. "The hellion followed me here."

Ah.

Peering between the trees, my stomach leaps as I realize there are indeed a pair of dark eyes staring back. "How long has he been out here?"

Anrai shrugs. Though his words indicated a clear intention to cease relations, his hands appear to have other ideas. He presses his fingertips into my hip bones with leashed possession, like his self-control may snap at any moment and he'll yank me closer. "As long as I've been. I don't think the boy sleeps."

Neither do you, I want to say. But instead, I hit him in the arm. "Anrai, he doesn't even have a coat on!"

Again, he shrugs, this time rather sheepishly. "He's eight. Don't eight-year-old's have enough sense to bring a cloak when it's cold?"

I roll my eyes. "Eight-year-old boys have even less sense than twenty-one-year-old men, if it's possible."

Anrai grins. "Point taken." He calls over his shoulder, "Helias, you may as well come out. The woman thinks you're apt to freeze to death over there."

The little earth-wielder steps out from behind the tree, a dark curl flopping in front of his eyes. His impish face is perpetually serious, even as he swipes at the errant tendril and sets me with a baleful look. "I'm not cold," he says obstinately, before swinging an accusing gaze to Anrai. "*He* doesn't even have a shirt on."

I tamp down a laugh. "*He* has fire magic and burns hotter than the sun." I tilt my head with a tut, and shed my own cloak, holding it out toward Helias. He watches it like it's something slimy, even as goosebumps rise on his skinny arms. I look to Anrai for help.

He signs in resignation, and without looking at the boy, barks, "Put the cloak on, hellion. You'll catch your death out here, and I don't want to have to go searching for another earth-wielder."

Helias immediately takes the cloak. The hem drags through pine needles and dirt as he pulls it around his small body, never taking his reverent gaze from Anrai.

The day we'd found him curled up in the middle of his own destruction, the ground had shaken violently in time with his screams, and the earth itself had risen up to protect him. Helias' father had been killed with the deserters, pinned to the wall of their quarterage by the Covinus, and his mother had been killed during the Dark Militia occupation. The Community around him watched his power with horror and suspicion, like his rage was contagious.

Helias was entirely alone, and the buildings around him began to crumble beneath the onslaught of his terror.

Until Anrai had walked slowly through the debris and kneeled down next to the boy. And when he whispered, Helias had listened. Maybe because Anrai knew the cost of everything Helias had lost, knew the burn of his anger and fear so intimately.

At the time, Anrai had hardly been able to stand beneath the weight of his soul. But when the earth finally settled and Helias curled into his arms, he'd picked the boy up like there was no pain and carried him back to the quarterage.

Since then, the little earth-wielder rarely leaves Anrai's side, much to the latter's bewilderment.

The hair on my arms raises as a Ditya wolf howls in the distance, followed by the yapping reply of its pack. Anrai glances east where the sky has begun to lighten on the horizon. "I'm just about finished here. Why don't we see if we can convince Cal to make us some hotcakes?" he says to Helias, ruffling the boy's hair gently.

While the little boy doesn't smile—he never does—his face lights at the suggestion. He nods enthusiastically and more inky black curls tumble over his eyes.

"Lead the way, hellion."

The boy hops ahead of us, his arms bouncing up at his sides like unruly bird wings. Anrai watches him streak toward the Boundary with something between relief and trepidation as we trail behind slowly.

"If he insists on being out here every morning, why don't you at least let him join you?" Though my voice is mild, the suggestion cuts through the air like a whip.

Anrai stiffens beside me, his fingers stretching wide before curling back into his palm. "I've told you. He shouldn't be around someone like me."

I furrow my brow. "Someone like you? You mean the kind-hearted man who comforts him every time he has a bad dream?"

Anrai glares at me sidelong, before rolling his gaze back to the tunnel in the Boundary rubble Helias just disappeared through. "You know what I mean, Lemming. He's only a child. He should have someone good to look up to." His jaw tightens, and I know he's thinking of Denver. What he meant to Anrai as a lost boy.

With a shake of his head, he pushes a sharp breath through his teeth. "His Community is already suspicious of him. He certainly doesn't need to be hanging around the man the entire continent hates. And rightfully so."

He doesn't say it mournfully, only as fact, but it turns my stomach all the same. Anrai has decided to do the work of living, but the weight of his shame hasn't eased. All the atrocities he committed while under his father's command press in on him every day, and sometimes, the dark heft of it still threatens to overtake him entirely.

It's why he doesn't sleep; why, when I look over at him, sometimes he is somewhere far from me, buried beneath black stone and horror.

But still, he fights. I can ask no more of him than that.

We duck through the Boundary and emerge into the empty field on the other side. Helias bounds through the remnants of the harvested cornstalks, twirling and kicking at the dirt like Anrai does in his morning routine, but with far less finesse. "Why don't you train him? If he's going to grow up without a Boundary, even you have to admit training would be wise."

Anrai makes a noise somewhere between a scoff and a bitter laugh. "I don't know anything about training a child." His eyes wander from me back to Helias, who's now taken to rolling through the dirt.

"You trained Cal."

"Cal was a teenager, and really gave me no choice in the matter," he mutters. "I know nothing about children, even when I was one. I was trained with broken bones and whips, with no choice but to learn if I wanted the pain to stop."

Tell me, I want to say. *Tell me all your pain. If you give it to me, it will be lighter. It won't hurt you so much.*

"Anyway," he continues with a sigh, "Cal's the one who's been running the Similian training sessions. I'm sure he has far better methods. Darkness knows, even Max would probably be a better teacher."

I take his hand, and he stops to face me, his wariness palpable. Like he's waiting for me to tell him he's right and Helias deserves better. Or waiting for me to tell him he's wrong, and to get out of his own head. "Helias doesn't want Cal or Max. He wants *you*. Exactly as you are."

Anrai's mouth tightens, but he doesn't argue, even as something akin to grief washes over him.

"He chose you because something inside you speaks to him. He probably doesn't even know exactly what it is, just that you are kindred spirits. He doesn't need you to be anything but yourself. He just needs *you*."

His hand tightens in my grasp, before relaxing once more. "I'll think about it," he concedes.

I try to tamp down my victorious smile, but Anrai sees it anyway, and tugs me to his chest. "Ah, Lemming. For someone who claims to hate my arrogance, you sure look smug when you win."

My grin breaks out into the open. "Only with you. It feels like the first time, every time."

His eyes darken, and his tongue darts out to sweep his lower lip. And when he catches me tracing the path with greedy eyes, his own smile slides over his face, the bespoken arrogance somehow infuriatingly tempting. "Hmm," he drawls, tilting his head. "It seems there are quite a few things that feel like the first time, every time."

I clench my thighs together as his words spark through me. A small, discreet movement, but nothing escapes Anrai, and his grin turns wicked. "So which is better, Lemming?" His tone is casual, innocent, even as his hands begin to move again, palms a hot brand along the thin material of my nightgown. "When you best me in an argument?"

Helias tumbles through the dirt a few yards away, so Anrai leans in close, his breath a whispered breeze against my throat. "Or when I best you, and make you come apart?"

I tilt my head, pretending to consider, even as wanton heat pools at my center. "That's a tough choice," I muse, tapping my finger against my lip.

Anrai's gaze flares as he watches the motion, and the low rasp of his voice rolls through me like a caress when he replies, "It didn't seem like such a tough choice when my tongue was buried inside you last night."

Images of the night prior flood through me, and his face lights in victory. My skin flushes as I remember his head between my legs while the salted taste of him filled my mouth. For a wild moment, I consider pushing him up against the nearest quarterage and allowing him to win. But instead, I shrug with casualty, even as my blood pulses. "As talented as your tongue is, there is no feeling that compares to defeating it."

A loud guffaw of laughter erupts from him, and his eyes glint at my challenge. "Later, Mirren, and you'll be eating your words." A threat and a promise that has the most reckless side of me hoping later comes soon.

Anrai pulls me into his side with another laugh, and together we follow Helias back to the quarterage. As Jakoby and Farrah have holed themselves up with the faction inside the Covinus building, we've been staying in my old home. When we duck through the door, Max sits at the table with an alarming assortment of weapons spread before her. The sight elicits an absurd giggle from me, as I imagine the look on Farrah's face if she could see what's become of her kitchen.

Helias has already taken Anrai's suggestion of waking Cal, evidenced by the loud grumbles echoing from his room. After a moment, he emerges, rubbing at his remaining eye as Helias tugs him into the kitchen. The earth-wielder may not have taken to Cal as he has to Anrai, but he's certainly taken to Cal's cooking. As someone who grew up with Similian food, I can hardly blame him.

Copper hair sticking straight up, Cal is bare-chested, a pair of loose gray pants slung low on his hips. He slumps into the kitchen with a pithy glare at the three of us, as Anrai and I take seats across from Max. "And I suppose none of *you* are capable of making the little urchin breakfast?" he snipes groggily, tugging on the embroidered patch he wears over his injured eye.

Max doesn't bother to look up from her whetstone.

"Just because Mirren and I are women, doesn't mean we should be the ones who cook, Cal. I thought you more enlightened than that."

"I wasn't—I didn't mean—" Cal scrunches up his face in frustration, pushing a loud breath through his teeth. "Anni's sitting there, too!" When Max only sets him with a bored gaze, he throws up his hands with a sigh of conceit. "Fine! But I'm only doing it because Mirren's Similian cooking is bland as hell, and you two both burn everything you touch."

"Hey!" Anrai protests indignantly.

Max shrugs as her attention returns to her swords. "It's true, Shaw. And you can't even blame the fire magic because your cooking was terrible long before you had it." She tilts her head thoughtfully. "Come to think of it, dinner was probably the first thing you ever burned."

I laugh loudly. Anrai slumps back in his chair and crosses his arms over his chest as he eyes Max. "I always hear about how delicious the food in Tahi is, but apparently I've befriended the one islander who didn't inherit their discerning tastes."

Max flips him off with a disarming smile, as the sounds of Cal moving around the kitchen begin to fill the quarterage. The three of them continue to trade barbs, occasionally dragging me into the fray, and as our laughter grows louder with each passing moment, so does the airy feeling in my chest. This quarterage, with its gray walls and sterile floors, has always been shaped like the emptiness of my heart. But now, with Anrai's smile, with Cal and Max's warmth, it feels full.

The door to the quarterage opens, and a crisp breeze sweeps through the room as Avedis and Harlan step over the threshold.

"Godsdammit, Avedis!" Cal huffs from the kitchen. "I just got this stove lit!"

The assassin looks entirely unapologetic as he slinks into the room and tosses a few errant weapons atop Max's heaping pile. He drops into the remaining chair, his hulking frame threatening to reduce the spindled legs to splinters at any moment. "I had so hoped to hear you say that Calloway, for that is exactly why I'm here." Avedis furrows his brow in disgust. "I cannot bear one more meal of Similian cooking. The lemmings seem to be offended by the very *idea* of seasoning."

As the quarterage is filled to bursting as it is, Avedis has been staying with Harlan for the time being. "I'm sorry my cooking isn't to your taste," Harlan says, shedding his overcoat and hanging it neatly on the hook near the door. Though his hair is Ferusian in length and his golden skin is still sun-kissed by travel, he's now back in a khaki Similian suit. I haven't determined whether it's because he's more comfortable, or because dressing as a Similian helps him appear relatable to them. Harlan has been the one to convince the Community to accept the Ferusians' help and shore up their defenses; to train; to adjust to life in the Darkness. And those outside the Covinus building have listened because Harlan has always embodied the best of the Keys.

"Knock off the apologizing, Goldie," Max bites out. "If Blood-Thirsty over here doesn't like your cooking, he doesn't have to eat."

Avedis presses a hand dramatically to his heart. "You wound me, dear Maxwell. I thought we were becoming the best of friends."

Harlan's gaze snaps between the two of them, torn between being offended on Avedis' behalf or bursting into laughter. After a hesitant moment, he shakes his head in defeat, and joins Cal in the kitchen.

Max raises a haughty eyebrow at the assassin. "I don't know what you mean. I've always hated you with the same level of enthusiasm." She fluffs her hair and gazes down at her perfectly shaped nails. "I'm nothing if not consistent."

"That you are, Maxi," Anrai replies with a laugh, tossing Avedis a whetstone. The assassin snatches it deftly from the air as Anrai goes on, "The longer you're around, the more her hatred will begin to feel like love."

Max rolls her eyes, but doesn't argue his point, turning instead to pluck another dagger from the pile.

Anrai nods to Helias, who's been skulking behind the table, eyeing the weapons and Anrai with curiosity. "Come here, hellion," Anrai says with a resigned sigh. "I'll show you how to care for your blade."

I press my lips together to keep from smiling as Anrai glances up at me with a twinkle in his eye, daring me to comment. I arrange my expression into a one of innocence as Helias eagerly jumps into Anrai's lap. He fixes his dark gaze reverently on every small motion, determined to commit each one to memory, as Anrai patiently demonstrates how to oil the small blade.

A knife skids loudly across the countertop, snapping my attention from the tender scene unfolding at the table, to Cal, who is now waving his arms in the air looking apoplectic. "Is that how they teach you lemmings to chop? You're liable to take off all your fingers and probably half on mine if you keep going like that," he tells Harlan, but there's no rancor in his voice. Only teasing adoration. "Here. Let me show you."

Cal moves behind Harlan, his chest pressed up against Harlan's back as Cal snakes his arms around him and curls his fingers over Harlan's to grip the knife. "Stance matters. Just like with a sword."

After a brief hesitation, Harlan relaxes into Cal. The tips of his ears turn pink as he allows Cal to lead the blade, the small smile on his face bringing one to my own. So much darkness exists in the world, so much more to be done, but in small moments like these, I can't help but be thankful. For the peace I've found in the turmoil.

The warmth in my chest is just as quickly swallowed by ice as my gaze travels to the boy standing in the hallway, frozen midstride.

Easton.

Usually, my brother leaves to assist with the rebuild efforts early enough to avoid us all, but today, he must have slept in. His mouth is fixed in a tight line, and his gaze is hard as it homes in on the bare skin of Cal's chest; on the intimacy of their position. Something like guilt winds around my ribs, though I have no ownership of it.

Harlan's relationship with my brother, or with Cal, is none of my business. And yet, there exists a gaping chasm between Easton and I, one I've covered with the vines of my guilt and my worry, until they've become so tangled, it's hard to tell whose hurt is responsible. He blames me for upending his entire existence but is grateful I'm home. I blame him for leaving me alone but am thankful we're together.

I want to protect him, and I want to punish him.

Easton's mouth presses tighter as his eyes trail from Cal and Harlan to the pile of weapons sitting on the dinner table. His disapproval only grows as he takes in Anrai and Avedis, and when those hazel eyes finally snag on me, my skin turns cold beneath them.

"Good morning, Easton." I try and fail to keep my voice light.

Abruptly, the merriment of the quarterage dies as everyone notices my brother's presence, the silence as deafening as when we grew up here. My brother swallows, his face working as he struggles to school his features into Similian contentment. He doesn't quite manage, settling somewhere between cool indifference and outright dislike. "Good morning, Mirren." He nods stiffly to Cal and Harlan. "Morning."

Cal doesn't reply. Only steps away from Harlan with the smooth grace of a cat and busies himself with plating Helias' hotcakes.

Harlan gives Easton a weak smile. "Good morning. I didn't realize you were still sleeping, or we would have been quieter."

Easton swallows again, this time so hard he may as well be swallowing a pile of nails. "The meetings with the Covinus faction went longer than expected. I didn't get in until late last night and must have slept through my alarm."

"That must mean they've decided to at least listen," Harlan replies hopefully.

Until now, the faction inside the Covinus building has refused all attempts at negotiations by those living on the outside, Harlan's parents among them. From the little he's mentioned of them, their decision to leave him to the outside world hadn't been a surprise as they'd been the ones to turn him in for his relationship with Easton. And though Harlan doesn't wallow in his misfortune, I know their continued refusal stings.

"They've done more than that," Easton says, stuffing

his hands into the pockets of his jumpsuit. "They're willing to work together."

My heart leaps. "Easton, that's wonderful they've agreed to work with us!"

A muscle jumps in his jaw, and when his eyes refuse to meet mine, I immediately understand my mistake. They have not agreed to work with us, because there is no *us*. There are Similians on the inside and those on the outside. The Boundary may have fallen, but a divide still exists in the marrow of the Community. There is no room here for anything different.

And though my brother has refrained from speaking the words aloud, it lines every polite greeting and every strained interaction between us: Easton is one of them. I am not.

"Their agreeance comes with conditions," he continues. His fingers twist in his pockets, and the dread unspooling in my stomach ratchets up to my throat. Easton rarely fidgets.

Anrai must sense the hesitation in my brother as well. He straightens in his chair, his eyes narrowing in assessment. Assessment of a threat. While he has never been outrightly rude to Easton, neither has he warmed to him, always keeping a healthy barrier of indifference between them. I'd thought it was to protect Easton, but suddenly, I see it for what it truly is—protecting *us* from him.

"They will work with us only if anyone who is not a Community member leaves Similis." Easton finally raises his gaze to mine, and though his hazel eyes swirl with emotion, I can't decipher their nature. And then he says, "And anyone with magic is not permitted to be a Community member."

CHAPTER TWO

Shaw

There are times life would be far simpler without a soul. Times like now, when hurt and confusion wash over Mirren's face. Put there by her brother's inability to adapt to the world around him. Mirren is nothing if not loyal, and for the past few weeks, she's stubbornly hung onto the hope Easton is slowly accepting her as she is. But love has blinded her to things very apparent to me.

Easton is too weak to accept the world as it is, let alone Mirren. He may love her, but he wishes her something different; something smaller that doesn't push at the edges of his boundaries. And if I didn't have a soul, I'd be able to light him on fire, and watch him burn for breaking her heart over and over. For granting the rest of the godsdamn lemmings the power to make Mirren feel like she's too much. Like she doesn't fit.

But as it is, all I can do is sit and watch as devastation falls over her.

"Easton, does that—this isn't..." She pushes a deep breath through her teeth, calming the power that swirls inside her at all times. I wish she wouldn't. "You want me to leave?" she finally asks, her voice small in the silence of the room.

There are a thousand reasons banishing the nature-wielders is a terrible idea, the topmost being that Similis is unprotected. They have no Boundary, and the twisted protection of the Covinus is gone. They have no militia, no war strategy. Even their fleet of trained guards has left them. It's only a matter of time before a warlord comes to claim the riches they've hoarded; comes to punish the Similians for living so long in the light.

But none of these reasons are what cause Mirren's eyes to shine with hurt.

Easton's jaw twitches. "Of course I don't want you to leave," he replies neutrally.

Relief blossoms on Mirren's face. "Then you refused the terms?"

His eyes flicker from Mirren to where Harlan stands behind her, his face uncharacteristically hard, and then to where I sit holding Helias. I'm familiar with the weight of Easton's disapproval, the heaviness of his dislike, and though his expression doesn't change, I feel it now. I stare back at him flatly, until he finally flicks his gaze back to his sister. "Can we talk outside?"

The rest of the sentence is implied. *Alone.*

After a hesitant moment, Mirren nods. Easton strides purposefully out the front door, probably certain he can sway her by removing her from her allies, which only demonstrates he still doesn't know her. Not truly. Mirren's heart cannot be swayed.

She brushes her fingers along my shoulders as she makes to follow her brother out the door. Shivers rise at her touch, and I grab her hand to leave a kiss on her palm. Her cheeks flush and she gives me a reassuring smile. Then she's gone.

Harlan drops his plate onto the counter haphazardly, the resulting clatter upending my thoughts. His jaw has gone so tight that for a moment, I think he may storm right out the door to follow Mirren. But with a grind of his teeth, he masters himself and says to the room at large, "This is ridiculous."

Cal laughs. "That might be the rudest thing I've ever heard you say."

Harlan inhales sharply, turning toward Cal with a look somewhere between amusement and exasperation. A look that often adorns my own face when dealing with Calloway. Instead of sniping back, however, Harlan softens. "They don't know any better. They don't know what they truly face." He shakes his head. "They're working against their own best interests."

Avedis shrugs mildly, running his whetstone over the blade of one of Max's daggers. "If they hate us so much, there is no reason to subject ourselves any further to their revolting food."

"They don't hate you," Harlan insists. "They don't all think that way. You know they don't, Avedis." When the assassin doesn't respond, Harlan rounds the kitchen counter. "You've come to the training sessions. You've helped them learn. They're terrified, but so many of them are open to change."

Avedis finally raises his gaze to Harlan, dark eyes glittering. "And there are just as many who would jump at the chance to slit our throats in our sleep."

Harlan pales, but Avedis isn't finished. "You do not hear the whispers as I do, or feel the heat of their hate. You do not know how the fear of *different* will drive a person to cut it down at the roots."

I don't need the songs of the wind to know of what Avedis speaks. While I've stayed far away from Harlan and Cal's training sessions, away from any of the rebuild efforts, on the rare occasion I do come across a Similian, their whispers are a physical thing. They wind around me, sliding down my throat and strangling the air from my lungs. *Firebringer,* they say. But there's no respect. Only fear.

Harlan raises his chin, as something steel slides through him. "I know better than most what it is to be different here." His words have a savage edge, and Avedis leans back in his chair with a tilt of his head. Regarding the golden boy with respect, even as Harlan continues, "But I also know people can change. Be better than they are. Isn't that why we're trying to break the curse?"

He looks to me imploringly. "I'll talk to them. I'll make them see reason."

I hate that his words settle beneath my skin—hate that I understand exactly why he and Mirren are life partners. The Covinus may have banned emotion to better control the population, but whatever algorithm matched Mirren and Harlan understood something of souls, because theirs are so similar. Stubborn faith, resilient love.

And just like I believe in Mirren, I also want to believe in Harlan's ability for change. Living in the light didn't protect Harlan from having pieces ripped from him, and still, he believes. He has no otherworldly power, but he possesses his own in the strength of his hope.

So, I nod. "We won't make any decisions until you get back."

Harlan smiles gratefully.

After he leaves, and we've all devoured Cal's breakfast,

we begin to work through the pile of weapons. Cleaning, sharpening, and oiling each in turn.

Helias wiggles in my lap. He's small for his age, and his tiny body is a constant flurry of movement, always bouncing or vibrating. Though he tries to tamp it down in order to follow my instructions, it still seems to move of its own accord.

The innocence of it draws a smile to my face, but a dagger to my heart as so many things with Helias do. As much as I try to pretend otherwise, since the very first day he curled up against my chest, I can't help but watch the little earth-wielder greedily. I wonder if I'd have moved the same if I'd been born somewhere other than the Castellium. Would I flap my arms like a bird when I ran, with no care to whether or not it made me slower? Would I shout odd sounds, for no other reason than the bubbly way they felt on my tongue? Would I bounce, light and airy as a cloud, if I'd never known the weight of violence?

I've spent most my life avoiding reflecting on what-ifs, because to survive, I needed to focus on what *is*. But now, I can't seem to escape them. A result of my healed soul, or my proximity to a child for the first time in my life, I'm still not sure.

But in Helias, I see all I've been denied.

And all he stands to lose if he grows up attached to someone like me.

The boy takes the cloth and runs it along the black blade of a dagger, careful to avoid the edge just as I showed him. He sneaks glances at me from beneath his long lashes, and when he notices my approval, he shivers and bounces even more rapidly. But he doesn't smile.

The Darkness stole his smiles when it took those he

loved. I've spent more time than I care to admit wondering if I could somehow get them back, even for just a moment.

But I never allow the thought to linger for long, as being tied to me will only further ruin his chances of happiness. He's already ostracized from his own people, an unfortunate result of the magnificent power that bursts from him on an unpredictable basis. Being friendly with the man who destroyed the Boundary, and half the continent last year, will do him no favors.

"If I didn't know better Maxwell, I'd think you were raised by a pack of Ditya rather than the royal family." Avedis' voice jolts me from my thoughts, as he watches Max shovel a last heaping forkful of breakfast into her mouth with a small frown.

Max rolls her eyes to the assassin, and the air seems to spark with electricity as she narrows her gaze. Avedis is aware of her true heritage, something only Cal and I previously knew. When Max and I escaped my father, we'd both shed the skin of our old lives and become someone different. Not even Denver has ever guessed at her true identity. And while this is the first the assassin has mentioned it, the idea of him knowing her secret at all surely makes her skin crawl.

We both know Avedis can be trusted, but for Max, it isn't a matter of trust; it's a matter of choice. So many of them were stolen from her, she holds the few she has dear.

"If I cut out your tongue, perhaps you'd be better at keeping the wind's secrets to yourself," she snipes, running her finger delicately along the falchion blade.

Avedis only smiles knowingly. "Ah, but you'd have to cut off all my fingers as well, because you assuredly know, my handwriting is exquisite."

Max raises an eyebrow like she's pondering slicing his

hands off at this very kitchen table, when the assassin suddenly goes still in that unsettling manner that means he's listening to the wind. His eyes flicker closed for a fraction of a moment, before snapping back open and finding mine. "Sura is here," he says with a curious tilt of his head. "In the Nemoran."

Ice crystals form in my veins, though I can't say exactly why, as the little Xamani is pleasant enough. Perhaps because it's been easy while in Similis, nestled in the isolation of the forest, to pretend like the rest of the continent doesn't exist. To imagine the Praeceptor's fall, and the return of magic, has blanketed the land in peace. Despite the suspicion of the Similians around us, when we're together in the quarterage, we've existed in our own world.

The arrival of Sura is a stark reminder of all that rages beyond these woods. The Covinus has ensconced himself atop my father's throne in Argentum, and though he's been quiet, he won't remain that way with the entire Dark Militia under his thrall. Rumor leads us to believe the return of magic has armed Akari Ilinka's people against her, and though she's been busy quelling the uprisings, even a rebellion won't keep the clever queen from exploiting the chaos power vacuums create. And there are dozens of other warlords, both of larger territories and lesser, that would sacrifice everything they have for a chance to claim Similis.

But truthfully, it isn't the threat of war that runs through my veins like lead.

Sura has come from Nadjaa. Which means she's more than likely been sent by Denver, as nothing happens in his city without his knowledge.

The father who first loved me.

The Chancellor who sacrificed me.

I meet Avedis' gaze, breathing deeply until all childish

imaginings leave me. Until there is only the iron in my veins, and steel over my heart. Because no matter how my mind dreams, I *was* born in the Castellium, and my body will never move with whimsy. It moves with death and violence, with fire and rage. "Let's go see what the Chancellor wants."

Mirren

My heart is lodged somewhere in my throat as I follow Easton out of the quarterage. It threatens to spill from my mouth, and I work to swallow it down before it stains him, and everything else around me, in shades of red.

To my surprise, he ushers me to the back of the building, and then up the small set of metal stairs that lead to the roof. When we reach the top, he sits on the same edge I've spent so much time dreaming atop. He motions for me to sit beside him, and for a brief moment, it feels as though the past six months haven't happened. That he's my little brother, and I'm his big sister, and my greatest worry is how to stay together.

But as I perch beside him, and take in the expanse of Similis around us, the feeling evaporates as quickly as it comes. Rubble lines the streets of the Community, a result of the collapse of the Boundary and the subsequent earthquakes. The traumas of the past few months slash through the once immaculate streets like scars on skin.

I used to sit and imagine the freedom of the Dark World, but now, there are no lights to ponder. And I know the sacrifices that freedom demands, the double-edged blade of its beauty.

There is no use pretending things are as they once were. And Easton and I are no longer children.

I take a deep breath. "Easton, how could you let them vote that way?"

He doesn't look at me, instead, staring out at the city. Perhaps taking his own inventory of the Community's wounds. "I am not the one who led the talks."

It's a weak excuse. Easton is only seventeen, so of course he hadn't led the meetings, but he's been invited to all of them. As far as the Community is concerned, my brother is a true believer of the Keys, his traitorous, nature-wielding sister notwithstanding. He's always embodied the best of them, always put the Community before self.

"Those in the metropolis will soon run out of food stores, and those of us on the outside need medicine. We have to be one Community if we're going to survive without the Boundary."

"But kicking out the nature-wielders, Easton…it's suicide. News of the Boundary has certainly spread across the continent by now. What happens when one of the warlords' militias comes marching through the Nemoran? How will any of you protect yourselves? You don't know the nightmares that exist beyond these trees. The atrocities people will commit for a little bit of power."

Easton swallows, his hands balled in his lap as he weighs his words. It's a habit that's always aided his kindness, and one I used to envy—the ability to consider what you're going to say, and each word's intended effect, *before* it comes barreling out of his mouth. But right now, it sets my teeth on edge. My brother should not have to guard his words with me.

After a long moment, he says carefully, "Their nightmare is living here, Mirren. The man who brought down their Boundary, their safety, now lives beside them. What is out there cannot be worse than what's right next door. The Community doesn't feel safe with him here."

I immediately bristle and my cheeks grow hot with indignation. Anrai took the knife meant for Easton, and still, my brother cannot forgive him for destroying the Boundary. "The Boundary was never meant to be there in the first place. You heard what the Covinus said. He twisted the gods' sacrifice for his own gain. And he left the rest of the world to rot beneath his own curse."

When my brother finally looks at me, I'm reminded so forcibly of my father, I wonder why I ever thought he resembled my mother. He does not have Denver's eyes or hair, but the set of his mouth and the slant of his nose are similar. So is the single-minded fervor that threads through each of his decisions.

"It doesn't matter how the Community was formed," he says resolutely. "It matters what we make of it. The Covinus was wrong, but that doesn't mean the Keys are. You've always fought against the ways they've held you back and never stopped to see the good in them. How they help people and bring us together."

"And what about Kindness before Truth?" I bite out.

"Shaw is not a Community member. You know the things they say about him, Mirren."

Fire-bringer. Destroyer. Scourge. Evil.

I've heard the whispers, the horrible names they call him. The rumors about me have grown tenfold since the Covinus left, but instead of winding around my heart, they now bounce harmlessly off my skin. Maybe it's grown thicker after my time in Ferusa, or maybe it's because now that I've found my true home, I'm not so desperate to fit into this one. But despite my newfound peace, whenever I hear Shaw's name spoken with disgust and hate, rage overcomes me and it's a struggle to keep a hold on my power.

Breathing deeply, I manage to get out, "And what about me?"

For the first time, Easton looks distinctly uncomfortable. "What do you mean?"

I dig my teeth into my lip, willing the heat of my anger to cool. Willing my *other* to calm. "You seem to forget Shaw isn't the only wielder."

"We're debating the details later today, but I'm sure they'll make an exception for you and Helias. You're both natural born Similians, and you haven't hurt anyone."

Except that I have, and I'd gladly do it again. My soul has been fractured by the curse, the lines of my morals honed and sharpened on the edge of desperation and love. How can Easton, the person who once knew me better than anyone, not sense my dark heart? Not sense its violent longings and ruthless loyalty?

"They won't, Easton. The Community has never made exceptions for those who don't fit, and they certainly won't start now."

"I'll convince them to see reason."

I emit a sound somewhere between a laugh and a scoff, pushing myself to standing with a disgusted shake of my head. My brother stares up at me with wide eyes. "Did they see reason when they punished Harlan for loving you? Do you think they'd see reason if they found out you love him back?"

A steel wall slams down behind his eyes, and suddenly, Easton no longer looks like a boy. He looks like a man, hardened and distant. "I can't do this on my own, Mirren. You have to try and behave. And you can start by not shouting about things that are none of your business."

His words are sharp and pointed, and I almost rear back at the brutality of his tone. I meant to shock him into understanding, and instead, I've only succeeded in further shutting him down. For a moment, I consider reaching for his hand like I would when we were children, hidden beneath the covers. *Don't leave me, Mirri,* he'd whisper. *Never,* I'd reply.

"If you and Helias agree not to use magic, they'll see reason. You'll be allowed to stay. I'll make sure of it."

My heart wrenches as my brother stares up at me, hesitant hope glimmering in his eyes. Hope that I will behave. That I will be less magical, less loud—that I will be *less*. Despite the sudden tremble of my hands, and the wave of emotion climbing my throat, my words come out steady. "My power is a part of me. You're asking me to be someone else."

Easton shakes his head vehemently, pushing himself to standing. He is so much taller than I remember. Will I always see him as the little boy I swore to protect? "I'm asking you to be my sister. I'm asking you to stay with me."

Don't leave me, Mirri.

Tears sting my eyes. "I cannot shrink myself any longer," I tell him. "Even for you."

Easton opens his mouth to reply, but his words are lost as a powerful gust of wind blasts across the rooftop.

Sura is in the Nemoran, Avedis' voice whispers. *She brings word of the Dead Prophecy.*

CHAPTER
THREE

Shaw

Mirren finds me at the edge of the Boundary, her curls wild around her face and her cheeks ruddy with the exertion of running here. She collides into me with a soft yelp of excitement, her fingers curling into my chest like it's been weeks since we've seen each other, rather than the half hour that's truly passed. Warmth radiates through me as I wrap my arms around her and bury my face in her hair, her scent of sunbaked waves swirling in my nose.

A hundred years could pass, and I'd never become accustomed to Mirren's enthusiasm for my presence. It lives in my chest like the strains of a song, soft and sensuously winding, its beat renewed each time that smile lights up her face. It does so now, playful on lush lips. My breath catches as she gazes up at me, and suddenly, I could care less about Denver or Sura or the Dead Prophecy.

All I want is to drag Mirren deeper into the forest and bury myself inside her. Devour every inch of her until my name is the only word she can remember.

Because though we are together, whole, and safe, we

still exist beneath the Darkness. And on the days when my soul is too heavy to bear, and the weight of the continent's hate mingled with my own threatens to crush me, the lessons woven into me with blood and pain echo with unrelenting malice.

You love her and so she will be taken from you.

"Do you think Sura truly knows the prophecy?" Mirren asks breathlessly, before hesitating. "Or do you think my father has sent her?"

The small hesitation sends a flash of flame shooting upward inside my chest. Because Denver's treatment of me is acceptable—understandable, even—but his continued abandonment of Mirren is not. "I'm not sure. But by now, he's definitely heard about the Boundary. Which means Jayan will have the People's Council in an uproar, demanding they come conquer Similis before anyone else can. Maybe Denver is using Sura to feel out the situation. He is a man that loves information."

"You think he's using her to see if we're still here protecting the city?"

I wind our fingers together, my callouses scraping against her soft palm. "Whatever Denver is, he isn't a conqueror. As long as he remains Chancellor, Nadjaa won't go to war against Similis."

Mirren nods, though she doesn't look entirely convinced, and I can't say I blame her. Like her, my feelings for Denver are a practice in dichotomy: love burning alongside hate. Respect alongside disgust. Gratitude alongside hurt. They are too entangled to sort out, each emotion stretching into the next, the line between them indistinguishable.

Denver saved me and Denver damned me, and I don't know which matters more. If he knows the Dead Prophecy, which side of him will win out? Will he help us, or sacrifice us on a pyre in the name of progress?

"Either way, it'll be good to see Sura," Mirren says as we slip through the Boundary and into the trees.

Even after the destruction of the wall, the presence of the Nemoran still feels heavy. Ancient magic wound in the roots and trunks, threaded through the leaves and soil. Every time we step inside the forest, it presses against us, searching through our veins and tugging at our magic. *Like calls to like.*

Though without the unnatural drain of the Boundary, the Nemoran no longer feels as ominous. In fact, as we venture further beneath the canopy, something in me begins to unwind. Though it might not be the trees at all, but rather escaping Similis.

If it weren't for Mirren, I'd have left the sterile gray prison for the wood the minute I was able to walk again. I hate everything about the city, even without the harsh glare of the lights. The hard lines, the endless monotony—it all makes my skin itch. And Darkness knows, I'd take the company of a yamardu over the lemmings any day.

Leaves crunch beneath Mirren's feet as she walks beside me, and a smile pulls at my lips. For such a small person, she makes an awful lot of noise. Reading my thoughts, she shoots me an indignant glare. "I'm quieter than I used to be!"

"If you say so, Lemming." I laugh as she shoves me lightly. "How'd your talk with Easton go?"

Her humor instantly fades, and she digs her teeth into her bottom lip. "He wants me to stay but only if I don't use magic."

I halt, turning toward her. "Then he doesn't want you to stay."

Her eyes shine. "He *told* me he wants me to stay," she insists. "And that took a lot for him...being vulnerable like that. It's hard for us—for Similians."

"Yes," I agree softly. "But you *are* your power, Mirren. So he isn't asking you to stay. He's asking the version of you in his head to stay. That isn't the same thing."

Her lip wobbles and her eyes drop to the ground, and I hate it. Hate that my words have caused it. But Mirren and I don't lie to each other, and I'll be damned if her simpering brother is the reason I start now. I cup my fingers beneath her jaw, gently raising her chin until she meets my gaze. The emerald green churns like crashing waves, their power echoing through my soul. "He doesn't get to choose what parts of you are acceptable. If he can't love all of you, he doesn't deserve any of you."

After a long moment, Mirren nods. "You're awfully wise sometimes. Maybe you should take your own advice every once and awhile."

I shoot her a wry grin and kiss her to save myself responding. Because as much as Mirren wishes it to be, it isn't the same thing. Mirren should be accepted in her entirety, but I should not. My crimes against humanity are not forgivable—*I* am not forgivable.

"Anrai—"

I tense, waiting for her next words. They will undoubtedly be full of faith and kindness, neither of which I deserve in the least, and I both love and hate her for them. But before she can finish, the ground beneath us trembles.

The trees begin to roll, as if their roots are sown in the waves of a sea rather than soil. My stomach heaves as I plant my feet, and though I keep my breathing even and try to determine which side of us the earthquake originates, panic shoots up my throat. Because if the ground is shaking, it means something is wrong with Helias. He's learned to wield his power well in the past few weeks, and usually, the only time he loses control is if he's extremely upset.

Mirren's eyes are wide as they meet mine, her arms thrown out to the side like bird wings as she tries to keep her balance. "It's coming from the gates," she says slowly.

I scrape my fingers through my hair in an attempt to smooth the tangled upheaval of my thoughts. I left Helias with Cal. They were going to training, which is nowhere near the Boundary gates. The earth shudders once more, a violent sigh that shakes leaves and branches loose. They rain down around us, and then the world goes still.

"Go," Mirren insists. "Make sure he's alright. I'll find Sura and bring her back to the quarterage."

I grind my jaw, indecision entrenching my feet so deeply in place, for a moment, I feel nothing like myself. I've never been plagued by hesitancy before, even when there were no good choices. I decided with my head, with sound strategy, and then I carried through. There was no wavering like there is now, that pulls my heart in two different directions when my body is only capable of one.

Mirren throws her hands on her hips and tilts her head. "I'll be fine. Go check on Helias."

She'll be more than fine. I've seen Mirren fight—have fought against her myself—and know that power of hers is unmatched. My hesitation isn't rooted in logic. It's embedded somewhere far deeper, where dread unfurls like a creature of the night, tentacles always reaching to strangle whatever hope I've allowed myself.

You love her and so she will be taken from you.
She loves you and so you will be punished for it.

"Be safe. Come back as soon as you find Sura." My

words are pulled tight, a band ready to snap. But when Mirren kisses me with a smile, everything inside me eases.

"I was thinking of stopping to have lunch with a few Boundary hunters first. Then maybe see if we can catch a yamardu with our bare hands."

I set her with an unamused stare. "Considering you share a bed with the man who kidnapped you, and are best friends with an assassin who once tried to slit your throat, it's really not a stretch to imagine you'd try to see the best in those bloodsuckers, Lemming."

Mirren rolls her eyes, a laugh playing at the edge of her mouth. "Go on," she urges, with measure patience. "I'll see you back at the quarterage."

The ground rumbles again. With a meaningful look and one last kiss, Mirren disappears into the shadows of the trees. I take off at a steady sprint, leaping over roots and through the underbrush with ease. I'm not at the level of conditioning I was before the weeks I spent in the dark bedroom heaving up everything I ate, but the burn in my muscles and the rhythmic expansion of my lungs feels good. Familiar.

A tether to someone I know.

Because whoever I am now is a stranger. The same heart I was born with still beats against my ribs, but it has been set adrift in my tumultuous soul. Mirren healed the Darkness, but how is something light ever to survive against the shadow of the things I've done?

I keep close to the Boundary, following the destroyed piles as closely as I can without getting hit by falling debris. The closer I come to the gates, the more frequent the tremors become, and the faster my heart pounds. "Avedis!" I shout into the silence of the wood.

The assassin doesn't respond. No breeze at all tickles my neck or rustles my hair.

It isn't unusual for Avedis not to hear something: he isn't clairvoyant. There are millions of people speaking on the continent at any given moment, and unless he's searching for something specific, he's bound to miss a few things. But his continued silence drops into the pit of my stomach anyway.

Did Helias run away from Cal and Max? Is Avedis busy searching for him? Has he been caught by Boundary hunters near the gates? Or worse?

My thoughts spiral, interrupted only when the ground suddenly lurches beneath my feet. Scrambling, I leap for the nearest low-hanging branch. The rough bark scrapes my palms as I pull myself up, leveraging my boots against the branch, and vaulting upward to the next limb. The dirt crumbles beneath me and a giant chasm opens up where I just stood, dark and seemingly endless.

The earth roars, the sound vibrating against my ear drums, and my heart pounds violently, as I pull myself further away from the vacuum of the hole. I balance my feet, but before I manage to grab the next branch, the entire tree, roots and all, tumble into the chasm.

My stomach wobbles as I fall into the darkness. Branches crash, and soil rains down on top of me in a blinding waterfall. All the air shoots from my lungs as my body hits the ground with a blinding shock of pain, and for a moment, I'm positive I've snapped every bone in my body. But there's no time to assess the damage, as I hurtle sideways just before the giant trunk shatters against the bottom of the hole with an earsplitting boom.

More boughs shower down, and I roll to my feet to avoid being crushed by another plummeting tree. Pain racks every bone, every muscle, as I pitch sideways and plaster myself to the side of the hole, and I know the only reason I'm still breathing is the fire imbuing my body. My wrist is swollen from the brunt of the impact, but I can move it. Probably only a sprain.

Finally, the earth stills, the sudden lack of racket almost as disorienting as the noise. Gritting my teeth and cradling my wrist to my stomach, I climb nimbly up through the debris.

My ears ring as I peer upward. The Nemoran canopy is so far away, the sky beyond isn't visible. The hole must be at least a hundred feet deep, and though the giant remains of trees litter the floor, the pile doesn't even scale half the distance. High above my head, roots slither along the walls, but down here, there is nothing. No footholds, no ledges. Only sheer rock and loose dirt, as if a god drilled straight down into the ground.

What in the Darkness happened?

"Helias!" I call out, hoping to see his impish face peer over the edge. He's destroyed things before when his emotions got the best of him, but this is certainly the first time he's sucked me into a giant hole in the ground. Anxiety threads through me again that something has gone terribly wrong, but as I regulate my breathing, I tamp it down. "If this was you, I'm gonna need a little help here!"

There is no answer from above. In fact, there is no noise at all trapped here in the earth. It is a thick silence—the silence of dungeons. Of Yen Girene. Of the Castellium.

Bile rises in my throat and I swallow it down roughly, blinking away the images. Flexing my fingers, I examine the walls. I've made higher climbs. When I murdered the Baakan warlord all those years ago, I scaled smooth trunks twice this high to infiltrate the palace. But I'd had rope then; the full use of both my arms.

And nothing to live for if I fell.

I could shoot flame skyward and hope Mirren's the one that sees my signal. But she was headed in the opposite direction on her way to Sura, and I can't risk someone else finding me vulnerable in this hole. I may be a fire-wielder, but I can just as easily die from a gunshot as anyone else.

Twisting my mouth, I'm still determining the best course of action when a stone clatters topside.

My gaze jerks upward. Another soft rustle. The snap of twigs beneath boots.

Someone is up there.

I grab two daggers from my bandolier and melt silently into the shadows.

And that's when the water comes.

CHAPTER
FOUR

Calloway

"Do you know what I miss?" I ask. Helias bobs beside me as we trail Max and Avedis toward the courtyard we've turned into a makeshift training ground. The little earth-wielder's excitement vibrates through his body, as his fingers trail repeatedly to the tiny knife Anni gifted him before he'd gone to meet Mirren. The blade is only three inches, hardly longer than Helias' small fingers, but the boy hasn't stopped admiring it. "Wine. What I wouldn't give to drink myself into oblivion right now."

The wide-paved streets are filled with Similians scurrying to their morning assignments with the quiet efficiency I've come to loathe. They give us a wide berth, keeping their heads down and carrying on with their lives like their Boundary, and the world beyond, hasn't come crashing down around them. Their lack of emotion is just as unsettling as the stories have always said, made even more so by the crumbling infrastructure around us. The mass graves at the edge of the city. The dead lights on their borders.

Max turns her head to grunt in agreement, and accidentally stumbles into a woman dressed in the same khaki jumpsuit as everyone else. Though the collision is entirely Max's fault for not paying attention to where she was going, the woman's eyes widen and she stutters, "Oh! I am so sorry!"

She skirts around Max with a small squeak, and hurries in the opposite direction.

Max's mouth twists in annoyance. "You know what I miss? People yelling at me on the street when I deserve it."

Avedis laughs. "Shall I yell at you to give you a taste of home? I assure you, it would be no trouble at all."

She scowls. "I'm sure we'll have all the wine and shouting we could ever want soon enough. There's no way Goldie convinces those bigots in the Covinus building to let Dark Worlders stay."

My heart stutters uncomfortably at the mention of Harlan, the mere name immediately conjuring images of his amber eyes. Our time here has made a few things regarding the Similian painfully clear: the foremost being I'd read him all wrong. He was never in love with Mirren. The second: he was, and still is, pining for Mirren's bastard of a brother. And the third: I have learned absolutely nothing of self-control. My heart still tangles itself with determination around those who could never possibly return my affection. Always staunching the holes in others while bleeding out itself.

And it shouldn't even matter because Max is right. Harlan will never convince the Similians to let any of us stay, even if it means their own destruction. And when the time comes to leave, I know it will not be Ferusa—or me—Harlan chooses. Despite everything they've done to him, Harlan still sees beneath it to the good that exists in everyone. A quality I can't decide whether to admire or despise.

Helias tugs on my sleeve, startling me from my thoughts. He looks up at me through a thick curtain of lashes, his large, upturned eyes sullen and serious.

"What is it, little man?"

The boy considers me for a moment, as he does with anyone who isn't Anni. In Helias' mind, Anni is safe; everyone else is undetermined. And I understand it, in the same way I'd found safe haven in my brother when I was fourteen.

Helias fidgets with his jumpsuit, pressing his lips together as he considers his words. Considers them, because until now, he's been punished for them. "I left my cloak at the quarterage."

I furrow my brow. Though it's autumn, the air heats soon after sunrise and it isn't particularly chilly. "I'm sure you'll warm up once we get through a few exercises."

Helias purses his lips and shakes his head. "Shaw told me to wear a cloak. I have to go get it."

I don't understand, but the earnestness with which he speaks tells me I don't need to. For whatever reason, it's important to him. I nod to Max. "We'll catch up with you guys in the courtyard."

Taking Helias' hand, we turn back the way we came. He skips alongside me, having immediately lightened at the promise of retrieving the damned cloak. Mirren's told me some of what it was like to grow up here—the whispers and the suffocating judgement, but feeling the ugly weight of it homed in on a child has thrown the meaning of it all into vivid perspective.

Everyone on the street avoids Helias at all costs, no matter that he's one of them—that he's a child. On the rare occasion a lemming accidentally meets our gaze, they immediately avert their eyes, like they've glimpsed something shameful. The earth-wielder is eight and orphaned, and rather than sympathy, they only eye him with suspicion. With fear.

I'm not a fire-wielder, but it's enough to make my very ordinary blood boil.

For a place that touts Community as its strongest value, it doesn't seem to know the meaning of the word.

I clear my throat. "So is this some sort of magical cloak, then? Is that why it can't be left alone for one training session?" Though I haven't been around children in a while, I'd helped raise my sister Vee, and she always loved when someone older than her dropped their adult façade and acted silly.

Helias sets me with a somber stare. "There are no such thing as magical cloaks."

"That's a shame, as a magic cloak would be a very good way to bother Max."

He watches me expectantly, as if to say he'll tolerate whatever story I'm trying to weave, so I oblige. "We could enchant it to tickle her every time she gets angry. Which you know is all the time, so she'd be laughing until her sides split."

Helias doesn't smile, but his eyes shimmer. "Do you think we could enchant it to tickle Mirren when she tries to baby me? I am *eight*," he sighs dramatically. "I'm almost a grown up!"

I guffaw, a thrill of victory pulsing through me. I may not have made Helias smile, but his participation in my whimsy is a step in the right direction. Ruffling his hair, we round the next corner, and the newfound lightness in my chest is promptly strangled by something much darker.

Because there, tucked between the small walkway between two quarterages, are Harlan and Easton. Their bodies are entangled, the constant movement of their limbs fluid and indecipherable. Heat rushes to the surface of my skin as I follow the sweep of Harlan's hand, the bob of his throat, the grind of his narrow hips.

Something the color of a summer's night sky burgeons in the recesses of me, and I don't stop to examine if it's anger, or something so much worse.

Only when Helias glances up at me curiously do I realize I've halted in my tracks. And then I decide anger is exactly what I feel. Anger at Harlan for putting his hand on someone who isn't me. Anger at myself for caring where Harlan's hands go.

Anger at Similis for not having better alcoves for secretive rendezvous, so I don't have to bear witness to them, a bundle of arousal and shame.

Helias tugs at the hem of my shirt and I begin moving again, my feet working robotically. The cloak. We're here for a cloak.

But I can't picture the cloak. I only see the pulse of Harlan's hips. The flush of his golden skin.

The ground rumbles, and I'm so far in my own head, it's only pure luck I don't pitch forward headfirst into the pavement. My stomach roils, and I shoot Helias an exasperated look as I steady myself. "We have *talked* about not shaking the whole city out of impatience, Helias. Just use your w—"

The words die in my throat as I take in the boy. Confusion and fear mingle openly on his face, and his small hands are clamped at his sides, like his body has frozen in place. "That—that wasn't you," I say slowly. "Was it?"

Helias shakes his head vehemently, and the heat racing through me only moments prior ices over entirely. "Come on," I grab Helias' hand, and tug him up the fire escape of the nearest quarterage. The metal stairs wobble beneath my weight, but I only slow to make sure the boy is still behind me.

It isn't the tallest building in Similis, but I can see enough of the city, to the empty agricultural fields and the Boundary rubble beyond.

To the gates, twisted and ruined as they are.

And to the army spread out before them.

~

Shaw

Water floods the chasm from above. An icy deluge, a dam unleashed. Panic squeezes my throat as the giant wave crashes down on top of me, the force driving the air from my lungs. My power is snuffed out amid the tide of fear, and even as I squeeze my eyes shut against the pressure, I cannot block out images of the Castellium.

It doesn't matter that my father is dead, his ashes scattered on the wind; his rage haunts me. No matter how far I run, I'll always be that wraith trapped in his dungeons. Extinguished by the malevolence of his never-ending need.

I thrash as the water hammers my chest, the pressure creating a vice around my ribs. Another wave crashes down, and my skull collides with rock. My ears ring, and it's all I can I do to hold my breath as stars bloom behind my eyes.

The current is relentless, lifting me up and tossing me to the bottom of the cavern. Pain radiates through me as my spine is driven into the sharp remains of the trees. I whirl my arms wildly, struggling to swim, to get to my feet—to do anything but lay here and drown—but the force is too great. The water drives ceaselessly against my chest, knocks against my lips.

My lungs feel like they're filled with acid as fear pulses through me, settling in my limbs like stone until they go numb and limp, even as another tree crashes on top of me. My leg is wrenched unnaturally between the debris, and a shameful part of me whispers, *no more fighting. Take a breath. Let the current wash you away.*

Because as heavy as the water is, it's nothing to the weight of the soul I carry every day.

And gods, I'm so tired.

Are you truly so weak you'd die alone at the bottom of a hole? Drowned, because you were too panicked to swim?

I can almost hear the ring of my father's laughter, cruel and cutting.

My head pounds, and my lungs burn with the need to inhale, but I force myself still. Even as the wave swirls around me, a constant deluge of unbearable pressure, I stop flailing. I relax every muscle in my body, down to the tips of my fingers. And then, I open my eyes.

This is not the Castellium. And I will not be afraid.

I repeat it to myself over and over again, a rhythmic prayer as the torrent of debris and water and mud swirls above me. I lay the words over my extinguished flame, kindling against the emptiness of terror. Heat against the cold trauma.

My head screams as my oxygen nearly runs out, but I tamp down the pain and peer up. Through the cloudy muck, the spinning branches. Far above me, there is the watery glow of daylight. I focus on the small pinprick, and then I grapple inside my chest, relighting the flame I allowed fear to blow out.

It flares to life, weak at first. The soft glow of a singular ember.

But the small bit of warmth in the icy barrenness of my chest is enough to remember that even when I was a dark void, there was always a light guiding me home. Mirren. I was never alone in the Castellium; I've always had her gentle touch, her powerful fury, curled up inside me, reminding me to keep fighting. Because we are not done.

I've worked to rebuild myself brick by agonizing brick, and I won't allow it to be destroyed now: not when I haven't had the chance to build her a library with more books than she can ever possibly read; when I haven't had the chance to bury myself inside her on the shores of a foreign continent; to hear the sounds of her pleasure ringing across the waves.

Not when I haven't had the chance to make her my wife.

The thought ignites the ember, and my flame flares to life in a spectacular explosion, bursting from my chest and racing to my fingertips. It burns outside my skin, a beacon of hope in the dark water.

Mirren and I aren't done, which means *I* am not done. There is so much more I want from this life, even if I have to wring it out with my bare fucking hands.

I burn. So hot the tree pinning my leg is reduced to ash and the water around me evaporates, giving me enough space to gulp down a few desperate breaths of oxygen. It won't last long, as my flame will eat up the little air available, but the small breaths are enough to clear my mind. I gaze upward through the swirling current to the sky above. To the roots that jut out from the top of the hole.

And then I stop fighting. I take a deep breath and relax, letting the water carry me. Though it is an element that holds so much pain, it is also Mirren. The thought bolsters my resolve as the current tugs me upward, carrying me toward the light, and with it, I feed my flame.

My love, my grief, my unrelenting anger.

My fire consumes them, rising higher in my chest. In the month since Mirren healed the rift between my power and I, we've floated aimlessly next to each other, neither entirely satisfied. Because though my father is gone, the things I've done remain, and I haven't figured out who I am next to them.

I am a killer. I am a lover. I am lost.

But maybe, I don't need to be entirely found to move forward.

The water around me begins to boil and steam rises toward the distant sun as I ride the current. It thrusts me upward, a spinning whirlpool of its own making. The sky comes closer and closer, and just when I think my lungs will burst, I finally break the surface. Still at least thirty feet from the mouth of the chasm, but climbable.

I stretch, reaching for one of the protruding roots. My fingertips slip against the soaked wood and my injured wrist smarts as I manage to grab hold. The water rages around me, trying to pull me back into its depths, but somehow, I keep my grip.

Gritting my teeth, I hoist myself up bit by bit. The root is slippery and bends beneath my weight, but I move before it can break, leveraging my feet and swinging to the next. I manage to catch this one with both hands, moving methodically until I'm halfway up. I don't look down at what swirls beneath me. Only up, as I climb slowly toward the sky.

When I reach the lip of the cavern, my nails scrabble at the loose dirt as I hoist myself up. Water plasters my hair and sluices down my face, blurring my vision. Thick mud coats my skin and grit scrapes between my teeth. My lungs burn and every bit of my body screams with exertion as I collapse onto the needle covered ground.

I flip to my knees, coughing and choking. I've barely managed to catch my breath when a snicker of laughter sounds from the other side of the hole.

My abyss flares as I realize three people watch me, the woman in the middle looking like a siren come to life. Her upturned eyes glitter and her red mouth pulls into a vicious smile as Akari Ilinka says, "We meet again, Fire-bringer."

CHAPTER
FIVE

Calloway

Adrenaline and panic course through me in equal measure as I hurtle down from the roof, Helias close on my heels.

"Avedis!" I shout wildly. How in the Darkness did an entire army get through the Nemoran without the assassin hearing their movements on the wind? And why do no alarms sound even now that the forces clash against the gates, their twisted remains no match against the giant battering rams?

There's no reply from Avedis as I whip around the nearest corner to where Harlan and Easton are still tangled together. They blink wildly, like I've startled them in the privacy of their bedroom, rather than a public alleyway. A mixture of shame and defiance and desire too potent to sort through at the moment flashes over Easton's face as he lurches away from Harlan.

A hot flush stains Harlan's skin, and the sight of it creates a war inside me between wanting to throttle him, and wanting desperately to taste it for myself. Unfortunately, I don't have time for either. "An army," I yelp, before shaking my head, and inhaling sharply in an attempt to order my words. "There's an army at the gates."

Harlan's eyes flare. "What? That isn't—"

"—possible? Well, they're here…and they're about to break them down. We have to move. Now."

"Who?" Harlan asks breathlessly, but I'm already shaking my head.

"We'll find out when we meet them, but right now, I need you to rally anyone you can who's capable of fighting. Anyone who's had some amount of training. And get everyone else into that Covinus building. I don't care if you have to bash down the doors with an axe."

Easton's eyes have gone so wide, for a moment, I'm reminded of a fawn. Naïve. Weak.

But Harlan nods, and without sparing Easton another glance, takes off running toward the quarterage.

Easton's lower lip flutters as he tries to gather his thoughts, and I have to dig my fingers into my thighs to refrain from shaking him. "H-hardly anyone has had training. How will we possibly keep an army out?"

I glare at him hotly, even as his fear radiates between us. "You know those wielders you hate so much? The Ferusians you despise? They're the only thing that stands between you and the Darkness. So I suggest you start by getting down on your knees and thanking them for their mercy. Darkness knows, you've done nothing to deserve it."

I've never craved the bitter taste of anger, never liked the acid of hatred, but something about Easton sends it hurtling to the surface. It shouldn't make me feel better—shouldn't cool the heat pulsing through my veins—but when the last bit of color leeches from his face, it does.

"By the Covinus…"

"The Covinus left you," I snarl so aggressively, he takes a step back. Pushing a leveling breath through my nose, I try to smooth my words. To remember Easton is scared and naïve, and that isn't entirely his fault. "I need you to watch Helias. Take him somewhere safe."

Helias shakes his head vehemently, twisting his mouth in a stubborn frown. "I can help," he insists, as I begin checking my quiver. Not enough arrows. There aren't enough arrows in this whole godsdamn city. "I can help you and Shaw! I can make the earth swallow them up."

My heart wrenches at his bravery. I kneel down to his level. "You are strong and powerful, and I'm not asking you to stay behind because those things aren't true. I'm asking because if the earth swallows them up, you'll have to pay with pieces of your soul. And you're far too young for that. Do you understand?"

His fingers curl into fists at his sides. "I don't care, I'm coming!" His chin wobbles, and tears line his eyes. "I can keep you all safe."

And now, the wrench in my heart becomes a gaping hole because I see lines of myself in his words. His family is gone, and he believes it was his fault. I was only a boy when mine was taken, but I spent years going over the moments in my head. If I'd just been older, stronger, *there*. It had never mattered that I was only a child, and my parents would have only been grateful I'd been spared—it had only mattered they were gone.

"I need you here," I tell Helias gently. Easton bristles as I jerk my head in his direction. "Most of your Community is like him. They don't know how to protect themselves. So while Shaw and Mirren and I go fight, I need someone powerful to stay with them. Can we count on your help?"

Helias straightens, lightened at being given responsibility, even if I hope he'll never have to use it. He lifts his chin and nods. "I'll keep them all safe."

I give Helias a small smile, before cutting my gaze back to Easton. "Don't let him out of your sight."

"What about my sister? She can't—she needs to be inside the Boundary. It isn't safe out there."

I laugh, but it isn't my usual good-natured chortle. "It isn't safe *in here,* Easton. And I'd like to see you try to keep Mirren inside the gates. In case you haven't noticed, your sister isn't afraid of the sacrifices it takes to truly love someone. She'll protect you and this damn city with everything she has."

Harlan returns, arms laden with the weapons we left on the kitchen table. He shoves a small sword into Easton's hands, ignoring the way Easton flinches when their fingers brush. I see it though, and turn away before I do something ridiculous like hit him in the teeth. "I have to go find Max and Avedis. We'll meet you at the gates."

I take off running through the streets. Every building, every corner, every brick of this infernal city looks exactly the same, and without landmarks, I've found myself lost more times than I can count over the past few weeks. But now, muscle memory takes over as I sprint between quarterages and through Sectors, toward the small courtyard we've designated for training.

Max and Avedis' bickering echoes behind them as they slowly amble up the street, Max swinging a falchion around in boredom. "AVEDIS!" I bellow, careening to a halt just before I smack into the assassin's broad back.

He shoots an irritated look over his shoulder, his eyes roving over my shambled appearance with slight distaste. "There is no need to yell, Calloway. I assure you my hearing is perfectly adequate."

"Considering there is an entire *militia* outside the gates, I'm going to have to respectfully disagree!"

Avedis' eyes widen in shock, and he immediately drops to the ground. His long legs curl beneath him, and he closes his eyes, his face furrowed in concentration as he listens to the wind.

Max watches as he goes perfectly still, that calculating fervor already shining in her eyes. "Are you sure?" she asks.

"You caught me, Max. I've been so bored by life in Similis, I thought I'd spice things up a bit by creating mass panic."

She shoots me a menacing look, but before she can snap a retort, Avedis leaps to his feet with a curse. "I cannot hear anything," he bites out, his voice uncharacteristically tight as he pulls his sword and begins to stalk angrily up the street.

Max and I stare at each other, before remembering ourselves. Max pulls her own blade and hurries after him. "How is that possible?" she demands at the same time, I shout, "There were at least a thousand of them out there, Avedis! With a battering a ram!"

Avedis ignores us both, striding in the direction of the ruined red square, his footfalls so hard they echo behind him.

"The Boundary doesn't block Mirren or Shaw's power anymore," Max says doubtfully. "It shouldn't be blocking yours."

"You have to let them know what's happening, Avedis! They're outside the Boundary!"

"I *cannot!*" he growls so savagely, both Max and I halt in place. It's easy to forget with all his smooth charm, and high-born manners, what Avedis actually is—a cold-blooded killer. But times like now, when his shoulders rise and fall heavily, and violence threads through every line of him, sharp and deadly, it's impossible to see him as anything else.

Max watches him with a steel gaze before something in her softens. Hesitating, she places a hand on the assassin's shoulder. "What's going on, Avedis?"

He raises his eyes to hers, lethal malice glittering in the dark irises. "The breezes are silent because whoever is out there—" His gaze snaps in the direction of the gates, like he can see past the metropolis, past the Covinus building and the ruins of the red square, to the forest beyond. "They have another wind-wielder."

∼

Mirren

The Nemoran canopy towers above me as I wind my way slowly between the thick trunks. Anrai must have found Helias quickly, as the earthquakes have eased, my anxiety with it. Avedis told Sura to wait where she was, so I walk at a decent pace and enjoy the quiet of the forest. The fresh air expands pleasantly in my lungs, the scent of moist soil and sharp pine mingling with something headier: what I now recognize as the Nemoran's inherent magic.

The forest has always had power, but without the Boundary's unnatural drain on the resting place of the old gods, magic has been set free. It rustles in the leaves and bubbles in the springs. It winds through the branches and roots; hangs in the very air. And while it's still heavy, an otherworldly pull, it's now tinged with something sparkling. Ethereal.

Dead leaves crunch beneath my feet as I walk, and I wonder what the Nemoran would have been if the Covinus had never constructed the Boundary. If the old gods sacrifice had been free to nurture as it was intended, instead of spoil in the Darkness. Would there still be twisted creatures skulking in the shadows?

"Mirren!"

My name rings through the forest in a spritely yelp, and I barely have time to turn before Sura barrels into me, her spindly arms winding around me in an exuberant hug. I laugh, hugging her back. "It's so good to see you!"

She pulls back, her eyes sparkling with a smile. Her long, dark hair is tied in two plaits, woven with the same straps of dyed leather that adorn Asa's. Though she's dressed for travel, a cloak of thick fur draped over her shoulders, the clothes beneath are far finer than her usual attire. Following my gaze, Sura shrugs sheepishly. "My training as a Kashan is almost complete." Though she says it casually, I don't miss the thick pride that edges her voice.

I hug her again, smiling back broadly. "That's amazing, Sura! Asa must be so proud."

Something flickers in her gaze. Something like sadness. "He—well, it was necessary. So I'm not sure it's something to be celebrated."

Wrinkling my brow in confusion, I motion for her to sit. "What do you mean?"

Sura settles on the ground, pulling her legs beneath her as she leans back against a wide trunk. She looks so much healthier than the first time we met, when she'd been half-starved and desperate—but there are dark smudges of exhaustion beneath her eyes that weren't there when I last saw her in Nadjaa.

"It's your father." She hesitates, picking nervously at the skin around her nails. *Father.* The word drops into my stomach like lead. So, Denver is the one who sent her. "He won't let Asa leave the valley, you see."

I snap my head around, anxiety and surprise threading through me. "At all? Sura, has Asa been arrested?" Asa helped Anrai and I escape my father's grasp, and if he's been punished because of it—

She shakes her head, and I release a breath of relief. "Not exactly. But he isn't entirely free, either. It isn't natural for the Xaman tribes to be tethered to one place, but your father will not allow us to leave Nadjaa. The return of magic has made the Chancellor more determined than ever to discover the prophecy. He keeps Aggie and the Kashan both under watch, so if they learn what it says, he will be the first to know."

Anger crashes against my lungs as my *other* rises up, somehow always ready when it comes to my father. Asa and Denver were both held hostage by the Praeceptor— their freedom stolen; their bodies violated. And somehow, my father cannot see the parallel as he takes something that doesn't belong to him under the guise of the greater good. Asa's autonomy.

Perhaps he's retained more of his Similian upbringing than I thought.

Heavy realization settles over me. "That's why Asa has been training you so quickly," I say slowly. "So he won't be the only one who knows the story."

Sura pushes a braid behind her shoulder and sets me with a furtive look.

My mouth drops open. "Sura—are you...are you saying you *know* the rest of the Dead Prophecy?"

She smiles, but again, it's edged with a sadness I don't entirely understand. "As much as I missed you, the prophecy is why I've come." Her smile fades as she begins to pick at her fingers more maliciously. "Mirren, I—Kashans can only tell the story. Words are the magic that tether the world together, but they are also individual. We cannot control how each tale affects someone, or how it settles in their hearts. That's between them and the story."

I nod slowly. "I understand," I tell her, though I'm not sure I do.

Abandoning her cuticles, Sura takes my hands in hers. Her palms are rough against mine, calloused by the work of the Xamani camps. Her eyes shine, and a part of me wants to shy away from her gaze, as she seeks to speak without words. "This story…it's important. But how you hear it is also important. Does that make sense?"

"Not really, Sura. You're starting to worry me. What does it say?"

Sura's shoulders rise with a deep inhale, and she squeezes my hand, something uncomfortably close to pity on her face. Anxiety tingles the back of my neck as she opens her mouth to speak.

But I never hear her words.

Because suddenly, my *other* is torn from me. Agony shreds through my bones, and I topple over. My face lands in the damp earth, and black edges my vision. My lungs are like sandpaper, and my muscles scream, and for a moment, all I can remember is pain.

Pain in a dungeon far from here, helpless as Anrai's soul was stolen from him. Where Max and Cal bled, my father strung up and tortured. Pain in a cavern of the gods, when everyone I love teetered on the brink of death. Pain of living as an echo of myself for months on end, a broken shard that cut anything that came near it.

The Boundary is gone, but the pain remains.

Because there is one person still capable of tearing the

world apart. The same one who stole magic, who spoiled the light, who ruined my family.

The Covinus.

Lungs on fire, and nerves singed, I claw at the damp soil and whisper, "Run, Sura. *Run.*"

CHAPTER SIX

Shaw

"Queen," I sneer with a derisive grin. "Brave of you to face me considering what happened the last time we met."

The witch-queen smiles, blood red lips tugging over ivory white teeth, apparently the memory of me trapping her in a burning circle not enough to dull her arrogance. "Not brave at all, as I'm told you have a soul now, Fire-bringer. Scourge of the continent, Heir of the Praeceptor... tamed by love, was it?" She laughs, a simpering sound that slices through trees.

"Look at the things you've done with a soul, Akari. Seems rather ridiculous to be assuaged by its presence when you're just as aware of human nature as I am."

The queen tilts her head, watching with mild amusement as I scan the trees behind her, searching for any sign of Helias. Is this why he shook the earth? Because he's been taken by the queen?

Rage billows through me as I imagine the little earth-wielder in Akari Ilinka's power hungry hands: hands responsible for the brutal death of Cal's family, for the slice through Avedis' eye and the theft of pieces of his soul.

If she's touched Helias, I'll gut her from throat to belly and show her exactly what lives inside me, soul or not. Because even after Mirren healed me, I'm still the same man. Always the boy who grew up with darkness over his heart and blood on his hands. And the witch-queen should know well—no one touches what is mine.

And as much as he shouldn't be, Helias is mine.

I run my tongue over my teeth, before shooting the witch-queen a terrifying smile. The kind that promises death. She lowers her chin, adjusting her stance as if readying for an attack. But she doesn't retreat.

"Where is he?"

It's her turn to smile, a wicked slash on her beautiful face, and flames explode in my chest at the sight of it. Vengeful, wild. "I heard you burned the Praeceptor alive. Tell me, how did it feel to watch him die?" she muses, ignoring my question.

My eyes travel to the two people standing behind her, both of whom have remained mute. A man and a woman, dressed in Siraleni fashion beneath thick teal cloaks. The color is almost an affront to the senses in the shadowed recesses of the wood, and completely impractical for blending in.

Which means whoever they are, they don't plan on hiding. Even from me.

"Where is he?" I repeat.

Akari makes an amused humming sound. "I must admit, when news of your father's death reached me, I was shamefully jealous. I so wish I'd been the one to send him to the Darkness. But alas, I suppose life is cruel that way."

The man shifts slightly, swiping his palm against his

cloak. I narrow my gaze on that hand as it comes to rest once more against his side, and dread winds through me anew. Because though he just wiped it clean, water beads there once more. Barely perceptible.

"Next time I plan on gutting a parental figure, I'll be sure to check if you'd like the first shot," I bite out acerbically. "Now, where is the earth-wielder?"

"I don't have him," Ilinka replies, tossing the curtain of shining, dark hair over her shoulder. She ducks her head sensually, gazing up at me through her thick lashes, but there is nothing warm about the invitation. Her eyes glow with greed as she watches me, and I resist the urge to scratch at my skin. She smiles. "Yet."

I bare my teeth, flames bursting from my hands and racing up my arms. The queen watches them with a covetous glint, the firelight reflecting in her irises. "Careful, Akari," I warn. "You know what happens to those who threaten what's mine."

The witch-queen practically purrs. "I don't think it's those who threaten that should be wary, Fire-bringer." She runs her tongue over her teeth, that gaze never wavering. A collector of all things powerful. Just like my father. "From what I've heard, it's those you claim who should take heed. Tortured. Kidnapped. Stabbed. I promise to be far gentler when I collect the young earth-shaker."

Flame swirls in my chest, even as her words beckon shame from the recesses of my soul. Shame that she's right. *You only destroy.*

I coax the fire higher, feeding it the thought before it can land. It's been so long since we've fed on anyone's pain but our own. Would it be a relief, to feel something we hold no ownership over? To escape the heaviness of guilt for just a moment—to relish in someone else's?

"I am, however, a pragmatic ruler."

I make a sound of disbelief. "Is that so?"

"I would make you an offer to spare your earth-wielder from my service." The witch-queen runs her gaze from the top of my head down to my feet in an assessment that feels like something crawling over my skin. "Even now that magic has returned, wielders are not so easy to come by since your...purge." She says the word delicately, as if discussing the unruly habits of a child and not the extermination of an entire people. Bile rises in my throat as she continues, "I, of course, have always had my ways of finding the rarities of this continent."

She trails a finger along her mouth. "But fire-bearers, *they* are the true prize. So rare, that someone is strong enough to hold flame. Since the fall of the Boundary, there has not been a single report of another."

Water threads through the man's fingers, and I cannot tear my eyes from it. The element that holds my heart, but also, the one that haunts me. That I cannot escape in dreams and waking. The queen means to coerce me into coming with her. And if I don't, if I fail, she'll take Helias as a consolation.

"I've seen what you do to those in your service, Akari. The people of your city you purport to protect who you only exploit. I'll have to pass, for both Helias *and* myself."

More water droplets rise from the damp earth, trickling into the wielder's hands. I cannot let Akari anywhere near Similis, not only for Helias' sake, but also Avedis'. She's hunted him for years, her lost prize—a wound to her pride that still smarts years later. Her and my father are more alike than she'd like to admit, and I don't want to know the lengths she'd go to force the wind-wielder back under her thrall.

My flames ignite, sparking from my palms and sizzling to the ground. They crawl over the underbrush slowly, their light a dance of consumption as they eat everything in their path. The witch-queen doesn't retreat, only watches them with a glint in her eye. And when my flame reaches her feet, biting at them just enough to remind her what they feel like on her skin, she motions to the two standing behind her. "I thought you might need convincing."

She steps deftly behind them, and the ground opens beneath me once more.

This time, I'm ready. It was never Helias causing the earthquakes.

Ilinka has found two wielders, water and earth.

But unfortunately for them, they didn't succeed in killing me the first time. And I learn from my mistakes.

Instead of leaping up, I jump forward, vaulting over the trembling ground as it crumbles. Dirt showers down like a cascading waterfall. I spiral through the air, twisting my body and landing directly in front of the water-wielder with a wild snarl. He aims a jet of water for my face, but it dissipates into steam before it hits my skin.

The earth-wielder stands a few feet away from us, her face screwed up in concentration, hands pushed out in front of her. The ground begins to crawl like the soil is a sentient being. It snakes over my feet, yanking at my ankles, determined to pull me into the earth. I unsheathe a dagger and slash through the tendrils, just as the water-wielder sends another stream blasting for my face.

I raise my flame just before it hits, cursing inwardly. I can't fight them both unless I burn them alive. I've killed no one but my father since Mirren healed my soul, and the thought of shattering it makes me ill.

So I'll have to use something other than violence. Cunning.

I duck beneath another stream of water and hurtle sideways to grab a low hanging branch. Grunting as my good arm takes the brunt of my weight, I swing my legs up even as the as tree trembles beneath me. Leaves and limbs shower down, a deluge of debris that burns to ash before it can land. The flames heat my heart, my skin, my brain, until all I do is burn. They wrap around me, leaving me both breathless and satiated.

Fire dances from me, winding through the branches, and then races down the trunk. Embers spark, and the tree ignites, a conflagration of destruction. Balancing my feet, I leap toward the next tree just as the first goes tumbling over.

Sparks fly everywhere as the massive tree crashes to the ground, and both wielders are forced to dart for cover. It's enough to break the concentration of the earth-wielder, and the ground stills, even as the water-wielder douses the flaming tree. The woman's pause is all I need, and still burning, I launch myself at her.

She claws at me as we go tumbling across the ground. Fingernails dig into my face as the earth rises to protect the wielder. Soil crawls over my limbs, and electric pain shoots through my injured wrist as the tendrils of earth yank it backward. But I don't relent, circling the two of us in a wall of flame that streaks upward higher than the canopy.

The water-wielder shouts, but his voice is lost in the barrage of chaos. He pummels the flaming wall with a stream of water, but has the good sense to stay back, even as I wrap my fingers around the earth-wielder's throat. When I meet her eyes, they're a light shade of hazel, wide and terrified. And somewhere beyond the roar of the abyss in my chest and the roar of fire around me, the memory lingers of what it felt like to be controlled. To kill for someone else, to shred your soul in the service of another's battle.

The soil snaps at my skin like whips, but despite the pain, I hesitate. We stare at each other, and as power floods my veins, howling and whirling, I keep it locked in my chest. My body shakes with restraint.

Are you truly so weak to leave her alive? Have you learned nothing, Heir? My father's voice, as clear as if he stands next to me. *Are you going to let mercy put everything you love in danger?*

End this. End her.

The earth-wielder squirms wildly beneath me, clawing at my wrist as her lips begin to turn blue. I should kill her before she kills me. End her before she has a chance to threaten the life I've poured my blood into rebuilding.

The abyss roars in approval, an echo of the fire around us. *Take from her before she can take from us.*

"Relent," I whisper, the word barely audible.

Her eyes widen, and then flick toward where the witch-queen inevitably stands watching. Safe from the bite of her own consequences.

"Relent," I say again as the ground beneath us surges. I have only a split second to make a decision; she'll open up another hole beneath the both of us, and I'll be doomed. But I know the harm the witch-queen has caused Avedis and Cal; know the price this woman's service carves. And beyond the dark slash of my father's death, beyond the Darkness edging my soul, is the light Mirren gifted me. "Relent, and I'll free you from her."

A slight hesitation, a fraction of a pause.

And then, the earth-wielder nods. Barely perceptible,

but her body stills beneath me. The ground settles. Meeting her gaze, I nod. And then press my fingers into her pressure point until she passes out.

Gritting my teeth, I stand and drop my wall of flame. The water-wielder stands before me, shielding the witch-queen from view with both his body and the whirlwind of water around them. Unlike the earth-wielder, he doesn't appear to have any reservations about killing for Akari Ilinka. He tilts his head, a malicious smile carving his angled face. "I've heard the tales, Heir," he says, a dark glint in his eye. "The almighty Fire-bringer, terrified of a little bit of water."

The droplets swirl higher, faster. How the witch-queen managed to discover my weakness, I have no idea, but I'm not surprised. It was only a matter of time before someone realized I'm not invincible—that I can be trapped in my mind by memories. I watch the man's storm with a face of stone as I call my flame back to me, curling it over my heart. I won't allow it to be doused by fear—not again.

"A little rain, and the Heir runs and hides. Cowers and cries, unable to produce even a spark." He pushes the water outward slowly, the droplets growing ever closer to where I stand frozen. He laughs, excitement and spite clear on his face as he taunts me. I watch the water, and in spite of my resolve, I can't help but remember the way it feels in my throat. Vomit surges in my stomach, and suddenly, I am choking, my lungs burning, unable to get any air.

"Shall we test how true the rumors are?" The man goads. "See what happens when a fire-bearer finally meets his equal?"

The water shoots forward, and the world seems to slow as I watch the wave race toward me. Glittering and cold.

Like my father's eyes. Like the steel of his blade and the edge of his obsession.

Like the dungeons of the Castellium.

The man cackles loudly, and it rings through my heart, as I don't move to conjure even a flicker.

Don't move to defend myself at all.

He bares his teeth as the water surrounds me, his face going red with exertion and madness.

I hold my breath, as my flames brush up against my soul, a soft caress. *Mine.*

I imagine how different the last year would have been, if only I'd been allowed to claim my own power. Feed it. I imagine burning through the Castellium, so hot, I melt the stone that's stood for centuries.

The moment the water touches my skin, I burst into flame. A conflagration of the guilt and the anger and everything in between. I've been shoving it down, struggling to keep my head above it all, but now, I let it all outside of myself. My power *shivers* with delight as I nourish it, and flames of the hottest blue ripple from me in shining waves.

Everything around me ignites, an explosion of light and heat so powerful, the very trees bend with its force.

Calmly, I draw the fire back to me. The tendrils curl up my arms and slither through my chest, their warmth imbuing my aching bones, as I survey the damage around me.

Acrid smoke fills the air, and ash rains down from the hole burning in the canopy. Ilinka is nowhere to be found, but the water-wielder is sprawled a few feet away. His blonde hair is now singed close to his scalp, his skin a mottled mixture of red and black. It peels away from his bones in some places and is entirely gone in others. His breaths come in ragged wheezes; the scorched remains of his lungs unable to absorb enough oxygen.

He blinks up to where I loom over him, his mouth opening and closing in whistling gasps. I tilt my head as I watch him, the abyss inside me rising and settling in turn. "Being a water-wielder does not make you my equal."

That was his mistake. Thinking a small amount of power could match the Darkness that has always burned in me, the fire, and the ruthless drive.

My eyes rove coldly over his ruined body. "I have only one equal. And you—you are not her."

∼

Calloway

The gates hold, but the Boundary does not.

Though we stationed as many archers as we could atop the ruins of the wall, our arrows are useless against the shield of wind protecting the militia. The archers are forced to retreat as the soldiers scale the Boundary. They stream into the agricultural fields, even as the landmines we'd buried there explode. Bodies fly and screams sound, and still, they come.

My heart pounds violently in my chest as Avedis and I slip soundlessly through the only field that hasn't yet been harvested, the stalks swaying with the slight breeze that follows the assassin wherever he goes. Normally, the sound would calm me—a sound of earth and home—but today, it only heightens my anxiety.

If we're going to stand any chance of survival, we have to find the opposing wind-wielder. Break through his shields and alert Shaw and Mirren. It's why Avedis and I left the paltry forces we mustered in the charge of Harlan and Max, why I keep putting one foot in front of the other, even as my heart desperately tries to yank me backward.

Though Avedis moves silently, it isn't with the same lithe grace I've become accustomed to of Shaw. Where Anni is a mountain cat slinking through the forest, Avedis is a bear: all claws and heft and teeth, his movements kept silent only by the wind that trails him.

When we reach the edge of the field, Avedis drops into a crouch. I kneel next to him, peering out at the expanse of soldiers. My breath evaporates in a rush of anger as I take in the sight before us. There are at least a thousand of them, all armed to the teeth and standing at the ready. Waiting for orders.

But it isn't their numbers or swords or spears that replace my blood with acid.

It's the color of their regalia. The white of the witch-queen.

"Avedis," I breathe. No other words are needed. The assassin's eyes have already sharpened, his affable charm having long given way to steel death. There is no mercy on his face as he watches the militia he was once a part of—there's nothing soft at all.

Because Akari Ilinka stole everything tender when Avedis was just a child. She took everything delicate and wrapped it in darkness; gilded it in death, until it could only be hers.

Mama. Papa. Lila. Vee.

They were *my* softness, and she stole them, too. And now she seeks to do the same to the innocents of Similis, all the in the name of more.

For a moment, rage squeezes my lungs so intensely, I can't speak. Half-choking, I manage to clear my throat. "I thought she was dealing with an uprising in Siralene."

Avedis spits out a curse, his face lethal as he stares out at the militia. "It appears she's culled her opposition." The corn stalks around us begin to shake as a strong wind whistles through, smelling like the edge of winter. Of starvation. And I understand it, because when Akari Ilinka handles dissent, she leaves no survivors.

I shiver against the cold, tugging my collar closer to my neck as Avedis closes his eyes. He grows completely still, something I've not been able to manage a single moment in my life. Even now, feet away from enemy combatants, and my knee bobs up and down of its own accord. Movement has always calmed me, the simple act of fidgeting usually enough to ground me to the present.

Now, though, even the motion of my body doesn't save me from falling into the past. From the smell of smoke, and the sights of complete destruction.

Avedis snaps his eyes open, and motions toward the back of the militia. The last of the soldiers have climbed the Boundary, but some still stand guard atop the ruins. And below them, three people dressed in teal, their cloaks a riot of color against the sea of white and the monotony of gray that is Similis itself.

"How in the Darkness are we ever going to get to them through that?" I ask incredulously. There are at least a couple hundred soldiers between our hiding place and the other wielders. "I mean, I know you've got the wind, but so do they. I'd bet anything those other two are wielders, too."

Avedis makes a humming noise, but he doesn't respond. Only stares at the other three wielders like he can see through them.

I scoff in disbelief. "Why would Ilinka denote her wielders so obviously?"

"Arrogance," Avedis replies, his voice oddly distant. "Arrogance has always been the queen's downfall."

He isn't wrong. Akari Ilinka subscribes to the same ideals as most of the power hungry: the world owes her, and so, she will take what she is owed. Though there is never any end to the debt, always consuming more and more.

"Can't you just do your obnoxious wind thing, and suck the air from their lungs?" I ask, motioning vaguely to the militia.

The assassin twists his mouth wryly. "The windwielder has a shield around most of the militia. That's how they managed to get through the wood unheard. I don't know that I'll be able to break it." He hesitates, the indecision so unlike him that I blink. "And I've never controlled an entire army's worth of air. I'm not sure if I'd be able to, to be honest. Or what it would cost if I could."

His soul. His body. Magic has been gone so long, no one is truly aware of its limitations. Or its sacrifices.

I yank an arrow from my quiver and grip my bow in its my hand. Its serpentine curve fits against my palm like it was carved just for me. The loss of my eye took some adjustment, but there was comfort in the fact the feel of my bow is always the same, even if I were to lose my sight entirely. "Alright then, how are we going to keep this army from annihilating everything until Shaw and Mirren can get back here?"

When Avedis turns to me, I almost rear back at what I see. Fervent excitement shines in his eyes, twists along his mischievous mouth, as if he can't imagine anything more fun than the prospect of facing an entire army alone. "You did lament the boredom of lemming life," he says lightly, even as he raises his eyebrows in challenge.

"Dying wasn't *exactly* what I had in mind to break up the monotony."

Avedis smiles, smooth charm edged with cunning madness, as the wind rushes around us. "You have to admit, even dying would be better than another day of food with no salt." He springs to his feet, pulling his sword from the sheath at his hip. So much about Avedis is ornate and dramatic, but his weapons are plain. Utilitarian.

He makes to step forward, but I jump up and grab his shoulder, forcing him to look at me. "And what if we meet Ilinka out there, Avedis? We're outnumbered a hundred to one. You've spent your life avoiding her. Are you just going to get yourself killed at her feet now?"

Avedis' eyes wander from my hand's place on the bulk of his shoulder, before finally rising to meet mine once more. There is no fear, no shame. Only pure defiance. "I have never been under the illusion that repaying the monster who created me would be easy. The world does not care of our losses, Calloway. It does not dole out merciful atonements for wrongs done. It is up to us to take it by the throat. To force it to give back what is ours."

For a wild moment, he appears far away from Similis, lost in another time. Another loss. "We must pull the thorns by the roots, or else we leave them to rise up and strangle someone else." He lifts his chin. "And if I die doing it, so be it. I belong to the Darkness as it is."

I purse my lips in annoyance, and mutter, "I think you've been hanging around with Anni far too much."

Avedis laughs softly, and even though his face doesn't soften, something in his eyes does. "Your soul is whole, Calloway. I will do my best to keep it so."

Something explodes in the distance, deep into the Nemoran. A tremor of power surges through the trees and over the Boundary, its heat brushing across my cheek like a deep summer wind. My heart trips over itself when I realize it can only be Anni. And that, maybe, he doesn't need to be alerted to the queen's presence after all. The power recedes like a wave from shore, and newfound determination threads through me.

Even after being nearly shattered, Anni is still willing to tear himself apart in service of a better world. Maybe it's his ruthless heart, or maybe, it's the stubborn hope in him he refuses to acknowledge.

Once, when we were seventeen, he offered to break his vow for me. To murder Akari Ilinka. He didn't know whether it would be the last piece of his soul, and still, he offered it up to me without hesitation. And when I asked why, he'd simply said I shouldn't have to tear my soul to avenge my family's death. I'd saved him and so he would save me. It was that simple to him. That pure.

I'd refused, and then gone to my room and cried.

Because as much as I wanted the witch-queen dead, I couldn't let Anni do it. He was willing to give up everything to honor our friendship, and I was willing to give up nothing, even for my family's vengeance. I was too terrified of tearing my soul; scared of seeing my family's murderer and facing the memories I'd tried so hard to escape.

I was scared of who I would become if I ever confronted the past.

It's always been easier to hide, to tell myself the witch-queen's death would ultimately change nothing.

My family would still be dead.

But now that she's here, am I still willing to say her death would change nothing? Do I still think protecting my soul matters, when I might be able to save an entire territory with its ruin?

I've never been brave like Anni, never been steadfast. But I'm not exempt from the Darkness, no matter how far I run.

I meet Avedis' gaze. "Don't worry about my soul. Let's go get those wielders."

CHAPTER SEVEN

Shaw

Vomit climbs my throat. *Fuck.*

All around me is destruction—ash rains down from the burning trees and the night sky is obscured by wreathes of thick smoke. The ground is blackened and dead, and both Akari Ilinka and the earth-wielder are nowhere to be found.

What remains of the water-wielder lies sprawled a few feet from me. Painful, wheezing gasps sound from his scorched chest, and as his last breath passes between his lips, a familiar agony tears through me.

The soul Mirren died to give me, shredded through once again.

I claw my hands through my hair, rub the heels of my palm into my eyes. I cannot be trusted with good things. I am not careful. I am not kind.

I brutal. I am ruination.

You love and so it will be taken from you.

Or I'll destroy it before it can be stolen. Without ever meaning to.

My nerves sizzle as my soul shreds, but I squeeze my

eyes shut and breathe through it. When I'd killed my father, I was out of my mind with grief, and far too gone to acknowledge the wound. I thought it might feel different to fragment a new soul, but the pain is the same as it's always been. Deep. Dark. Acidic.

I gulp down a few quick breaths and wait until the agony passes before opening my eyes. I pull two daggers from my bandolier, their blades crafted from the same carved, black metal as my father's sword that hangs in a sheath at my hip. Mirren offered my old knives back, but as much as I've missed the feel of them, I choose to wield the Praeceptor's weapons instead. A reminder. A penance.

I give myself two more breaths of regret, then straighten my spine. Because the witch-queen lives and I can't let her anywhere near Similis.

My flames flicker in my chest, licking at my heart and feeding on the abyss as I begin to hunt. Ilinka is quick and clever, a warrior in all senses of the words or she never would have kept her territory this long. But she was born to the sands of Siralene, not the shadows of the Nemoran. She doesn't know its oddities, or the way the smallest broken twig will lead me in her direction.

Her trail is nearly invisible, but I find it in the compression of the leaves and the sweep of branches. I race between the trees, silently following the trail as dread unspools heavily in my stomach.

Just as I feared, she's headed in the direction of Similis.

A moment later, I catch sight of her. A spill of dark hair, a flash of tawny skin. She spins, raising her sword in a deadly arc, but it's too late as a wall of fire rises around her. Akari snarls, stepping toward me, and her prison shrinks, the flame licking at the toes of her boots. She keeps her blade raised like she's preparing to cut herself out, and her eyes dart around her, searching for an escape.

"Well, this looks familiar," I drawl, slowing my pace to an arrogant saunter.

Her red lips twist in a snarl as she tracks my movements. "I suggest you keep your distance, Heir. Unless you'd like to add a thousand more deaths to your already sizable list."

Irritation flares that I don't know what she means, that she's a step ahead of me again. But there's a reason the witch queen has never been deposed: a cutting mixture of cleverness and brutality that's hard to beat.

Flames conflagrates in my palms. I tilt my head and smile, taking another prowling step. "Go on."

The queen steps back the fraction my flames will allow and her teal cloak catches on a wiry bit of underbrush. She snatches it away, glaring at me insolently. "I've always hated this infernal forest with its horrible trees and bloodsucking creatures. Someone should have burned it a century ago."

I make a noncommittal noise. "I think you'd feel right at home among those creatures. Now, quit stalling, Akari, before I lose my patience."

Akari licks her lips, examining me anew. "Have you not wondered why your air-wielder has gone silent, Heir?"

Something ice cold slithers through me. It isn't abnormal for Avedis not to hear everything, but an explosion of flame right outside the city walls? I was too caught up to think about it clearly, but the queen's gloating smile is enough to swell my dread.

"I am heir of nothing," I tell her, buying time as my mind races. *What has she done?*

"Ah, that isn't quite true, is it? You slayed the warlord. Is that not how the line of succession works in Argentum? Whoever has the most kills, the biggest cock, or some other odious rule decided by small minded men?"

The queen is technically right. Even before my father's reign, the Argentian warlord seat has always been passed to whoever is the most vicious. The higher your body count, the higher your chances. And my father ensured no one will ever be able to best mine. "I have no interest in Argentum," I reply flatly.

She lets out an incredulous laugh, her dark hair spilling over her shoulder. "You're truly going to allow a man who has lived his life beneath electric lights take what's rightfully yours? What you've earned by blood?"

I level a blank stare.

"He's creating another Similis, you know. Another city filled with mindless followers. Because truly, are the lemmings any different than the soulless? And the almighty Fire-bearer is just going to sit back and let him, in the name of what? Being gentle?" She laughs again, this one ringing through the trees. "You can pretend all you want with your ocean-wielder. Pretend you're a peaceful man. But beneath your skin, you will always be what you are. The monster who slaughtered his way across the continent, who *earned* his father's seat."

"I have no interest in Argentum," I repeat brusquely, even as my skin begins to crawl with her words.

The queen throws her hands up. "Men!" she spits as if it's the worst insult she can imagine. "The world thinks women to be the weaker sex, always ruled by their emotions. But can we not agree, it is men who are always weak minded enough to bend to every impulse? Your daddy didn't love you and so you reject power? Pathetic."

Absurd laughter bubbles in my chest, and I have to

press my lips together to keep a straight face. "It's a shame you were always trying to murder each other. You would have gotten on really well with my father." I coax my flame casually up the length of my arms, before setting the queen with a cool gaze. "And I think you're stalling, Akari."

The flame around the queen flares, the bright tendrils winding and dancing higher around her legs. For the first time, I see a hint of fear. The unbearable pain, the smell of cooked skin. Being burned is not something one forgets, a stain always in the back of the mind. Much like drowning.

The fear in her eyes doesn't reach her voice. "I'd be careful if I were you, Heir. The wind hears everything. I'd hate to see what my militia does if it hears my screams."

Wind. Militia.

Ilinka's face glimmers with satisfaction. "Go ahead and kill me, Fire-bringer. Split that shiny new soul. But my army has orders upon my death, and you'll have no one to help you protect Similis." She runs her tongue along her teeth, looking entirely too smug for someone outmatched and surrounded by flame. "You'll have to kill them all and give up your soul completely."

She stands straighter, adjusting her cloak primly. "Don't tell me a part of you doesn't want to. Souls were not made to carry the weight of crimes such as yours." The queen runs her eyes from the top of my head to my feet in assessment. "It must be *excruciating* to live as you have the past few weeks."

I snarl, snapping my flames higher, but she only laughs.

"I'd beg you to spare yourself the horror of becoming that soulless wraith once again, but I fear it's already too late for you. You've already let the Darkness in. It's only a matter of time before it's stronger than you. I suppose the only question that remains is whether it will be today or tomorrow."

The witch-queen cocks her head. "Do you think your sweet little ocean-wielder will stand by your side when you shatter what she gave you?"

The abyss in my chest billows, it's roar reverberating against my ribs as crimson flame shades my vision. The queen is taunting me, but it doesn't make her wrong. I may have a new soul, but the curse is a compulsion, and it has already begun to spread, beginning the moment I shoved a flaming sword into my father's chest.

You'll lose her anyway. Give in, give in.

I grin at the queen, madness and wild, agitated fire burning in my eyes. "I choose today, Queen."

∽

Calloway

We're halfway to the wielders when everything descends into chaos.

Something shifts in the air around us, and Avedis whirls to me in warning. And then, whatever tether kept the militia in stasis snaps. With a reverberating cry, the force surges forward toward the city.

"Godsdammit!" I shout, all thoughts of remaining invisible gone. I've barely managed to yank my swords from their sheaths, and Avedis is already darting out into the open. He raises his hands and squeezes his eyes shut, and the wind rises to his call. It whips into a cyclone, whirling along the outer edges of the city. The militia may be shielded, but the buildings of Similis are not. A deafening *crack* resounds as the quarterages are ripped from their foundations and rise into the air, where they hover for only a moment. Then, with a slight grunt, Avedis sends them careening into the front lines of the enemy.

My mouth gapes open as quarterage after quarterage is ruined, and the debris piles in a giant blockade. But I don't have time to marvel at Avedis' power as soldiers begin to shout and run toward him. The assassin sways on his feet, his breathing labored, and I leap between them, slicing at the nearest one's thighs. He goes down with a shriek, but I'm already on my knees, sliding toward the next, my blade swinging in a lethal arc.

The militia's surge forward is waylaid by Avedis' blockade, but it'll only hold for so long. Even from here, I see people fighting atop it and something like panic wends through me. I don't need to see their faces to know Max is one of them, slicing down any soldier who manages to make it to the top. The Similian arrows still bounce harmlessly off the air shield around them, and my heart wallops against my chest as I think of Max and Harlan defenseless against the onslaught.

"Avedis, we gotta move faster or our only line of defense is going to fall. We have to get to those wielders."

The assassin doesn't acknowledge me, only runs his blade perfunctorily across the nearest soldier's throat and collapses three more by pulling the air from their lungs. If it tears his soul, he doesn't let on, moving from one soldier to the next, a blur of wind and violence. His dark brow furrows in concentration, and his gaze never wavers from his next opponent, never searches for the wielders. And suddenly, I understand why.

We don't have to find the wielders. They've found us.

Two women and a man dressed in teal cloaks stalk through the ranks, their hands stretched in front of them and their faces bloodless and pale. I can feel the call of their combined wind, the hard press of air they keep around the militia.

Avedis' lips pull back from his teeth in a snarl as he dips his head toward the wielders, a predator sizing up its opponent. And then, he unleashes himself and the strength of a hurricane shreds straight through the shield.

The wielders are forced to pull the shield back, pressing it closer to themselves like armor. There are heartened cheers from the front lines, where finally, Similian arrows find their mark. And it isn't enough, but just maybe, our paltry forces will be able to hold their ground until Anni arrives.

Tree boughs ripped from the Nemoran fly through the air around us. Beams from destroyed quarterages circle above, before spearing for their marks, impaling some and crushing others. The wielders shout for reinforcements, and a fresh wave of soldiers breaks from the larger group and surges toward Avedis.

I yank my bow from my shoulder and send arrow after arrow flying into any who manage to claw their way toward the assassin. *Thwack, thwack, thwack.* The familiar sound sings against my ear as soldiers fall. Heartened, I push forward, slicing with my sword, and then send another wave of arrows raining down.

But rather the scattering beneath the onslaught, the three wielders raise their hands as one. A giant gale howls across the field, barreling into Avedis and I. It's all I can do to keep hold of my bow as I watch every one of my arrows freeze in midflight and fall listlessly to the ground. Another wind rises, pummeling against whatever shield Avedis erected. He groans as the pressure steals his breath, and his feet skid along the overturned dirt as they push him back.

They aren't as strong as he is.

The thought pummels into me as I watch the synchronicity with which they move. Together, they are able to stand against him, but apart—

I duck, lowering my stance as close to the ground as I can manage, and begin to stalk forward. They don't bother with a simple, powerless man, their eyes only on Avedis. And isn't that the irony of the powerful? Always underestimating those weaker until they've fallen on their sword.

I spin, swing, dance backward and then spiral forward, all to the rhythm of my heart. Anni has always compared fighting to a dance, and while his habit of staining even the most beautiful things with blood has been a long-standing source of annoyance, in this, he isn't wrong. I never wanted a sword in my hand, nor a bow—just a farmer's shovel.

But those days are long past, and after all these years, I can see the music in the battle.

The wielders bear down on Avedis as I draw closer.

"Hold on," I grunt, walloping another soldier over the head. I don't know if Avedis can hear me, but the words hearten my drive.

Until the wielders break through his shield.

My stomach leaps into my throat as Avedis is thrown to the ground. The wielders hands clench and release in time, and I know I have only seconds before they steal the air from his lungs.

I lunge forward, falling to my knees and twisting beneath the last guard's blade. And then I sink my sword into the soft spot just below the smallest wielder's ribs. She gasps, and her mouth gapes open as I jump back to my feet and run the blade over her throat.

Blood sprays everywhere, speckling my hands and face as she topples backward, her body oddly heavy for her small stature. And somewhere in the distant recesses of my mind, I know I should keep moving. That stillness is death.

But sharp agony spreads from my heart outward, as if someone has taken every bone in my body and cracked it in half. I stumble beneath the dead wielder's weight and clutch desperately at my chest as we both collapse to the ground in a heap. I stare into her unseeing eyes, even as my veins pull taut and shining hot pain radiates through every molecule in my body.

The other wielder screams, a high-pitched harrowing sound, as she realizes her friend's blank stare is permanent. Her attention momentarily strays from Avedis to where I lay, prostrate and trapped beneath her dead comrade. Horror flashes in her eyes, followed by rage. Her mouth twists and she lifts her hands.

A stray branch rises beside me.

With a snarl, she stabs the branch into my stomach.

Suddenly, it is not just my soul in agony, but my entire physical body. Hot, electric, blinding pain.

Stars bloom behind my eyelids and ice spreads from my abdomen to my limbs.

I hear Avedis' roar of fury and take heart in the fact it sounds so distant. He is alive and he is powerful enough to save Similis. To protect Harlan, and Max, and Helias. I hear the strength of his anger, but I cannot feel his wind as it blasts the remaining wielders.

I can't feel anything at all.

CHAPTER
EIGHT

Calloway

Is this the Darkness, then?

Endless void, resolute nothingness.

There is no light. No tormented souls. No vengeful gods. Only emptiness.

How anticlimactic, I think ruefully as the numbness gives way to an unbearable chill. My body shivers violently, and the Similian sky sharpens and fades from my vision. Caught somewhere between life and infinite night.

I've never died before, but I know enough to realize the blood pouring from my wound should feel hot. So, I close my eyes and imagine another sky, stained in shades of cottony pinks and watery blues. The sky I was born beneath.

If I'm going to the Darkness, I'm sure as hell not going to do it surrounded by the ugly monotony of Similis. I'll die surrounded by vibrant splashes of color and laughter, where the sun shines all year, and nothing is ever gray.

As if I've willed it into existence, a blinding light flashes above me.

It stains my closed eyelids with splotches of neon color, and then flashes again, the heat of it so dazzling, I'd shield my face if I could move any of my limbs.

And then, my cold shock is replaced by excruciating pain. It radiates from somewhere near my stomach to every nerve in my body. I scream, in my head or out loud, I can't be sure. Breath shoots from my lungs and my eyes fly open.

It is not the sun of Siralene beating down on me, but a ring of pure flame, the tendrils licking up higher into the sky than the Nemoran canopy. I blink up at them, wondering if this is perhaps the end people speak of, when Anni's face comes into view. All the blood has leeched from his skin and beneath a thick layer of mud, his expression is tortured.

I wheeze as the smell of burning flesh fills my nostrils, and the sound of it snaps Anni's gaze from where his hands press into my wound, to my face. Relief washes over his panic, a cresting wave, as we stare at each other in shocked silence for a few long moments.

My throat feels like it's on fire as I attempt to swallow. "Did you—" My voice cracks. "Did you *burn* me?"

At the accusation in my voice, Anni lowers his brow and leans back on his heels, removing his bloodstained hands from where, only moments before, a tree limb had protruded. Now, an angry burn bubbles up in splotches of pink and black, the skin peeling away in grotesque layers. A wave of nausea overcomes me, and I gulp down small sips of air to keep from puking.

"I wouldn't have had to if you hadn't been about to die," he snaps hotly. "What in godsnames were you thinking? You know never to let your guard down like that. It was sloppy and reckless."

His words are sharp, but I know they're cut by the

blades of his panic. I roll my eyes at his self-righteous tone, and immediately regret it, as my vision begins to swim. "I know you've always been threatened by my good looks, but permanently marring me twice in one year...it's really beneath you, brother. Petty, even."

Anni's mouth twists, and he pushes an irritated breath through his teeth. "Calloway—" he mutters in warning, but the world has begun to feel oddly light, like my body may very well float off the ground at any moment. My words feel much the same as they pour out me in a bubbly, convoluted mess.

"Perhaps the next time *you're* about to die, I'll shave all your hair off as revenge. Avedis can pull the look off, but I really don't think you have the head shape for it—"

"Calloway, the witch-queen is here."

This silences me and sends me crashing back to earth with cruel accuracy. I meet Anni's clear gaze. Flame reflects in the pale irises, and whether it's the fire burning around us, or the one burning within him at all times, something about it grounds me in the present.

I am not dead. And there is still more to do.

"I know."

Anni breathes deeply and nods. "I didn't kill her." His words are oddly tangled, as if he doesn't know whether he's confessing a sin, or the complete opposite.

And indeed, I don't know whether I feel anger or gratitude. So, I reply, "I killed one of the wind-wielders."

We stare at each other for another prolonged moment, even as the sounds of battle rage around us. It's then I remember why we're here, why I got myself stabbed in the first place. Anni opens his mouth, but I shake my head. There is more to say, but with him, I've never needed to say it. He knows the gaping wound in my soul left by the witch-queen. And he knows the new laceration gouged by the wind-wielder's death.

"You should probably stop wallowing at my bedside and go help Avedis and Max."

He scowls at me, which is as good as an *I love you* where Anni is concerned. He releases the flames around us, and I blink wildly, attempting to clear the stains of light from my vision. The battle has surged closer to the city. Though the wielders' shield has fallen as they battle Avedis, the Similians are still far outnumbered, and the witch-queen's militia has broken through the rubble. Now, they stream into the city proper.

I attempt to sit up, but as a fresh wave of agony sizzles through me, I settle for dragging myself toward an overturned tree trunk and prop myself against it with an undignified groan.

Anni's gaze homes in on where Avedis battles the remaining two wielders. "Which one?"

I shake my head, already knowing what he means to do. My brother does not allow those he calls his to be taken from him, never gives up an inch whether the Darkness demands it or not. And I've been his since we were fifteen, and he'd stopped growling long enough to teach me to spar.

But now I understand the price his protection demands; the agony of giving up a piece of your soul.

When Anni flicks his eyes back to me, they are fathomless. Like the heart of a star that burns so hot, it turns to ice. "Which. One." He grits out through his teeth.

I don't answer, only stare up at him solemnly and press my hand to my wound with a hiss. A grin pulls at his mouth. He knew I wouldn't tell him.

"Both then," he says perfunctorily, unsheathing two black daggers from his bandolier.

He hesitates only once, and I know it's worry for me, half-dead and undefended. I motion vaguely to my bow. "I can still shoot. Go."

Anni steels his spine. A lone muscle twitches in his jaw as he nods to me once, and then sprints toward Avedis.

My killing hadn't been in vain, as it turned the odds in the assassin's favor, but it still wasn't enough to overpower them completely. Not as soldiers run at him from all sides and both wielders barrel down upon him with fury. Dust whirls around them in blinding clouds, sandblasting Avedis' eyes, even as he cuts down three more militia members.

Anni races into the fray. He moves like his own wind, a spiraling storm of grace and power. Where his body dances, where his blades flash—soldiers fall. He cuts his way toward Avedis with single-minded determination, no longer a man at all, but a creature of destruction and chaos.

And when he reaches the wind-wielders, I hardly have time to blink before a blade sprouts from the first's throat. A blur of movement, and Anni has already dropped low to slice through the back of the last wielder's knees.

Dread crawls through me, winding alongside relief. A swift blade across the throat, and the woman who stabbed me falls to the ground in a pool of her own blood. The feel of the Darkness' knife when it carves its price is debilitating, never-ending pain. But my brother doesn't even flinch. Instead, he bursts into flame, throwing a shield around himself and Avedis. The soldiers who run at it, who try to cut through it, burn alive.

As more soldiers stream into Similis toward Max and

Harlan and Helias; as more circle around Anni and Avedis, it is not my injury that spreads ice through my veins.

It's the realization that the only way to win is if Anni kills everyone on this field.

And he never loses.

~

Shaw

"Have a nice, leisurely stroll through the Nemoran, did you?" Avedis grunts as he brings his longsword slicing down through a half-burned soldier who somehow survived the jump through my shield.

"Very relaxing," I shout back over the roar of flame, the clamor of battle around us. A fiery arm reaches through, and a scream sounds as I hack down across the wrist. "I particularly enjoyed my time in a hundred-foot hole being partially drowned. Extremely enlightening."

Avedis only raises an eyebrow and lifts his hands. I oblige, lowering the wall only long enough for him to direct what remains of a quarterage door into an encroaching group of militia. They tumble backward under the force, colliding into one another with bellows of anger. "Have time in the hole to figure out how to defeat an entire army without losing both our souls in the process?"

As if in demonstration, he rubs gingerly at his chest. While I was dealing with the witch-queen, Avedis has been giving over pieces of himself bit by bit for a place that would never do the same for him. My resolve surges anew as I push the flame out further, just to give us a chance to breathe. In the distance, the head of the army disappears into the city, a flood of bodies and weapons.

I'm sure Harlan and Max have done their best to get

everyone to safety, but I've seen what happens when warlords conquer other territories. Total destruction. Ruination of everything that makes a place what it is. Beginning with its people.

And those were territories that haven't been hated for centuries.

We're on borrowed time.

I'd known the militia would attack whether I left the witch-queen alive or not. And while she's no longer in any condition to lead them, her current state won't allow her to call the attack off either.

And every soldier we leave alive is another body to rise up and stab us in the back.

But if we kill them all, we risk creating a far worse monster. Avedis and I with no souls and an endless supply of power.

Strike, parry, move.

My abyss flares and acid pumps through my veins. "Can't you just suck the air out of them all?"

"Why do people keep asking this like it's never occurred to me? Do I give the impression of being too stupid to suffocate someone?" Avedis snipes. He knocks the sword from a protruding hand, before yanking the attached soldier through the flame. We both watch in disgust as the man collapses at our feet with a pitiable cry. "I spent too much on the wind-wielders, and my depths are running dry. I'm afraid I do not contain enough."

The assassin speaks of the spirits in a way only another wielder would understand. And indeed, he looks ragged—and terrifying. As I examine the deep circles beneath his eyes and the blood spattering his face, my gaze snags on the scar that runs from his forehead to his ear. An outward scar, the mirror of which runs invisibly through me, bonding us together in a way I would have never imagined when I tried to gut him last year.

The Darkness, it seems, has a sense of humor.

Bound.

The word sparks a memory, the story unwinding just as it did the first time Asa told it. "Alone, you don't, but what about together? We're the first four...we're all connected."

Avedis furrows his brow in confusion, his shoulders moving up and down with exerted breaths. "Much to my infernal irritation, I suppose that's true," he admits.

I grin wickedly. "Fire cannot live without air."

The assassin's dark eyes sparkle in amusement as I repeat the words he once spoke to me. Then he dips his head in acknowledgement. "So it cannot. What would you have me do?"

Avedis was raised in the same pits of Darkness as I was—was taught the only person in the world he could trust was himself. I don't take it lightly that he is willing to defer to me now, when both our souls are on the line.

I plant my feet and breathe in deeply. The scent of smoke and blood is thick in my lungs. "Ready?"

Avedis sheathes his sword with a quick nod.

I close my eyes and raise my hands. The abyss rages in my chest, singeing my veins, lapping at my lungs. When I was soulless, my power had been something outside of myself, something that could only be fed by spearing out. But now, it is *mine*. It feeds on my emotions, and billows against my ribs demanding more.

I am lacking in so many aspects of life, but in this, I have enough. Rage, love, terror. All the feelings that have always spilled out of me in waves, too much for any person to contain, now flow into the abyss.

And from it rises a wildfire.

It surges from the depths of me, shooting into the air like a geyser of lava. And when it meets Avedis' wind, it explodes.

His power brushes against mine, so oddly foreign in its crisp gusts. Where I crawl and flicker, Avedis caresses and billows, a gale of whispers intertwining into a song of both melancholy and power. Words and sounds rush around my flame, a deafening cacophony so overwhelming, for a brief moment, I want to stuff my hands over my ears and cower from it.

I open my eyes and peer upward as Avedis' wind skitters over my flame, coaxing it higher, brighter. Together, our power races across the sky, a radiant detonation of light and heat. The militia cries out as the flame curls over them, around them. Waves of fire snap at them like whips, until they are corralled on all sides, trapped in a burning prison.

The rush of power leaves me slightly breathless. It is hard to think beyond the burn, and when I turn to Avedis, I know he feels the same. His eyes have gone from brown to the howling depths of an angry storm. It's the same surge of strength I saw that first night in the manor, though I hadn't recognized it then. I'd only felt a call in my soul I couldn't explain. But now, as he sends his voice on the wind, the powerful sound a tangle of every voice that speaks on the continent, I understand what lives in him.

Your queen has surrendered. His voice is both the sound of rustling breeze and a rageful storm's lament. *We will allow you the chance to do the same. Leave Similis, and we will grant you safe passage.*

My blood boils, and I let out a shout as more power channels through me. There is no limit to its magnitude beyond myself. I create, I shape. I expand the cage of flame, bringing the tendrils a hairsbreadth away from the soldiers.

Panic ensues as soldiers scramble to get away, trampling one another to save themselves from burning.

Any who stay will be met with the Fire-bringer's justice.

Fire has no innate mercy, and for a moment, I cannot remember my own. But buried deep in the embers of my heart lies a fragment of the ocean, soft and healing. It cannot be burned or consumed, so I grasp it, dig in with my nails and squeeze it tight, until I'm able to feel my humanity once more and open up a small path to the Nemoran.

The army surges around us, shouts of anger and bellows of fear weaving alongside the echo of flame and wind. The abyss flares and my body becomes a current of electric sparks that wind their way through me, coaxing my fire higher and higher as I feed it every terrible and wonderful feeling.

My father's blood coating my hands. *You think I hesitate out of love?*

The curve of Mirren's smile. *You are mine, Anrai Shaw. Now and forever.*

Each memory, each feeling, lashes inside me. Their own flame, their own shadow.

Until every last militia member has fled the city.

Avedis staggers on his feet as his wind whips around him, a frantic flutter, before dying to little more than a soft breeze.

I breathe fire as I call my power back to me. It rolls across my tongue, but I swallow it down gulp by gulp until I can feel my human body once more. I coil all of its fury back in my chest where the only person it can burn is me.

CHAPTER NINE

Shaw

We find Cal still propped against the same trunk, his bow laid out across his lap. His face is worryingly pale, the freckles splashed across his skin far starker than usual. But he hasn't lost any more blood. Hopefully, Mirren will be able to fix the mess I made of closing his wound.

The moment the last of my flame curled into my chest, every bit of energy drained from me. My limbs feel a hundred times heavier than normal, and all I want to do is curl up on the blood-soaked ground and sleep for a week. Avedis looks much the same, his ever-present arrogance given way to something far quieter as he limps to Cal's side.

Together we haul Cal up between us, and stagger slowly toward the city. Bodies litter the field, and scavengers already circle above, their caws a song of death. Cal groans in pain with each movement, and though I'm wasted, emptied out and exhausted, the sound spurs me to move faster. I won't let him die on this godsforsaken field. The faster I get him to Mirren, the better off he'll be.

We haven't made it more than a few feet, when two figures come streaming out from behind the rubble of ruined quarterages. Even before I can make out their features, a wash of relief cools some of the burn in my throat. Max. I'd recognize her lithe sprint anywhere, the shape of her movements, the measure of her strides.

I hadn't let myself think of her during the battle, hadn't allowed an inch of terror take space that I'd come back to find her dead, but as she collides into us with all the grace of an angry bear, every bit of fear I repressed crashes down on me. I can hardly breathe as she attacks Cal with a deadly combination of a headlock and a hug. "What in the Darkness is the matter with you?!" she cries into his neck.

Her terror of losing him mirrors my own, but when she pulls back and throws her hands on her hips, her face is all anger. "Throwing yourself into the middle of the militia like you're immortal or something! Are you trying to get yourself killed?!"

Cal wets his lips like he's trying to find the strength to respond. "What's the matter with me? You should be asking what's the matter with him!" He jabs his thumb in my direction. "He just split his shiny new soul. *Again.*"

"I knew you weren't going to let that go," I mutter irritably, hefting his weight further against me. He hisses through his teeth at the jolt of movement. "She tried to kill you, Calloway. What did you expect me to do?"

Max shakes her head in exasperation, and I get a clear look at her for the first time. Her face is covered in a gruesome mask of blood and gore, and it's impossible to determine which bit of it is her own. Her bottom lip is split, and beneath a tear at the thigh of her pants, a nasty welt is already blooming. One of her falchions is sheathed at her back, and the other still clutched in her hand is crusted crimson.

I tilt my head at it. "What about you, Maxi? It doesn't look like you stayed on top of the Covinus building."

She twists her mouth in annoyance. "They were streaming into the city. We had to do something, or they would have overrun everything."

Harlan jogs up beside her, his breathing far more labored than hers. His Similian-style gun is slung over his shoulder, and his hair is coated in a thick layer of blood and ash like he was fighting right alongside Max. But it isn't the golden boy's willingness to get his hands dirty, to fight to protect what he loves that lodges in my throat like warm coal. It's the way his eyes immediately find Cal's, and then break apart as he takes in the grievous injury. Like the thought of Cal being injured has shattered Harlan just as surely as any physical wound.

"I'm okay," Cal assures him softly.

Harlan's throat works, and for an absurd moment, I think he'll do something ridiculous like throw himself at Cal's feet. But he only nods.

And I may not understand what in the Darkness is happening between Cal and Harlan, but I understand that look. The way the fear of someone you love being hurt can threaten to unravel you entirely. "I cauterized the wound," I explain hurriedly in an attempt to assuage his terror. "It was only battlefield triage, but I stopped the blood loss. Mirren will be able to heal everything properly."

At the mention of her name, the world goes oddly still. It's a heavy stillness, one that settles over my heart like a weight; that pulls it so taut, every beat is suddenly painful.

For a moment, no one moves.

"Where is Mirren?" I breathe, my voice so tight it could snap.

Something roars, and I don't know if it's a beast of the Nemoran or my own blood rushing in my ears, but it rises like a crest of fire. *Where is she, where is she, where is she.*

I hardly hear my friends' worried mutters as they begin to realize Mirren hasn't returned with Sura. Someone takes Cal from me, and I don't feel that either, only the scrape of breath in my lungs.

"It's a long walk from that side of the Boundary," one of them says from somewhere far off, "I'm sure they'll be back soon."

But I'm shaking my head violently because I already know what they do not. Can feel it in the depths of my soul, in the untethered beat of my heart against my ribs. *She's gone. They've taken her from me.*

Because if she were here, she would have found her way to the battlefield. She never would have allowed those she loved to face that militia alone, would never have left Similis unprotected to hide somewhere.

There have been very few times in my life panic has overruled the killing calm of the abyss, but it does so now, beginning with the squeeze of my chest and then clawing at my nerves until each end is a frayed current of electricity. I can't think beyond the static, beyond the howl in my head, beyond the weight of my soul barreling down on top of me.

I run at Avedis and grab him by the shoulders. Fingers digging into his skin, I shake him and roar, "Where is she?!"

Avedis doesn't try to assuage my madness. He only closes his eyes and goes still. I stare at the way his dark lashes span across his pale cheekbones, at the slight pull of his gnarled scar, at the determined press of his mouth. I focus on small things to ground myself as the flame inside me rises, because if I don't calm down, it will burn through me, outside of me, until I am nothing but fire.

It feels like before when I had no soul. Drowning in hunger, the voracious ache suddenly consuming. Because Mirren tethers my power to the earth. And without her, we are both left wanting.

Avedis' eyes flick open, his pupils expanding and then shrinking once more. If it was anyone else, they would back away from what burns in my eyes, and wisely so. But the assassin only raises his chin and says calmly, "The Covinus has taken her."

All at once, the rushing in my head, in my soul, explodes.

I squeeze my eyes shut as rage billows out from me, a conflagration of anger and desperation that burns everything around me to ash. Avedis throws up a wall of air just in time to protect my friends from being scorched as I try to pull it back toward my heart.

But the flame is too consuming, too determined; my rage given form. And what is more enduring than my wrath? What is more devouring than my constant need for vengeance? My father is dead, but my anger remains, always seeking to punish even with the source of my pain gone. It is why I've lost Mirren, why I *deserve* to lose her. When will it ever be enough to quell my burning? Does the whole world need to burn so that I won't?

Panic flares as my fire rages, and I force two short breaths into my lungs. I reach out for the third time in as many hours, feeling for Mirren's soul. I sink into its velvet depths, its cool veracity soothing the burning in my throat.

Because even when she's gone, I hold her close. We are forever, entangled. I will not break beneath my anger, will not give in to the pull of my rage. I need to remain whole, so she'll have something to come back to.

Once I'm able to take a few more deep breaths, my flames recede and curl inside my chest. They still burn—they *always* burn—but they don't consume.

They lie in wait.

I will need every bit of flame to get Mirren back. We will scorch everything between here and Argentum, anything that stands between me and Mirren.

When I finally open my eyes, my friends all stare back at me with bated breath, their eyes wide and wary. The earth around us is ash-ridden and gray, the smell of smoke and destruction heavy in the air. Flame has no innate mercy, and I *am* flame. So there is only unending determination when I say, "Gods help the Covinus for taking what is mine."

∽

It's oddly silent as I tear through Similis, which only amplifies the sound of my heart crashing against my ribs like a sledgehammer. The pavement buckles in places and completely crumbles into the ground in others. Entire quarterages have been reduced to mere splinters, while bullet holes pepper the few remaining walls. Littered between the wreckage are the injured and dead.

Even so, there are no sounds of mourning. None of the heart wrenching keening or desperate wails I associate with the devastation of battle. The lemmings load their dead into red vehicles in near silence, while others work side by side to clear a path for the injured to be taken to the

Healing Center. Despite the quiet, the Darkness has left its mark on many of them, evidenced by their tear-soaked cheeks.

I hardly spare any of them a glance or stop to consider there are no longer whispers trailing after me as I sprint toward the quarterage. Cal and Max tried to follow, but without Mirren to heal him, Cal's injury is far more deadly than I first hoped. I'd barked at Harlan and Max to get him to the Healing Center and then taken off into the city. I should feel shame for leaving my best friend behind in that state, but my panic has shattered every rational thought until they all float before me in indistinguishable fragments.

Only one remains. *Get her back.*

I fly through the metropolis, over the red bricks still scorched black in places from my battle with my father, and am just about to turn down the main street that leads to Mirren's quarterage when someone shouts my name. As much as I want to ignore it, to remain focused before I lose any more time, Helias' voice halts me in my tracks. I turn just in time to see the little earth-wielder rushing toward me, Mirren's cloak tucked beneath his chin, the hem dragging along the bricks behind him.

He crashes into me with such force, I'm left temporarily breathless. He wraps his skinny arms around my waist and buries his head in my stomach, his face hidden between the disgusting fabric of my shirt and his mass of tangled curls. My heart twinges as he allows me to lift him up and hold him tight to me. I breathe in his scent and let it blanket my panic for just a moment.

When he pulls back, his face is twisted in fear. "I thought you were dead," he says. "I thought you were gone like them."

His parents. The words embed themselves somewhere deep, the isolated holes left by the loneliness of my childhood. Helias needs a promise I won't leave him; he needs reassurance he'll never be alone. He needs someone better than me because I can't give him either of those things. "Listen, hellion, we need to have a talk. Grown-ups always think kids can't handle the truth, but I know you can. You know I'll never lie to you, right?"

Helias nods, his bottom lip quivering like he senses what's about to come.

"I have to go away for a little while. And I can't promise I'll come back. But I can make you another promise. Do you know what it is?"

He shakes his head, his dark eyes shining.

"I promise you won't ever be alone. You will always have Max or Cal or Avedis or Mirren. You won't ever be on your own again. Do you understand? I can't give you more than I have, and it isn't a lot. But I can give you my family. They found me and loved me, and they'll do the same for you. So there's no reason to be afraid. Okay?"

Helias' makes a desperate sound at the back of his throat, and it threatens to undo me completely as he grips me tighter. His small body is so warm, so breakable. "I need you to go with them while I'm gone. Protect them while I can't. And let them protect you."

The little boy doesn't cry as he gazes up at me, and I wonder at the strength already imbuing his spine. He shouldn't have to weather the Darkness so young, shouldn't have to bear the brunt of its malice, but gods—it makes me proud and breaks my heart at how well he does.

"Helias," Easton scolds from a few paces away. His cheeks are red and chapped, and his breathing is winded like he's chased the boy through half the city.

Judging by the wry glance Helias gives me from beneath his lashes, the assertion probably isn't far off. I set him down gently and ruffle his hair, before turning to Mirren's brother. The writhing abyss settled when I held the boy, but it roars now, furious and agitated as I stare at Easton. It isn't his fault she was taken, but suddenly, I can't think beyond the way he looked at her this morning.

Like she was something to be fixed.

And if I fail to get her back, I won't ever have time to show her how wrong he is.

"Shaw," Easton says, his tone as metallic and sterile as the city around us. His eyes rove from the mud caking my face to the blood and gore staining my clothes and blades. His lips purse in distaste, and it takes everything in me not to skewer him right here in the middle of the square.

Breathing deeply, I give Helias a quick wink and turn back toward the quarterage. Mirren was most likely taken hours ago, which means the Covinus has a large head start. I've already wasted enough precious time. Helias deserved it, but Easton doesn't.

"Shaw, we need to talk to you. It's important!" he calls behind me. "This is Jakoby. One of the main voices in the Covinus building. They've come to a decision!"

"I don't have time for this," I bark over my shoulder, not bothering to turn around or slow my pace.

"They've agreed to let the wielders stay! To allow both you and Mirren to live here."

His words ignite something in me, something flaring and explosive. I whip around, and Easton yelps in surprise, skidding to a stop just before he collides with my chest. The man beside him blinks at me in horror. Middle-aged, slightly balding, unassuming.

I wrap my fingers around the man's throat and slam him into the nearest wall.

Easton cries out in protest, as I narrow my gaze on Jakoby, drinking in his acute fear. He claws uselessly at my hand as I bring my face closer to his, breathing in the stink of his cowardice. And then I smile malevolently. "Oh, you'll *allow* it, will you?"

I laugh humorlessly as Jakoby squeezes his eyes shut, like I'm an imagined monster he can wish away. As his body begins to shake, trembling like leaves on a tree, I realize who the man is. Mirren and Easton's adopted father.

I squeeze harder. "How very gracious of you to allow us refuge *after* we saved your sorry city." I yank a dagger from my bandolier, and Easton lunges toward me, shaking his head desperately. He digs his fingers into my upper arm in an effort to pull me back, but he may as well be an errant insect for all it affects me.

"Shaw, stop!" he cries.

I press the dagger to Jakoby's throat. "Look at me!"

The man opens his eyes reluctantly, gaping up at me in terror. I can't imagine what I look like to him, blood-soaked face, and mad eyes, but it's enough to leech every bit of color from his face.

"Your Boundary is gone, lemming. And apparently, you haven't learned what that means, so let me enlighten you. You don't have the power to *allow* us anything. The Darkness doesn't give a damn about your silly Keys, and neither do I. For centuries, you've let the Ferusians around you starve, and if it were up to me, I'd let that entire militia overrun this godsforsaken place and leave you to experience a little of their mercy."

I press the knife into the skin of his throat, hard enough that blood begins to well at the tip. Jakoby whimpers in pain. "Lucky for you, it isn't up to me. You continue to exist on the mercy of the woman who's spent her entire life being told by pathetic little shits like you that something's wrong with her."

Digging the dagger in further, I level Jakoby with every bit of the abyss burning in my eyes. "I should gut you where you stand for ever thinking yourself worthy of commanding her. You don't deserve her protection. And sure as the Darkness, you don't deserve her mercy."

I bring the hilt of the dagger down on his head, and Jakoby crumples into a graceless heap.

When I turn back toward Easton, his face is a comedic mix of horror and revulsion. "By the Covinus, what is *wrong* with you? That was Mirren's chance to stay in her home!"

Snarling, I stalk toward him with barely leashed fury. He measures my steps, backing up slowly. And when I spit at his feet, his nostrils flare wide. There are so many things I want to say to him: *you aren't worthy of the ground your sister walks on. You don't deserve her pure heart.*

I *am her home.*

But I settle on the worst of them all. "While you've been sniveling around your Community, your sister's been taken by the Covinus. And you've already wasted enough of my time."

Easton's breath catches in his throat, a miniscule noise of desperation and disbelief. But I've no time to coddle the Similian, nor the patience. Let him stew in his consequences. He deserves far worse.

"Mirren's been taken?" Easton repeats, his voice oddly distant. "To Argentum?"

I don't answer. Instead, I say, "Make sure Helias gets to Harlan. You can at least manage that much, can't you?"

Without waiting for his response, I sprint toward the quarterage.

When I crash through the door a few minutes later, I head straight to Mirren's bedroom. The bed is unmade, the dull gray comforter thrown wide, and the sheets rumpled. I'd left her sleeping here so many hours ago, driven outside before sunrise by the dreamed smell of burning skin. Why had I left her? Why hadn't I stayed and wrapped myself around her, held her while she slept? Why hadn't I run my fingers through her hair until she stirred with a sleepy smile? Worshipped every inch of her until she made those delicious squeaks that always burrow beneath my skin and light my brain on fire?

Why, when I was so scared of losing her, had I ever let her go?

I tear through the room, throwing every weapon I can find into my pack.

You love her and so you'll lose her.

I've thought it with every breath. Felt it with every heartbeat. And somehow, still not managed to fight against it hard enough.

The front door crashes open just as I emerge from Mirren's room. Max storms through the threshold, her cheeks flushed, not from exertion, but from pure fury. Shame immediately washes over me that she's not only had to chase me through the entire city, but that she's had to leave Cal to do it.

"You should be with Cal."

Max shakes her head and rolls her eyes, as if I'm the most ridiculous person she's ever had the misfortune to encounter. "I would be," she bites out furiously. "If our best friend didn't insist on barreling through the city to go murder a thousand-year-old dictator...alone!"

I don't reply, instead beginning to shove the morning's leftover food into the bag.

"Shaw," Max tries, her voice far softer. It's the softness that edges me closer to madness, as Max is hardly ever gentle with me. She places a hand on my shoulder, coaxing me the way she would a feral animal. "Shaw, just wait a minute—"

I whirl around so fast she rears back in surprise. "Wait for *what?!*" I hiss. "He has her, Max! He could be torturing her right now!"

Max nods. Tears spring to her eyes, and I'm struck with the urge to throw myself at her and let the comfort of her arms protect me from the world around us, at the same time I have the urge to throttle her. "I know," she says patiently, her composure only serving to set my teeth further on edge. "But we need to plan. You can't go storming Argentum by yourself. The Covinus has the Dark Militia under his power, and Avedis says he has the coin. Magic is back and he could have other wielders on his side as well. It's too risky."

Max bites her lip, the movement uncharacteristically uncertain. "For all we know, you getting yourself caught is exactly what he's after. If he has you and Mirren, he controls the prophecy. He controls everything."

My breaths come rapidly as flame begins to rise in my chest. Max watches as I struggle to tamp it down, to contain my rage, my fear.

"It won't be like it was with Ilinka's forces. You know the Dark Militia. They do not surrender. Ever. You'll lose your soul again, Shaw, and we just got you back—"

I shake my head furiously, in an attempt to drown out her words. "Then I lose my soul. I don't care, Max, I'm going to get her. If I leave now, I might be able to catch them before they reach Argentum."

"Shaw—"

Blood roars in my ears as I turn toward the door.

"Mirren wouldn't want this, Shaw. We need to plan—"

"She came for me, Max!" I roar, half mad, my panic and fear and anguish rising up until I feel like I'm drowning on dry land. Like the Castellium dungeon, my lungs burn, and it's only the thought of moving forward that keeps me from curling up in a useless heap. Cursing, I dig my fingers into my palms and breathe wildly. "She always comes for me. She came for me when I didn't deserve it, when I'd kidnapped and hurt her. And she came for me when I was lost in the Darkness, despite everyone, even me, telling her it was hopeless. She always comes for me, Maxi, and I'll be—"

My voice breaks, and I swallow roughly as acid climbs my throat. "I'll be damned if I don't do the same for her."

Max doesn't break beneath the onslaught of my anger —from the moment we met, she has never once feared the power of my fury or the way I've blazed through the world. She's only accepted me as I am, destruction and all, and she does so now in the resigned way she nods, like she knew exactly where this conversation would end, but had to try all the same. And gods, I love her for it—for being strong enough to tell me things I don't want to hear.

"Well then, I'm going with you."

I shake my head and take two large strides back toward her. Max's gaze is pure steel, that same haughty regality that looked at me from behind a mask in my father's dining room and dared me to be brave enough to change my fate. "You can't, Maxi. I need you here with Cal. I can't stand to leave him without knowing you're here to make sure he survives."

She nods, again like she already knew the answer.

"And then I need you to go home."

Now, her eyes widen in surprise. "What? Home to Nadjaa?"

"Denver needs to know what's happening in Ferusa. Because if the Covinus has Mirren, he has the Dead Prophecy. And Nadjaa isn't safe."

"He isn't going to listen. The Nadjaan guard probably won't even let us over the pass," Max remarks doubtfully.

I meet her gaze. "Then do what you do best and *make* him listen. Take Helias to Aggie's. Don't let Denver or anyone else find out what he is. I promised him he wouldn't be alone, and I need you to keep it for me."

Max watches as I sling the pack over my shoulder. "I'll meet you there when Mirren is safe."

Or only Mirren will. I'm under no illusions I'll come out of this with my soul intact. I've seen the Dark Militia in action, and that was before magic. I'm powerful, but my soul is just as easily shattered as anyone else's.

Max frowns, reading my thoughts, but she doesn't protest. She knows me too well, knows the guilt of staying behind would be far worse than any other fate. She swallows roughly, her eyes shining, and then slowly nods.

It's the license I need to leave without guilt. The knowledge my friends understand the depths of me and will always be there to help me crawl back to the surface. "I left a gift for Cal in the Nemoran, on the south side of the city."

The agonized acceptance in her eyes gives way to curiosity.

"Please tell him it's his to do with what he wishes."

Max's face grows more consternated, and when I shoot

her a genuine smile, she looks positively alarmed. But I don't explain further, and instead, wrap her in a hug. She digs her fingers into my shirt, not shying away from the mud and gore, and when she pulls back, her gaze is carved from stone once more.

"Don't be stupid," she bites out.

When I emerge into the sunlight, Avedis is already there, lounging between two mares and looking bored as he picks dried blood from beneath his fingernails. Dahiitii trots toward me cheerfully and nudges my hand in search of her favorite blossoms. I run my fingers along her withers, the warm strength of her muscles seeping into my own. "There aren't any flowers here," I mutter to the horse. "And there certainly aren't any where we're headed."

She gives me a perfunctory look as I take the reins from Avedis and tosses her head impatiently while I secure my pack to the saddle. Then she stomps and nickers, as if to say she's as ready to be free of this gray hellscape as I am.

Avedis swings himself up on the remaining horse, a tall mare with a shining black coat. I raise an eyebrow at him in question, but he only shifts primly and sheathes his longsword behind the saddle. "I do hope you aren't going to try and tell *me* what to do."

I purse my lips in irritation. "You should go protect Nadjaa. War is coming."

He adjusts his reins with a flourish. "I have no loyalty to the Moon City or its Chancellor." When Avedis finally raises his gaze to mine, it glints like the Bay of Reflection. Bottomless and dark. "To the Darkness' final calling. That is what I told Our Lady of the Deep. And I won't be made a liar just so you can go all noble and get yourself killed. Or whatever other odious thing it is you seek to do."

I open my mouth, whether to argue or laugh, I can't

decide. So I close it once more with a defeated shake of my head. Avedis answers to no one; follows his own path with the freedom of the wind. Arguing with him will only waste more time, and probably lead to us pummeling each other again.

I give him a stiff nod.

A grin crawls across the assassin's face, a slow promise of the death and pain to whoever stands in our way. "Let's go get our girl."

CHAPTER
TEN

My retinas burn when I emerge from the mineshaft out into the sunlight. I blink wildly against the sting as my vision blurs with tears, and greedily gulp down the air that hasn't been staled by being trapped for hundreds of years beneath the mountains. It's odd that things like the sun and fresh air have become so disorienting when they keep humans alive, but that's what life in the mine does to men.

The world is at once larger and smaller in this memory. Buildings tall as the mountains tower into the sky, stretching toward machines that fly through the air like metallic birds. Machines that link our continent to far off lands. Foreign places that were once only stories and legends now destinations to visit. To conquer.

I shiver as my eyes finally adjust and turn my gaze to the sky. Bright cerulean, a mirror of the sea sparkling in the distance, and streaked with the vapor trails of the machines. I began working only a year ago, the day I turned sixteen, but it feels as though I've been trapped beneath the earth for much longer. I don't particularly miss the heat of the sun, but I do find myself longing for the glowing light of the moon that blesses our valley.

Iara and I used to spend hours staring up at that moon, but the mine saps most of my energy, and now, I spend my nights sleeping away the exhaustion.

I miss lying on the rocky cliffs, our fingers interlocked, palms sweaty against each other's as we debated whether the moon looked the same hanging over the foreign shores the flying machines traveled to. Iara thought the moon would appear different in their skies, remote and cold rather than warm and beautiful like ours. I determined it didn't much matter what the moon looked like.

It mattered what she *looked like, when I finally made enough money for us to ride off in the machines. The cost wouldn't matter either; I would pay a king's ransom to watch the smile on her bowtie lips as the world opened up for us.*

It had been a grand fantasy back then, one that had fed my heart with happiness and nurtured my soul with hope. Now, on the rare occasion I venture from the hole in the ground long enough to glimpse those flying machines, I watch them leave with greedy eyes and a hungering heart.

My want has become something that crawls beneath my skin like tentacles. They grow thicker and darker with each passing year, fed by the state of the world around me: the nature wielders and business tycoons that have so much, while those born without have little more than table scraps. The rich flit off to exotic locations, while we toil beneath the earth, break our bodies and our souls, to feed their electricity.

I've always held jealousy like a crutch, something that both helps and hinders me, but since I took my place beside my father in the mine, it's become something more like armor. Something that sprouts from my skin and threatens to strangle those around me. To use their bodies as stepping stools to climb to the heights I desire.

It hasn't seemed to matter that Iara and her brother are both part of the wielder class, water and fire, respectively. The gods have blessed their family with so many riches, they can not only fly to another continent, but buy the whole godsforsaken thing. It hasn't mattered that they use the powers they've been gifted to help, their charity unable to temper the anger of injustice pulsing through me.

Perhaps it's because Iara has always been kept separate in my mind from the rest of the world. She is different, exemplary, and unprecedented. A spot of brilliance in a dull curtain of monotony.

Someday, I'll marry her. We'll have a multitude of extraordinary children with her power and my mind, and none of their ribs will be visible through their skin, none of their bellies ever swollen with hunger. None of them will ever know what it's like to breathe coal into their lungs.

"Aye boy!" My father has just ambled out of the shaft, the thick lenses of his glasses coated in a thick layer of soot. "Get back down in the hole or we'll never meet today's quota."

My father's eyes are perpetually squinted against the sun, and he's buried beneath tattered layers of clothing despite the heat of the summer sun. It's always cold in the mine, no matter the season. The kind that stays in your bones long after you've returned topside, a constant malady that turns even the youngest miners into frail, brittle things. And my father has been working here since he was my age.

I take in the weathered set of his skin and the unnatural curve of his spine with a twist of disgust I don't hide well enough. My father immediately bristles, his beady eyes narrowing on me. For someone who's allowed the path of his life to be dictated by the circumstances of his birth, he is a proud man. "I've already told you, Aurelius, you ain't no better than the man digging next to you."

Except I am. My father is a stout man, with lumbering mass and broad hands made for manual labor, but the sharpness of my mind indicates I was born for so much more. He's known since I was a boy that I am far cleverer than he, and he's always despised that I am destined to be above him.

Men like him accept circumstances as they are, never striving for more because they are too weak to climb. But I am not weak.

"You think yourself too good for coal because some teacher told you you was smart. Well, lemme tell you somethin', son... Books ain't gonna put food on your table. Words don't keep you warm durin' long winters and math figures ain't gonna save you from being cast into the streets. You'd do well to get your nose out of the sky and back in the shaft where it belongs."

I heft the pickaxe in my hand as my cheeks begin to blaze. My father has earned a certain level of superiority in his thirty years of work. Other miners have begun to stop and stare, to watch as he brutally shoves me back into my place beneath him. Shoved back in among the rest of them, another cog in the machine; one easily replaced if I lose my efficiency.

Satisfied, my father turns back toward the mine shaft. "We'll be in that sky someday," *I mutter softly, the words not meant for him, but for Iara.*

He hears though, and the line of his jaw hardens in a way that has the back of my neck prickling. Because while my father is mostly bluster, there are times when he is more. When the indecencies done to him on a regular basis stack up and spill out of him, aimed at someone smaller. Since I've grown, it hasn't been me as often, but I can feel the aim of his cruelty now. "You think that girl of yours is gonna stick around, do you, Aurelius? You're gutter trash to her, nothing more than a dirty roll in the hay to laugh with her rich friends about. And when you ain't as amusing as you used to be, when the coal and the stink and the *trash ain't funny anymore, she gonna chew you up and spit you right back into the sewer."*

Nausea and dread barrel into my mouth, like my father's reached inside my chest and yanked my worst fears up my throat. "Iara isn't like that," I grit out, the only words I can manage beneath the building pressure of rage.

My father smiles, but it isn't a kind one. It's lined with pity, and something close to glee. "Spoiled cunt, just like the rest of them wielders. You may see yourself as high and mighty, but that girl sees you for exactly what you are. And soon enough, she'll go find herself someone better suited. Maybe another water-wielder. And you'll be all alone, boy, with only the mine to crawl back to."

The other miners have wisely scuttled back into the depths of the shaft. It is just me and my father, alone with the sunshine and my shame. It blooms inside me like a storm, its dark clouds growing and swirling until they spill from my eyes and my mouth and my fingers. Iara will never leave me; I'll never give her the chance.

My father thinks to help me by reminding me of my place, but he's only helping the rich uphold theirs. Because if they have no one to kneel on, they'd tumble into the dirt with the rest of us.

One block out of place, and their carefully built prison will come tumbling down.

If I'm ever going to be more, I have to start somewhere. Tear apart their world brick by brick and use the ruins to build myself something new. My father is only a small piece, less than a fragment of the foundation, but the smallest crack can breed the largest destabilization.

I glance around, my mind whirling quickly through the possibilities of each scenario. In less than a second, my decision is made.

With a cruel-hewn smile, I shove the blunted edge of the

pickaxe into my father's chest. His face wrinkles in confusion, and then smooths in rage. He makes to grab at me, his lumbering hand sweeping toward the axe, but it's already too late, as he loses his footing amidst the rubble.

He's always said shoddy footing was a death sentence in the mines. I wonder if he remembers his own advice as he falls backward into the shaft.

Screams echo far below, and then the unmistakable sound of a body colliding with rock, but I hardly hear any of it. Instead, each breath I heave feels lighter than the one before as I watch another machine fly away.

∽

Mirren

I drown in dreams.

An ocean-wielder cannot drown, and yet I do, as memories pour down my throat and fill my lungs. Some mine, some not. But they all overcome me.

My father's twinkling laugh as he whispered stories to Easton and me, stories of fantastical creatures and adventures so brave, they filled our hearts with unforgivable longing for something of the same. A mineshaft I've never seen fills me with hatred, the hole so dark and dank, I think I've gone blind. The wicked grin set at the corner of Anrai's mouth; the shape of him moving above me, in me.

A raging want that never ceases, that consumes everything in its path. Never full, never satisfied. It *needs*.

I cannot cry or scream, filled as I am by the remembering, hunted as I am by the want. I can only writhe desperately, scratching at the wooden bottom of the wagon carrying me. I search in vain for my *other,* but instead of its cool embrace, I only find more memories.

Where are you? How have they taken you from me?

No one answers. There is no sound except the wagon wheels and the roar of the wanting creature. It comes from inside my head and outside the wagon. It comes from the past and the present, the sky and the earth, until there is nothing but its rage.

"Mirren." My name sounds far away, soft and pleading. "Mirren, please wake up. You have to wake up."

But I'm not asleep, so I cannot wake. I'm lost in the tide of remembrance, swimming and swimming, and never reaching the surface.

"Mirren, we're getting closer to the city. You have to wake up!"

The voice drifts somewhere above me. I want to follow it, but everything hurts. There is nothing to hold onto inside of myself, nothing to leverage myself out of the depths.

"Wake up, Mirren. The Covinus is bringing us to Argentum."

Sura. It's Sura's voice that speaks. Panic squeezes my throat, fear for Sura being anywhere near the Covinus.

I peel open my eyes, feeling like shards of glass are embedded beneath the lids, to find I'm lying face down on the rotted floor of the wagon. When I turn my head, Sura peers back at me, her face pale and fearful even in the shadows. The wheels roll over the ground, jolting and jerking, as I struggle to push myself to sitting. My bones are like dry twigs, brittle and poised to snap, and my muscles are atrophied and weak.

But the feeling is no longer a surprise, its horrid presence entirely too recognizable. My *other* has been muted, taken from me. Just like in the caves of Yen Girene and inside the Boundary of the Covinus.

"How long have I been asleep?" I manage, my voice a rough scrape against my throat.

Sura shakes her head heedlessly. "I can't be sure. They only allow me out of the wagon to relieve myself. But we haven't stopped traveling. We're no longer in the Nemoran, and we're heading north."

The Xaman tribes called the utmost northern point of the continent home before Cullen drove them from it, so if Sura believes we're heading that way, I have to believe her. "I think he's taking us to Argentum," she continues.

Dread curls low in my belly. Argentum. The Praeceptor's territory. The place that carved pieces from Anrai until he could no longer stand it. His blood fed the stones, his pain stained the walls. And now, the Covinus, the man who's stolen everything from me, from the continent, has declared the place his home.

Shaw and I's nightmares, come together.

Before I can respond, the wagon jerks to a halt, and the fabric door is abruptly pulled open. Daylight sears my retinas, but I barely have time to shade my eyes before large hands grip my upper arms and wrench me out into the open. A scream lodges in my throat, but my mouth is so dry, it comes out as a silent release of air.

I'm shoved down by the head, my knees and palms scraping against the rough ground. There is no soft loam of the Nemoran here, only jagged stone and dry dirt.

I blink rapidly, attempting to find my bearings as Sura is shoved down beside me. She snarls at our nearest captor, black hair streaming around her as she claws at his arms. The man shoves his boot into her stomach, and ice crackles in my veins as I stare up at him.

I recognize him as a Similian Boundary man, but it isn't this that stuns me into submission. It's his eyes—

fragmented, tortured, depthless. The man no longer has a soul.

What has he done for the Covinus in the weeks he's been gone to lose it?

Baring my teeth, I grip Sura to me as he lifts his boot to level another blow, but a reasonable voice freezes both of us in place. "That will be enough, thank you, Gideon."

The Covinus steps out from behind the wagon, his prim appearance disorienting against the rugged landscape. With his neatly combed white-blonde hair and his crisply pressed clothes, he looks like he belongs in the sterile metropolis rather than the Argentian tundra. His flat gaze finds mine, and it takes every bit of remaining strength not to flinch.

"Hello, Ms. Ellis," he greets amiably, like we've met over lunch, and he hasn't dragged me into the middle of nowhere. "I do apologize for the discomfort you're experiencing with the loss of your nature spirit. I know it to be severely disorienting."

I glare up at him, mashing my lips together to keep from speaking, even as my mind races with questions. How would the Covinus have any idea what it feels like to have my power torn away?

A ghost of a smile tugs at one corner of his lips, an echo of amusement so faint, I'm unsure whether I've imagined it. "All will be answered in time, Ms. Ellis. When we get to Argentum, I will gift you with the knowledge you've so desperately craved." His eyes glint. "And in return, you shall get on your knees for your Covinus."

His words slither up the back of my neck. "Let Sura go. She has nothing to do with any of this."

The Covinus tilts his head. "The carrier of the Dead Prophecy has everything to do with this."

Sura stiffens beside me as I thrust myself up with a snarl. I don't care what he does to me; if the Covinus touches a hair on her head, I'll drown him with the rage of the Storven Sea.

"Relax, dear one. The girl won't be tortured for the prophecy." He tilts his head, examining me. "I take it you don't know it was me to whom the words were first spoken. In the beginning of my reign, before I knew how to use the Darkness, I admit, I sought a way to reverse it."

I gape up at him, uncertain whether he speaks the truth. The queen's curse was meant for him, and if he'd wanted to reverse it at one time, why wouldn't he still want to?

The Covinus raises his chin. "The Xamani girl isn't here for what she knows, Mirren. She's here so you will give me what *you* know."

I stare at him. "I—I don't know what you mean."

Now, he smiles. It begins at the corner of his mouth and curls into his cheeks like a divot carved into candle wax. A grin of madness and destruction. "You will. Oh, how you will," he says softly. Then he nods to the man hovering over us.

The man wedges a rough hand under my arm and hauls me upright, shoving me forward into the Covinus.

I grip at his shirt, trying to keep my wasted legs beneath me. This close, the Covinus' smile is even more terrifying. His eyes are depthless pits, fragmented and *wrong,* and it only takes me a moment of being so near to realize the wanting beast I felt in the wagon was not in my dreams. It is standing in front of me in the form of a man.

The cliffs. The mine. The desperate greed. It's all *him.*

The want plunges down my throat, and suddenly, the fresh Ferusian air is bitter and rotten. I gasp loudly, which only widens the Covinus' smile. At the direction of his gaze, the Boundary man kneels beside us.

Something about the robotic movement sets me on edge, the vague reminder of a puppet on strings tugging uncomfortably. I've only seen movement like that once before: in the gods' cavern when the Praeceptor had control of Shaw's soul.

"You see, I have no interest in breaking a curse that has given me everything. Iara and the meddlesome gods intended it to be my downfall, but it has been my second coming. Every soul in the Dark Militia is now mine to control as I wish."

The Covinus' tongue darts out of his mouth, and he runs it slowly along his top lip as his eyes light with fervor. "And soon, yours will be as well."

CHAPTER
ELEVEN

Shaw

We ride through the Nemoran in silence. There is no direct route north from Similis to Argentum, as the Old Road skirts along the south and west borders of the forest, so our progress is slow through the thick trees. We stick to a few winding footpaths carved from years of travel, but none are wide enough for a horse at full gallop.

Avedis seems completely unbothered by my quiet. His eyes are distant as he rides atop the black mare, listening to the song of the wind only he can hear. For once, I'm thankful for the assassin's company as I have no interest in making small talk, and don't think I could manage it even if I wanted to. A thick knot has fixed itself in the pit of my stomach, its inky black tendrils winding their way through my ribs and squeezing all words from my throat.

Desperation.

A familiar feeling, one that's plagued most of my relationship with Mirren, as all our interactions since the moment I met her have been marked with urgency: to kidnap her. To take her. To love her.

Even during the past few weeks, when we lay in bed and I languidly explored every inch of her body, the frenzied urgency has always lived just behind the gentle touches. Because I am a son of the Darkness, and I knew too well there was no world in which we'd be allowed to live peacefully; no world in which the goodness wouldn't be stolen from us at some point.

So every time I touched her, every time I took her lips beneath mine, it had been desperate.

If I'd lived in the present, treated it more gently, would I still have it? Or should I have held on even tighter, with claws and fists?

Avedis curses loudly, startling me from my thoughts just in time for an arrow to whiz between the trees.

With a snarl, I swing myself off Dahiitii, and land in a soft crouch as another arrow flies above my head. The assassin flattens himself atop the mare, yanking the reins so tightly she rears up before making a tight circle to head in the opposite direction and hopefully catch the assailant from behind.

Dahiitii nickers unhappily, pawing at the ground as I melt into the shadows of the trees. Another arrow sails through the low hanging boughs, the shaft slicing through the leaves with impressive precision. Whoever it is, their bow skill rivals even Cal's.

I prowl forward as more arrows rain down, one whistling so close I'm forced to duck and roll through the thorny undergrowth. I'm halfway back to my feet when I notice the soft rustle of a branch a few measures away. The breeze here has gone silent thanks to Avedis, so the movement is unmistakable, even in the dim light of the forest.

Pulling two daggers, I send one flying into the underbrush. The blade sticks into the gnarled trunk just above where the person hides, a warning. I'm already lining up the next when I stop short in surprised recognition, dagger frozen between my fingers, sword gripped in my other hand. The assailant shares no such hesitation, leaping up from the foliage with another arrow already notched, even as Avedis appears behind him.

The boy lunges for me with a wild snarl, his feet sliding across the soft earth as he stops just short of being impaled on my blade. But he doesn't lower his bow.

The first time Luwei had been on the receiving end of my wrath, he'd been fearful and desperate. But now, he glares up at me furiously, his lip curled in a snarl and his dark eyes churning with disapproval. We stare at each other for a frozen moment, my sword at his throat, his bow leveled at my chest. Avedis has gone entirely still, watching the exchange with poorly contained amusement.

"You were supposed to protect her," Luwei snarls. He spits at my feet. "The almighty Fire-bringer. They've sung songs of your power, of your untouchable wrath. No one can defeat you, and yet—" Now, the boy's lower lip wobbles, the first sign of the true emotion simmering beneath his anger. "You didn't protect them."

I rear back like he's leveled a punch to my chest, dropping both my weapons to the ground. Because Luwei knows what the others refuse to acknowledge: that I am not, nor have I ever been, worthy of Mirren. The protection of my sword, my fire, was the one thing I had to offer her, and when she needed it, I wasn't there.

Mirren has come for me through fire and blood. She clawed her way through my father, through the Darkness, through my own malevolence to bring me back from the edge. Every time I've fallen, she fought for me. And the one time she needed me, *I wasn't there.*

My vision tunnels and my knees threaten to buckle beneath me as my soul presses down heavily. I breathe through it, attempting to focus on the rest of Luwei's words. *Them. You didn't protect* them. "Who else was taken?" I ask, dread sinking low in my stomach, because I already know.

Luwei's face crumples, his anger washed away by the power of his grief. "Sura. The Covinus took my sister."

Shame washes over me that in all my panic, I hadn't once considered the Xamani girl. The girl who, more than likely, has information the Covinus won't hesitate to torture out of her. Mirren told me what he did to Harlan last year, and that was when he was still pretending to be a benevolent leader. Now, he has no reason to be anything other than what he is: a soulless monster.

"Asa has found the story of the Dead Prophecy, and he sent Sura to tell you and Mirren. We were beset by a pack of Ditya while traveling through the wood. I told my sister to go north so I could lead them away, as she's the one who matters. By the time I finally lost them and traveled back, Sura and Mirren were gone. I tried to track them through the woods, but they were moving too fast—unnaturally fast. And I lost the trail."

I nod to Avedis, and the wind-wielder sinks to the ground behind Luwei. I pluck my weapons from the ground and sheathe them both, even as Luwei still holds his bow tightly strung. The boy is a threat because of his grief, and in the same way I understand him, I know he doesn't actually mean to kill us. Killing me will not get his sister back, and he knows I'm the best way into Argentum. That's why he tracked us after he lost the Covinus' trail.

Avedis opens his eyes, his face grave. "The little Kashan is with Mirren, but I cannot see where they are or anything beyond. The air around them is wrong, like the air in the gods' cavern."

Which means the Covinus is using one of the coins to stifle Mirren's power. But was it Sura he originally came for? He was weakened by the loss of the Boundary, and perhaps he seeks to control the prophecy like the rest of the Ferusian warlords.

A branch snaps behind me, and I whirl around, daggers in hand once more.

Easton steps out from behind the nearest trunk, arms held high in surrender, hazel eyes wide. I curse again. "How is it that you didn't manage to hear *him*?" I snap at Avedis.

The wind-wielder shrugs, his face so unaffected I begin to wonder whether he *had* heard him and allowed him to approach all the same. I've never been able to guess at Avedis' true agenda, flighty and unpredictable as it is, but even so, *I* should have heard Easton behind us. Have I truly been so caught up in my own panic that I haven't paid any attention to the world around me? Am I only able to hear the absence of Mirren's heartbeat, to feel the gaping hole where she usually resides?

Being too caught in my emotions is a sure-fire way to end up dead.

I say nothing, just point my sword at Easton's jugular with a glare.

Normally, the Darkness in my eyes and the violence on my face is enough for most to back away, especially an untrained Similian. But Easton's feet stay planted where they are, and his eyes lock on mine. "I'm coming with you."

"You sure as hell are not," I scoff derisively.

Easton raises his chin, and I notice he's dressed in a large Similian overcoat and a sturdy pair of boots, an over-stuffed bag slung haphazardly over his shoulder. But none of this is what gives me pause. It's the set of his face, usually so wretchedly passive and pleasant, now twisted into something like determination. His brows are lowered, and his eyes practically spark like he's daring me to stop him.

For the first time, I see his relation to Mirren.

"I'm coming," he says again, louder.

I laugh, the sound humorless and mocking. "I know you resent your sister, Easton, but I thought you'd at least want her saved. A useless lemming like yourself with absolutely nothing to offer is only going to be a liability. And liabilities will get Mirren killed."

He only repeats, "I'm coming," before stepping forward to plant his throat more firmly at the tip of my sword. I raise an eyebrow, examining the indent of the black blade against his pale skin.

"If you'd like to get yourself killed, do it on your own time, Similian," I growl back, digging the blade further into the soft hollow at the base of his neck. A small bead of blood blooms, but Easton doesn't relent.

He sets his jaw. "I may not have fire, or weapons, or a complete lack of morality," he says, eyes flashing, "but I will *not* leave Mirren alone. She saved my life, and as vast as our differences are, she can't think—" He stumbles over his words, and then huffs a deep breath as acute regret washes over him. It looks so out of place on his normally emotionless face, for a moment, I'm struck dumb by it. Then it fades like a wave from a shore, but it isn't the passive acceptance I've come to know from him that replaces it. It's pure will. "I won't let her think she doesn't deserve the same."

As we stare at each other, an unwilling understanding passes between us. Mirren has come for us both, over and over again, driven by the unrelenting strength of her heart. And neither of us ever deserved it.

I sheathe my sword. "Fine, but you'll ride with Avedis."

The assassin looks offended. "I think not, Fire-bearer."

"I have Harlan's horse," Easton explains hurriedly, motioning to the trees behind him. "But I—I don't know how to ride very well."

I push an irritated sigh through my teeth, wondering again how a useless lemming who can barely even mount a horse managed to keep up with us. A testament to the heights regret can drive a man.

I roll my gaze to Luwei, who's taken my momentary distraction to gather up his arrows. At my consternated look, he shrugs. "No use wasting good arrows."

"You could have refrained from shooting us in the first place," Avedis quips helpfully. "Haven't you heard of using words instead of violence? I thought the Xamani to be more diplomatic than the rest of us."

Luwei rolls his eyes, his face unapologetic. "I'd shoot him again for letting Sura and Mirren come to harm."

I have no defense, so I don't bother. "I suppose you're going to insist on coming along as well?"

He only levels me with a hard stare.

When I glance at Avedis, he only shrugs. Though he's since washed and changed into clean clothes, the wind-wielder still looks decidedly weary after our spend of magic against the militia. His scar is a stark red against his sallow skin, a representation of my own exhaustion. I feel tired in every part of myself: the scream of my bones and the burn of acid in my muscles. Everything is tight and sore, like one well-placed hit will shatter me to pieces. We spilled every part of ourselves onto that battlefield, and there was no time to gather any of it back up.

What remains will have to be enough. Because to get Mirren back, to face a man who's been soulless for a millennium—who has orchestrated wars and famines and death—we will have to be more. And our only reinforcements are a peace-loving lemming and a teenaged boy.

I glare at them both. "You can ride along. But neither of you will be coming into Argentum."

They both open their mouths to argue, Luwei's face flushing a cherry red and Easton's brows lowering over his eyes, but when I raise my hand, their arguments die in their throats. "I understand," I tell them both, my tone far gentler.

Because I do. I understand it in the way my skin began crawling the moment I realized Mirren was gone, the way it won't stop until she's in my arms again. The need for atonement. The need to *do* something.

"But we aren't just fighting the Covinus, we're facing the Dark Militia. My father is gone, but his legacy lives on. And we'll need every bit of our focus to save Mirren and Sura and survive. I won't risk their wellbeing by splitting my focus and worrying about you two. You'll provide support from outside the city, and if you can't agree to that, I have no problem knocking you out right now and leaving you tied to a tree."

"They'd probably be drained by a yamardu," Avedis points out lazily, "as you've already bloodied that one up."

"Not my problem."

Easton swallows, looking mildly ill, but Luwei straightens. Because only he has truly seen that I abide by my word. Always.

"Do you agree to follow my orders?" I challenge.

"Are you truly the Heir?" Luwei challenges back, his eyes narrowed. "The fire-bearer of stories? That takes no prisoners and burns through any who challenge him? Are you the man who will do whatever it takes to get back what's ours, even if it means tearing the entire world apart by its seams?"

I nod solemnly. Because soul or not, I remain.

Luwei slings his bow over his shoulder, appeased. "Then order away, Fire-bringer."

I slide my eyes to Easton, who's been watching the exchange with an unreadable expression. Luwei is familiar with the slant of the Dark World and the price of mistakes here, but Easton has never known the sacrifice it demands. "And you, lemming? Are you really going to debase yourself by following a murderer? The man who burned the entire world and is ready to do it again? Or would you rather crawl back to your civility and uselessness?"

The corner of his mouth twitches, and I get the distinct feeling if he hadn't grown up behind the Boundary, I'd get an earful in response. As it is, he only says, "I'll crawl as far as I have to, to get my sister back."

"Then let's crawl."

∽

Calloway

I groan as Harlan sticks a needle into my skin. He presses down the plunger with his thumb, and something akin to acid shoots through my muscle. Gritting my teeth, I shift on the threadbare couch, trying to focus on the scratch of the worn fabric rather than the fire in my veins.

It's the third one today, and though I'd normally enjoy the feel of Harlan's soft hands on my skin, I can't say I much enjoy this. After Max took off to keep Anni from doing something extremely stupid, Harlan had taken it upon himself to get me back to the quarterage without reopening my wound. And when he'd peeled back the tattered remains of my shirt, his eyes blazed in a way that both warmed and scared me.

Though I suppose being terrified can also feel warm, if you conflate the adrenaline with something else. Something that flutters and burns in equal measure.

"Sit still." A command, but a gentle one. A measure of strength and softness, as most things with Harlan are.

"I *am* sitting still," I retort obstinately, even as I shift once more and bob my foot. Surely a small amount of fidgeting is better than me screaming at the top of my lungs and shoving Harlan to the floor, which was my reaction to the first injection.

A small smile tugs at the corner of his mouth, but he presses his lips together firmly and lowers his brow, examining the grotesque wound once again. His fingers follow his eyes, dancing lightly over my stomach, both shivers and sweat blooming in their wake. I've imagined the way Harlan's gaze would feel focused on me with increasing frequency over the past few weeks, but I hoped to be far less mangled when it happened.

"I wish you'd let me take you to the Healing Center," he says again with a consternated sigh.

I make a noise in the back of my throat that falls somewhere between a laugh and a scoff. "I'd rather be dead than become an experiment for the lemmings. Knowing them, I'd end up strapped to a table with my insides splayed open so they could see if the Darkness is in my actual blood."

Harlan's jaw ticks. "They don't need to cut you open to see that. They'd only need to observe you for five minutes."

A surprised guffaw bursts from me, accompanied by a sickening wave of pain. "Why, Harlan...was that a joke?"

His eyes flick shyly to mine for only a brief moment, before returning back to my wound. "Cal, I know Shaw stopped the bleeding, but there's no way for us to know he stopped it all or if he damaged something important unless you go to the Center for surgery."

"What have I been suffering through those infernal injections for if not to keep me from keeling over?"

He levels me with a patient look that reminds me so much of Vee, it almost hurts. *Come now, Calloway,* she'd say, *this isn't the time.*

It's always the time, I'd quip back, ruffling her hair until she yelped.

"The injections will stop infection, but they aren't going to magically meld your insides back together," Harlan says sharply. "Only Mirren can do that."

His words are heavy with worry. No one is more familiar with the Covinus' cruelty than Harlan, and I wonder if he's here with me to keep the memories from eating him alive. *Share them with me,* I want to plead, before remembering I'm not the one he shares anything with.

He pushes a beleaguered sigh through his nostrils, and removes his hands from my skin, folding them neatly in his own lap. I feel the absence of them more acutely than their actual touch, and to keep myself from examining that thought any further, I shove my elbows beneath me and try to sit up.

Unfortunately, the muscles that allow me to do that have been scorched to high hell by my best friend, and even the subtle movement sends a fresh wave of agony and nausea through me. I collapse back onto the couch, pinching the bridge of my nose between my fingers to keep from retching. "What is the point of living in this hellish gray-scrape if they don't even have medicine that sews your insides back together?"

Harlan ignores me and climbs to his feet. Then his hands are back on my skin as he props me up gently, wedging a few throw pillows behind my back. When he meets my gaze, his eyes remind me of amber whiskey, and they leave the same feeling swirling in my belly.

"Calloway," he says softly. His eyes slide down to my mouth, before quickly snapping back up again. But not before the tops of his cheeks flush. "If you don't have surgery, you won't be able to ride. You might not ever be able to use those muscles again. And your skin—burns are horrible to recover from. It's going to be extremely painful."

I stare at him. "I'm no stranger to pain, Harlan."

I'm also no stranger to burns, though admittedly, I've never witnessed recovery from them. Only death.

Harlan watches me, his face so close, I can take in the slight indentation in his plush lower lip. For a wild moment, I imagine dipping my tongue into the hollow and rolling it softly until I taste his moans. But then, I imagine Easton doing the same, and another wave of nausea swells, this one having nothing to do with my injury.

I swallow roughly and close my eyes.

"But you don't have to. They can help you. You don't have to be in pain."

I almost laugh because he couldn't be further from the truth. Pain has been my familiar since I was fourteen and discovered the charred remains of my family. It had been seeing Vee's hand still clutched in Lila's that had burrowed that pain permanently into my bones, as Vee was too tough to ever need a hand. But they'd broken her in those last moments, and it was something I could never get over.

I've drowned the pain in drink and laughter and merriment, but it's never left. There's always an echo, Darkness-edged and perpetual, that will never leave me no matter how far I go.

And ever since, I seem to live my life only to reinforce that which is embedded in me. I am drawn to the broken things; the ones so fragmented their pieces cut whoever comes close. And I thrive on being the one to be cut, the one who can take a bit of their agony. Because if I'm inundated in theirs, it becomes more difficult to feel my own.

So, ignoring the pain in my body, and the newfound one blooming entirely too close to my heart, I grin wickedly and say, "Clearly you've never—"

Harlan shakes his head, halting my words with a pleading look. "Please, Calloway. You need the Healing Center. You need help."

I steel my jaw. "I won't go where they hurt you." The words come out with far more rage than I intend, but it can't be helped. The same reason Harlan fears for Mirren is the same reason I'll be dead before stepping foot in that cesspit. When he'd finally told me what he went through those months after helping Mirren escape, it had taken a concerted effort not to go burn the entire place to the ground.

Harlan blanches, at my ferocity or the words themselves, I can't be sure. "You can't—I mean—" He swallows and shakes his head, before trying again. "Cal, you can't let yourself die for me. For what happened to me, I mean. Especially when I—" His cheeks flame. "When Easton and I—"

Something hot and dark fills my stomach at the memory of his body pressed against Easton's, but I stop his words with a shake of my head. "Don't. You don't have to *earn* humane treatment."

He drops his head into his hands, shoulders rising and falling in a deep rhythm. It's the only emotion he shows, and I watch it greedily as the implication of my words press into him. I spoke the truth. My avoidance of the Healing Center has nothing to do with my attraction to Harlan, and everything to do with his value as a human being. No one should ever be treated as he was. What kind of friend would I be if I condoned it, simply because I may or may not be dying?

After a protracted moment, Harlan says into his hands, "He's gone, you know."

"What do you mean 'he's gone'?"

He lifts his head, his mouth twisted. "He went after Shaw. To save Mirren."

A surprised laugh bubbles out of me, and scorching pain radiates from my wound. Laughter gives way to a groan, and even as I press my hand to my stomach, it does little to ease the agony. "Good for him," I gasp honestly. "I'm only sorry I'm going to miss the look on Anni's face when he finds out."

"About the alleyway, Cal—"

I shake my head and lean back into the pillows. I don't have the strength to sort through the mess of Harlan and me. It was easier when I thought he was in love with Mirren as I love her too. My affection for her created a physical wall that I'd never thought to cross, because I wouldn't do anything to hurt her. But when I realized it's her brother Harlan loves, the wall crumbled almost instantaneously.

I have no allegiance to Easton. In fact, quite the opposite: I disliked him before we ever even met, as he'd made it clear neither Mirren nor Harlan is a priority. Easton is a slave to the whims of society, and I still don't understand how Harlan can love someone like that, when he deserves someone strong enough not to bend to the world's demands.

The door to the quarterage bursts open, and I don't even need to look to the threshold to know it's Max. I haven't seen her since she took off after Anni hours and hours ago, and it's clear from her appearance, it wasn't a successful mission. She's still filthy from the battle, the smell of blood wafting into the living room as she stomps inside and slams the door behind her.

"I almost hesitate to ask what you've been doing that required postponing a bath."

Max throws a hand on her hip, and stares down her nose at me. "You don't exactly smell like a bouquet of flowers," she snipes, before whipping her head to Harlan, her eyes sharp with accusation. "I thought you were taking him to the Healing Center."

To his credit, Harlan doesn't crumple beneath Max's scrutiny. He only fits me with another exasperated look. "He won't go."

"Gods save me from men with a death wish," she mutters, confirming what I already knew. She couldn't stop Anni from tearing after Mirren. I don't fault my brother for going, but a bitter part of me wishes desperately I wasn't stuck on this godsforsaken couch when I should be at his back.

Max paces wildly, before halting in front of me. I stiffen, waiting for the onslaught of fury, but instead, she flutters her hand in dismissal. "Well, I'm actually glad you're both here."

I furrow my brow, suspicion prickling at my spine. "Why?"

She shifts from one foot to the other and worries her bottom lip between her teeth, which only furthers my alarm. Max is rarely hesitant, and I'm not going to like whatever has made her so. "Before he left, Shaw left you a gift in the Nemoran. I was...well, I was out retrieving it."

My confusion only grows as I run my eyes down her person. She isn't carrying anything. "Was it his love and good wishes, then? He could have spared himself the trouble. I already know how amazing I am."

Max rolls her eyes. "It's outside."

"Please tell me it isn't the branch I was impaled with," I implore, flicking my eyes to the ceiling in false prayer. "I love Anni more than life, but the man is a terrible gift giver," I explain to Harlan. "He'd probably think it was meaningful or something."

Max huffs another sharp sigh of annoyance, before disappearing back out the front door without another word. Harlan glances at me uncertainly, but before I can respond, she returns, this time, dragging a person behind her.

Harlan's mouth drops open so it wide, it would be comical, if I hadn't just realized what Anni meant by 'gift'. *Who* he meant.

Pink gag tied tightly around her mouth, hands and feet bound in rope, Max deposits Akari Ilinka, witch-queen and star of my nightmares, at my feet.

I stare down at the queen. I've never been this close to her, have never seen the shrewd cut of her eyes or the cruel turn of her lips so intimately, but her face is unmistakable. I don't know whether to be horrified or relieved that my memory has done nothing to soften or harden her edges. It has not made her more monstrous nor more beautiful. She is exactly as I picture when I wake up screaming.

The queen glares up at me, her face showing no sign of recognition nor contrition. Her signature red lipstick is smeared across her cheek, and her hair has been singed on one side, its flowing silk now falling raggedly to her chin. But it isn't any of this that turns my stomach, that causes it to leap with both disgust and excitement.

Anni told me he didn't kill the witch-queen, but I should have known, he'd still find a way to take a little of what's owed.

A jagged cut runs from Akari Ilinka's forehead, through the now empty eye-socket, all the way to her ear. A brutal mockery and a hallowed tribute of the exact same scar she gave Avedis.

Savage and poignant, a signature of my brother. And now, he's handed her to me, retribution, or forgiveness mine to give or withhold.

I both love him and hate him for it.

Her death wasn't his to take, but in giving it to me, he's thrust my worst failings into my lap. I've avoided thinking about the queen for years, but there's no ignoring her now. I'll have to make a decision, and I'm not sure I have the strength. Shame winds through me. Anni's always held himself up as the worst of the Darkness, influenced by its power, but to me, he has always been the epitome of strength.

Unflappable. Immovable.

He's never asked me to be strong for him, or even to be strong for myself. He's always just done it for all of us without question, his quiet faith that we'd do the same always unassailable.

Will I do the same? For him? For my family?

And what kind of person does it make me if I can't?

I swing my feet slowly to the floor with a hiss of pain. Harlan jumps to my side to help, understanding without my saying that I cannot be lying down for this. My head swims as I grit my teeth. "Take out the gag."

Max does as I ask, but not before unsheathing her gore-covered swords and pointing both blades at the queen. "You make one wrong move, and I'll gut you where you stand. Am I clear, *queen?*" her voice drips with derision at the self-appointed title.

Akari Ilinka only glares up at Max with her remaining eye, her back straight and chin raised as if she sits on her throne in Siralene. When the gag is pulled, she licks her lips and swallows demurely, somehow managing to look regal despite the blood crusted on her face and neck. "Maxwell," she acknowledges, her voice edged in venom. "I'd thought you too strong to do the Heir's bidding. It seems even a queen can misjudge."

Max rolls her eyes. "It isn't me you should be worried about, Akari."

The queen twitches at the marked disrespect but doesn't comment as she follows Max's gaze to me. I stare down at her, the war of emotions in my chest threatening to burst through my ribs. What would it look like in the dim light of the quarterage, all my despair and hate and rage displayed for everyone to see? Would it look like my family? Would it smell like smoke?

"Am I supposed to know who you are?" the queen asks disdainfully.

"I'd be more surprised if you did," I answer honestly, my voice sticking in my mouth. "When you destroy lives every day, it wouldn't be sensible to keep track of names. There certainly wouldn't be room for them all."

Ilinka narrows her eye, as I continue. "It doesn't matter who I am. What matters is your fate has been gifted to me, and I'd rather die than allow you another chance to use your insane quest for power as justification for destroying lives. Max, hand me my sword."

Max solemnly places the pommel in my hand. It's grip molds to my palm as an extension of my arm, a result of Anni's incessant training. It's because of this same training my hand is steady as I lift the blade and prepare to split my soul for the second time.

The witch-queen doesn't balk; only smirks and cocks her head to one side. "You're fool enough to cut my throat rather than bargain for riches? For land? You're as foolhardy as the Heir himself."

I curse myself for not being able to stand, for experiencing this moment sitting on my ass on an ugly old couch rather than towering above her. I settle for sitting up straight and laughing. The sound blooms in my chest and mingles with my heartache, until it comes out as a dark and cutting thing, madness given form. Because that's what I've done—driven myself mad with thoughts of this moment until I could no longer stand them. Until I had to move, to drink, to fuck, in order to escape them.

Her mouth turns down in indignation. "And just what is so funny?"

Swallowing down another bubble of laughter, I sober my face. "You've always touted yourself as supernaturally clever, and yet, here you are, thinking I would want anything to do with your riches or power. I can't be bought."

"*Everyone* can be bought for the right price," she snarls.

I dig my blade further into her throat and laugh again. I stare at the small indent, the minute trickle of blood, as memories swirl around me. "Let me tell you a story, queen. There's a large swath of land off the Siraleni coast with fertile soil and verdant hills. A family settled there, hundreds of years ago, long before a power-hungry witch ever declared herself ruler of those shores. The family bled into the land, ground their bones into the dirt, and in return, the land blessed them with bountiful harvests."

"Until the queen grew envious of their prosperity, and decided she wanted the land for herself. The farmers refused, as the land was theirs by birth and blood. So, the queen came for them while they slept. Barricaded them in the house they were born and burned them alive."

I watch as the queen's eyes go wide in remembrance, and then narrow on the copper of my hair. An odd color, not quite red and not quite brown.

"Allow me to assist the gaps in your memory. I'm Calloway Cabrera." My full name rolls off my tongue easily, like the last time I said it was this morning rather than when it truly was: seven years ago. "And you slaughtered my family."

Taking a steadying breath, I steel my spine. Grip the pommel tighter. And when I let it out, I release all the shame that's built up these past years. For Lila. For Vee. For Mama and Papa. They will finally be able to rest, knowing their son remembers.

"Wait!" Akari shouts, the sudden desperation in her voice ripping me from my thoughts. "You need a healer. I can get you one."

I laugh ruefully. "There is no healer that will be able to fix this, queen. We both know that. And if I'm to die, I may as well take you with me."

"A water-wielder would be able to," she replies, shifting on her knees. "A wielder would be able to heal both of us."

"Unfortunately for you, our Ocean-wielder is otherwise occupied at the moment. Something I'm sure you had a hand in."

Akari's jaw tightens. "I did not say Ocean-wielder, as she is one of a kind. But since the fall of the Boundary, wielders have begun to emerge all over Ferusa. It just so happens I know of one who owes me a favor."

Max lets out a noise of frustration. "Of course you do," she snaps with an exaggerated eye roll. "How convenient." When she notices my hesitation, she says, "Cal, you may not survive the ride to Siralene."

She's right. I may not even survive the night.

But the witch-queen isn't deterred. "Oh, but the wielder isn't in Siralene," she purrs. "She is in Havay, healing my injured militia as we speak."

I stare at her. The witch-queen has had a long-standing alliance with the warlord of Havay, but that doesn't mean she has control of its citizens. "What's to keep me from finding the wielder myself?"

Now, the queen smiles. "I hold something dear to the girl, and to keep it safe, she will not use her power in service to any but me."

"And what do you want in return?"

Akari Ilinka straightens her shoulders, her mutilated gaze darting around the room. She notices Harlan, and the sudden glint in her eyes has the sword in my hand twitching closer to her jugular. "My freedom."

I allowed the Darkness in when I split my soul on the battlefield. A compulsion, Asa said. And perhaps it's this that has me leveraging my morals to say, "You have yourself a deal, witch."

CHAPTER
TWELVE

Shaw

The ride through the north side of the Nemoran is painstakingly slow. The whispered hush of the leaves pull at my heart, urging me faster, further, but there's no way to be quick when leading four horses through the thick wood. Especially when one of the riders can barely hang on to his saddle.

Easton shifts, pulling awkwardly at the pant legs of his jumpsuit and attempting to hoist himself into a different position. It would be comical to watch his clear discomfort if the need to move wasn't pulsing through me with every frenetic beat of my heart. For the thousandth time today, I consider digging my heels into Dahiitii and leaving him far behind. Not stopping until I reach the black gates of Argentum and have watched the whole city burn to the ground.

But Easton's ill ease also serves to remind me of another's. With her loud feet and clumsy gait, every stride through the forest reminds me of the first time Mirren and I traveled these woods. Her, unprepared for life in the Dark World; and me, unprepared for *her*.

The irony isn't lost on me that I now travel with another ill prepared lemming, but I find Easton's ineptitude far less charming. There was something about Mirren's innocence that called to me, but in her brother, it only turns my stomach.

We reach the edge of the wood just as night falls. After a paltry meal of the leftovers I'd stuffed into my bag, I offer to take first watch. No one bothers to disagree, as the adrenaline of the past few days fades and exhaustion takes over.

Sitting down to lean against a tree, I tug my cloak tighter around my neck and spread my sword over my lap. The air is already cooler here than it was in Similis, edged with the icy promise of winter.

It'll be colder still once we reach Argentum, the ice season already having decisively fallen that far north. Acid barrels up my throat as I imagine Mirren in the frigid dungeons of the Castellium, alone and powerless. *Because you weren't there.*

I've already given up hope of catching them before they reach the city. As far as Avedis can tell, the Covinus has only a day and a half's head start but has somehow managed to make up far more ground. The traveling party has not stopped to sleep, but even so, their fast pace isn't natural, and I've given up trying to puzzle it out. Another facet of magic I don't understand, and one that doesn't matter—it only matters that I get to her. That I have the chance to make up for my failure. That I punish every person who's touched her.

Avedis plops down beside me.

I glare at him irritably. "I said I'd take watch."

The assassin shrugs, laying his own sword beside him.

"My thoughts are too loud to allow sleep." He eyes me in challenge, but I find I don't have it in me. If he wants to spend the entire journey awake, who I am to argue?

Especially when the idea of closing my eyes, even for a moment, sounds impossible, though every bit of my body aches and my fire has sputtered down to embers in my chest. "Well, you look like shit."

Avedis only shimmies primly, smoothing his crisp black tunic with a grin. "We both know I always look flawless, no matter how tired." His gaze travels to the two bedrolls a few feet away. "Quite the traveling party you've acquired."

"Unwillingly," I bite out. Luwei is already asleep beneath his blankets, accustomed as he is to sleeping under the open sky. Easton thrashes about uncomfortably, his disgruntled sighs drifting all the way over here. Shaking my head, I look back to Avedis. "When we get to Argentum, it's only me and you."

He nods, the black tresses of his hair dancing over his forehead, though I feel no breeze. I'm still watching them when he says, "You met the witch-queen today." Though his tone is neutral, casual even, what lives behind it is not. It blows with the rage of an ocean storm battering against the coast.

I roll my shoulders in an attempt to soothe the ache of my muscles. "Ask me, Avedis." I don't say it to be cruel. It isn't my place to thrust Avedis' trauma into his lap. He should be able to choose how deeply he wants to wade.

The assassin is silent so long, I'm sure the conversation is over. But then, "Did you kill her?"

"No."

I'd wanted to. The abyss roared for her blood, demanded we punish her for everything she's taken, and everything she would take in the future if she were allowed to live. But her death wasn't mine. Avedis' breathing hitches, and his shoulders go still as I turn to look at him once more.

"However, I did bestow her with a bit of her own mercy."

His gaze snaps to mine as I use my finger to mimic a slice through my eye. A dark grin spreads over Avedis' face, morbid appreciation of Dark World justice. "And where is the queen now?"

"I gave her to Cal."

The assassin raises a brow. "You believe Calloway capable of such things? His heart is soft, and I've never gotten the impression he has a thirst for vengeance."

"That's exactly why Cal is better suited to justice than the rest of us. He doesn't let the wrongs done to him spoil his heart or his judgement. I think he's the perfect person to deal with the queen, at least until you get your chance."

Avedis clears his throat and stretches his legs out in front of him, examining the shine on his boots. How they remain so pristine after days of war and traveling, I'll never know. "Is it easier...now?" he asks after a long pause, the words rough sounding, like they've been pulled from the depths of his throat.

"Is what easier?"

He keeps his eyes trained on the forest, and though they don't stray from their line, I get the impression he's closely observing my reaction. Pushing out a beleaguered sigh, he gestures vaguely. "I don't know. All of this. Is it easier, now that he's gone?"

I realize what he's asking. Has pulling the roots from my thorns made life easier to live? "I don't know." The only honest answer I can settle on. The weight I've carried since I was a boy was lifted with my father's death, the heft of which I never truly understood until it abated. He's gone. He no longer waits in the Darkness plotting my ruin, and I no longer spend my time dreading the day it will come.

But even in death, he took something of me with him. And now, he isn't here to answer for it. My wounds are my own, my traumas like forgotten stretches of tattered silk left floundering in the winds of the world. Tying their ends is now solely up to me and I haven't found myself up to the task.

Because who am I without my rage?

The last time I asked myself that question, I was twelve and had just stabbed my father. In slicing through his skin, I cut through everything that made me who I was. I'd had to rebuild myself into something new, but I'd had Denver to guide me through it. Now, it's only me and the weight of my crimes.

I stare at Avedis. I've always had my friends to talk to, but I've never met someone who so fully understands what it's like to be cut into a shape as a child, wielded as a weapon, and then have your entire sense of purpose upended. "Some things are easier," I begin slowly. "I'm not looking over my shoulder every minute of the day wondering when he'll find me. I don't spend my hours worrying he's in the shadows ruining someone else. But nothing fixes the hole."

"Until your ocean-wielder."

"She healed my soul, Avedis. But the abyss remains. Always. I would never deny you the blood debt the witch-queen owes you, but just know—it won't heal what was done."

Avedis bows his head, before shifting his gaze back to the shadowed trees. "All for the best, I suppose. You're going to need those extra pieces of soul if we're ever going to make it out of Argentum."

Dread sinks into the pit of my stomach. "About that, Avedis—"

The assassin's eyes flash and his jaw stiffens. "Do not condescend to me, friend. I know what I risk, just as well as you do."

I trap my warnings behind my lips, because Avedis is right. He's lived with the knowledge the next kill could be the one that damns his soul since he was a boy. Souls don't split evenly, so you never know how much remains, the uncertainty part of both the high and the dread. It isn't up to me to dictate what he does with the little remaining—he risks it for what he deems important, just as I do.

I can only be thankful Mirren garners his risk.

Easton pushes himself up with a loud sigh, and stomps over to us. The Nemoran is never entirely still, alive as it is with creatures and magic, but somehow, the sound of Easton's boots drowns it all out.

"It's freezing," he bites out, his voice so loud in the night air Avedis winces beside me. "Will you please build a fire?"

His words are polite enough, but they're laced with barely contained disgust. Avedis smirks and tips his head to me mischievously, like he can't wait to be entertained by my response.

"If you want a fire, you'll need to learn to build one yourself," I snap, irritation settling pervasively beneath my skin. "But even so, a fire will lead every creature in this forest straight to us."

Easton straightens his spine. "We are not *in* the forest. And according to Mirren's stories, lots of people have fires in the Nemoran. Including you."

I roll my eyes lazily. "Sure they do. When they have more than two people to fight off a yamardu. But as Avedis and I are stuck with your useless company and there is no invisible fence keeping the beasts to the trees, it's a risk we don't need to take."

Leaning my head back against the trunk, I cross my arms over my chest. "And if your delicate sensibilities can't handle the cold, you may as well turn around now. It's only going to get worse."

"Surely, the fire-bearer would be able to handle some paltry forest creatures," Easton replies. And though a normal person would allow their frustration to leak into their words, the boy keeps his locked behind a sterile gray wall.

When I don't bother to answer, he huffs loudly and turns on his heel to stomp into the trees. Undergrowth crashes where he walks, and I lurch to my feet with a muttered curse. Avedis laughs again, as I chase after Easton. "Where are you going?" I demand.

"To the bathroom!" he snipes back, somehow managing to walk even louder.

I grit my teeth, moving my gaze warily to the trees behind him. If I allow her brother to be attacked by a Ditya, Mirren is going to begin to think it's a pattern, but Easton isn't finished. "As useless as you think I am, I can most certainly *pee* by myself!"

"Debatable," I hiss, just as the boy trips over a root. He bats wildly at the branches of a bush, as a springy twig snaps across his cheek, leaving behind a small scratch. "As loud as you are, you're going to attract every monster in the wood. You're going to get yourself lost or killed."

Memories bubble to the forefront of my mind. *Are you trying to get us caught?* At the time, I'd only been trying to protect Mirren from the Boundary hunters and had gotten kicked in the jaw for my trouble. It seems trying to keep her brother from his own worst impulses is going to earn me much of the same.

"Surely even a *lemming* can find his way back from the bathroom," Easton gripes from where he crashes through bushes in front of me.

But it isn't only his feet that crash. I peer into the shadows, cursing inwardly that I left my sword sitting on the ground next to Avedis. "Easton, be quiet."

The boy is too indignant to listen. He whips around, his eyes flashing with the first outward sign of anger. "Just because I don't burn through entire populations doesn't mean I'm useless. Some of us have other ways of solving problems."

His words pierce through something vulnerable and have me snapping my gaze from whatever lurks in the shadows back to his face. My flame rises in my chest as I take in the flush of his cheeks and the breathless way he watches me. Whether he realizes it or not, the little Similian is angry. And something in me wants to poke at it until it pours from him; to watch him drown in his anger and fear as I drown in my own.

"Tell me, Easton," I sneer. "Are you going to *talk* Mirren out of Argentum?" I take a menacing step toward him. "Are you still stupid enough to believe your power-hungry dictator will listen?"

The flush floods Easton's face, washing down his neck and up to the tips of his ears. "Shall we set the whole city on fire instead?" he challenges, his volume rising. "I'm sure you've just been *waiting* for another excuse to burn children."

Flames fill my veins as I stare at the boy, trying desperately through the heat to remember Mirren loves him. I focus on the set of his mouth, the angle of his eyes: features that remind me of my soul-bonded enough to calm the building rage. But the boy isn't done.

"As a matter of fact, why don't you do it your way, Firebearer? Burn the whole city and lose your soul again. Maybe my sister will finally see what a vile monster you truly are."

Anxiety threads through me as the boy plucks my worst fears from the depths of my dreams. But I only let out a cutting laugh and take two large strides until I'm in Easton's face. He tilts his chin up to look at me, and when I take in the twisted snarl of his mouth, I laugh again. "So the little lemming has feelings after all," I taunt, baring my teeth. "And your sister knows *exactly* what kind of monster I am."

"Lower your voices," Avedis hisses from behind us, as exasperated as if he is scolding children.

But just as Easton's words pierced me, mine have found a weakness in his Similian armor. His face twists in rage and his fists curl at his sides, and half of me hopes he hits me. Hopes he'll give me a reason to pummel his smug lemming face; to forget my panic and worry for just moment, drown it in petty violence. "The kind of monster who will burn through anyone who touches her and revel in their pain."

"Shaw—" Avedis says in warning, but I don't take my eyes from Easton as his fists turn white at his sides.

"You think yourself above the scum of Dark Worlders, Similian? *That* is why your sister will leave you."

Easton blanches. "Mirren would never leave me for a child-killer like you."

An arrogant smile curves my mouth as I lean in close

enough to whisper. "I would get down on my belly and *crawl* for your sister. Through blood and fire and darkness, I would shred every bit of my skin to get to her." Tilting my head with predatorial malice, I continue, "You won't even get your clothes dirty. *That* is why she'll leave you alone. Because you know nothing of love, nothing of sacrifice. You're a pathetic little child who clings to civility as if it's a life raft and not the wave that sinks you."

"SHE WON'T LEAVE ME!" Easton screams, his face wild as his rage and fear finally break out into the open. Freed from its Similian cage.

I step back with a satisfied laugh, but I don't get the chance to enjoy the Similian passivity broken and undone, because at that moment, the shadows behind him begin to shift and grow.

And a yamardu shreds its razor-sharp claws through Easton.

∼

Mirren

I stare at the cracks crawling through the dark stone of the Castellium dungeon, and imagine they are ocean waves. Always rolling, stretching endlessly toward the moon and stars. The tides pulled toward the night sky, just as I am.

Because even trapped, I still feel the tug of *my* tides—Anrai. My friends. Nadjaa. Easton. My heart is dry as a wasteland without my *other,* but the insistence of their tether remains. It is lodged under my ribs, embedded in my skin. And no matter what the Covinus has planned for me, the call of what is mine will never relent.

The door to the cell opens, the corroded black metal eating up the miniscule amount of light that spills in from the corridor. The Covinus strides in, his crisply pressed clothes contrasting against the grime of the small space. I resist the urge to shrink back into the wall, to curl up and make myself smaller. *Don't make yourself less than what I love.* I let Anrai's words filter through me, pulse through my blood and beat in time with my heart. Whatever happens, there will be no more hiding myself to appease the man before me.

"Where is Sura?" I demand.

He runs his grey eyes down the length of me, and though it isn't lecherous, it feels wrong all the same. Like he's assessing what exists beneath my skin—and determining how to devour it. "Do not fret, Ms. Ellis. You will see the girl after we talk."

Dread sinks into my stomach at his agreement. Mercy is not in the Covinus' nature. If he's allowing me to see Sura, it won't come without cost.

The door opens again, and a member of the Dark Militia, his rank of *legatus* denoted by his red regalia, brings in two metal chairs. He sets them down across from each other, and with a quick nod to the Covinus, retreats back into the hallway. The unmistakable scrape of a lock echoes in the silence, the sound akin to a gunshot.

"I see you've made yourself at home in the Praeceptor's city," I observe levelly. "What happened to disapproving of violence? Of greed?"

The Covinus' eyes twinkle with laughter, but it does nothing to soften him. "There are many ways to control a population. Admittedly, the Praeceptor's was often far too messy for my taste." Though his face remains smooth, his nose twitches with mild disdain. "But the strong adapt, as you well know. You would have died the moment you stepped foot outside my Boundary if not for your willingness to change your skin and bones. To shape to your circumstances and become something new."

He sits in one of the chairs, crossing his legs smoothly. "In that, we are the same."

"I may change, but I still have the same heart," I snap. I have changed, and it has been a painful process. The stretching and breaking; healing and growing all while holding on to what's true.

The Covinus makes a humming sound of neither approval nor disapproval. "You may fool others, but there is no need to lie to me. I know the feel of power in your bones…am intimate with the addictive nature of the elixir pulsing through your veins with each beat of your heart. Do not pretend you do not waste away here without the feel of it, empty and wanting."

Rage rushes past my ears as the Covinus regards me dispassionately. He doesn't fidget or smile, the only sign of emotion being a hint of curiosity. Like suppressing my *other* is an experiment, and he intends on recording the results.

I tense as he reaches inside the pocket of his crisp white shirt, but he doesn't pull out a weapon. Instead, he threads a simple gold chain through his fingers. My coin. The one I found in my brother's drawer all those months ago, that's followed me through the Dark World. "I have been preparing for your arrival for centuries," the Covinus says softly, his eyes glinting as he rubs the coin gently between his fingers. "Since the prophecy was first spoken."

For a moment, he appears somewhere far away from this dungeon. "Gods are too powerful to die human deaths, and because of this, fragments of their essence still exist. I harnessed most of it into the creation of my Boundary, but there were filaments that escaped." Now, his eyes come to rest on me. "Like the one living inside the witch you call a friend."

The Covinus' doesn't smile, but I get the impression of sick amusement. "And the gods do like to play, don't they? The god who first spoke the prophecy is the same essence who spoke another, that would bring you out of the safety of my Boundary and spark the end of the world."

"The Dead Prophecy isn't the end of the world. It's the beginning of it. A reversal of the Darkness. Wouldn't you want that too, if the Darkness was meant to curse you?"

For the first time, an emotion flickers in the depths of his eyes. A flash of something dark and rotten, an eerie mirror of the wanting beast from my dreams. "For centuries, I thought it was what I wanted. But then, I built Similis and got everything I wanted in spite of Iara's curse. And I lorded not only over my city, but over the entirety of the Ferusa. I was the only one with electricity and modern technology, and with it, I armed warlords and decimated others. They have always been so busy fighting themselves, they never stopped to question who was truly controlling the tides of the land."

The Covinus' face smooths. "I suppose in that respect, I've already beaten Iara and become exactly what she sought to stop. All-powerful." His eyes flash black and I realize I didn't imagine the color that day on the Boundary when I healed Easton.

"Why didn't you just kill me, then? When I came back to Similis?"

The Covinus runs his tongue along his lower lip as he watches me. "It seems once again the nature spirits have chosen those who have no grasp on the cost of power, or how to wield it. Magic wasted on those too weak to ever do what's needed to rule." He lifts his chin. "There is always more power to be had, Ms. Ellis. If magic was destined to come back, was it not better to keep it in my control? I had you within my walls, and the Praeceptor controlled his son. You were ours to do with what we wished."

Abruptly the Covinus stands, his movements as smoothly robotic as the rest of his mannerisms. I wonder vaguely if it's living for over a millennium that has stolen all aspects of humanity from him—the clunky movements, the loud emotions—or if it's the fact he's lived those years without a soul.

He knocks on the door, two succinct raps, and the outside lock clicks open. The same militia man appears, this time dragging two bound women with him. The first is unmistakably Sura, her hands and feet clasped in thick iron shackles, a gag shoved into her mouth. Her wide eyes shine when they find mine, fear and defiance mingling equally as the soldier shoves her to her knees beside me.

I grip her to me, the feel of her warmth calming me slightly. Sura is alive—alive and unharmed. For now, at least, the knowledge is enough to keep me from breaking apart entirely.

I don't recognize the other woman. Her long silver hair hangs in a matted curtain down her back, and her face is spattered with half-healed bruises, and fresh cuts. When she sees the Covinus, her lower lips begins to wobble in a silent sob and her feet fail her entirely as she crashes against the Dark Militia member, clawing desperately at his uniform. "No, no...please..."

Her voice cracks as she begs, her terror raising goosebumps on my skin. The remnants of a khaki jumpsuit hang off her emaciated body, and horror spreads through me. The woman is Similian. Easton said there were people missing after the Boundary fell, people who'd disappeared from their homes at the same time as the Covinus. I thought they'd been loyalists following their leader, but this woman does not appear to have come willingly. Not at all.

The soldier brushes the woman off his clothes with a look of disgust, and she collapses to the floor in a sobbing heap. Without a word, he turns and leaves the cell once more. The lock clicks into place again as the woman cries, her wasted body unable to even peel her face from the dirty floor.

I glare up at the Covinus hatefully as he stands, looming above the three of us with the same serene look he used standing above us in the Community Center. My coin still clutched in one of his palms, he fishes in his front pocket with the other hand and pulls out its twin.

My eyes widen as he holds both coins out before me. "It is almost comical how the lines of time unspool, is it not, Ms. Ellis? If I had never Outcast your father or killed your mother, I wouldn't have lost the second coin. And if your brother had never gotten sick, if you'd never thwarted all the rules to save him, I would have never found it again."

"You see, one is enough to stifle your power. To root out those who have the potential to host a nature spirit. But when you put them together, they are capable of so much more." That same wanting greed spills into the room, starting at the black of his eyes and pouring into the air like poisonous smoke. "You've already witnessed their potential."

I stare at him in bewilderment, and he obliges my confusion with relish. "In the Praeceptor's Heir."

Fury clogs my throat as understanding presses down on me. The Praeceptor stole my coin from Yen Girene, and the Covinus must have given him the other. Is that how Cullen was able to capture Anrai's soul, able to wield him like a puppet?

Armed with both coins, is the Covinus able to steal *anyone's* soul?

As if I've projected my fear into the space between us, the Covinus flicks his hand casually. As though attached to invisible strings, the silver-haired woman jerks upward with a cry of pain, coming to her feet before Sura and me. The Covinus sets a small black dagger in her palm. Her entire body trembles and twitches, but despite the woman's desperate sobs, no tears stain her dirty cheeks.

The soulless have no tears.

Anrai's words come back to me, settling with a newfound horror as the woman's body goes eerily still. Then, she takes the dagger and drags the blade across her own throat. Blood blooms, a crimson necklace that grows and grows. With a small gasp, the woman falls to the ground.

Despite the ache of my bones, I scramble toward her and press my hands to her throat, desperately trying to staunch the bleeding. To do *something*. My hands are awash in scarlet, the blood vitally hot even as it leaves her. When her eyes go glassy a moment later, I leap backward. My hands are sticky, and I wipe her blood on my filthy clothes with a dry sob.

My own tears are trapped in the barren absence of my *other*, too dry to even cry at the loss of this poor forgotten woman. Another life senselessly stolen.

The Covinus watches me with that penetrating gaze, his face impassive as if a woman doesn't lay bleeding at his feet. I want to hurtle myself at him, to claw at his eyes and his skin until I feel his blood beneath my fingernails. Will it be hot like hers? Or as cold as the ice shrouding his humanity?

"Is that why you've taken us? To take our souls and control the prophecy?"

Now, the Covinus actually smiles. An eerie echo of twisted humor as his eyes flash black once more. "I will only take dear Sura's soul if you decide to be uncooperative. We both know your history with authority, Mirren, and I have found it is better to provide you with clear motivation to behave."

Ice runs up my spine as his horrible gaze presses into me, his endless want burrowing into the empty spaces where my soul once resided. "From you, Ocean-wielder, I want so much more than your soul."

CHAPTER
THIRTEEN

Shaw

Blood sprays as the yamardu's claws sink into Easton's shoulder. The beast screeches, and they both go tumbling to the ground in a tangle of muscled wings and pale limbs. For the first time since I realized Mirren was gone, I feel like myself as the abyss rises up. There is no more panic, no more hesitation. Only the killing calm and the feel of hot acid pumping through my veins.

My ear drums rattle in my head as the yamardu screams again. I duck and roll, coaxing flame from my heart and into my hands. The beast's wings extend and flare, their powerful slash through the air enough to buffet me back and send my fire skittering out, as it lowers its beak toward Easton's throat. The whites of his eyes flash as the boy struggles and writhes, pinned between strong black talons and the forest ground.

Aiming for the yamardu's head, I shoot a torrent of flame. I ready myself, expecting the beast to rear up in agony and set its sights on me, but it doesn't even bother to look around. Only screeches once more and adjusts its grip on Easton. And when I pull my fire back, indeed, the black leather skin of its wings remains intact. Completely unmarred.

Dread sinks in my stomach. Yamardu are fireproof.

Pulling two daggers from my bandolier, I roll beneath the beast's wings and slice out at its scaled legs. It yowls in fury, but before the sound can deafen us all, it's abruptly cut off. The yamardu gasps, struggling for air, as Avedis appears behind it, his face scrunched in concentration. At least someone's power is still useful.

"My hold won't last!" the assassin shouts.

Heart hammering against my chest, I thrust my blade up as the beast bears down. Hot blood and gore rain down on my face as my blade pierces the thick hide. Avedis' hold breaks, and the yamardu's scream of fury reverberates through the forest, through my bones. My ears ring and I struggle to regain my bearings, my balance, as my hearing goes fuzzy.

The beast spreads its wings and leaps into the air. I barely manage to roll out of the way before it crashes back down. Whirling, I bring up the other dagger and slice through the wing.

The membrane splits like paper, and more blood gushes as Avedis leaps in from the side with his sword raised, his power having faltered. He slashes at the other wing, and with another screech, the beast pumps the injured wing and sends Avedis flying backward. The assassin slams into the trunk, just as an arrow comes flying from between the branches. It sticks into the wing, and I turn just in time to see Luwei send another whistling into the fray.

Each injury weakens the yamardu, but it isn't enough. At this rate, it will take all day of this to actually bring it down, unless we hit something vital.

When Mirren set the yamardu on me, it wasn't the first I'd taken down, but it was certainly the first I'd felled alone. The only way to kill one for certain is to cut its throat, which, unfortunately, towers far above my head. To best a yamardu by yourself, you have to let the beast come to you. Allow it close enough to tear your throat out with that sickly beak.

It isn't something most sane people would attempt.

Before, I was driven by fear that Mirren was headed straight to my father's cruel grasp, the power of my desperation so strong, I probably could have killed three to keep her from him. But I was stronger then. Now, my breaths come in labored huffs, and I curse the ragged state of my body. I feel wrung out, like my insides have been emptied and my skin sags on my bones. Hot pain shoots up my sprained wrist as I grit my teeth and race toward the beast.

My jaw rattles with another earsplitting shriek as the yamardu's powerful wings lift it into the air. Never taking my eyes from its throat, I brace myself for impact. There's no way to lessen the pain, but I try my best to go pliant in order to keep from breaking every bone in my body as the yamardu's heft crashes down on top of me. Rancid breath buffets my face as it bears down, and black talons pierce the ground on either side of my head. Clawed feet wrap around my legs, and it's all I can do not to panic at the suffocating feeling of being trapped. Trapped like I was on my father's table, weak and hopeless.

The abyss rises, burning away the thoughts as I bring up my blade. The knife-edged beak brushes my throat, just as I shove my dagger straight into its jugular. Its maw opens, but no scream sounds now as I slash my other blade across the yamardu's throat. I squeeze my eyes shut against the spray of blood and brace myself to be crushed beneath the beast's slumped weight. It never comes.

Peeking my eyes open with an exhale of relief, I see the beast hovering above me, held in place by Avedis. With a rough swallow, I crawl quickly from beneath the carcass, blinking the sticky sting of blood from my eyes.

I shoot the assassin a grateful smirk, as words are still buried somewhere deep in the recesses of myself. My head throbs and the sounds of the forest are muffled behind a constant ring as I attempt to recoat my tongue with saliva. When I finally manage to stand, I sway on my feet and half-trip, half-limp toward Easton.

The boy lays sprawled on the forest floor, his body so still my heart leaps into my throat. *Don't be dead. Don't be dead.* His chest moves upward with a slow breath, and relief shoots through me. His lashes flutter when I kneel beside him, his face entirely too pale as I gently examine his wounds.

One large talon mark dissects his upper arm, and another scrapes over his collarbone. And while I'm sure they feel like hell, nothing appears punctured. If I can stitch this, he'll survive.

Avedis and Luwei come beside us, the latter dropping my pack beside me. "Do you want me to..." he trails off, the offer hanging in the air.

I shake my head, pulling the pack toward me. "Both of you sleep." I nod to Avedis, who looks as awful as I feel. Like he may keel over at any moment. "I'll wake you later for watch. No use in all of us being tired."

The assassin doesn't bother to argue this time, which only demonstrates how deep his exhaustion runs. He also doesn't point out that Luwei would probably be far better qualified to stitch the wounds, as the Xaman tribes often specialize in healing. But as I'm the one who lost my mind long enough to get Easton marred, I'm the one who needs to fix it.

I rifle through my bag, pulling out supplies and setting them in a neat line. Easton watches silently, his eyes wide. When I press my fingers to his chest, he winces, trying half-heartedly to shove me away. "I'm fine," he mutters weakly.

I don't even bother to roll my eyes. "You will be, but these need to be stitched." I thread the needle. "And it's going to hurt."

I pour the antiseptic Harlan swiped from the Healing Center over Easton's wounds. The smell is unnatural, biting but clean, and I wrinkle my nose as it bubbles up. To his credit, he doesn't punch me; only grits his teeth together with a muffled moan. "Hold still," I instruct, as I splash the needle with the antiseptic, the past and present suddenly colliding together in a weird storm above me.

Mirren's hands on my skin for the first time. The pierce of a needle, the haze of blood loss.

She'd been kind to me when I didn't deserve it, soft when I was hard. And now the lines of fate tease me, challenging me to the same. *You've got a new soul. Can you be pliant instead of rigid? Gentle instead of rough?*

I press the needle into Easton's skin, and he flinches with a sharp cry. Agitation rises and I level a breath, before meeting the boy's eyes as calmly as I can manage. "This is going to feel like absolute shit, but dying is worse, which is what will happen if we don't close these up. Okay?" I wait for his agreement.

A long beat passes, before Easton steels himself and nods. After that, there is no more moaning. Only the hard grind of his jaw, and my steady movements as I sew up the wound on his arm.

When he can no longer bear the pain, or perhaps the silence, he says, "Those creatures are fireproof."

I nod with a grunt of annoyance. Just another of the Nemoran's mysteries I'll never understand, some remnant of the old gods that granted the horrid creatures armor against the nature spirits.

"But you saved me anyway."

Again, I don't answer, pulling the thread out and then pushing it steadily back in.

"Did you do it for Mirren? Or because you truly wished to?"

"Probably both," I mutter honestly. "I don't imagine Mirren would be pleased with me if I stood by and watched a yamardu drain her brother. But I don't wish you dead, either."

The boy mulls this over for a few moments as I finish closing the first wound. I tie the thread into a knot and clip the end neatly.

"You also saved me beneath Similis," Easton says and though his words are tight with pain, when I meet his eyes, he appears oddly earnest. "I never—" He clears his throat. "—I never properly thanked you for that. Probably because it speaks to your character more than I'd like to admit." When I raise my brow, he clarifies, "Endangering yourself to save someone you hate."

I stare at him for a moment, swallowing down my laughter when I notice the gravity of his eyes. "I don't hate you."

"You don't like me."

"I'm not Similian. I have the freedom to dislike anyone I please. And I know you think all Ferusians are bloodthirsty animals, but my ire for someone doesn't dictate my morals. I saved you because you didn't deserve to die. Now or then."

Easton's mouth twists as I begin sewing up the laceration across his chest. This one is both shallower and longer, and will require quite a few more stitches. "Do you need a break?" I know firsthand how much stitches hurt, and Easton's face has gone even paler. But he shakes his head with determination.

Respecting his tenacity, I resume my ministrations.

"I don't like you either," Easton says after a breathless moment. His words are a huff of excitement and horror, and his eyes grow wide with disbelief, like he can't quite understand how the sentiment escaped from the depths of his brain, let alone his mouth.

I laugh. "Is that the first time you've ever said that to anyone?"

"It's the first time I've ever allowed myself to even think it."

I tilt my head, a smile tugging at my mouth, feeling oddly proud of the fact that someone actively dislikes me. "Well, you clearly have much more self-control than your sister, who openly despised me the moment she met me and made damn sure I knew it."

The memory warms something in my chest and as Easton watches it bloom across my face, sadness flickers in his eyes. "She's always been braver than me. Always protected me." He drops his eyes. "I was trying to protect her for once...in my own way."

"The question isn't whether you're protecting her, Easton. It's the cost. What she has to hand over and give up in order to earn it. There are a thousand ways to protect someone. You chose the easiest for you. Not the best for her."

At this, Easton's face grows dark. "You all think staying true to my beliefs is because I'm weak. It takes strength to have faith when the world around you tests it at every turn. I have sacrificed so much to keep true to that faith, Shaw. That isn't weakness."

A year ago, I would have laughed in Easton's face. I would have decried my faithless heart with pride, certain that nothing was worth handing it over to be skewered. But even then, it would have been a lie. Even before Mirren took my empty heart and filled it with home, I knew better. Max and Cal and Denver had gifted me faith, and even when it was challenged, it held true.

"It takes strength to have faith, but it takes more to admit you've placed that faith in the wrong things. You may think I'm a savage who doesn't understand, but trust me when I say...I know what it's like to realize everything you were taught is wrong. I know what it feels like to have the earth torn out from beneath you. And I know the courage it takes to begin again with nothing."

Shame washes over Easton. It presses into his skin and bears down on his chest, and gods, it's so recognizable in its strangling fervor. I don't need to punish Easton for his frailty of character, because he punishes himself with it every day. Quietly, maybe. But fervently enough that I can see the imprint of his mistakes on his skin.

Harlan, who he loves, betrayed and driven away by his convictions. His sister, cut down and sacrificed on the altar of those same beliefs. And if he admits his folly, that perhaps he misplaced his faith, what will it have all been for? I understand it in the same breath I despise it.

I stitch the rest of his wound in silence, before dousing it with more antiseptic and leaning back on my heels. With help, Easton manages to sit up, his eyes traveling to the yamardu's heaping corpse, huge wings limp and sprawled in odd angles across the forest floor. With a labored breath, he flicks his gaze back to me. "Thank you," he says softly. "For letting me come with you."

It isn't forgiveness or apathy that settles around my heart. It is something more akin to understanding. Because I hear the words he doesn't say—

Thank you for allowing me the chance to redeem myself.

∼

Mirren

Drip, drip, drip.

The sound burrows into my ears, and laps at the edges of my mind. The proximity to water is both taunting and soothing, so near and yet out of reach from the metal chair I've been strapped to.

I climbed up willingly; allowed a soldier to chain my arms and feet. Shame courses through me at my compliance, mingled with a warped sense of pride. I'm giving into the man who tore my family apart, who rent a jagged wound in the fabric of the world, but in doing so, I'm keep Sura alive. And in her continued survival, the promise of completing the prophecy and destroying the Covinus' hold.

I remind myself I'm only giving in physically. I've spent my life rebelling against the Covinus, and most of it was done inside my head. I retreat there now, to the dark recesses of myself where anger and abandonment have been nurtured, and I use them to bolster my resolve. It doesn't matter what he plans to do to me—I'll never truly give in.

At first, the Covinus does nothing to me at all. He only sits in the chair across from mine and watches me in silence.

He watches me for hours, every minute flicker of my

mouth, every fractional dart of my gaze. His eyes are like knives, sharp and destructive, and they pierce through the fabric of the jumpsuit he's dressed me in to my skin beneath. He wants the rough fabric to remind me of obedience—of the submission and defeat I've felt my whole life—but it has the opposite effect.

It reminds me of my vow to never shrink myself again.

Drip, drip, drip.

The sound delves into me, and I imagine it's my *other* calling out. The coins do not steal power, only suppress it, but no matter how far I dig, I feel nothing but dry emptiness. *Where are you? You are mine and I am yours and we should not be alone.*

My muscles ache and my empty stomach roils as nausea climbs my throat. I have no idea how long it's been since I've eaten, and my vision swims as I try to focus on the man before me, on the Xamani girl chained to the wall behind him, but they blink in and out of existence as I grow weaker.

Like none of this is real. The dungeon, the pale fiend before me. All a dream, dredged from the depths of my greatest fears.

On the few occasions the Covinus leaves the room, I try to catch Sura's eye. She can't speak through the gag, but the warmth of her gaze heartens me. But soon enough, Sura is unconscious more than she is awake, and without her tether, my mind wanders.

While the doors of the Castellium are pure black, the stone of the building is light enough that stains are visible on the cell floor. Blood, vomit. Stains of misery.

I wonder which of them belong to Anrai, pieces of himself carved out by his father and left as a reminder of his horrors. A morbid part of me wants to lay down on top of them, dirty floor be damned, and meld myself with his forgotten fragments. *How did you survive down here all alone? How will I?*

The cell door scrapes open, and I squint against the searing light of the corridor as the Covinus returns. Something unsettling glints in his eyes as he regards me. "It is time. Are you willing, Ms. Ellis?"

My mouth is too dry to speak, my tongue stuck thickly to the roof of my mouth. Despite my waning strength, I slowly turn my head once to the right. Once to the left.

The Covinus' mouth turns down so slightly, it isn't a true frown. But his disapproval is clear as he takes two large strides toward where Sura lies curled up against the wall. "Shall I remind you why your compliance is mandatory?" He grabs Sura by the hair and yanks her upward.

She jolts awake with a whimper of pain, and fresh tears spill down her cheeks. But she doesn't resist. Thirst and hunger have rendered her too weak to struggle.

I lick my lips, even as there is no saliva to be found. "Give her...give her something to drink. Something to eat," I manage, my throat feeling like it's been scraped with small pieces of jagged glass. "And I'll do whatever you want."

"You will do whatever I ask regardless," the Covinus replies calmly, pulling Sura up to her feet. "Hunger is temporary. Soullessness...well, we both know that is far more permanent. You nearly killed yourself repairing that monster's soul. I doubt you'd be able to manage another and survive."

If I had any moisture left in me, I'd cry at the unfairness of it all. Scream and thrash and claw until the Covinus' skin broke beneath my nails. But as it is, I only steel my spine and nod.

Satisfied, the Covinus lets go of Sura and she curls back

up on the ground with a whimper. Then he moves behind me and unlocks the shackles around my wrists. My shoulders scream as they release into a more natural position, but my own scream, of anger and devastation, stays locked tightly in my throat.

The Covinus takes his seat across from mine, and I stare him down without blinking as he situates himself. I may not have my power, but I have my rage. My grief. My heartbreak and love. I let him see everything he's tried to take from me, everything I'll stubbornly hold onto until my last breath. My rebellion has always been keeping hold of myself against all odds, even when he tried to erase everything that made me who I am.

The Covinus lays the two coins flat in each of his palms. "Take my hands."

It's a struggle to do as he asks as weak as my muscles feel, but after a moment, I grit my teeth and manage. The Covinus' palms beneath mine are cold and clammy, but his skin feels no different than anyone else's. I can't decide if it's a relief that his body somehow remains human, or if it's an affront that his physical appearance doesn't match the toiling depravity within.

He doesn't move for a few long moments, watching me with a slight tilt of his head. His face is completely devoid of emotion; he doesn't look victorious or excited, pleased or disdainful. He doesn't look like *anything*.

I shift in my seat as anxiety threads through me and wish desperately to pull back my hands. If I die in this dungeon, I don't want him to be the last one to touch me.

The thought has barely settled when the room shifts, and suddenly, I'm drowning once more.

CHAPTER
FOURTEEN

Calloway

The ride to Havay is agonizing.

I spend most of it asleep, lost in a haze of pain and fever, in a tiny wagon Harlan commandeered from one of the Similian factories and Max rigged behind my horse. It's slow going and painful as the rubber wheels bump over tree roots and rocks, through small streams and over hills, and by the end of the first day, I'm convinced I won't survive.

The wound in my abdomen radiates between shooting ice and scorching acid through my veins. I am festering from the inside out, the rot leaking from my stomach and poisoning the rest of me, including my thoughts. It's colored them in unnaturally dark tones, each one more dire than the last.

If Anni were here, he would make a self-deprecating joke and tell me to snap out of it. *There's only room for one self-loathing sap in this relationship and I've already claimed the title.* But instead, my only company in the cramped wagon is Akari Ilinka.

The wheels hit a particularly large root and the witch-queen tumbles into me, her weight sending a fresh wave of agony and nausea barreling up my throat. I curse loudly, thrusting her off me with a disgusted grunt.

She careens backward and almost out of the wagon, held in place only by the shackles Max has tethered her with. The queen blows her hair huffily out of her face, her golden skin flushed with fury. "How dare you touch me," she snipes venomously, glaring at me from her one good eye.

The jagged wound in the other has begun to puss and ooze, no doubt set with infection. The sight of it sends an odd mixture of satisfaction and disgust plummeting uncomfortably in my stomach. I have never taken pleasure in someone else's hurt before, never thought there *could* be any pleasure to take.

But here I am, staring at a grievous injury, a part of me wishing it was worse.

"You touched me first," I snap. A comeback far beneath my usual wit, but irritation and teetering on the edge of death will apparently sour even the most humorous of men.

"You forget, Calloway Cabrera, that you may hold the upper hand now, but it will not always be so. And a queen never forgets."

I cock my head, something between a snarl and a smile playing on my lips. "Apparently that isn't entirely true as you forgot an entire family you murdered."

Akari straightens. "It was not murder. It was business."

I laugh ruefully. "Well, if I push you out of this cart and you die from the fall, I'll also consider it business. The business of needing more space."

The witch-queen sneers, her lips having returned to

their natural color as her signature rouge has long since faded. I now see it for what it was: armor. Because with it, she looked regal and impossible. But in the dim light of the forest, with her bare lips, sloppily shorn hair, and torn clothes, she looks like any other Ferusian woman. Knife-edged, slightly vulnerable. And lost.

"It would be foolish to kill me before we reach the healer, but then again, most men are far too driven by the brain in their pants than the one in their heads to be anything but foolish."

I roll my eyes, wondering why I'm bothering to reply, even as I do. "As opposed to you who is driven by what, exactly? The need to drink blood?"

Akari scowls in a decidedly unqueenlike manner. "That was a rumor spread by my opponents meant to destabilize my reign." She smiles, but without the lipstick, it softens her face rather than hardens it.

I look away with an inward curse. I don't want to see anything soft in the queen, anything that paints her as human. Because she's not. None of the warlords are, their humanity sacrificed in the name of power. The name of *more*.

And yet, old habits die hard, my propensity to ferret out the softest parts of people. I've never seen it as a weakness, but here in this rickety old wagon, it certainly feels like one.

"Though I used the rumor to my advantage, sowing fear into my enemies and reverence into my subjects," Akari continues haughtily, adjusting herself as best she can while chained to the rotting wooden floor.

"I'm sure you did," I mumble grumpily, scooting as far from her as I can manage without throwing up. "Though it seems you didn't sow it well enough."

Ilinka narrows her eyes dangerously. "And just what is that supposed to mean, boy?"

I hum noncommittally. "Just that I've heard the rumors. The return of magic caused upheaval in Siralene, and the people have begun to rise against you. Guess they no longer believe in your supernatural powers, now that they've witnessed true magic."

"Nonsense spread by rebel sympathizers and opposing warlords."

Her throat bobs ever so slightly, and I narrow my eyes. "Ah, witch. I don't think it's at all nonsense. Not when you've treated the people of Siralene like slaves for so long. When they bleed for you and still die with nothing. Your people have turned against you, and rightly so. What I don't understand is why you've taken your militia to Similis rather than staying to defend your throne."

Akari swallows roughly and her face twists in disgust like she's tasted something foul. "You know nothing of politics or what it takes to hold power. You follow your Chancellor's pathetic path, preaching peace and other inane ideas."

"Say what you will about the Chancellor, Akari, but his own people don't want to string him up from the city gates." The queen stiffens, ever so subtly. But it's enough. I smile. "That's why you left, isn't it? You may have a fearsome militia, probably the most powerful in Ferusa since the Praeceptor's death, but even they are no match to the people you've wronged."

The queen says nothing, just glowers as if she's imagining my head on a spike. Even as she plots my death, I feel infinitely lighter. Because I've gotten under her skin, crawled beneath her hardened exterior and unsettled her.

And more than that, the edges of a plan are beginning

to come together in my mind. If I can just stay alive long enough to see it through.

∼

Mirren

The tide is strong.

I swim against it until my limbs are numb and my lungs burn, but no matter how much effort I exert, I get no further. The current tugs at my hair, pulls at my feet. *Come to me.*

A part of me wants to. I am the ocean, its rolling song a salve to my heart. But the current that beckons is no ordinary sea. It does not want me to dance in its waves; it wants to devour me whole.

When I scream into the whirling void, it is not water that fills my mouth.

It is memory, filmy and sleek, sliding down my throat and into my chest like swaths of silk. I try to cough it up, to push it away, but it is relentless. Inescapable.

I watch the slices of sunshine flicker across the walls of the kitchen as I kick my feet against the table leg. Morning is one of the rare times of day the quarterage is not simply gray, but a million colors of glowing warmth, and instead of eating my oatmeal, I tilt my head and imagine they are painted there. Splashed permanently so I could look at them any time I wanted.

Easton sits across from me, shoveling food into his mouth. The majority of it winds up smeared across his cheeks, while other bits splatter across the table. I curl my lip in distaste and shake my head, readying myself to scold him, when he glances up at me and giggles softly. His teeth are full of oatmeal, but his eyes shine, so I close my mouth.

He has not yet learned that such things are not acceptable.

By five years old most children have already lost their laughter, but Father has always encouraged us to keep ours, safe and secret. To hold it close inside our chests, and let it light us from the inside out.

Sometimes I think Father is brilliant. And other times, fear for him roots itself so deep in my stomach, I can't breathe. Because what if the Covinus somehow discovers his ideas?

I tell myself I'm being silly. No one is Outcast because they laughed.

But when my eyes wander to Father and Mother in the kitchen, the unexplained fear remains.

They are supposed to be getting ready for their morning assignments, but instead, their heads are bent low, and they speak in whispers. Jealousy threads through me that Mother is getting to hear a story I'm not, because Father tells the best stories. But then, she smiles at him so brightly, the dark feeling is replaced with a burgeoning warmth. Embarrassing and foreign.

I stare as his nose brushes her ear and nuzzles into her neck, and I imagine what that might feel like. His fingers graze the small of my mother's back, the touch so light it is more of a whisper, but a fresh heat stains my cheeks. And then, Father leans in close and brushes his lips against the smooth skin next to Mother's mouth.

Easton babbles on through the smattering of oatmeal, some of which is now plastered in his hair, oblivious to what's happened in the kitchen, but I cannot stop staring.

A part of me wants to tear my eyes away, to ignore the squirming in my belly. It is full of things I don't understand, thoughts that writhe like snakes. Kissing is wrong. Touch is wrong.

But why doesn't it feel *wrong?*

Mother doesn't push Father away or scold him and recite the Keys. She smiles and wiggles her body into the crook of his arms, the place that is safe and warm. And this I understand. Everything in Similis is gray and cold, but Father's arms are soft and full. It is where imagination blooms in the middle of the night, where I am wrapped in stories of far-off worlds.

"Six months is no time at all, Azurra," Father says.

I strain to hear her whispered response, which sounds something like, "What if—"

My father shakes his head and smiles. "None of that. Count down the days and know I will come for you." And then, more softly, "We do this for them." His eyes skip over to the table and my cheeks flame as I drop my gaze to my uneaten oatmeal, now gone cold.

I don't hear my mother's response, hoping by some miracle my father didn't notice my eavesdropping. But footsteps pad toward the table, and then I am surrounded by the familiar scent of him. I peek up sheepishly, my skin hot and flushed. He doesn't smile, but at the twinkle in his eyes, some of my shame eases. "My Mirri," he coos, "too clever for her own good."

He pats my shoulder. "We better go before we miss morning assignments. Grab your coat."

My Mirri. My Mirri.

Even in the midst of the current, the words dredge up forgotten parts of myself. Tender places I've covered in thorns so no one would ever touch them, but in doing so, I made it so I would never touch them either. I let them be darkened by the whispers of my Community, and the prickly feelings of abandonment. I didn't protect them as I should.

But I will protect them now.

Those aren't yours, I scream at the current. But opening my mouth is a mistake, as it dives into me once more.

I run my hands down Anrai's chest, fingers bumping over scars both old and new. I trace them delicately, his skin seeming to glow with warmth in the setting sun. Somehow, his presence makes even the drab monotony of the quarterage appear bright with flame, and even now that we've had more uninterrupted days together than we have since we first met, I find that everything about him still hitches my breath.

His smile is lazy, but there is nothing lazy about the way he watches me. His eyes are devouring, sparking with a madness I've come to know well. One that brings a flush to my skin and warmth pooling at my core. Because it is a madness that will never be satiated, one whose flame burns within us both.

"If you keep doing that, neither of us is going to get any sleep," he drawls, as my fingers trace the gnarled knot above his heart. He doesn't flinch like he once would have, and the knowledge that in this, at least, he has begun to heal eases into me.

I hum in response, trailing my hand down over the ridges of his stomach. Though he keeps himself perfectly still, a remnant of his father's training, a growl vibrates in his throat. A satisfied smile curls my lips. I've found there is nothing more pleasing than breaking Anrai's self-control; in making him shake and yearn for me until he throws everything else aside and gives into the most primal aspect of himself.

"If you want to sleep, maybe you should crash in Cal's room," I tease as my fingers dip below the waistband of his pants, just for a brief moment, before crawling slowly back up.

Anrai's eyes spark. "Do you think a hallway and a door are enough to make me forget what it feels like to be inside you?"

Faster than I can react, he grabs my wrists and pins them above my head, rolling me beneath him. I yelp as he presses into the cradle of my legs, the sharp bones of his hips digging into the soft flesh of my thighs. The weight of him settles something in me and he holds none of it back, knowing I was meant to take all of him. "A thousand-year-old wall wasn't enough to keep me from you, Lemming. And that was before I tasted you." His eyes darken. *"You don't want to know what I'd do now."*

He grinds his hips into me, the thick length of him pressing into my heated core, only a thin wall of fabric preventing me from feeling all of him. I want to rip it away, to end the agony of being apart, but with my hands pinned, I can only settle for wriggling my hips. Anrai laughs, its deep sound rumbling over my skin.

"Tell me," I demand breathlessly.

He runs his lips up the curve of my throat lightly, before flicking his tongue behind my ear. "Hmm," he muses, keeping my wrists pinned with one hand and setting his other roaming down my body. His long fingers splay across my breasts, and I push them up toward him with a needy whimper. "What would I do for this..."

He traces his thumb in small circles over the tip, and before continuing down the roll of my stomach. Anrai never takes his eyes from mine and beneath his reverent gaze, I no longer feel the cold of the coming winter. Because with his attention on me, I am my own ray of sun. My own flick of flame. Dancing and writhing; a multitude of color.

His hand dips between my legs, where he finds me wet and waiting. I gasp as he pushes two fingers into me, the feeling of fullness exquisitely sumptuous. Anrai's own breath hitches as I raise my hips, pushing his fingers deeper. "This is home," he rasps against my throat, and satisfaction threads through me as his body trembles above mine.

This is my favorite Anrai: undone, needy, controlling.

"My home," he says again, pumping his fingers in and out. "And I would shred my soul to keep it."

Our home. This is our home.

But instead of warmth, something icy slithers through

me. The current. It pulls and pulls, trying to claim what's ours. What's mine.

That's not yours, I scream into oblivion. *You can't have that.*

We have fought and bled for our home, and the current has no right to it. I thrash and claw, trying to keep the memory close to my chest. *Not yours, not yours.*

But the current is relentless, and the memory slips from my grasp. I want to cry, but the current takes everything, even my tears.

Soon, Ms. Ellis, everything that is yours will be mine.

CHAPTER
FIFTEEN

Shaw

The Argentian wastes spread out before us, the landscape cut with jagged canyons and spires of black rock. The sky has turned gray and stormy, and this early in the morning, a thin layer of ice coats the ground. We've already been traveling for hours, only stopping to water the horses and relieve ourselves, and it still hasn't been fast enough. Though the coin keeps Avedis from being able to see clearly, he's been able to track the Covinus' progress through the words of others, and according to the accounts, Mirren has been in Argentum for more than a day.

It shouldn't be possible. It's a four-day journey from the Nemoran to my father's territory, three if you were to ride through the night. In order to have made it so quickly, the Covinus must not have stopped at *all*. As an ageless wraith, perhaps he doesn't need rest or food or water. But our traveling party is entirely human, and with the pace we've been keeping, exhaustion pulls at me more heavily than ever.

We're still half a day from the city, but it already feels like the sky itself has crawled beneath my skin and turned my veins to lead. I was born to this land, shaped on the keen-edged rocks and the point of my father's blade. I was torn apart here, honed into a nightmare, and wielded like a weapon. My father may be gone, but the echoes of him still linger like bruises on skin.

And here, they feel far too corporeal.

My thoughts spiral, even as I try to drown them out. What will happen when I enter the Castellium itself, the birthplace of all my horrors? Will I be able to descend into the abyss and quiet my thoughts? Or will they run rampant and get us all killed?

"One of my favorite cliffs!" Avedis declares loudly, gazing at the cliff edge beside us like it's a long-lost friend.

I glare at him, even as Luwei asks in bewilderment, "You have a favorite cliff?"

Avedis grins so widely, I consider throwing a dagger at him. "Of course I do, young friend. For this is the cliff I had the pleasure of tossing the fire-bearer off of only a few months ago!" He shivers with dramatic rapture. "Such a warm memory."

Luwei snickers loudly, before shooting me a conciliatory look. Easton tenses, as if expecting me to burn Avedis to a crisp without bothering to stop my horse. If only I was able to accomplish it before he sucked the air from my lungs.

I settle for rolling my eyes at the assassin, even as something like gratitude wends its way through me. Avedis has a distinct talent for shooting his mouth off every time my thoughts begin to drown me, his obnoxious arrogance effectively damming their incessant waves. I've begun to suspect his timing isn't at all a coincidence. Even without the ability to read thoughts, Avedis is apt at reading mine, a fact that simultaneously calms and infuriates me.

"After this is over, my top priority will be figuring out how to unbind myself from you," I tell Avedis with a chuckle. The assassin only winks in response.

"Bound?" Easton repeats curiously.

Avedis frowns in disdain. "Not in the loathsome way you lemmings mean it."

When he doesn't explain further, Easton looks to Luwei for help. It's the first I've seen him share Mirren's natural curiosity for the world, and it does something to soften me toward him. Luwei obliges, adjusting the reins of his thick black mare. "They are the original four elements, and the stories say they are bonded. The Covinus stole the term and twisted it for his own methods, but the original Binding ceremony was that of the gods. To keep what little balance remained in the world intact."

Asa's story, told in the warmth of Aggie's cabin. *If one fell, so did the others.*

For some reason, the words set my teeth on edge. "We already proved it's just a story," I mutter skeptically. "Gislan died and the rest of us didn't." Traitorous piece of shit.

Luwei shrugs with a casualty I wish I felt. "Maybe he wasn't the Bonded."

"What do you mean? You think there was just an extra earth-wielder running around? That doesn't make any sense." My frustration rises, because *none* of this makes any sense. I understood the Praeceptor—what drove him, what he was after. But everything about the Covinus and the old gods and the curse still remain stubbornly unclear.

I've focused only on the fact that the Covinus took Mirren; I haven't stopped to consider that I have no idea *why.* How am I going to outwit a thousand-year-old enemy when I can't even begin to fathom his motivations?

"I'm not a Kashan, I don't know the stories like Asa and

Sura. But she said being Bonded was important. Like combining your spirits makes you more powerful, but also gives you a greater weakness."

Avedis' face has grown solemn as he mulls over the information. "It was an...odd feeling. To combine my power with yours in Similis. Perhaps it truly is the bond that allowed it."

I hardly hear him, for the iron in my veins has suddenly grown claws. Because if the stories are true, and Gislan wasn't our bonded—what if it was another little earth-wielder? One who brought down an entire city block because he was scared and alone?

One who's power manifested *before* I destroyed the Boundary. I never believed the whispers that he shook the earth in the spaces of time the lights were out, but what if there was something to them?

The assassin watches me shrewdly before turning to Luwei and asking, "What else has Sura told you about the prophecy?"

Luwei shifts uncomfortably as he realizes how intensely we're all staring at him. "Um, not much. Just that all of the bonded are needed to break the first queen's curse."

The boy isn't telling me anything I didn't already know, but it makes me abruptly angry, now that its set against the realization Helias' may also be tangled up in the Covinus' mess. It's bad enough Mirren and I are embroiled in a centuries old battle, but we're strong and capable. Helias is only a child, too young to be forced into life-or-death decisions. Too young to hand over his soul piece by piece to save the world from itself.

He should be the one protected, not the one doing the protecting. And as hard as I try, I can't protect any of us against something beyond me, written in the lines of time before any of us were even a thought in the ether.

"Ghost stories and whimsy," Avedis replies lightly, as much for my sake as his own. He stretches his neck lazily, moving his gaze back to the landscape before us. "If the gods truly wanted the curse broken, it would have been far more prudent to leave a letter of instructions. A cave carving, at the very least. But instead, they chose the far more dramatic option. And while normally, I'd applaud their penchant for theatrics, you'll forgive me if I don't take their *stories* at their worth."

We ride until the sun begins to dip in the sky and the city of Argentum spreads out across the wastelands, a seeping black plague on an otherwise gray scape. This close to the city, the glow of civilization rises up into the swirling violet clouds. Smoke from the hearths curl into the air, and as the first snowflakes begin to fall, Argentum appears softer than ever. Cozy, slightly dimmed, nestled into the icy air.

I know better. Snow may soften even the harshest of cities, but it cannot change what festers beneath. Steel, stone, and rot.

"We'll stop here and wait for night to fall. Then we'll make our move."

No one argues, dismounting their horses and leading them inside the small cave mouth. There are thousands of caves like this along the west side of Argentum, carved by years of erosion and mining that have hollowed out the mountain range. Most stay clear of the tunnels themselves, as it's been said they were dug too deep and one wrong move will leave you trapped beneath the earth for eternity. But I never heeded the warnings as a boy, using them for travel and more importantly, for a place to hide from my father.

Easton shivers beside me and yanks up the hood of his overcoat. With a roll of my eyes, I toss him an extra cloak from my saddle bags. He catches it with a grateful grunt.

"You want a fire, Similian?"

He glances up at me with guarded hope that instantly dies at my rueful smirk. "Then start building one."

Easton presses his lips together so hard all the blood drains from them. But he doesn't protest, and instead, begins to gather an armful of wood. It's the first fire we've had on the journey, as there wasn't time, and I hadn't wanted to call attention to ourselves. But this close to the city, hundreds of fires spread out across the mountains and the wastes below. Merchant traveling parties, thieves, and families alike either trying to enter the Argentian gates or trying to escape them. One more fire will hardly be noticed.

I laze against a rock, and an icy breeze nips at my nose and cheeks as Avedis comes to sit beside me. Together, we watch Easton struggle with the wood, numb fingers attempting to build it correctly two or three times. Without a word, I toss him my flint, and though his ears turn bright red, he still doesn't argue. Only works again in silence.

"You are truly monstrous to make him struggle instead of just lighting the damn thing with a thought," Avedis muses.

I shrug, running my fingers along the handles of my daggers absently. "He should learn to survive without electricity, or all the lemmings will freeze inside their homes this winter."

"Good riddance," Avedis contends, but there's no bite to his words. He risked his life to save the city from Akari Ilinka, but it certainly wasn't because the Community endeared itself to him. It was because Mirren had. The assassin's morals are dubious at the best of times, but it seems once his loyalty is earned, it doesn't waver.

Easton yelps in excitement at the small flame that flickers at the base of the wood, pride shining in his eyes. I coax the paltry fire higher with a lazy wave of my hand. Luwei drops the last of our stores into an iron pan, along with a few dried herbs from his pack, and soon, the mouth-watering scent of *hajan* fills the small cave. A traditional Xaman stew, the scent burrows into the recesses of my mind and warms my stomach, one of the few smells from my childhood that doesn't accompany a horrifying memory.

It reminds me of Nehuan, the Xamani man who shared his lunch with me as a child in the Castellium. My father had him killed for being kind to me, and though his death still brings a wave of shame, remembering him is still something of a comfort. He was the only warmth I ever found in this city.

By the time our bellies are full, the snow has begun to swirl around us in thick, white sheets. Winter has not arrived in the north with a soft tease, but instead, a roar of majesty. Avedis raises a shield at the cave mouth, protecting us from the worst of the storm, and as I watch the flames dance, mirroring the ones in my chest, and wait for night to decisively fall, I begin to feel drowsy.

If only I didn't know what awaits every time I close my eyes. Burning hair. Melting skin. Screams.

And there will only be more of it in a few hours. More horror to live with.

Avedis and Luwei burrow into bedrolls to get a few hours sleep before we venture into Argentum, but to my surprise, Easton comes to sit beside me at the cave mouth.

He tucks his legs close to his chest, and stares at the city sprawled out below us.

Moments of silence stretch between us, fragile and thin, before he finally says, "I want to come tonight."

I expected the request, but it still sends a breath hissing between my teeth. "No."

For the first time, there is no disapproval on his face when Easton looks at me. Instead, there is pleading hope, and somehow, it's so much worse. "Mirri is in there because of me. The Covinus could be—he could be torturing her right now...he could be doing to her what he did to Harlan." He swallows roughly, and for a terrifying moment, I think he might cry. "And it's my fault."

I furrow my brow, even as his words leave me breathless. I haven't allowed myself to imagine what Mirren's endured in our time apart, because it would shatter me completely. She is alive, and my girl, she fights. Always. The knowledge has been enough to keep me moving, to keep me together.

"Easton, I know I said a lot of things when I was angry, but what happened to Mirren isn't your fault." I don't say it to be kind, as kindness is a frivolous luxury in the Darkness.

"It is," he insists, tugging uncomfortably at the bandages beneath his shirt. "She told me before she left what the Covinus was, and I didn't believe her. I *couldn't* believe her. If I'd just been stronger—or, or...braver. If I'd just left with her then, she wouldn't have even been in Similis. We all would have been safe in Nadjaa."

I watch the heavy pull of Easton's shoulders. So much shame. "You can't know that's what would have happened."

"She was under the Boundary because she was trying to protect me. Because I stayed behind."

I nod slowly. "Yes. But, Easton...even if you weren't there, Mirren still would have gone back."

He shakes his head stubbornly, and I understand it. Sometimes, it is easier to place blame, even if the blame lies with yourself. Because if it is no one's fault, we are admitting there's no control—no way to dictate what happens, all of us only leaves on the winds of time.

If I was someone else, I might place a comforting hand on Easton's shoulder. If he was someone else, he might want me to. But as it is, both of us remain still, straddling the delicate space where dislike and begrudging respect reside.

I inhale sharply. "You said you know Mirren better than anyone, right?"

Easton nods miserably.

"Would Mirren have stayed safe in Nadjaa if there was even the slightest chance she could save Similis? Save Ferusa? It wouldn't have mattered if you were there or not, and it didn't matter that the Community shunned her for most of her life. Mirren's heart is pure. She would have gone back no matter what."

"Doesn't that scare you?" he cries desperately, bringing his gaze to mine. "I've spent every moment of my life fearing Mirren's heart is going to be the end of her. That it's going to drive her to do something heroic—something she can never come back from. Look at her now, Shaw! She'll die if she thinks she can save Sura—if she thinks she can save a stranger—and it *terrifies* me."

Easton heaves a leveling breath, his eyes slightly wild with his confession. "You claim to love her. That she has your heart. How are you not afraid?"

A year ago, I would have said nothing in the Darkness scared me beyond my father. I'd already seen the worst of humanity, and there were no surprises that would ever horrify beyond my own self.

But I've come a long way since then, and I'm man enough to admit fear is now my constant companion. *You love her and so she will be taken from you.* Fear of the Darkness stealing her away somewhere I can't follow. Fear of being unable to keep myself whole for her. Fear the prophecy will demand something of us we cannot possibly give.

"I am," I confess, "but not of Mirren's heart. Never that. It's infallible, Easton. And if there were more of what makes her heart and soul in this world, there wouldn't be monsters like the Praeceptor and the Covinus. There wouldn't be Darkness."

Easton purses his lips. Now that he's allowed his terror outside of himself, it balloons around him in a cloud. "And what if we get her back only for the prophecy to demand her death? What then, Shaw? Because you know she'll do it. You know she'll lay herself down and cut open her own throat if it means breaking the curse."

Anxiety threads through my chest, slimy and unsettling, but when it meets the heat of my abyss, it curls away to ash. One battle at a time.

Get her back. Slit the Covinus open from throat to groin. Then worry about the curse.

Because I don't care what the damned prophecy says, today isn't the day I give Mirren up to the Darkness. We found each other through the lines of time, the depths of night; bled and fought to protect what we have. And I will claw my way through whatever I have to, to get her back.

The abyss roars its approval, and flames crackle in my chest, licking up my throat and pooling in my mouth until I feel as though I could breathe fire. A beast of the old world, dragon of blood and flame.

And gods help any who stand in my way.

~

Mirren

The Covinus never relents.

He does not stop to eat or drink, only sits in the chair across from me with the two coins positioned on each of his palms. I squirm, trying to pull my hands away, trying to stop the unending agony ripping through my brain, but his grip is iron and in my feeble condition, struggling is useless.

With each memory he takes, his hold on me grows stronger, until it feels like he kneels on my mind, everything that makes me who I am crushed beneath him. I have no tears to cry, but sobs come anyway, wheezes of desperation and pain. And still, he comes.

Easton wiggles his small body closer to mine and the icy air of the quarterage seems to relent. Blankets pulled up over our heads, we are our own source of heat, cocooned in the only thing that still makes sense in the wake of our parents' banishment: each other. We have separate bedrooms in Farrah and Jakoby's house, but most nights, my brother sneaks into mine, and for a few merciful hours, we disappear into our own world beneath the covers. The only place where the whispers cannot touch us.

"Mirri," he says softly. His fingers are curled in mine, palms sweaty and warm. "You won't disappear, will you?"

Will you, Mirri? Will you disappear like they all disappear, dissolving into dust and air? Bones, heart, skin, all gone like it never existed in the first place. Sometimes, I think the only thing keeping me grounded is Easton's hand: his fingers my tether to the world, his heart strapped to mine.

Not yours. This isn't yours.

I thrash wildly, desperate to dislodge the talons digging

into my mind. They are anchored into my deepest thoughts, embroiled around my most precious memories, and I bleed under their sharp hold. The Covinus will take them all, and I'll be left with nothing. Alone, untethered. Lost.

Music twinkles around us, and Max looks ethereal in the soft glow of the lantern light. She winds her fingers through mine and twirls me around and around the living room of the quarterage. Our laughter begins deep in our bellies and swells outside of us, until it tickles our very skin, and then we laugh more. She bows, her face suddenly serious in a precise impression of one of Anrai's sullen moods.

Anrai stands next to her, but he is not sullen. He is luminous, poking Max in the side until her impression breaks and we all dissolve in another fit of giggles. Max's feet match mine as the beat of the music pumps in time with my heart, thumping in my chest, and I think I might die from happiness. Certainly, there is not enough room between my ribs, not enough space in my heart for how full I feel.

The memory is swept away before it even settles and I cry out, my fingers gripping at the empty air. *It is mine, it is mine.*

"Nothing is yours," the Covinus' emotionless voice drifts somewhere above my head. "Your history, your heart, your power. You will give it all to me."

Somewhere distantly along the edges of my agony, thoughts pull together in a crushing realization. He is taking everything that makes up my heart, everything that sustains my power.

The Covinus is not stealing my soul. He is stealing my *other.*

No. *NO.*

The thought resounds in my mind with a residual clang, and I burrow down into the depths of my heart, sinking into the parts long gone dark. It is all that's left, these twisted parts, warped by abandonment and loneliness. The black vines spear out from my heart, twine around my lungs and dive into the talons digging into my mind.

The claws screech and struggle, desperately trying to escape, but my dark vines are far too powerful. How ironic that the Covinus is responsible for their very creation, for their nourishment every passing year.

The vines squeeze, pulling tighter and tighter, until the talons are forced to loosen their grip.

But my darkness doesn't stop. It keeps the talons in its hold, squeezing so hard, we tumble into another memory, this one not our own.

Iara looks beautiful.

She always looks beautiful, but with the angry tears magnifying her chocolate eyes and the hot flush staining her cheeks, she is even more magnificent than usual. Her hair tumbles down her shoulders in waves of gold, and though her ire is directed at me, I don't feel shame. I only feel vindication.

"Aurelius, where is Xander?" It is a demand, but I hear the desperation lingering behind it. She refers to her brother, the sniveling fire-wielder who was never strong enough to hold the power the gods gifted him. It was easy to catch the boy off guard, and even easier to take everything he was and make it mine. By the end, he'd been begging me to send him into the Darkness. And I, being the merciful man I am, granted his wish.

Iara will be better off without the weakness of her twin constantly siphoning her own blooming energy. She may not see now, but she's been blinded by her love for him. I will show her the folly of her misplaced affection. She will soon learn that I am the only one worthy of it, the only one equal to the demands of such a strong heart.

"He's in a better place, Iara," I tell her gently, watching as

her lower lip wobbles and her face dissolves into a picture of anguish. I drink that in too, reveling in her beautiful pain.

"What have you done?" she says, her voice no longer the gentle hush of a wave, but a crash of stormy surf. Her power begins to swirl at her fingertips, and I watch it with affection, loving the way her eyes whorl with the sea. She is a sea goddess and soon, she will realize the things I have sacrificed to become her equal.

"I have restored balance where it was lacking," I tell her casually, strolling toward the marble bar of my house and pouring myself a drink. She watches me with narrowed eyes, before her gaze flickers to the luxurious trappings I've surrounded myself in. Every piece chosen for her in our time apart.

Our separation had been horrid, each day without her feeling like a millennium. But it was necessary.

She runs her fingers along a velvet couch that cost more than three of the hovels I grew up in, before grazing them across a gilded table. I wait for her to speak, to ask how it is I've climbed my way above those who sought to keep me trodden beneath their feet. But instead, she asks, "Has it been worth it?"

I turn, startled. "Has what been worth it?"

Her lips settle in a firm line as her power crawls up her arms. "Having a fancy house and money to burn? Was it worth the price of your soul? This isn't you, Aurelius."

Anger rises in my throat. Iara looks as perfect as I imagined she would in my house, surrounded by the luxury she's always been accustomed to. And instead of gratitude, she means to preach to me? When she was born with a silver spoon in her mouth, one carved by the bleeding hands of thousands of destitute before her?

My father's words come racing back to me, and my skin heats.

I take three charged strides toward her as anger flames to life in my chest, dark and twisted and cold. Something happened when her brother handed over his power in the final moments of life, something that warped the heat of his fire into ice, cold but equally as deadly.

Something new, worthy of someone like me. Iara's eyes widen in horror as she bears witness to my newfound power, but I don't give her a chance to contemplate it. I know what's best for her, and I will shred her apart and put her back together until she understands how well we fit. I grab her throat and squeeze until she gasps, but I don't yield, even when she claws at my hands.

I am only doing what I have always done—protecting Iara, even if it's from herself.

"Does it bother you that someone you deemed inferior has fought his way to your level? I thought you better than this, Iara, but you're just as pompous and spoiled as the rest of them." I contract my hand as her face begins to turn blue. "You wielders only want to keep everyone else beneath the steel of your boot."

Iara's power rises, and I shake my head with a rueful laugh. "Ah, ah. Keep that power curled away, little sea witch. Or I will burn not only you, but everyone in this godsdamn city."

Instantly, her water fades back into her skin, but her anger is just as powerful as any flame. I drink it in like a fine wine, its sustenance more potent than any elixir. Because anger is better than indifference. In my time since the mines, I have forced even the most important of the wielders, the richest of citizens, to stand up and pay attention.

I have destroyed their businesses and fed on the carcasses. I have monopolized almost every source of energy on this continent and now, if any of them want the comfort of electricity, they are forced to grovel at my feet.

"Aurelius, Xander trusted you. He was your friend." And

then, angrier, "His power doesn't belong to you. You were not chosen, nor were you born to create fire."

Keeping one hand around her windpipe, I run my finger along the curve of her throat, as I've imagined doing so many times in the years we've been apart. I've dreamed up so many things when it comes to her smooth skin. Tasting it with my tongue, tearing at it with my teeth, consuming it until she is only mine.

"It is mine now, Iara," I bury my nose in her hair and inhale sharply, as her body stiffens beneath my ministrations. No matter. We have all the time in the world for me to teach her where her place is. Beside me, always.

Flame bursts in my palm, and she whimpers as the heat lingers uncomfortably close to the skin of her cheek. "The power is mine, the continent is mine, and you *are* mine,*" I growl, before running my tongue along her jawline. "I didn't need to be chosen, Iara. Life didn't bless me with what I deserved, so I tore it out with my teeth," I tell her snapping at the thin skin, hard enough to leave behind red marks. "And no one will keep me from what is mine," I promise.*

Iara meets my gaze, her irises whirling with an oncoming storm. It lights in my chest. I have missed the thrill of conquering. I can't wait to conquer her.

"You will never have me," she growls.

I only smile. "Dear Iara. I already do."

The Covinus' talons buck so violently my vines of darkness tumble back into my chest. I scream, trying to readjust my grip, to find anything to hold onto, but it is as if I am lost in a slick metal tunnel. There is no purchase, nothing to save me from the fall.

"That was not yours to take," the Covinus says calmly. His claws relent and abruptly, the dim light of the dungeon comes snapping back into view. The temperature has plummeted, and my breath comes in icy puffs before me, my skin aching from the bite of cold. Sura is slumped against her chains, sleeping or unconscious, and I can only be thankful she's spared from witnessing the misery I've become.

Everything hurts, everything is pain, and I am so tired.

The Covinus runs his eyes from the tip of my head, down the tangle of hair plastered to my neck with cold sweat, and to the blood that's begun to pour from my nose. Satisfaction flickers subtly across his face. "You have broken a Key by taking what was not given to you, Mirren. And you know there are consequences for breaking the Keys."

He is stealing my power like he stole Iara's brothers', and in doing so, is draining me entirely of myself. Because I am my *other,* and without it, whatever fragments remain will wither and die. He preaches to me about the Keys, while taking something that doesn't belong to him. *I will never belong to you.*

The Covinus stands, rapping once on the cell door. The soldier hands something through the opening, before closing the door once more. When the Covinus turns back to me, he smiles as nausea climbs my throat. I recognize the instrument in his hands from the Education Center videos, but worse, I recognize it from Harlan's stories; from the scars that line his inner thighs. A switch.

Panic flutters in my chest as he disappears from my view, circling around the back of me. I squirm in the chair, trying to angle away from him despite the shackles around my ankles. But my limbs are jelly, and I list forward, slumping to my knees on the cold ground. My shirt is yanked up, and I don't even have time to level a breath before the first lash lights across my bare skin.

I bite down so hard, I'm sure my teeth will crack, keeping my scream trapped in my throat. The Covinus brings the switch down again, and agonizing fire blazes across my back. I try to hold onto the burn, to transform it into a different sort of flame, one that brings comfort and light.

Shaw, I am trying to be strong, I think into the ether, as the switch lashes down again. *But I am so tired.*

The only response is silence, only the faint sound of the *drip, drip, drip.*

And when the Covinus finally sets the switch down after what feels like hours, and takes my hands once more, my screams drown out even that.

CHAPTER
SIXTEEN

Shaw

"How did you escape before?" Avedis asks, staring down at the bustle surrounding the Argentian gates.

Merchants move in and out in a slow stream, each cart and traveler checked thoroughly by a member of the militia. Soldiers stride along the top of the wall surrounding the city, while others take shifts in the guard stations located throughout the various districts. Despite my father's death, Argentum is still a well-oiled machine. And a deadly one at that.

I wonder if my father ever realized how perfectly primed his territory was for the Covinus to steal. The warlord's seat has never been passed by birth, but by blood. Cullen thought he'd ensured my place as Heir as no single person would ever manage to best the number of deaths on my hands.

My father never looked to the seemingly benign leader inviting him into the gates of utopia. Cullen's thirst for power blinded him to the truth—that the Covinus has thousands of years of deaths on his hands, and no one could ever challenge his right to the seat.

"Max," I reply frankly, shifting ever so slightly on my belly. Sharp pieces of shale dig into my skin, and the bones of my hips are sore from being frozen in this position. "I was half-dead, and she dumped me into a death cart, and hid beneath me."

Avedis makes a humming noise in the back of his throat, a dire acknowledgment of what I already knew—making it to Argentum was the easy part. Finding our way into a protected city, armed with wielders, militia, and Similian guns, is going to be much more difficult.

The wind-wielder closes his eyes and breathes in deeply as a crisp breeze feathers around us. When he opens his eyes once more, it's with a frustrated shake of his head. "I still see nothing. It's like Similis all over again."

Unease pricks my skin. "It's the coins. It has to be. We have to be prepared to do this without our power." Prepared to fight as agony tears through our bodies. "But if we don't have power, at least the other side doesn't either."

Avedis nods, his brow lowered thoughtfully as he stares down at the city. "It doesn't seem to extend to the wall itself, so I believe I'll be able to get us over it. After that, we'll be moving blind."

"Not blind," I amend with some measure of misery. As much as I've tried to forget my time within those dank black walls, the memories are carved in stone. "I can find my way around the Castellium with my eyes closed. The tricky part will be the dungeons, as that's where he'll have the most guards stationed."

"The dungeons," Avedis muses, cocking his head. "For a man who projected civility for a thousand years, he's certainly been quick to turn to the ways of the Darkness."

"His civility was only ever a façade. Similis has their own dungeon to torture their citizens, they just call it a Healing Center." Fresh anger burgeons in my chest. "Say what you want about Dark Worlders and warlords, but at least we don't pretend to be anything but what we are."

"Speak for yourself," Avedis *tsks,* "I am the picture of civility."

"You've got blood on your cloak."

He shoots me a roughish grin. "Ah, but it brings out the exquisite color of my cheeks."

I roll my eyes, thinking of how much Cal would appreciate Avedis' penchant for the finer things in life. And then I slam a steel wall down around the dull ache that pulses through me at the thought of my friends. Max and Cal have been part of everything I've had to do since I was fourteen, and though their absence is a gaping hole, a part of me remains thankful for it.

They are far from the wretched gray city, far from the twisted reach of the Covinus.

"I should burn all of Argentum to the ground," I snarl savagely. "It's only fitting I keep my last promise to my father."

If Avedis is startled by my sudden violence, he doesn't show it. He doesn't even look at me, only continues watching the flurry of activity at the gates. "The city is made of stone. And you—" His voice is edged with sadness, the kind that burrows holes into your heart and fills them with loneliness. "You are made of soul, friend."

I dig my fingers further into my palm, reminding myself Avedis is right. But the morose sight of all my experienced horrors, and the thought of Mirren—beautiful, luminous, Mirren—trapped inside makes it hard to care about things like souls. It's hard to think of anything beyond the flame of rage billowing in my chest: rage at the Covinus for taking Mirren; rage at my father for being too dead to punish for the events he set in motion.

Rage at the world for never ceasing. Always pressing closer and closer and refusing to allow even an inch to breathe.

"Soul or not, Avedis, I'll gut every single person who's touched her. I'll melt the skin from their bones and savor every piece of myself given in service of avenging her."

The assassin nods. "Let's go then."

The storm swirls around us as we climb stiffly to our feet. Luwei and Easton stand beside their horses a few feet away. The Xamani boy looks at home in the ice, bundled as he is in furs and hides. In contrast, Easton shivers uncontrollably even tucked inside the borrowed cloak.

But he doesn't complain. Only mounts his horse and meets my gaze with uncharacteristic ferocity. I've seen the Darkness drive even the most docile of people to the depths of violence, but love can do much the same. It can temper even the weakest resolve into reinforced steel, and for a moment, I wish Mirren could see her brother like this.

It takes a few hours to reach the northernmost edge of the city, where both the wall, and the Castellium inside it, are built into a large rock formation, the giant spires piercing through the white snow and reaching toward the sky like knives. As a child, the black rock reminded me of my father's sword, but now, they look like fingers clawing their way out of the snow. Souls trapped forever beneath the horror of the Castellium.

"Come no further than this rock, not even if you see us bleeding out in the snow. Do you understand? Only break cover if you see Sura and Mirren, and even then, keep your guard up."

Both boys nods solemnly. Luwei adjusts his grip on his bow, setting me with a determined look. "Bring back my sister, Fire-wielder. Or I won't rest until I've spilled your blood in payment."

Something like pride wends through me. Since we met at the base of the Shadiil mountains all those months ago, Luwei's jaw and body have filled out, the result of both being properly nourished and approaching manhood. Desperation no longer edges every line of him, pushed to the edge of humanity by the Darkness. Now, it is only pure will in his eyes.

I nod once, and then turn toward the city.

An icy breeze flits around Avedis and I as we prowl silently toward the wall. The snow swirls up around us, shielding our presence to any who happened to look this way. While we are far from the bustle of the front gates, Boundary men armed with guns and Dark Militia alike patrol the top at regular intervals, sending signals to the guard houses spread throughout the interior of the city.

As we grow nearer, the two closest patrolmen both topple over unconscious. I twist my mouth, remembering how unpleasant the experience is, and have hardly had time to steel my spine when the breeze swells to a robust wind. I resist the urge to squeeze my eyes shut as I'm lifted from my feet, instead, forcing myself to watch the wall above for guards.

When my feet hit stone, and my stomach stops wobbling somewhere up near my throat, Avedis joins me on the top of the wall. His footsteps are feather-light and soundless, his raven hair dancing wildly across his forehead as he unsheathes his long sword. For once, it feels like fate has favored us, as the blizzard not only shrouds our presence, but has driven most every Argentian into their homes.

The curving streets are all but abandoned as we land silently in the powder. The Castellium looms above us, the towering spires a dark shadow against the winter sky. For a moment, the world feels hushed. Snow has a way of softening even the harshest of places; of muting the sharpest of screams, shaping them into something softer.

Shrouded by wind, we sneak around the back wall of the fortress. The vines are thicker here, climbing upward in giant, verdant ropes, leaves the size of my palm fanning out over the black rock. The plants were younger when Max and I escaped years before, but now, they're nearly impossible to brush aside. Avedis watches my back as I resort to hacking at them with a dagger, in search of the small crack in the stone.

After a few tense moments of slicing through the plants, a sigh of relief rushes through me. The hole is still here, eight years later. My father never discovered the route Max and I escaped through. Places of beauty, especially forgotten ones like this garden never interested Cullen. He was so sure he'd ruined this garden for me, so certain I would never come back, that he probably hadn't even bothered to search it.

The hole is much smaller than I remember. Or I'm much bigger, as Max and I were only children when we ran from the Praeceptor's wrath.

With a nod to Avedis, I contort my body, managing to wiggle my head and then a shoulder through. I follow it with the other shoulder, wriggling slowly and trying not to think of how easy it would be to get trapped inside the rock. My skin stings as it scrapes against the shards, but finally, I manage to slide the rest of my body through.

Avedis, who didn't spend almost an entire month vomiting while relearning how to be human, has a far harder time. His bulk far outweighs the tight space of the crack, so we both take turns hacking at the rock until small pieces of it give way. The echoing sound in the night heightens my anxiety. We make slow progress, made slower by our attempt to muffle the noise, and the tortuously stagnant pace feels like nails beneath my skin.

I haven't allowed myself to imagine Mirren's experience in the Castellium, haven't allowed myself to picture her staring up at the same walls that held me, trapped beneath stone and agony. But now that I'm here, close enough to run to her, wild images lash at my mind despite my best attempts to silence them. I feel the pull of her here like a physical tether, and it's only through pure strength of will that I don't burn my way straight down to the dungeons, soul be damned.

Finally, the hole is large enough for Avedis. I hold out a hand to help him to his feet, try to focus on the feel of his palm against mine to calm the flame beginning to spiral out from my heart. It burns so hot, so out of control, for a terrifying moment, I think I'll scorch everything around me again.

"Not yet, friend," the wind-wielder whispers softly.

I meet his gaze and will the fire to relent, but before I can pull the flames back into my heart, a giant shadow snuffs them out.

I gasp, clawing at my heart as my power is ripped from me. Ice crackles through my veins, encases my lungs and bones. Avedis stumbles beside me, his desperate wheezes harrowing in the silence of the snow.

"Hello, Heir," a voice growls behind me.

Agony ripping through me, I struggle to place the voice.

Struggle to understand why it sounds like a ghost risen from the Darkness itself.

Turning, whatever breath I still have left leaves me completely.

For there, cloak billowing around him, stands Nehuan. He appears far older than he does in my memories, gray now tinging his temples and lines delineating the skin around his mouth, but there is no mistaking him. My first taste of kindness in the world, the Xamani slave who befriended me in this very same garden.

Even as I struggle to breathe without my power, my eyes cannot drink in enough of the friend I thought I'd lost forever. His face no longer holds the gaunt edge of submission it did when I was a child, and he isn't clad in the tattered garb denoting enslavement.

Now, Nehuan is clad in red—the red of a Dark Militia *legatus*. My eyes snag on the clothing for so long, it takes far too many beats for me to realize what he wears around his throat on a gold chain.

The coin.

∼

Mirren

"You are a light, Mirri. Not the lights of the Boundary that blind any who look at it, but the light of the moon. Shining in the Darkness." My father's voice drifts from memory, his dreams painting a watercolor across the room of my quarterage. Tales of adventure and bravery and love.

The memory stretches and warps until it is misshapen and wrong, until it feels foreign in my mind. And then, it is gone. The memories rush faster now, an endless wave. And I have no more strength to fight against them, to keep them from him. The Covinus has bled it out of my back, has starved it and crushed it beneath the force of his evil.

I try to curl up in my mind, to brace myself against them, but still they come. Each one as potent as the last, each scraping out the inside of me with their claws as they're pulled from me. I sob and I scream, but none of it sounds in the endless crash of the current.

Anrai's smile, his face luminous with delight as he crouches, readying himself for a sparring match. Flames spark over his skin as he beckons me forward. "Give me all of you, Lemming," he tells me, his low voice sliding through my lower belly like a soft caress.

Another wave. Another memory washed away.

Easton's wide eyes filled with hope as we wait in the Education Center. "Mirri, when are they coming?"

When are they coming. When is someone coming. Give me all of you.

I have nothing left to give.

Cal's long fingers running across the keys of a piano at the manor, his sparkling smile mischievous as he begins to sing a bawdy song. His look of delight as he succeeds in making me blush. His laugh as he pulls me down onto the bench beside him and begins to teach me how to make my own music.

My father caressing my mother's cheek with his lips, the pretty blush of her skin. The shy smile pulling at her full lips.

Those lips smiling at me in the dark of my room, her arms warm as they came around me. The warmth drives the bad dreams away and I think, Mother's hugs could keep even the curse from me.

Anrai's pleading whisper, "Open for me. Let me home."

Let me home, let me home.

I have no home. Adrift. Lost. Nameless. Nothing is mine, it is all *his*.

I am sinking into the depths of oblivion with nothing to hold onto. And soon, I will be disappeared.

No. *NO.*

With one last burst of rage, I gather up the remaining pieces of myself tightly. I hold them together, even as their jagged edges pierce my skin, even as blood pools in the palms of my hand. And then I explode, thrusting their sharp points out into the chasm like blades of pure energy.

The Covinus screams, and as we tumble into his memory once more, only one thought resounds: *I will make you bleed as you have bled me. I will never belong to you.*

His memory is steadier than mine, still whole. But when I realize it is my mother's face that stares back at me, I almost lose hold of it. The lush set of her mouth, the clever spark in her eyes; it is all the same even through the Covinus' thousand-year-old eyes.

She is beautiful and spirited, tied up at my feet. Her eyes gleam in defiance, and I'm reminded of another whose defiance was both my poison and my salve, so long ago.

I take the gag out of her mouth, and Azurra spits at my feet. If I still felt humor, I would laugh, but the years have muted even the brightest of emotions. They've been buried somewhere deep in time, now faint whisps of themselves. I no longer feel rage, or lust, or love. I only feel an echo of satisfaction at my defeat of the dead gods. Of the nature spirits. Of Iara.

Of everything that once tried to break me.

I defied them all.

"Do you have anything to say to your Covinus?" I ask Azurra, drinking in the way she looks on her knees. "You have been in the Healing Center longer than anyone else, and still, the Healers tell me you have not learned."

She laughs. "I have learned much, Covinus. But it is not the lesson you are trying to teach me."

I tilt my head to the side, an echo of curiosity blooming somewhere in my chest. It feels like fluttering wings in the empti-

ness that normally resides there, and for a moment, I'm struck dumb. I haven't felt its like in so long, haven't felt the glimmer of an emotion since Iara cursed me.

I had stolen hundreds of nature spirits by the time Iara figured out how to stop me. She'd died at my feet to take my soul as I had taken so many others, punishment for my selfishness. But in her agony, the curse had magnified. It did not only take my soul, it took anyone's who allowed the Darkness in.

The emptiness had almost driven me to madness, but I adjusted. Adapted, as I always do.

Azurra's eyes practically spark as she glares up at me. Her Life Partner was Outcast for love months ago, and by all accounts, the woman is an upstanding Community member. But when she was brought in for questioning, something about her had unsettled me.

She should have been kneeling before me, kissing my feet, her milky skin tinged pink with contrition and admiration. Instead, her hazel eyes had been grossly clever and her face overtly defiant. So instead of allowing her to go back to her children, I'd sent her to the bottom most levels of the Healing Center.

Hidden behind heavy metal doors and electric locks, where the education I so graciously bestow upon my followers is reinforced through whatever means necessary.

"I know your secret," Azurra whispers, her face glowing with rebellion. "I know what you've done with the Boundary. And I've made sure you'll never be able to create anything like it again."

I stare at the woman—at her dark fringe of lashes and the determined set of her lush mouth—as something far more dreadful than curiosity rises within me. Something like anger.

The sting of the switch rips me from the memory. I cower on the cold dungeon floor in a sticky pool of my own blood. No tears come even as sobs rack my body, great, heaving tremors that feel like they'll pull my heart right up my throat. Squeezing my eyes shut, I try to claw my way back to my mother, to trace the outlines of her face with my fingertips until it's carved into my soul.

It wasn't until I saw her in the Covinus' mind that I realized my memory of her has been warped with time. The edges of her have grown fuzzy, her features frayed and dulled. But when I saw her in the same office I'd almost died in, she was suddenly as vibrant as a summer day in Nadjaa.

My mother hadn't left us. She never wanted to abandon me.

The Covinus took her like he's taken everything else.

He brings down the switch again, but this time, I hardly feel it. Whether it is the cold or the shock, I can't be sure.

When I don't respond, don't even lift my head, his satisfaction vibrates through the room. I'm no longer shackled with irons, but I have no strength to save myself. To keep fighting.

He took my father and my mother. He took my brother and my sense of self. Now, he'll take the rest of me.

I am going to die in this room, stripped of everything I am.

"Get her cleaned up," the Covinus tells the guard outside calmly. "The last few moments are key, and I want her to be present. I need rest before the final stage."

Then the door closes with a soft metallic snick.

Sorrow washes over me as I shiver on the floor. Because the Covinus is not done taking. And when he comes back, I will cease to exist.

CHAPTER
SEVENTEEN

Shaw

I stare and stare, feeling as though I've been kicked squarely in the chest. My breaths are painful against my ribs, and somehow, it has nothing to do with my fire being suppressed. "Nehuan?" I finally whisper in disbelief. "I—I thought you were dead." My voice breaks. "I thought he killed you for your kindness."

Nehuan had been a slave in the Castellium, and the only person to ever show me kindness. He'd sat with me when I'd been hurt and comforted me when I was scared. He'd shared his stories and his language. He had been the only bright spot in the dark of my father's shadow.

And then he'd been gone. I was certain Cullen was behind it because to my father, love was a weakness, and I had loved Nehuan.

Nehuan dips his head and smiles, but it doesn't contain the warmth I remember. It is razor sharp, like the tip of a blade, and when I move my gaze to his eyes, I understand why. He is soulless.

"I was punished for my kindness," he says, the tenor of

his voice hurtling me back to this same garden, years before, though now, it is edged in danger. A small fracture that delineates into madness. Avedis shifts beside me and though his breaths still come in painful gasps, he grips his sword with clear wariness.

And I know he's right. Something feels wrong. But I cannot unfreeze myself, cannot stop from greedily taking in every detail of the man I thought I'd lost.

The first person to be sacrificed for the mistake of loving me.

"Your father discovered our friendship and stole me away to a militia training camp in the northern wastes. It was torture in and of itself...being so close to home and not being able to see it. But that was not the end of it. The Praeceptor captured and interrogated my tribe."

I want to scream at him to stop talking, to cover my ears and keep whatever horrors he endured from weighing on my heart. But I keep still and force myself to listen to every bit of his pain, of his torture. Because his suffering belongs to me, just like so many others.

"The Praeceptor lined them up in front of me and made me kill every one of them. Brothers and cousins. Aunts and uncles. My Kashan. All their bodies piled at my feet until I finally lost my soul. I have been kept imprisoned ever since, driven mad by the inability to feed the emptiness."

He tilts his head, drinking in my agony. "Until the Covinus saw fit to free me. To allow me the opportunity to nourish the hollows with revenge and pain."

Vomit surges up the back of my throat. Nehuan had always been a gentle soul. Hands rough with work but curled in kindness.

"I hope the shame of what became of me eats you alive

for eternity, Anrai, but do remember...I could have turned the pistol on myself. I chose not to because the Darkness was in me long before I met you. The Praeceptor simply peeled back the layers of humanity I used to hide it from the world."

My body trembles without my fire, and Nehuan watches with detachment: with the same barren eyes I know so well.

"You weren't—Nehuan, you were good to me."

He lets out a pitiful laugh, mocking and cruel. "It isn't hard to be seen as good by someone the world has abandoned. Give them the least bit of attention, and you become a savior in their eyes. My life before and after you left me stained black, and being soulless was both a fitting end and an apt beginning."

Nehuan's dark eyes flicker toward Avedis, who's managed to raise his sword. "Calm yourself, wind-speaker. The Covinus is resting at the moment, and I have not yet alerted him to your presence."

"It is the fact you haven't alerted anyone that arouses my suspicions." The assassin turns to me, his gaze sharpening at whatever he sees on my face.

At this, Nehuan smiles. The first day I found him in this garden, I'd had broken bones and a bruised ego. Tears striped my cheeks and blood was caked to my clothes, but unlike everyone else, he didn't look at me with fear or disappointment. He'd offered me a seat next to him, a few bites of *hajan,* and a story. Sitting beside him had felt like sitting behind a hearth after years of winter.

But now, it feels like a forge gone long cold.

"The Covinus has been waiting for your arrival, Heir. He knew you would come for the girl, just as he knew that when you did, I would want to be the one to greet you. To steal your power and drink your pain. Tell me, how does it feel, Shaw?"

He tilts his head in an inhuman manner, his eyes narrowing on my every miniscule reaction. The flare of my nostrils, the tremble of my hand. "To know that everyone who loves you ends up in ruins?"

My breath hitches as agony flares through me—not just the absence of my power, but the sharp point of Nehuan's words. Words I've tortured myself with over and over, now resound even deeper in the sound of his voice.

"How does it feel to know it's about to happen once more?" He *tsks* in mocking pity. "So close to your ocean-wielder, but not close enough to save her?"

I bare my teeth, the shadows in my chest beginning to smolder. The Covinus understands enough of emotion to have sent Nehuan here; to break me with my failures. It's what makes him more dangerous than my father—the way he wields emotions like weapons, binds them around souls until they're suffocated.

Nehuan steps closer, raising his blade. He was a peaceful man when I knew him, but he grips the sword with a certainty that only comes from years of practice. As if reading my mind, he smiles. "I had a lot of time trapped in your father's prison. To learn the art of violence—to imagine the day I'd get the chance to break you." He widens his stance and plants his feet, his eyes glinting maliciously. "If you take one step further, your ocean-wielder will lose her soul. Get on your knees before me, Heir, and allow me to drag you in front of the Covinus. Bow to him, pledge your eternal service, or everything you love about the girl will be gone."

He runs his tongue along his bottom lip. "And we both

know you aren't capable of healing her as she did you. *You only destroy."*

My father's words echo through me, ringing against my skull and tugging at the dark recesses of my memory, as I realize the Covinus may understand emotion, but he doesn't understand enough. Time has pulled him too far from them.

Nehuan bearing the coin isn't enough to keep me from Mirren. It was never my fire that made me powerful, wasn't nature that brought down the Boundary. It was the flame of my heart, crafted of shadow and darkness, the flame that burns for her.

I don't only destroy. I *create.* Fire-wielders have always been different, even in the old stories. We are our own source of power, shaping it to our wills, even as the coin would sap others' ability.

And so, as agony shreds through me and my legs shake beneath the weight of my soul, I pull my father's sword. Nightbringer has been strapped to my side since my father's death, the blade's weight a constant reminder of every evil I've wrought, every sin. The Covinus can't break me with Nehuan because I punish myself with him every day—him and every other soul I've hurt.

I lift the heft of my soul every day, and it has made me stronger than before. For a moment, I stare at the blade, the dark metal looking entirely wrong against the pure white snow. I imagine the blood imbued in the steel: mine, my mother's. The thousands of others whose last breath lingers on its edges.

Am I strong enough to add more? To bear the weight of another's death? Of more ruined love?

Nehuan only laughs once more. "You mean to best me,

cut down and weak? With no power?" He pulls his own blade, a standard militia issued sword.

"Let us pass, Nehuan," I plead quietly.

Avedis goes still at the desperation in my tone. I don't beg, do not get on my knees for anyone, but Nehuan was the first person to show me kindness. And in honor of that, I can take a moment to try—even when I know it's useless. There is no pleading with the soulless, no mending the wounds of the Darkness.

"You're the reason I am this wraith," he snarls savagely, taking two charged strides toward me. "You caused this pain, the unbearable hunger. Not everyone is blessed enough to satiate it with the ruin of entire civilizations."

With one deft movement, he whips my hand, knocking Nightbringer into the snow. Then he presses his own blade into my throat. "Submit, Heir."

His eyes flash with hunger, a hunger I recognize all too well.

For a moment, grief threatens to overtake me. But then, the abyss reaches for it, tendrils of the shadows that once brought down the Boundary flickering as its entirely consumed. And when I raise my gaze to Nehuan's, I know only Darkness stares out as I thrust the shadows into his heart.

He screams in agony, a scream that will linger long after tonight, as his ribs and chest collapse beneath the force. He falls, the red of his cloak sprawled around his head, the crimson of his blood soiling the white of the snow. I yank the coin from his body and stuff it into my pocket, before turning back toward the looming shadow of the Castellium.

I do not grieve. Only burrow further into my shadows and darkness.

Because the man I loved has been gone for a decade,

and there is no place for regret within these stone walls. There is only space for blood and vengeance.

~

Mirren

We fight, Lemming.

I dig my fingers into the cold stone floor.

With or without power. You and me? We never give up.

My arms shake beneath my weight. My hands slip in my own blood, and my cheek collides once more with the cell floor.

Even if we have to crawl.

I try again, this time managing to draw my belly along the stone. Inch by agonizing inch, Anrai's words pulsing through me, I move myself slowly back toward the chair. The Covinus has given me a reprieve, but something tells me it's the last one. The next time he leaves this room, I won't have my power, my soul. I won't belong to myself.

So, I crawl. My back is an open wound, seeping and raw, and my bones grind as I dig my elbows into the ground and drag myself forward. My throat aches, and my tongue sticks thickly to the roof of my mouth. I've been deprived of water for so long, I am turning to dust from the inside out.

But I am the daughter of Azurra Ellis, who fought against injustice until the day she died. I am the soul-bonded of Anrai Shaw, who overcame the Darkness itself. I have the heart of the ocean, and I refuse to give another inch of it to the man who has already taken so much from me. Not without a fight.

Finally, I wrap my fingers around the cold metal of the chair and try to pull myself up. My legs are flimsy beneath me and my head swims as I rear back with a crash. Stars bloom behind my eyes as the back of my head cracks against the floor, and a fresh wave of nausea barrels up my throat.

Fight, Lemming!

I get back up, swallowing down the rising acid and squeezing my eyes shut until my vision levels. The metallic lock scrapes outside the cell. I grit my teeth, as blood rushes past my ears. And when the door opens, I swing the chair as hard as I can at the soldier's head.

He shouts in surprise and stumbles backward into the wall, his nose furiously spurting blood, as I raise the chair again. But I am no match for him in my weakened condition, and he grabs the leg before it makes contact. With a snarl, he throws the chair out of reach, and it clatters loudly against the opposite wall.

"You bitch," he growls, one hand clutching his nose as the other pulls a pistol from the holster. "You're going to pay for that one." He tilts his head and cocks the gun. "Let's see how much fun we can have before the Covinus gets back."

But the threat of death no longer means anything. I fly at him with a cry of rage and dig my nails into his face. He slams backward into the wall, yelping in pain, and the pistol goes flying as he tries to yank me off of him. Tripping, we both fall to the ground. Something like madness overcomes me and I claw at every bit of him I can reach. His skin under my nails, his blood on my fingers, I don't stop until something squelches, followed by a rush of more blood.

The soldier screams in fury, and his fist comes flying at my face.

Light explodes behind my eyelids as it crashes into my jaw, and I'm knocked to the side. He blindly grapples for a dagger sheathed at his chest. He scrambles to sitting, his eye and nose grotesque and mutilated as he swings the blade in my direction. Throwing myself at his arm with a feral scream, I pry at his fingers. The sounds I emit aren't remotely human, all desperation and rage and agony.

The soldier pounds at my chest, and I wheeze as the breath whooshes from my lungs. With one final tug, I pull his hand toward me and tear into his flesh with my teeth. The iron taste of blood explodes in my mouth, and with a sharp cry of pain, his grip on the dagger loosens.

I wrap my fingers around it. The first time I stared down death, I hesitated.

There is no hesitation now.

I stab the dagger as hard as I can into his throat. Blood sprays my face and stings my eyes, but I hardly notice it. Yanking the blade out with a snarl, I stab again, and this time, the blade sinks into the soldier's face. Agonizing heat rips through me as my soul tears, but I keep stabbing, again and again and again, the weapon becoming an extension of my rage, of my terror.

When my arms finally give out, the dagger falls from my grip and clatters to the floor. I am coated in blood and gore, as I stare down at the man's corpse. He is unrecognizable now, as grotesque and monstrous as what pulses through me. Vomit surges up my throat, and it's all I can do to roll off his body in time to retch.

There is nothing left in me to expel, but my body tries anyway. Painful spasms wrack my stomach, and the gaping slash through my soul radiates to every nerve ending. I swallow, and holding my breath, scour the soldier's body for keys. My fingers shake as I find them and shake even more violently when I try to fit them into Sura's shackles.

Her head bobs, and her eyes blink open slowly. We've

gone so long without water terror strikes through me that it's too late.

"Sura," I whisper desperately, my throat shredded. "We're not dying in this cell. Wake up!"

Her lashes flutter again, and her tongue darts out over her cracked lips. When she finally opens her eyes fully, she rears back at what she sees. Matted hair, blood-coated face. A monster.

But when her shackles pop open at last, recognition flares in her eyes.

I claw my way up the wall, and the world sways wildly as I work to get my feet beneath me. Everything hurts, and there is so much blood, I don't know how much of it is mine. But what I told Sura was true. We aren't dying in this cell. And I'm going to take out as many of the Covinus' followers as I can before I go.

Sura rubs her wrists and ankles, before crawling toward the door. She pauses at the soldier's mutilated body, her throat working roughly as she takes in what I've done to him. He looks like he was attacked by an animal rather than a human, but instead of commenting, she gingerly picks up the pistol at his feet.

She stares at the gun for so long, she barely notices me come up behind her. I know she's imagining having to use the gun. Take a life. Split her soul.

There are no smiles here in the Castellium, but I squeeze her shoulder and take the pistol from her, replacing it with the dagger. Sura wraps her fingers around it and blinks up at me gratefully. She pulls herself to standing, and though we tremor and quake, we both walk out of the cell.

For a moment, it feels like enough; like victory in itself. Because so many others were not lucky enough to make it this far—those cell walls the last thing they ever saw. And even if we die now, at least it won't be trapped in that misery-stained cage.

My fingers are squeezed so tightly around the pistol, they turn white as we stumble into the corridor. The nearest militia guard looks up, his eyes widening in horror as he takes in my appearance.

I can't imagine what he sees: a gore-covered specter of the night, a monster of blood and death. A terrified, desperate girl. But I don't wait for him to figure out which one I am. I raise the pistol, easing my finger over the trigger the same way I've watched so many others do. The sound explodes in the stone hallway and more blood sprays as the man falls where he stands. My ears ring, and I nearly topple over as acid washes through my veins and my soul shreds.

We fight. I won't get on my knees again. Not alive.

Shouts sound from both ends of the corridor and I raise the gun again, keeping Sura tucked behind me as we move forward. Doors line each side of the hall, the dim lantern lights reflecting off the black metal. The floor slants upward, made of the same light stone as the cell floors, and similarly marred with dark stains and deep gouges.

I ease my finger over the trigger again, aiming for the mass of guards streaming down the hall, and hope to the dead gods we're going the right direction. The soldiers scatter as the shot ricochets through the narrow corridor, winding through screams of fury and pain. I shoot again, and my soul tears as the round pierces something vital.

This time, I keep to my feet through the shatter. Because everything is pain. My heart, my skin, my hair, my lungs—all of it burns in such agony, it is impossible to delineate the pain of my soul from any other.

Five guards rush us from the opposite end of the corridor, and Sura spins, swinging out with the dagger to slice across their wrists. Two of their swords clatter to the ground, and Sura lunges for them with bared teeth. Her grip is natural, and her face is pure death as she arcs the blades toward the remaining three men. Her dark hair flies behind her in a halo and metal sings as their blades clash. Asa told me the Xamani were warriors when circumstances forced them to be, and I am both immensely thankful for Sura's presence at my side and horribly sad.

Because even if we manage to make it out of the dungeon, there's no way we'll make it out of the Castellium alive. The most I can hope for is making it far enough away from here that I find my other—that somehow, after everything the Covinus stole—there's enough left to take as many of his followers with me as I can.

I shoot off three more shots. Two of them lodge in bellies, and another ricochets off a cell door with a deafening ring. And that's the end of the ammunition.

I pilfer a sword from a woman bleeding at my feet. Six more soldiers swarm us, three from one side and three from the other. Despite the way my arms shake, I grit my teeth and raise the blade. I don't swing for joints and tendons like Shaw taught me in order to spare my soul.

I aim for throats and arteries and organs. I aim for death.

Sura screams behind me, the sound harrowing in its reverberation through my chest. I turn in time to see her disarmed, and soldiers surging. One has her by the throat even as she thrashes against his iron hold, while the remaining two restrain her wildly kicking ankles.

My blood surges, white hot and acidic. It rushes past my ears and clouds my vision in the same shade of crimson as the blood that stains me, the cell, the corridor. And though it leaves my guard open, I turn, and with every bit of my remaining strength, thrust my sword into the soldier's spine. He lets go of Sura as the blade sticks, the resulting force tearing the pommel from my hand. My breath hitches and my soul splits, as the remaining guards tackle me to the ground.

I throw my hands over my face, a pathetic shield against the fists and boots. Then my arms are pinned above my head, and someone lands a sharp blow to my ribs. Something cracks, and I don't know if I hear it or feel it as another kick lands. I cough and choke, as more soldiers restrain my legs, keeping me from curling into myself. Another hand grips my jaw roughly and I snap my teeth around the nearest finger, grinding down until blood spurts across my tongue.

But it isn't enough.

Sura screams again, having disappeared from my sight amid the crowd of militia. I thrash to get to her, just as a large hand comes around my throat. Grip like an iron vice, it squeezes until the world around me flickers and dims.

And then everything goes mercifully black.

CHAPTER
EIGHTEEN

Shaw

We slip soundlessly through an old slave corridor, the route abandoned long before my father's reign. My blood has begun to boil in my veins like magma, even as my teeth chatter in the absence of my flame. Only a small torch lights the stone stairs, sending odd shadows contorting over the walls and ceiling.

They mirror the growing darkness in my chest, the abyss of which I fill with everything I don't think of. My father and the things he did between these walls. Nehuan and the look of relief that filled his empty eyes as he bled out at my feet.

I only think of Mirren.

Somewhere in the depths of this hellhole, my soul-bonded waits. The thought burrows into me, burning at the center of my chest. It radiates to each of my fingertips until I'm my own source of nature, my own swirling void of Darkness. I need no fire to destroy everyone who's dared touch her.

The Castellium is thankfully quiet this time of night, for

though Avedis has mastered his lack of power well enough to jog beside me, I need him to save his strength for the dungeons. The few guards we meet on their rounds are silenced with brutal hits to the head, a process far more cumbersome without Avedis' control of air.

When we finally reach the entrance to the dungeons, it takes everything in me to keep the abyss balled tightly in my chest. It wrestles me, attempting to spear from my skin, demands to bury the place of my hurt with darkness and horror. It wants to blow apart the entire Castellium, destroy every stone that bore witness to my pain.

Stones that now hold the other half of my soul, keeping her buried in a place so cruel, it snuffs out even the brightest of lights. My chest is frozen over without my fire, somehow so cold it burns, and though it's agony, I hold onto the rage surging through me; that rushes past my ears in a roar of fury.

"Ready?" Avedis asks, his voice far more winded than usual. He's crouched next to me, sword in one hand and a dagger in the other. His hair is entirely still, the normally wild aura around him now stagnant. But his dark eyes are restless, hungry, Avedis' brutal nature he normally keeps hidden beneath his civil façade now worn openly on his face.

I grind my jaw, and nod. "Cover my flank."

He stiffens at my order, but then nods. It isn't in the nature of assassins, particularly ones with the power of the wind, to take orders. They go wherever the currents take them, following their own whims and desires. Avedis is not here from some ingrained sense of altruism; he's here because he wants to be, because Mirren has made herself his just as much as she's made herself mine, Max's, and Cal's. And I am so damn grateful for it.

"We're going in blind and powerless, aside from my shadows. My father kept at least fifteen guards in the dungeons, but the Covinus knew I was coming, and we have to expect at least twice that. The only bright side to us not having our power is he can't have any other wielders waiting for us."

"In the dungeons," Avedis says. "I'm sure he has them stationed in the city, beyond the coin's reach."

"One mountain at a time, Avedis."

Out of habit, we both check our weapons once more. And then, crouching low, we move toward the dungeons.

The Castellium shadows welcome me into them just as they did when I was a child, before I knew of things such as fire and smoke. Before I knew I was capable of bursting into flame and chasing them away; capable of scorching the sins from the stone. My father's and my own.

I know now, and ruefully, I wish for the heat of flame in my chest. A flicker of warmth. But the ice remains.

Two guards are stationed at the top of the stairs, and when I leap from the shadows, they don't even have time to react before two daggers sprout from their throats. The time for restraint is past; the Castellium only respects savage cruelty, and I'm far too happy to oblige. To destroy any who've touched Mirren, who've deigned to fucking look at her without her permission.

My soul rips, but I'm already moving, yanking my daggers from their throats, and racing down the stone steps to the bowels beneath the fortress. The last time I was here, I was empty and emotionless, but now, I am entirely too full. My rage and worry and anguish burst from me, unable to be contained beneath my skin any longer.

More guards run up the stairs, only to be impaled with sharply edged shadows. Their strangled cries echo eerily through the hall as the shadows overtake them entirely: crawl grotesquely over their skin and down their throats. The temperature of the stairwell drops at least thirty degrees, like the ice of my heart has frozen everything around it.

And still, the abyss crows for more.

More blood, more destruction.

Take from them what has been taken from us.

When we reach the landing, guards rush down the corridor. "The Fire-bringer is here!" "Kill him!" "...evil! "--grab the girl!"

Avedis ducks as gunshots crack, his blades gleaming in a deadly arc as they take down two of the nearest. Shadows wreath my fingers and my heart as I lift my hands above my head.

I am rebirth and destruction.

Three more guards fly at me, weapons raised, but their blades don't even brush my skin before they are consumed. Shadows crawl off the wall and leap up their legs. Others constrict around their throats, soldiers falling unconscious where they stand.

"He has power!" Someone screams, as the rest of the force forms a barrier of shields and weapons.

Avedis breathes heavily as he comes up behind me, staring down the militia with a look of death.

The frontmost of them sneers and raises his sword. "You'll die down here, Heir, just as your father meant you to."

And then, his eyes flicker behind him for the briefest moment. A fraction of a second.

At once, the abyss explodes from me, a detonation of every horrible, terrified thing I've fed it since Mirren was taken.

Because she is there, curled on the floor behind the soldiers, her pale skin stained the color of rust. The color of pain.

I thought I knew rage; thought I was intimate with violence.

But it is nothing to what courses through me now. It shatters every piece of myself, my teeth, my hair, my bones, my skin, into jagged fragments, each one heated with the force of my anger, honed with fury. I fly apart at the seams, ripping through the soldiers, even as my soul shreds, over and over. I hardly feel the icy pain, the echoing emptiness, through the rush of savagery pulsing from my chest.

Because what is the pain of losing my soul to the pain of losing Mirren? A pale echo, a whisp of a winter wind. It is nothing, and I move through it as such.

I snarl as the throng of militia crowds me. I descend down, down, down, into the abyss where shadows burn like ice. Crimson shades my vision, and I don't know whether it's my fury or the soldier's blood, but I don't stop to ponder it as I shove my dagger into bellies; as I rip through cloth and skin; as insides spill onto the stone floor, blood feeding the Castellium's never ending appetite for misery.

There is no thought to the dance of violence, no thought of anything except getting to Mirren. Because we are tethered, her heart to mine, and I cannot think beyond the pull of it. I can only follow its tug, can only cut down anything that threatens to sever its cord.

I am no longer Anrai, or Shaw, or Heir. I am primal, a maelstrom at the center of a wildfire. And as I cut through the last soldier, all I can think is, *I am made only to destroy. And I will destroy all of you.*

And when the last soldier falls at my feet, I stare through a mask of blood at the Covinus.

He stands over Mirren, his crisp white clothes nearly blinding in the dim dungeon light. He tilts his head slightly as I stalk forward, his face entirely emotionless even as I draw near to him with a feral snarl. The sound isn't human and neither am I as I raise my sword, but he doesn't move to draw a weapon, or even to run away. He only mutters a soft, "Interesting," before I thrust Nightbringer through his throat.

The Covinus collapses in an entirely human heap, his blood the same red as everyone else's, spilling out along the stones.

I don't spare him another thought as I fall to my knees beside Mirren, panic and relief clogging my throat with equal measure. She is curled into herself, knees and elbows pulled tight to her chest, childlike and vulnerable. Her hair is matted with blood and her clothes are shredded, and in spite of the deathly cold bite of her skin, the moment I touch her, something eases in me.

I settle back into myself. Piece by piece, the primal monster I just inhabited falls away, leaving only the mess of the man I am remaining; the man who thinks and feels beyond the need to destroy.

Sura crawls over to us. The little Xamani's face is gaunt and streaked with dirt, and though she limps, she appears to be in far better shape than Mirren. "He hurt her, Shaw," she weeps. Giant tears pour from her eyes though she doesn't appear to notice them at all, as she spits in the direction of the fallen Covinus. "She was protecting me, and he hurt her so badly. We have to get her out of this dungeon and get her power back or she'll never heal."

Because even though I put a sword through his

throat, the coin's hold still hasn't broken. A sob of rage and grief climbs my throat as I gently brush Mirren's hair back from her forehead. But it's her violent flinch that threatens to undo me completely. *What has he done to her? What has he taken that she shies from my touch?*

I have never seen Mirren as small, because to me, she's always been larger than life itself. Her spirit steals the air from every room she's in, and shamefully, it's never occurred to me how breakable she is. But here in the pit of my nightmares, she looks tiny. Fragile.

Her body goes taut as I gently gather her to me, careful to avoid the myriad of welts and lacerations on her back. A pained whimper sounds from her throat and her fingers dig into my chest like she's ready to claw out my heart, to fight her way out. I press my face into her hair and breathe her in. "I'm here, Lemming. You're safe. You can stop fighting now."

At my whisper, Mirren relaxes into me, her body going instantly pliant in my arms. Her breaths are shallow as she nuzzles her head into my chest, and her lashes flutter like she's lost in the depths of some unimaginable dream.

I'm here, I'm here, I'm here. I whisper the words over and over again into her hair, pouring them over both of us until the roughshod pound of my heart slows. Until I can think beyond the terror of losing her, the rage at what's been done. She's alive and I'm alive, and at the moment, that's enough.

I lift my head from Mirren's hair to see Avedis helping Sura to her feet. The girl lifts her chin and steels her nerve, leaning into the wind-wielder gratefully. Now that the adrenaline has passed, Avedis looks sicklier than ever, and his hands tremble as he wraps his fingers tightly around

Sura's waist. But together, the two begin to limp up the corridor.

Whatever otherworldly heat my rage temporarily granted me has ebbed, leaving my body feeling ice cold and frail without my fire. My shadows have receded with my strength, and each breath is like breathing in shards of ice. But I force myself to my feet with Mirren gripped in my arms. Every step takes concentration as pain shoots up from my feet and into the bones of my hips, and more than once, I almost topple over entirely.

It is only the feel of her against me that keeps me going. Only the thought of getting her out of this horrific place that fuels me.

The journey felt so short when Mirren was in danger, but now, it feels like an eternity. When we finally come to the garden, past Nehuan's bleeding body, and through the wall, I want to cry out in relief as my power floods back into me. It imbues my muscles with a rush of heat, races through my veins, and conflagrates at my heart. Mirren only sighs against my chest, and worry squeezes my stomach that she is too weak to use her power. To even feel its return. But her heartbeat is strong, the organ as stubborn as she is, and I take comfort in the fact that Mirren and I are the same. She'll fight until her last breath.

Avedis slips through the crack, his eyes immediately darting to where Mirren is still tucked into my arms. Rage washes over him and as his power returns, a violent wind whips the snow around us in a blinding storm.

Tamping it down with a restraint I envy, the assassin helps Sura through the wall. She leans against him with a strained smile and together, we start toward the city. With each step, my flame flickers in my chest, but no longer with the need to destroy. It shines like a signal fire, a way home.

Because Mirren made it out of the Castellium, and through her escape, somehow, I've accomplished my own.

I have been trapped here for so long, even after my father's death, unable to see beyond the cracked stone walls. But now, I can see everything. The future stretched out before us, the one I've always been too afraid to claim.

I'm not afraid now. I'm going to take Mirren back to Nadjaa and give her a home. I'm going to get down on my knees in front of her and make her mine forever, and I'm not going to worry anymore about how long that may be.

There is no more time for fear. Because the Darkness is swift, and however long I have left before its final calling, I will cherish all of it.

CHAPTER NINETEEN

Mirren

Warmth seeps through my clothes and beneath my skin. I nestle closer, wanting to crawl into it; to forget the frigid ache of the dungeon and the biting pain of emptiness. Shivers wrack my body, and even as I feel my *other* come back to me, it is not a crashing wave of power. It curls up beside my wrecked soul, too weak to do anything but lap softly against my mind.

And I have nothing to give it, nothing to imbue it with strength.

"I've got you, Lemming, I've got you," Anrai's voice whispers above me, into me.

I whimper because everything is pain and I'm so tired, but his words settle into me along with his warmth. Because if Anrai is here, I am safe.

I am safe. This is home.

The thought dissipates before it lands, and I let out a desperate sob at my frailty. *I tried to hold on,* I think to Anrai, *but I couldn't.*

And I lost it. Lost everything.

Anrai presses his lips to my forehead as he carries me. "Shh," he says softly. "There is nowhere I wouldn't find you. No place I wouldn't come for you." His words are a soothing susurrus against my mind, the deep tenor of his voice caressing my skin just as surely as a physical touch. His iron will, his ruthless determination, it all wraps around me along with the bite of his fire.

And for a moment, I let Anrai do the work of holding me together. I give him my pieces and trust he won't let any of them slip away.

Snowflakes pepper my face as he wraps me in his cloak, and then pulls me tighter against his chest. I breathe in the scent of smoke, of wild, of spice and my *other* rouses beneath his power, until it is as warm as a sunbaked summer shore. It trickles slowly from its place at my heart, heating my veins until I finally have the strength to open my eyes.

Glacial blue irises stare back, and even in my feeble state, I find no pity there. Only stubborn fortitude and fierce faith. That arrogant smile curves Anrai's mouth, and embers spark in the depths of his gaze. "Why is it that you're always saving yourself before I can get there? You could let me play the conquering hero at least once. I didn't even get to kick down a cell door."

A soft laugh escapes me, the sound so discordant in this brutal place, but the remaining cold in my limbs evaporates along its edges. Relief flickers on Anrai's face, because despite his bluster, he is still terrified he wasn't here in time. That I'm too far gone. And suddenly, all I want to do is ease his worry.

My *other* is not powerful enough to heal the wounds from the switch, starved and dehydrated and numb as I am, but it is enough to heal my cracked ribs; to imbue my stubborn heart. "I think I can walk."

Anrai has the good sense not to question me, even as his jaw ticks. Instead, he sets me down gently, not removing his hand from the small of my back until he's positive I'm steady.

Avedis and Sura come up beside us, and the windwielder dips his head toward me. "O Lady of the Watery Grave," he intones with a small smile. My *other* is fed by the small gesture, by the acknowledgement of Avedis' friendship. Of everything he risked to come here.

The assassin summons a snowstorm around us, the icy wind shrouding us from the eyes of the Castellium above and Argentum below.

"Are you ready?" Anrai asks, watching me closely as he presses two daggers into my hand. One, the black of the Dark Militia. And the other, the dagger he gave up all those months ago in a mountain cave, with its delicately carved hilt.

I grip their handles tightly, staring down at the dichotomy of the blades. Light and dark, like Shaw. Like me.

Hefting a breath that feels more like glass than air, I nod and buckle my bandolier. The brisk air stings, but I relish each inhale, as there'd been a moment in that cell I never thought I'd breathe fresh Ferusian air again. Sheathing the black dagger, I curl my hand in Anrai's.

Horns blare from the city walls, four rhythmic beats answered by a singular note from the guard houses spread through the city. Though he keeps his flame curled inside him, concealing us in the darkness, Anrai's jaw tightens as he listens.

"They know I'm here," he translates. His eyes meet

mine in the shadows. "And that you've escaped."

"But you killed the Covinus—" Sura begins frantically, even as Anrai shakes his head.

"It doesn't matter. The Dark Militia is a beast straight from the Darkness. Even if you cut off its head, it still lives."

More horns sound, and he spits out a curse. "They're sending the other wielders after us."

As if conjured by his words, a heavy wind whistles high above, whipping atop the towering city wall. It is not as high as the Boundary or Yen Girene, but feels just as imposing, a dark specter against the glowing sky.

Fear squeezes my throat as I remember how the Covinus directed the Similian woman like a grotesque puppet. Bile floods my mouth, and my fingers shake as I grip Anrai's chest. "We can't—Shaw, all those people the Covinus stole from Similis. They're wielders! We can't fight them all!" A panicked sob rips from me. "I won't go back down there, I can't—"

Anrai lifts my chin. His gaze is fierce but steady, just as it was on the first night we met, when I couldn't see him in the dark of the Nemoran, but something in me eased. Even then, my body had responded to his, irrevocably tied. "Listen to me, Lemming. You got yourself out of that dungeon—" He stares at me until I finally nod. "—And you will get yourself out of Argentum."

His eyes spark and embers flicker softly at his palms, before skittering over my chin and down my throat. "But know this..." His lips peel back from his teeth, and suddenly, he is the lethal Dark Worlder I first met; the man who will shred through anything that stands in his way. "I will burn this entire city to cinders before I let anyone take you from me again. I will make the streets run red with blood and laugh on top of their corpses. And I'll leave only one person alive, so he'll tell the story of what happens to those who try to touch you." His words, his fire, stokes my own, the relentless fight burning in the depths of my chest. "Until there is no one left on the continent who doesn't know the extent of my destruction."

His words are terrifying, but there is comfort in the brutality. Like sleeping with a blade under my pillow.

Anrai leans down, pressing his forehead to mine, and whispers against my lips, "I'll gladly send my soul to the Darkness if it means you're safe."

I nod, inhaling sharply and willing my panic down. My exhaustion. *Only a little further, Mirren.*

Anrai sets his jaw and stares up at the frenzied storm building on the outer walls of the city, his mind whirling. "We'll have to find another way out of the city."

I follow his gaze to the city sprawled beneath us, the light of hearth fires and torches glowing against the blustering storm. Isolated, harsh, and beautiful. I wonder what he sees when he looks down at the place he was born; if he can see the beauty in its harsh lines, or only the horror living along its edges.

His face gives nothing away. The weapon that lives beneath his skin, the predator that prowls his heart is all he allows to shine beneath his mask of death. And when he looks to Avedis, there is no worry, no hesitation. Only cool calculation. "They aren't going to make it across the city on foot." He nods to Sura and me.

Sura furrows her brow stubbornly, but she doesn't have it in her to argue, and neither do I. Starved and beaten, the only thing keeping me to my feet is the little power I have trickling through my veins. The city is massive, a maze of curling alleys and dead-end streets.

Anrai listens for another long moment, and his eyes

spark. "They don't know you're with us, Avedis."

The wind-wielder starts shaking his head before Anrai's words are even out of his mouth, but Anrai presses on with a hard look. "I'm going to cause a distraction, and when they send the other wielders after me, you're going to get yourselves over the wall. And then you're going to run like hell."

"And how in the Darkness are *you* going to get over the wall, Shaw? Last I checked, fire was not a particularly helpful method of flying." Avedis shoots back, an angry flush rising up his neck.

Anrai's throat works fiercely, but he doesn't relent as he glares back at Avedis. "I'll burn the whole godsdamn city to the ground if I have to. But you need to get them out of here first." And then, a flicker of something vulnerable, there, and just as quickly gone. "You're the only person capable of doing what needs to be done, assassin," he says gravely. His lips twist in terrifying snarl. "And you're the only person I would trust her with. The only one who can keep her safe."

Avedis looks as rattled as if Anrai has punched him, his dark eyes flaring in dreaded understanding, and I want to scream at them both that I'm not worth it. Not their souls, not their lives.

I tear my hand from Anrai's, my desperation and terror curling my fingers into a fist. I pound at his chest, shaking my head wildly. "No, *no!* We stay together—you and me... I'm coming with you!" My words are swollen with unshed tears, strained with terror. Dry sobs shake my body, tremors running up my ruined back. "I won't let you leave me!"

Agony washes over Anrai's face, and he catches my wrists in his hands, pressing them to my sides, before ensnaring me tightly against his chest. His breathing is ragged, but his heartbeat is a steady rhythm against my ribs, and all at once, the fight drains out of me. My next words come out as a broken whisper. "I won't let you go where I can't follow."

Anrai wrenches my chin upward. His raven hair falls in untamed tendrils over his forehead and dark circles stain the skin beneath his eyes. A jagged cut splits his lower lip, and bruises mar the strong line of his jaw. He looks wild and terrifying, and it's this, more than anything, that finally calms me.

He doesn't fail. He'll come back to me. And if I force him to drag me with him through Argentum, I'll only be a distraction. Potentially a fatal one.

I swallow down the rising wave of panic, digging my nails into his chest. "You come back to me," I practically snarl at him. "You come back to fight another day with me. Do you understand?"

A brilliant smile breaks his face open, luminous, and rare. "I know what happens to those who cross you, Lemming. I wouldn't dream of disobeying."

He lowers his mouth to mine. The kiss is desperate, a clash of tongues and teeth, horror and love mingled together.

"You and me, we're forever. I'll always come back to you," he whispers. And then, Anrai is gone, disappearing into the night like a whisp of smoke.

Avedis watches his receding shadow and spits out an angry curse. "Honestly, the gallantry is enough to turn my stomach. I don't know how you tolerate it," he says with no small amount of disdain.

I laugh weakly.

Anxiety winds through me as we wait for the sound of Anrai's distraction, still hidden by a swirl of wind and snow. Sura huddles against me, her shivering body providing a modicum of comfort, as time stalls, halting and jerking in a disorienting parade. It's been minutes since Anrai left, and it's also been hours, the polarity between the two a jarring truth.

Just when I'm considering damning Anrai's plan to the Darkness and running after him, an explosion rocks the ground. Across the city, a torrent of flame shoots up into the night sky. A conflagration of heat so bright, that for a moment, Argentum appears to be bathed in daylight.

And then comes another. And another.

Sura shields her eyes next to me against the blinding show, but I can't tear my gaze away. I've witnessed Anrai's power so many times before, but somehow, the intensity of it still manages to leave me breathless. The burning fury that's always lived inside him made physical; destruction and rebirth.

And though his power is a magnificent, it is also a beacon. Fear roils through me, because now every member of the Dark Militia knows exactly where to find him. No longer the invisible assassin, or the forgotten Heir. Now, he is the Fire-bringer and his father's militia will do anything to either control Anrai, or end him.

The beat of the horns becomes louder, more frantic as the guard beckons reinforcements to the north side of the city. Their eerie call sounds from the top of the Castellium itself, as another explosion rocks a lower sector.

The swirl of storming winds atop the wall above us ceases, as more and more wielders answer the call for help.

Flames race from rooftop to rooftop as Anrai moves through the city. And where he goes, screams follow.

Screams of terror, of pain.

Screams that once would have ravaged my soft heart,

that would have embedded into the soft tissue. Now, they bounce harmlessly off my skin, and I can only think, *they are not my screams.*

Avedis helps Sura and I to our feet, just as more explosions sound from Anrai's side of the city. Cracks of gunfire. Whistling winds. And torrents of water.

My heart twists in panic. The wielders have found him.

But Avedis gives the thought no time to take hold as he ushers us closer to the wall. It towers over us, militia and Boundary men alike running along the top, shouting orders.

"Avedis, we have to go help him—"

"Forgive me, lady, but you will only be a liability right now. The best thing we can do is keep you safe, so his attention isn't divided by worry."

I grit my teeth, hating that Avedis is right. Hating the weakness in my bones and muscle, in my heart.

Hating that just when Anrai found me, the world forced me to give him up again.

Avedis nods to the dagger in my hand. "I will try to shield us as best I can, but be prepared to use those at the top, just in case."

I nod. Sura, who's armed herself with two daggers of her own, heaves a leveling breath, staring up at the movement on the wall.

"You first, little Xamani?"

Sura glares haughtily at the nickname, but she holds up the blades with surprisingly steady hands, even as she's lifted off the ground. After a few painstaking moments, she lands on the top of the wall in a flurry of her own snowstorm, crouching down and disappearing from view. A gentle breeze winds around my ankles, and Avedis flashes me a shameless grin as I'm lifted upward.

My stomach surges into my throat, and I'm reminded just how much I hate traveling by wind. But unlike when I was floated off a cliff, this journey is over as quickly as it begins, and my feet hit the solid ground of the wall. Avedis joins us a moment later, his long legs stepping lithely onto the stone.

A frozen wasteland spreads out before us. The night seems to eat up and swallow the landscape, the barren land disappearing into the night sky. Giant black rock spires pierce the white snow like daggers from dead skin, their towering heights dwarfed only by the mountain range looming behind them. Avedis points to a particular spire, far in the distance. "Your brothers await with horses. I will shield you as long as I'm able."

Breath freezes in my lungs. "My—my brother? You let Easton come to Argentum?"

Avedis looks entirely unapologetic, and meets my gaze in challenge. "And here I thought you had renounced your Similian ways. I am no one's prison warden, and it is none of my business if the young lemming has debts to settle."

I glare at him, hating how astute his words are. How do I expect my brother to change if I insist on keeping him caged in the same surroundings?

Rustling clothing tears my attention away from Avedis and toward the two guards that are now barreling toward us. Avedis whips his head toward them, and they both collapse where they stand. "Hurry now," he says briskly, nodding to Sura.

The wind lifts her, slowly carrying her over the wall. When she is safely on solid ground, the assassin dips his head to me. "Be swift, Lady of the Deep. Get as far away from here as you can."

I watch Avedis shrewdly, from the determined set of his

mouth to the glint in his dark eyes. With the tendrils of hair blowing wildly around his face, he looks almost boyish, the impression at odds with the cut bulk of his muscles and deadliness of his stance. "You...you aren't coming with us, are you?" I ask slowly.

Avedis tilts his head, the echo of a mischievous smile tugging on the corner of his lips.

"Shaw is gonna kill you," I exhale, the words landing halfway between a laugh and a scoff.

Now, the wind-wielder does smile, devilishly charming. "The fire-bearer will have to get in line." His face sobers. "The winds' whims are mine, and I go where they take me, lady. Right now, they blow me toward that arrogant bastard you call yours." Something dark flashes in the depths of his gaze, a glimpse of the same darkness Anrai has carried with him since he was a child. "I won't leave him to his dungeon alone."

A sob climbs my throat, words and tears lodged so solidly I cannot begin to untangle them. And so, I throw my arms around Avedis, squeezing him as tightly as I can manage. The assassin tenses, before relaxing into my embrace and circling me with his own.

When I pull back, his eyes glisten. He clears his throat and smirks. "And please do stay safe. I would hate to save Shaw's life only to turn around and have to end it in self-defense."

I laugh and nod as my feet are lifted from the wall. I sail into the air, hardly noticing the height as my emotions snarl inside me. I am so grateful and so terrified. I am so tired and so lost.

When my feet hit solid ground, I turn my face upward, searching for Avedis.

But the wind-wielder is already gone.

CHAPTER
TWENTY

Calloway

I am lost somewhere between pain and relief, life and death. My skin burns with fever and my dreams take on an unnatural hue, painting them in strange colors and warped images. I manage a few moments of consciousness every few hours, only long enough to take the few sips of water Max forces down my throat before falling back into the depths of black.

"Calloway," a small voice says from above me, breath hot on my face like whoever speaks is entirely too close.

The name sounds sharp and stilted in Helias' Similian accent, but it rouses me all the same. I slide my eyelids open and almost jump backward when I see how close the little boy's face is to mine. He has one eye squeezed closed, and the other pressed up against mine, as if he can peer straight into my brain. "Gods, Helias. Personal space," I bark out, my voice pathetically weak.

The boy doesn't move an inch, only shoves his face closer to mine, until his mouth is plastered up against my cheek. "I thought you might be dead," he says slowly, as if still unsure I'm not.

"Yeah, me too," I mutter morosely.

Helias moves his face away, only to poke a sharp little finger into my cheek. "You feel sort of dead," he pronounces matter-of-factly. Well, he isn't wrong there. I've never been dead, but I imagine this is exactly what it feels like. Immobile, useless, and boring.

"Leave him be, Helias," Harlan says gently from beside the wagon.

It takes me a few moments of blinking up at the clear blue sky to realize we are no longer in the wood, and few long moments after that to recognize the grizzly streets of Havay. The city has never been beautiful, its low-slung buildings constructed to withstand the wild winds of the Breelyn Plain and the even wilder creatures of the Nemoran, rather than to be aesthetically pleasing. And that was before Anni's rampage.

Now, the city is little more than ruins. Charred houses line the street, their wooden remains crumbling into piles of black ash. My stomach churns, and I blink away the stinging in my eyes.

Max hops down lithely from the horse and comes to stand beside Harlan. Her face is strained with exhaustion and dark circles smudge the skin beneath her eyes. She peers into the wagon, her mouth turning down as her gaze runs the length of me. I tense, almost waiting for her to fall before me and weep at my untimely death.

But Max only fits me with a haughty look and says dryly, "If you're done wallowing, Calloway, we're here."

Laughter bubbles out of me in rough fits. Max doesn't waste her time with pity, and she sure as hell doesn't weep. I know the story of her and Anni's escape from the Praeceptor: she won't accept death even when it's staring her directly in the face, her stubbornness a thing of beauty.

"Well, my darling Max, I'm afraid I'm not quite fit for my usual dramatic entrance."

Akari Ilinka sniffs beside me, and Max's humor gives way to a lethal look. After the first few hours of listening to the witch-queen's snide voice, Max had stuffed a gag into her mouth and given us all a reprieve from the thinly veiled threats of death.

Rounding the cart, Max edges her sword beneath Akari's chin and forces the queen to meet her gaze. "If you try anything while we're with the healer...if you so much as breathe the wrong way, I'll see to it that both your eyes match. Do you understand me, *queen?*"

Ilinka sniffs again primly, but her queenly composure has fractured in our time together. The shackles on her wrists clink together as she paws at strands of hair that have been plastered to her forehead by grime, sweat and blood. Between her disheveled appearance and the ghastly gape of her destroyed eye socket, the queen doesn't look anything like the woman who commands armies—who guts rival warlords and orders the death of entire family lines—she looks pitiable.

Max unlocks the iron chain that's kept the witch-queen affixed to the wagon, and she stumbles to the ground. Harlan raises his gun as Ilinka rises to her feet, prodding her forward with the barrel, and I heave a deep breath. The queen has held her warlord seat as long as she has as much by her cunning as by force, and even if she looks human at the moment, I remind myself she isn't. She's a monster, fed by her drive for power.

And if she's led us willingly to this healer, there's a good chance it's a trap.

Max seems to follow my thoughts. "Helias, I want you to go hide. If the witch comes out of the house without us, you have my permission to suck her straight into the ground."

The little boy's eyes light, and he nods enthusiastically. The maniacal glint in his eyes would probably be concerning under different circumstances, but as it is, it only soothes me. Anni charged me with keeping the boy safe, and I've been in no condition to honor that promise. But Helias isn't helpless, and whatever happens in this hovel, he's able to protect himself.

Max watches as he darts down the alleyway, her frown growing deeper. Max's face is as known to me as my own, the lines and tics as easy to read as an open book. She doesn't like the idea of walking into a trap with a half-dead best friend, a hostage queen, a Similian, and a child.

"Have you decided what we're going to do with her?" Her eyes flicker hesitantly to my wound, and then stubbornly back up to my face, like she won't allow herself to dwell on the festering state of it. "After?"

This is the first she's mentioned my decision to spare the queen, and I haven't determined if it's because she understands or simply because she doesn't want to scold me while I'm actively dying. Either way, I appreciate her restraint as I haven't had the energy to examine the decision closely yet. "Forgive me for not having had much time to properly plan, what with my guts hanging out of my stomach and all."

Max sighs sharply through her nose, and without further ceremony, slides her arm around my middle. I grit my teeth so hard I'm sure they'll break as she maneuvers me to sitting. If she feels at all badly about my pain, it doesn't show. Just perfunctorily slides me forward and shoulders the heft of my weight.

Pain and nausea radiate through me, and a scream lodges in my throat. The only thing that keeps it trapped is Harlan's gaze on mine, his brows squeezed together, his worry pulsing from him. While I adore being the reason Harlan glows, I can't stand being the cause of his fear. So, I keep my agony hidden behind a horribly weak smile and try desperately not to puke on Max as I lean on her.

Thank the dead gods her physical strength rivals that of her stubbornness, because otherwise, we'd both go toppling to the ground. But Max just grunts and heaves me up, even as my feet wobble beneath me and the sky spins above me.

She scans the deserted alleyway, her eyes taking in each of the squalid houses. Everything is still, coated in the same thick layer of gray ash as the rest of the city, and though I try to follow her gaze, the simple act of standing has black edging my vision. My limbs feel foreign and clumsy, my skin clammy but cold.

If this mysterious water-wielder can't heal me, I'm going to die in Havay, which somehow seems even worse than Similis. At least there, I wouldn't be surrounded by ash.

As if sensing the direction of my thoughts, Max flicks an irritable gaze to me. "You know, I expect the dramatic brooding from Shaw, but I really thought you better than this."

I narrow my eyes. "Does he have the only claim in Ferusa on being miserable? Seems a tad unfair to those of us dying of sepsis," I pout, sounding far too much like an obstinate child.

Max heaves a winded sigh, hauling me toward the healer's hovel like I'm an overlarge ragdoll. "Really, Calloway." Her voice is scolding. "The sepsis is what you're choosing to focus on? Where are the ridiculous demands for your funeral? The debate about which ostentatious outfit you want your body dressed in?"

If my limbs were functioning, I would cross my arms stubbornly, but as it is, I only manage to furrow my brow and stick my tongue out at her. "Obviously it's going to need to be something tailored and made of silk. Have I taught you nothing?" My feet tangle beneath me and a fresh shock zaps through my nerves as Max jerks me upward. "Now I have to live just so you don't bungle my funeral and turn it into some morose bore."

Max doesn't bother to answer, instead rapping her knuckles on the wooden door. A moment later, the door swings open and a pair of watery-blue eyes gaze out at us from the small crack. They scan us fearfully, before zeroing on the witch-queen. A small yelp sounds and the owner falls to the ground in a deferent bow.

I can almost feel Max's eye roll beside me as she pushes the door open wider, revealing a diminutive woman still crouched low, swaths of a ratty dress haloed around her. She presses her nose into the dirt floor of the hovel, and strands of hair the color of dishwater hide her face from view as she squeaks, "My Queen."

Her entire body trembles as she stands. The woman is no taller than Mirren, but where Mirren appears strong, this water-wielder is so slight, it looks like one good breeze is all it would take to knock her over. A canteen is slung around her throat like an oversized necklace, and I tense as she moves her shaking fingers toward it.

"Touch your water, and we'll shoot your queen in the head," Max says.

The woman freezes, her face unreadable of everything but fear.

"My friend is dying. And if you want your queen alive, you'll let us in without trouble."

The girl's bottom lip tremors as her red-lined gaze whips between us, but she takes a step back to allow us to step inside the sagging threshold. The two-roomed house is dim, having no windows to allow in natural light. The candles have all been burned down to their quicks, and the sole lamp is empty of oil. It isn't odd for the impoverished to go without in Ferusa, but the woman has had powers for over a month—it's strange she's earned no coin for her services.

Harlan prods the queen forward, and the door slams shut behind them with a loud squeal, dousing the room in semi-darkness. The only light is what pours in from the large gaps between the walls and ceiling, a result of shoddy construction. I groan as Max hauls me forward and deposits me on a wobbling kitchen table.

I heave a breath to keep from passing out, but the motion only serves to send more pain shooting through my stomach.

"What are you waiting for?" Max demands somewhere above me. "Heal him. Now. Or your queen will be nothing more than a blood stain on your floor."

The girl makes another squeaking noise, dancing uncertainly in place. With a haggard sigh, Max yanks Ilinka's gag out. "Tell her, Queen."

Akari's tongue slides to rewet her lips, her hateful glower pinned on Max. When she addresses the water-wielder, it's without bothering to look at her. "Do exactly as your queen commands you, Verena."

The girl, Verena, trembles more violently, and her body

bows further toward the floor like an invisible weight is pressing into her back. Something tugs at my brain as she shuffles over to me, something beyond the dizziness and infection.

Verena lifts a shaking hand and the water in the canteen rises to her call above me. It is a paltry show of water compared to what Mirren wields, but as I stare up at the undulating pool, I think how easy it is to drown. The droplets slowly slide toward me and Verena squeezes her eyes shut with a small sob.

Like she doesn't want to bear witness to what happens next.

Max lunges forward, but I raise my hand, even as each breath becomes more painful than the last, and address Verena. "She no longer controls Siralene."

It's barely a whisper, but Verena's eyes snap back open. Surprise and distrust mingle on her face as the pool of water freezes inches above my face. But beneath her wariness is something for more potent: hope.

"The Siralenis have staged a coup and driven her out of the city."

Verena's breath hitches and her eyes widen.

"If she's threatening your family, she no longer has access to them. She can't hurt them, Verena."

"Her militia is camped just outside the city," Verena breathes, seeming to remember herself. A few droplets sprinkle my face. "They have ears everywhere. They'll know she's here. Know that I've helped you."

"We can get you out of Havay safely. Help you find your family."

I don't ask her to trust me, as trust is a ridiculous request in Ferusa. She has no reason to put her faith in a stranger, especially one that's begun to bleed freely all over her kitchen table. Instead, I appeal to that seed of hope, rooted in the want of freedom. Because for a continent with no law, so few of us are actually free.

Too many are chained by the Darkness, by greed and violence and oppression. "The queen has exploited so many for so long. Don't help her continue. Your family has a chance because the brave rose up against injustice. You have the same chance."

The water still writhes in midair like an oddly shaped puddle. Verena watches it for a moment, before straightening her spine, like whatever kept it pinned to the floor has been lifted by news of her family's freedom. And when she finally slides her gaze to Max, her lip no longer wobbles. "You can chain her over there."

Verena nods to the thick support pole in the middle of the room. "It's the sturdiest thing in this shithole."

The witch-queen lets out a howl of rage as Max drags her across the floor. "Looks like your power is dwindling, Akari. Drop by drop."

Harlan shoulders the Similian rifle with a look of relief and comes to stand beside me. His gait is stilted and sore—from both the battle and so many days of travel—but when his eyes meet mine, there is no sign of exhaustion or pain. Only sure warmth, like a midday sun. "How are you?"

It's only because he speaks with such sincerity that I manage to hold back the absurd laughter threatening to erupt. "The brink of death is oddly refreshing."

He grimaces as Max returns to the tableside, his annoyance at my continued insistence on making light of everything apparent. But he only nods like he expected nothing less. And truly, if the Darkness is going to take me, I may as well go out with a laugh.

Max looks at Verena expectantly. The water-wielder

shivers, and her entire body tenses as she blurts out a muffled word that sounds oddly like, "Payment." She swallows roughly, an attempt to gather her courage, no doubt, and clarifies, "I mean—if you want me to heal him, I need payment."

Max arches a brow. "Freeing you of the queen's service and ensuring your safety isn't payment enough?"

"Max," I say softly. She relents with an irritated huff and reaches into the pocket of her cloak. A moment later, she pulls out a gold doorknob.

I squint at it, recognizing it's unique etching from the Achijj's palace. "I'm sorry—have you been carrying a *doorknob* around in your pocket for months?"

Max shrugs, as if pocket doorknobs are perfectly reasonable. "Never know when you'll need something to barter with. Or when you'll need to lob one at someone's head." She tosses the knob to Verena with impeccable aim. "It's pure gold. Now quit wasting time and heal him before he dies on this table."

Verena, who has frozen staring at the knob in awe, jolts to life like she forgot we were in the room. And I can't say I blame her. The doorknob is certainly worth more than this entire hovel, and if she grew up in Siralene, probably more than she's ever seen in her life. She wraps it up carefully and stows it in the pocket of her apron.

She takes a small pair of scissors and begins to cut through the bandages Harlan so carefully wrapped around my wound. The fresh air against my hot skin sends another spasm of pain wracking through me, so to keep myself from sobbing, I say weakly to Max, "I wonder what else I'll find when I rifle through your pockets. Faucets? Hinges?"

Max only shoots me a look, as Verena's calloused

fingers gently prod my mangled stomach. "Who did this to you?" she asks in awed horror.

"My best friend," I mutter, enjoying her furthered dismay. "Great dancer, terrible healer." My teeth clack together as Verena's water trickles into the wound. Icy, but soothing, I force myself still as I'm struck with the distinct urge to scratch it.

It feels both similar and immensely different to Mirren's power. Like Mirren is an ocean of the south and Verena is the north, whatever it is that makes up its core colder somehow. Max grips my hand in hers, vulnerability flashing in her eyes for the first time since we left Similis, as if being forced to stare at the grievous extent of the injury has crumbled her wall of steel determination.

I grip Max's hand hard, and as agony radiates through me, I find Harlan's gaze and lock onto it. His eyes don't stray to the festering wound, or the wailing queen in the next room. They are a steady solace in the night, a soothing balm against the turbulence of the world, and they stay where they belong: on me.

I hold tight as heavy waves of agony wash over me, the pain of new growth. Of knitting the old back together. More ragged than before, battered and bruised, but functioning. Verena gasps as power flows from her fingers and into me, and I wonder vaguely where humanity got the idea that healing is a form of relief.

It is gritty work, painful and messy. There is nothing soft about it.

And then, the pain recedes like a wave from a beach. I gulp down a few breaths of oxygen and swallow, feeling momentarily like the acute absence of agony is some sort of fever dream. Like one wrong movement will cause it to crash over me again, inescapable, and fatal. I stare up at

Max and Harlan, absorbing the relief in their eyes, and it gives me the courage to sit up.

My muscles protest the movement, and I clutch at the soreness in my side, tensing as I look down at my stomach. The wound is mostly healed over, now a snarl of scar tissue. I stretch, more gingerly this time, testing the limits of my body's patchwork.

Verena watches me fearfully, like I may strike her at any moment. "I got all the infection, but don't have enough to leave you with no trace of the injury," she explains hurriedly, twisting her hands nervously together. "I am still learning and there were so many of the militia to heal, and I —my power is feeble as it is. I-I'm sorry."

I breathe in again, becoming accustomed to the newfound pull of the scar. Then I shrug, swinging my legs off the table and coming slowly to my feet. "There is nothing to be sorry for. I'm thankful for your help." I shuffle my feet in a cheerful, but terrible jig. "Works as good as it ever did."

Verena nods, but her relief at my approval is short lived as her eyes flicker to the other room, where the witch-queen is tied up. "Her militia is camped on the plain. I didn't see any wind-wielders, but she has a deal with the Havian warlord and has eyes everywhere. I don't know how we'll make it out of the city unless we kill her."

I smirk as Max hands me my bow and quiver. The grip feels alive in my hand, curvaceous and welcoming as a warm body. "We aren't going to kill her," I answer. "We're going to heal her."

CHAPTER
TWENTY-ONE

Shaw

The horns bellow again—one, two, three sharp beats—their eerie tenor echoing along the sharp stone walls of the city I was born. When Max and I escaped all those years ago, it had been to the same call, one reserved for only the direst of occasions: the song of the traitor. A harrowing hymn that not only summons the militia, but *every* Argentian citizen to do their duty to their territory.

Kill the enemy in our midst.

It's been almost ten years since our first escape, and still, the song reverberates in my chest with the same veracity. My father is dead, but nothing has truly changed. I'm still hunted, still forced to give up the things precious to me to keep them safe. I'd had Mirren in my arms, felt her heart beating against mine for only a few moments before it was gone. And the further I run away from her, the more I want to scream at the unfairness of it all.

Instead, I funnel my rage into the abyss, turn it into a torrent of flame that spews from my chest like lava. The snow, which has begun to whip through the streets with renewed fervor, evaporates long before it touches me. The coin in my pocket pulses darkly, its unnatural call answering the shimmer of power in the air. The wielders are close. Too close.

Which means Mirren is safe.

I halt abruptly.

Emotion on a battlefield gets you killed. It was one of the first things my father ever taught me, and one I've clung to long after I left him. But there is no disassociating now, no amount of training in the world that would be able to erase the sight of Mirren on that dungeon floor. Desperate, alone. Broken. It is imprinted on my eyelids, carved into the bones of my chest.

So this time, I don't push it away or drown it out. My power *demands* my anger, my hatred. It rises up and devours it whole, until I am not simply a wildfire burning out of control, but an inferno made in the deepest pits of the Darkness.

And when I erupt, it is not only flame that explodes out of me. It is the Darkness itself, a white-hot wave of destruction.

It eviscerates everything in its path. Wooden structures crumble instantly to piles of ash, and the stone of the buildings towering around me cracks and shatters under the force. The tallest one, a house of pleasure, begins to sway tenuously and I am already running when it comes toppling to the ground with a crash so violent, I'm blown from my feet.

I claw at the moving ground, scrambling upward. I have to keep moving, lead them as far away as possible before they realize Mirren isn't with me.

Screams ring out in the night as the wave of fire follows my path. Flame races along the tops of buildings, and shoots into the night sky in a torrent of light. The coin shudders again as a giant wave of water crests behind me, dousing some of the fire, and for a moment, my blood sings as it remembers. Threading my power through the otherworldly relic; the delicious heat, the unnerving swell of darkness and light.

The coin is repulsion and desire at once, and for a terrifying beat, I don't know which will win out. I could use the coin and feed on the other wielders' power, glutton myself on the fullness of it.

No. You are enough, my own power reminds me as flame imbues my bones, my exhausted muscles. *You claw from the air; you shape the world according to your will. You need nothing more.*

I breathe deeply, and with my acceptance of the words, the coin's pulse fades. I run faster, making a sharp turn to the left to avoid the militia running from the front gates. The city has changed in the years I've been gone, but not enough to disorient me. The roads, with their curving senselessness and abrupt dead ends, still feel as familiar as ever. My blood is in these pavers, my pain in the shadows, and I let it guide me through the never-ending tangle of roads.

Without Avedis, there is only one way out of Argentum. The front gates. When I left Mirren, I'd known the odds of making it through them without dying or losing my soul. The Dark Militia is not like most others: they cannot be threatened or swayed. I could surround every Argentian citizen in a circle of fire, and the militia would just as soon let them all burn if it meant apprehending me.

The black, jagged points of the gates come into view just as a wall of water shoots into the air. Wielders and militia members alike swarm in front of me. Gun shots ring out and it's only my flame that keeps the bullets from tearing through me. The metal melts on contact, falling like molten rain around my feet.

I spit out a curse and slide to a stop, glaring up at the large tenement house on one side of me and the expanse of the city wall on the other. Raising a wall of flame between myself and the militia, I know I'm on borrowed time as they begin testing their boundaries. Throwing themselves into the flame and tearing my soul, bit by bit.

Gripping my chest like I can pull the pain out of it; I tip my shoulders back and breathe in.

Through fire and blood, my choice will always be her.

Baring my teeth, I draw the flame back into my heart. The heat builds against my skin, burns my nerves, and scorches my lungs, and still, I feed it. When I can hardly stand it, when my grip on it is slipping and the only thing to do is let it go in a conflagration to kill them all, a shadow skids into my periphery.

A furious mix of gratitude, rage and fear punch me in the gut as I realize who has managed to follow me through my path of destruction. "I'll fucking *kill* you for leaving her!" I snarl at Avedis.

The assassin doesn't bother to answer me, his scar twisted and pale in the light of my fire. Instead, he raises his hands and I understand too late what he means to do. "Avedis, NO—"

But the words are strangled from me along with the air. I am still clawing at my throat as everything goes dark.

∼

Mirren

Sura and I lean on each other as we run away from Argentum. My cheeks have long gone numb in the whipping winter wind, my hair frozen in icy tendrils down my back. Snow tears at our cloaks and bites at our legs, and more than once, we lose our footing and topple face first into it. The horns of the militia blast across the wasteland, their harrowing song reverberating against my heart, echoing my own terror back to me.

Shaw and Avedis are still trapped inside with the entirety of the Dark Militia after them. And though I take heart that at the very least, their leader is dead, I cannot shake the feeling of dread that presses down against my chest.

My *other* has curled into a frozen pond, as feeble and weak as my body. But somehow, I keep my feet moving. I told Anrai I would be there when he came back, and I won't let him down.

There is no cover on this side of the wall, just a white blanket of thick snow. Though Anrai managed to lure most of the Dark Militia to the other side of the city, there are still the patrols along the outer boundaries to worry about.

Get to the rock, Mirren. Just make it to Easton.

An arrow whizzes past my cheek, and I lurch to the side. More begin to rain down, along with shouts of commands from on top of the wall. My legs feel like they are mired in cement, but I force them to move faster. One foot in front of the other. My breaths are sharply painful in my lungs and my muscles scream with every movement.

Another arrow slices at the ground in front of us and Sura stumbles. And though I try to haul her up, this time, we both collapse to the snow. I claw her arm with icy fingers, trying to yank her back to standing, but hunger and pain have sapped her strength. Her body has no more to give.

I let out the combination of a sob and a howl as another arrow sails past me.

In my desperation, it takes me entirely too long to understand this one doesn't come from the wall. It's been sent from somewhere in front of us.

I crouch down next to Sura and scan the night for the source, as I readjust the grip on the daggers Anrai gave me. Light and dark. Why is it I only feel the dark?

Two more arrows sail through the darkness, their shafts slicing through the air and finding their mark on top of the wall with morbid *thunks*. The two guards slump where they stand, and then—

"Mirri!" my brother's voice echoes through the night.

Two riders appear like spectral hallucinations, and for a moment, I wonder if perhaps that's what they are. Imaginings of my dying brain, as there is no sensible circumstance my brother would be on this wasteland, so far from the quarterage. And on a horse, no less.

Easton doesn't wait for the horse to stop to throw himself sideways, collapsing into an ungraceful heap a few feet away from me. He scrabbles at the ground and his feet slip in the snow before he manages to regain his bearings long enough to hurtle into me. We both go tumbling, and he is so warm and terrified and *alive* that the tears that abandoned me in the depths of the Castellium rush to my eyes now. They freeze before they can fully fall as Easton grips me to him desperately, any thought of the Keys left behind in Similis.

He wipes at my eyes and runs his fingers reverently over my face with a shattered expression; broken open like a glass box dropped from a tall tower. Through the cracks shines his terror, his worry, and most of all, his love. I allow it to seep into me with a sob, as Luwei jumps from his horse to help his own sister.

"I thought you were going to die," Easton cries, as his own tears fall. I have not seen Easton cry since he was a child, and the sight of it only makes me sob harder. "Mirri, I was terrified you were going to die without knowing how much you mean to me. I'm so sorry—I'm so sorry!"

We're alive and we're together, and none of the rest of it matters. Not now. I grip him to me to soothe his panic, but he pulls back with a shake of his head. "No. You don't need to protect me from my own actions. Mirri, I love you. Exactly as you are. You are not too little or too much. You're mine."

A fresh sob breaks from my throat, raw and unshaped, as if pulled from the deepest recesses of me.

"There'll be more guards coming on the wall," Luwei says desperately, lifting Sura onto the horse. His face is pale and panicked and his gaze flickers toward Argentum as more fire lights the sky. "We need to move. Now."

Easton winds an arm around my waist, taking my weight as we stand until I manage to steady my feet. His grip is surprisingly strong as he helps me into the saddle, and it occurs to me that I have always seen my brother as a child—as someone who needed my protection—but Easton is very nearly a man.

"What about Shaw and Avedis?" Easton asks, their names in his accent causing shivers to race up my skin. I can't remember Easton ever referring to Shaw by name, let alone with the modicum of worry and warmth lining the word as it does now.

"His orders were to meet him at the cave," Luwei replies, but even as he says it, he looks to me in question. The Xamani boy has never warmed to Shaw, but I see in his eyes there is a life debt owed: for risking himself to save his sister. And perhaps the debt is weighted heavily enough, that if I ask Luwei to go into Argentum, he'll do it.

Another explosion of flame rocks the northern side of the city, followed by a geyser of water. Unease prickles at the back of my neck. So many of Anrai's nightmares are of drowning, and now, he faces his greatest fears alone.

There is nowhere I wouldn't come for you. Nowhere I won't be able to find you.

He trusted me to make it out of the city. I can trust him to do the same, even if his absence hollows out my chest and roils my stomach.

"Then that's where we meet them," I reply.

Luwei nods, circling his arms around Sura and cradling her into his body as he takes the reins. Easton hops up behind me, his movements stilted and awkward. He nods to the horse sheepishly. "You'll probably do better at controlling this infernal beast than I do," he says affectionately.

Though I smile in reply, the humor doesn't reach my eyes. Because even as I turn away from Argentum, the tether binding my soul to Anrai's pulls taut.

And all I can do is hope it is strong enough not to break.

∼

We ride until the ringing horns of Argentum are swallowed by the thick snow, leaving only the sound of heavy hooves and our own frozen breath. When we reach the mountain range edging the west side of the city, Luwei leads us up a hidden path that winds behind large black formations of rock spearing into the sky. And behind them, a perfectly hidden cave.

From here, we can see the city proper below. It has gone

oddly dark in the hours since we left. There are no more explosions, no more fire. It seems that even the street lanterns have been shrouded by a thick layer of ash and smoke. The stillness feels eerily like death, so I turn toward the cave before I can consider it further.

The city is quiet because Anrai and Avedis are on their way back to me. I won't let myself imagine the alternative.

Luwei helps Sura to the ground, his throat working as he takes in the state of her. He's seen his sister starved before, but it isn't only hunger haunting her now. Desperation is woven into the lines of her face, horror etched into the spaces where her smile used to reside.

I allow Easton to help me from the horse, but I find no solace in our safety, even as he wraps me in a thick bed roll. Anxiety skitters over my skin, burns at the ends of my nerves, and I don't know whether I want to sob, or laugh, or run.

I hiss in pain as Easton eases me against the cave wall. The wounds on my back are raw and sticky, and as the adrenaline of the night fades, my head swims with each movement.

To my surprise, my brother builds a fire. His hands are clumsy with the wood, and even clumsier with the flint, but when it sparks, I see his pride.

Sura and I gulp down water, and tear into a few pieces of dried jerky from Luwei's pack. The smell of spices fills our small camp as he cooks, but even when it's finished, and the delicious broth warms me from the inside out, my sense of disquiet only grows.

Sura and Luwei fall asleep tangled against one another, arms and limbs wound tightly together. Even in sleep, Sura's fingers clutch at Luwei's chest like he might disappear beneath her at any moment. And maybe that's why I stare at her hand for so long, like she might be able to hold on tight enough for the both of us.

The sun glows behind the horizon teasing the morning, and still, sleep doesn't come. Easton sits next to me, his shoulder bumping mine, and the feel of him is enough to bring a lump to my throat. Whatever hesitation he feels about touch has been lost to his panic. I want to tell him how much it means to me, to feel his presence, to hear his words of acceptance.

But no words come, buried too deep beneath my exhaustion and worry.

"He'll come, Mirren," Easton whispers into the frozen dawn air. He circles his arm around me, and I lean my head on his shoulder. I have always taken care of my brother, taken his worries as my own, but it feels good now to allow him to do the same for me. The relief of it courses through me, of sharing the burden, of my feelings being known without having to speak them. I have always loved my brother, but now, I understand the rarity of intimacy. And I don't take it for granted.

It's because of this, I finally admit my worries aloud. "What if he doesn't? What if he's lost his soul again because of me?"

"Did he tell you he'd come?" Easton asks, tucking my head beneath his chin.

I nod miserably.

"Then he'll come," he repeats, sounding far more confident than I feel. "If there's one thing I've learned about Shaw, it's that he keeps his word. Whether you want him to or not."

I smile weakly, blanketing his words over my panic. *He'll come.*

There is no place I won't find you.

But as the sun rises higher, and Easton nods off, the words begin to fracture in my mind. My eyes are dry and stinging, my throat swollen and painful. The skin on my back burns, and though my exhaustion goes bone deep, sleep doesn't come.

I watch the horizon steadily, willing Anrai to appear. Hardly daring to blink, like even the briefest of pauses will cause me to lose him forever. I burrow deep into the warmth of his soul, and tug at the tether between us. *Come back to me.*

When the sun reaches its peak in the wintry sky, and the snow sparkles like diamonds beneath it, despair threatens to crest over me like a wave. But then, movement tickles the place where land meets sky, and the first full breath I've taken since Similis expands in my lungs.

Buttery rays shine behind him in orange streaks, bathing him entirely in shadows, but I'd know the shape of him anywhere; his lithe prowl, the graceful lines of his gait as he leads Dahiitii up the small path toward our mountain cave.

I thrust the bedroll aside and jump to my feet with a desperate yelp, ignoring the hot wave of pain that radiates from my back. Snowflakes flutter down around me and my untied boots log with slush as I tear across the moor. My *other*, fed by relief and love and terror, spears ahead of me with fervor. It runs along his skin, searching for any source of hurt, for every wound, every bruise.

And when the shadows finally relent, a sob barrels up my throat. His face is smudged with ash and blood, and his hair is a dark halo around his head. He is all colors against a landscape leeched of vibrancy; so handsome it feels like a physical blow, all the uncontained, brutal beauty of a wildfire.

Embers spark along his skin, his power dancing happily with mine as his gaze locks on me.

He drops Dahiitii's reins and breaks into a sprint up the rest of the path. And when we collide, a sharp breath shoots from his lungs—of relief, of terror. Everything I've felt in our time apart, mirrored in the sound. I leap at him, wrapping my legs around his waist and digging my fingers into the hard muscles of his chest. I kiss every bit of his skin I can reach, frantic and wild, and as his arms come around me, his embrace solid and strong, a jagged part of me smooths over.

Anrai's mouth comes over mine, and I inhale him like his expelled breath is the only sustenance I need. He smells of smoke and snow and wind, and I collapse against his chest as the tears I haven't been able to shed finally come pouring out of me.

He gently tips my chin up, and as I take in that pale gaze, clever and ruthless as always, everything in me settles. Because his eyes are not the empty pits of the soulless. Though fragmented by the pieces of himself he's given up, they still flicker like a torch, a beacon of home and hope.

"Don't you ever do that to me again," I scold, swatting his arm halfheartedly. I hiccup, swiping at my cheeks to clear my tears even as more pour down.

He cocks an eyebrow in amusement. "Me? You're the one who gets yourself kidnapped every time you step out of Similis."

And though his words are teasing, Anrai's expression is shattered. There's no sign of the confident mask of the assassin, no stone wall of the vigilant soldier. There is only raw hope and terror, everything he hasn't allowed himself to feel in the time I've been gone.

He tightens his embrace, pressing me closer to his chest

as snow gathers along his dark lashes and melts on his lips. "There is nothing in the Darkness that can keep me from you, Mirren. Your soul is my soul, your heart my heart, and I would tear apart the very fabric of time to get to you."

His words are beautifully carved and brutally edged, just like Anrai himself. Like me, the light made brighter by the darkness it accentuates. And for a moment, on the edge of ruin, I allow myself to feel the truth of his words and to let it be enough.

CHAPTER
TWENTY-TWO

Shaw

My heart pounds uncomfortably hard against my ribs, unable to settle anywhere but where it belongs—in Mirren's hands. She looks awful and beautiful at once, and the sight of her fuels a maelstrom of rage and relief so strong, it leaves me far more breathless than any injury. I cannot stop running my fingers over her skin, burying my face in her hair: clutching her to me like she may disappear at any moment, a conjured imagining of my deepest desires.

Luwei peers out from the cave, and as I meet his eyes over her shoulders, he bows his head in respect. But when he opens his mouth to speak, I shake my head. "There is no life debt owed, Luwei. We've all paid enough."

The boy swallows roughly, turning back toward where his sister still sleeps, but not before I miss the look on his face: hollowed out, gutted. Grateful. Each emotion flitting indeterminably into the next. After a long moment, he asks, "Can you ride? I don't think we should hang around here any longer than necessary."

I hardly hear his question as Mirren's gaze has finally looked past mine, searching. Her expression goes hollow as she realizes what feels so wrong about my return.

I'm alone.

Her eyes snap to mine warily. "Where's Avedis?" she demands.

She seeks reassurance, but all I have is the truth: that I don't know.

I was ready to sacrifice my soul, and Avedis had rendered me unconscious to save me from it. When I awoke, I was on the outside of the wall with a few bruised ribs and no sign at all of the wind-wielder. The horns had gone silent, the smell of smoke and ruin acrid in the still air. Eerily still. Like there was no breeze at all.

It had taken me most of the night to skirt around the edge of the city to my horse, and I'd spent the majority of it vacillating between cursing the assassin and whispering prayers to the dead gods that by some miracle, he made it out of the city.

"He's coming," I finally reply, the tone of my voice brooking no room for argument.

Because he is. I won't consider the alternative, have not allowed it one inch of space in my mind. Avedis has avoided being caught since he was a boy, and I won't doubt him now.

Luwei hesitates. "You said if you weren't here by sunrise, we needed to leave. It's already been too lo—"

"He's coming," I snarl, glaring at the boy. There is no world in which we leave Argentum without Avedis, no world that he'd sacrifice his own soul to save mine.

When I glance down at Mirren, her small body still tucked in my arms, I find her watching me intensely. And I know she sees more than I say, more than I can verbalize.

"He's coming," I say again. Softer this time, so only she can hear.

Mirren knows the edges of my soul: the way they fray, thread by thread as the world tries to unravel me completely. And how Avedis sacrificing himself will undo far too much.

She sets her jaw and nods. "We'll wait until sundown. We owe him that much."

Luwei relents, shouldering his bow with a sigh. "We'll be able to see the militia coming from here and can disappear into the caves if we need to. I'll keep first watch."

I set Mirren down gently, but don't take my hands from her. I've never been a restless person by nature, always in control of every muscle in my body. But now, my fingers trail across her lips, sweep up over her cheekbones, relentlessly searching.

For the ways she's been hurt. The places she's been shattered.

And as I gaze into her eyes, I can trace the many pieces of her soul that have fragmented in our time apart, torn by the horrors she was forced to endure—and the ones she was forced to perpetrate.

My chest burns. "He should have suffered more," I snarl. I feel the abyss flare in my eyes, as I run them over the bruises on her wrists, the welt on her cheek. And finally, the myriad of lacerations on her back, wounds all too familiar to me. Wounds I suffered in the same dungeon. "I should have taken my time. Made him watch as I melted his organs."

The Darkness inside me colors my words, lines them in echoes of shadows and pain. And I don't try to soften them, because with Mirren, there is no pretending. She knows the blackest parts of me, and she doesn't fear them. "Tell me," I demand softly.

Because I have to know. Have to know exactly what losing her has meant. The price it's carved.

So, we settle onto the floor of the cave, and as I tuck her beneath my cloak, she tells me. Her words are soft, but only a fool would mistake them as weak. In them is evidence of Mirren's strength, of the fight in her heart. And as she tells me of everything the Covinus took from her, pride swells alongside my vengeance.

There is nothing humble about it as it expands in the recesses of my soul until it feels like it may escape through my pores. Cullen once said Mirren was my equal, but he was wrong.

I burn brightly, consuming until I am obliterated, leaving nothing left but smoke; a flash in the night just as quickly gone. But Mirren—Mirren endures. She's the ocean, the waves crashing against the shore. So patiently quiet, some may not notice, but when they finally look up, she's changed the very shape of the land.

She is not my equal. She is my better. And in this moment, I am so damned grateful for it.

Easton has kept a respectful distance since my return, but even from where he sits on the other side of the cave, he listens. Horror shines in his eyes as Mirren recounts her time with the Covinus. But instead of denying the truth, of stubbornly holding on, Easton lets go. He crawls slowly to us and settles beside his sister. And as she speaks, takes her hand in his.

Choosing her as she deserves to be chosen.

Mirren's body trembles in my arms, but her breaths are steady, like speaking aloud has released the pain's hold on her. "The Covinus gave the Praeceptor the way to control your soul. There's two coins, and he's using them to control the other wielders."

I start, suddenly remembering the coin I took from Nehuan. Searching my pockets frantically, dread sinks in my stomach as my search proves futile. The coin is gone. *How in the Darkness did I lose it?*

"His death would break the control," I say even as unease spirals through me. The Covinus' death should be a relief, and yet there is something about it I cannot quite touch, something heavy. "But even so, they'll still be under the thumb of the Dark Militia."

A beast bred in the Darkness and forged against the steel of my father's blade. The morbid desire for pain that writhes within its forces, a mirror of my father's own soul: unending and fathomless. But how do I stop it without taking my place as Heir? How do I sever the head from the beast without getting close enough to do so?

The idea of it, of stepping into the shoes my father crafted for me, makes me want to scratch through my own skin.

I grit my teeth and push the thoughts away. There will be time to scheme later, once we're safe and far away from the bowels of Argentum. My eyes fall on Sura's sleeping form.

Denver has always believed the prophecy is the only way to restore balance. And perhaps, if we can destroy the Darkness, the beasts born within it will be defeated as well.

With a sigh, I tuck Mirren into my lap. She feels as fragile as she looked on the floor of the dungeon, and when she curls against my chest with a small exhale, my throat grows thick even as flames wash over my heart. I try not to think of the wounds scouring her back, if only to keep myself from riding back to Argentum and burning the entire city to the ground.

Instead, I hold her tighter. "Sleep now. I've got you," I whisper, the same words I gave to her in the dungeon.

I wish I had more: *You're safe. No harm will ever come to you. I'll protect you always.*

But none of them ring true this close to my father's city, with Avedis missing and the Dark Militia preparing to hunt us down. We've been spared until now solely because the change in leadership takes time, but the slight will not go unanswered for long. So I keep the words trapped behind my lips, rolling listlessly along my tongue.

Mirren doesn't appear to need them, as she nestles closer, her smell of rain overpowering even the smell of blood.

∽

Mirren and Sura sleep through the day, their exhaustion bone deep. Easton offers to take watch from Luwei, and though he hasn't slept in two nights, I allow it. To keep Mirren close, and because something has shifted in the boy. While his expression is still guarded, it's no longer apathetic and cold. His jaw is set in a stronger line, and a new fire burns in his eyes.

Whenever they stray from steadily watching the horizon for Avedis, they find Mirren and anchor there. Though everything he believes has been upended, he's found one true thing to hold tight to, even as the world spins on its axis: his love for his sister.

And it's this love that keeps his faith in Avedis' return, as much for Mirren as for himself. Even as we watch the Dark Militia form ranks and begin to filter through the plains in search parties of twos. As the sun begins to dip behind the mountains, Easton still stares out fiercely, willing the assassin back with his gaze.

My own faith is a flimsy thing, made of gossamer and silk that rips and splits beneath the weight of each moment Avedis doesn't return. We cannot afford to wait any longer than sunset with the militia so close, but am I truly to leave the wind-wielder behind in this wretched city when he's only here because he refused to leave me?

The wind has been quiet since the storm abated, the only sound in the hush of the cave the trickle of melting snow outside. I tell myself Avedis is quiet only because there are so many other wielders to eavesdrop. I tell myself he was forced to take a different way around the city to avoid detection. I tell myself a lot of things, but as the hours pass, they become harder to hear through my dread.

Dahiitii nickers, her impatience pricking beneath my skin, mingling with my own. My limbs twitch with the urge to do *something,* anything to relieve the agony of waiting.

I am as uncatchable as the wind itself, I once heard him say. But even the strongest winds die eventually.

When the sun is nothing more than a glow in the distant sky, and the horror of having to leave has iced me over from head to toe, Easton yelps outside. He jumps up with an excited whoop, a smile cracking his normally taciturn face. "It's him!" he shouts, darting toward the moor.

Mirren stirs, blinking up at me slowly as I untangle myself from her and help her to her feet. My heart thumps somewhere near my throat, hope burning through my dread like a candle in the night. *Avedis is here. We made it out.*

My ribs throb as I sprint after Easton, out of the dark shadows of the cave and into the dusky night. It only takes me a moment to spot Avedis: his mare's reins clutched in his hand as he limps alongside her. The mouth of the cave, which has been silent all night, suddenly howls as wind whips over it, a melancholy song.

Easton laughs excitedly as he runs to greet the assassin, but something halts me in place. Even from this distance, the rhythm of Avedis' movements is familiar, his upright posture the same as it always is. But as his wind buffets against me, it feels...different.

Empty. *Wrong.*

"Easton, no!" The words tear out of my throat as I break into a sprint, but they never land, even as I lurch forward to grab Easton's collar.

The boy is too far away, and my hand only grasps at empty air as Avedis sends a knife spiraling into Easton's chest.

A cry of anguish sounds, and for a moment, I don't know if it came from inside or outside of myself. Then I realize it's Mirren, her heartbreak and shock mingled into one desperate note. I reach Easton just as he stumbles back. His eyes are wide with fear and shock, as his fingers scrabble weakly at his chest. I stare at his hands in frozen horror; long, lithe fingers, untouched by the malevolence of the world, now stained red with his own blood.

Mirren can heal him. It isn't fatal. The words beat in my head as Easton collapses against me. I stagger under his weight, and we both tumble to the ground, his body sprawled awkwardly in my lap. *It isn't fatal,* I repeat, pressing my hands around the dagger to staunch the bleeding. But the words refuse to take root as warm blood spreads over his chest, over my fingers.

As the wind, empty and howling and wrong, buffets so

hard against us, I'm forced to dig my fingers into the dirt to keep us both from being pushed off the cliffside.

It isn't fatal, it isn't fatal.

The words are lost on the wind. Easton's eyes pop and his hands move to claw uselessly at his throat as the breath is ripped from his lungs. A horrible, squealing wheeze sounds from the depths of his chest.

And then, all is silent.

CHAPTER
TWENTY-THREE

Calloway

"You cannot be serious," Verena says, a newfound edge to her previously meek voice. Her tattered skirt swirls around her legs as she plants her feet and raises her chin stubbornly. "I won't do it."

Max tenses, watching the exchange closely. I haven't told her my plan, as it hadn't been fully formed until now, but when she draws her fingers along the daggers hidden at her sides, I know she has my back.

"Verena," I start calmly, lowering my voice, but the girl shakes her head voraciously.

"I won't heal that demon woman," she hisses. "My family was too poor to pay her taxes and her militia came in the middle of the night and stole them to a workhouse. She's held me hostage ever since to work off their debt, forcing me to commit every depraved act that comes to her mind." Verena's lower lip wobbles violently. "I'll drown her and be glad to watch her die."

I study her for a long moment. "Have you ever killed Verena?"

The girl doesn't reply, only makes a soft noise at the back of her throat. But I already know the answer, because if she'd split her soul before, she wouldn't speak of it so casually now.

"Take it from someone who knows what it feels like," I say, sliding my gaze to where Harlan has gone still in the corner. I expect to see horror or disapproval, but he only tilts his head slightly, his gaze as steady as ever. When I look back to Verena, it's to find her watching Harlan as well. "That woman has stolen enough from us. We won't give her a piece of our souls as well. She isn't worth it."

Verena tears her eyes away from Harlan and her lip trembles again as her eyes grow shiny. For a terrifying moment, I think she may burst into tears in the middle of the room. But she sucks that lip into her mouth, gnawing on it as she masters herself.

"What *is* worth it, then? If sparing the world from her horrors is not?"

It's Harlan that speaks, and though we've hardly spoken more than a few sentences since Similis, somehow, he knows the lines of my mind. Those eyes are terrifyingly observant, which is probably the exact quality that got him locked up in the Healing Center in the first place. "We don't know what happens to people when they meet the Darkness, Verena. She may find torment there, or she may find peace. In keeping her alive, we can force her to atone for her evils."

Verena stills at his soothing voice, listening intently as he continues, "We are the keepers of her fate now. And we can demand she pay the debt she owes. To every Siraleni."

Avedis' words drift back to me. *The world does not care one way or another, Calloway. We must take what we're owed.*

Surely, the assassin meant the witch-queen's life. But it

isn't just me or Avedis or even Verena she owes. There have been so many destroyed by her hand, ruined by her greed. And they all deserve a chance to for payment.

"I promise, miss—we won't allow her the chance to harm you again." Harlan finishes softly.

"Call me Verena," she mumbles hurriedly.

Harlan smiles, and color blooms high up on Verena's cheeks. The flush makes her look far less pinched. Less like a doll and more alive. But annoyance chafes at my ribs nonetheless, which is ridiculous. I have no authority over Harlan's smiles, and I shouldn't even want to.

But I do.

In a way that feels desperate, and somewhat frenzied, like the world spins around me even as I stand completely still.

"We're going to take her to Siralene, and make her stand trial for her war crimes. She'll be punished by the very same people she's hurt," I explain. "People like your family."

Harlan nods sincerely, and after a long moment, Verena agrees, "Okay, I will do as you ask and heal her."

"We thank you for your bravery," Harlan replies, and I have to turn my head away at the way Verena practically purrs beneath his praise before I do something impulsive like throw myself between them. It wouldn't matter if I did—if it isn't Verena, it's Easton. And if it isn't Easton, it's the purity of Harlan's intentions, which would never allow him to love me while he loved someone else.

In that we are similar; I also don't love in halves. Ever.

I sigh loudly, attempting to ease the sudden friction behind my eyes. Apparently, I've gone from wallowing in thoughts of death to ruminating in ones of self-destruction. Not much of an improvement.

Throwing my bow over my shoulder, I stalk into the next room where the witch-queen has been thrashing against her shackles. Verena, Max, and Harlan all follow, and the little water-wielder makes to summon the water from the canteen around her neck, but I stop her with a quick shake of my head. "Not here," I say, eyeing Akari Ilinka with disgust. "She's going to lead us out of the city and away from the militia quietly, or she doesn't get healed."

The queen's glare from her remaining eye is mutinous, and when Max hauls her up by the scruff of her cloak, she is positively apoplectic. Together, we all step out of the sagging threshold and into the street. As soon as he sees the door open, Helias bounces up to me, feet skidding on the loose dirt as he stops just short of barreling into my chest. Swaying, he blinks up at me from under a curtain of dark lashes, and if I'm expecting a heartfelt proclamation that I'm no longer on the edge of death, it isn't at all what I receive.

Instead, the little boy kicks mournfully at the dirt. "I didn't even get to suck anyone into the earth," he gripes sullenly.

"There's still time," I tell him with a grin, ruffling his hair. Looking considerably lighter, Helias bounds toward Max, who snags him by the waist and plops him atop the horse, before climbing up behind him.

Harlan mounts the other, and Verena and I both trail behind Akari, me ready with bow and her ready with her power in case the queen has not been quite convinced to behave.

We walk in mostly silence through the city, winding through the ramshackle alleyways of Verena's residence, and out onto the main street. As we wind down the cobblestoned thoroughfare, drawing closer to the center of Havay, evidence of Anni's destruction grows more apparent. There is no averting my gaze, no avoiding the pure devastation, as it's everywhere I look. Homes and businesses reduced to little more than mounds of rubble; lives reduced to piles of ash blown about by the wind.

It feels obscene to gape at the ruin, but Darkness loves company. After my family died, Siralenis would ride past the still smoking wreckage with hurried whispers. There is something morbidly addictive about horror, something that draws people to witness it even as they cover their eyes. Because in someone else's ruin, they are able to whisper: *It wasn't me. I am still whole.*

My stomach roils as I stare. Even the wind of Havay is ruined, no longer the crisp, invisible harbinger of the winter months to come. Now, it is tainted with ash, smearing even the air around us in muddied shades of gray as it whips through the empty streets. When we come to the square, the epicenter of Anni's attack and the place where I found Mirren lying unconscious all those months ago, I'm positive my stomach will leap right out of my mouth.

I've come to a stop without even noticing, staring at what's left of a once lively market, and trying desperately not to see another time, another place, another pile of ruination. Harlan glances back at me, pulling his horse to a stop and motioning for Max to do the same.

Meanwhile, Akari's hateful glare has twisted into a knowing smile as she watches me, the curve of which sends something akin to slime running down the back of my neck. "You pretend you're above the Darkness, Calloway, and yet you're bonded to the one who did all of *this*."

My breath freezes in my chest.

"You would punish me for burning one family, for doing what I had to in order to ensure my power, but you are the same as the rest of us toiling away beneath the curse." Her smile is serpentine, and her eyes flash. "You've just never been strong enough to do what it takes yourself. You have someone else do the dirty work for you, and follow him around like a pathetic little disciple, excusing all the violence he's committed, because he committed it for you rather than against you. You are just the same as I am."

Max opens her mouth hotly, a scathing response no doubt ready on her lips, but she quiets when I hold up a hand. The queen is my problem, my personal retribution. And as clever as she is, in this, she's missed a glaring fact. I don't follow Anni—I *love* Anni. I know his heart better than my own; know that though I am devastated by the state of the Havian square, he is thoroughly destroyed by it.

It's something the witch-queen will never understand: intentions matter. Anni may have caused this ruin, but he never wanted it. He breaks beneath it every day, his heart an open and wounded thing. I do not excuse Anni's violence, nor punish it, because I don't have to. He punishes himself far worse than I ever could.

On the other hand, the witch-queen has never once drowned in the depths of the hurt she's caused. She pushes ever forward, righteous in her own sense of purpose, of her gods-given right to take whatever she pleases.

That was before she met me. Because I swear to the dead gods, I'm going to force her to reconcile the things she's done.

When Anni dropped her at my feet, I was set adrift, drowning in guilt and indecision. But now, in the ruins of the square, a sense of purpose settles over me. What I said to Verena was true: the witch-queen has taken enough from me. And I will have my revenge for my family, for so many families, without giving her one more piece.

I take a deep breath of ash-ridden air and set her with a toying gaze. "If I was the same as you, Akari, I would have gutted you in Similis and spiked your head to the gates. You should be thanking the old gods that I'm nothing like you. Now keep walking, or I'll shoot you where you stand."

∽

By the time we make it through the city and out onto the rolling grasses of the Breelyn Plain, dusk has fallen. The sun is little more than a soft glow over the distant Shadiil Mountains, the ocean of land sparkling in waves of amber and gold. There is no cover on this side of the city beyond a few shallow dips of earth, and though the militia is camped miles away on the west side, their fires are visible even from here.

I can only hope the loud howl of wind and the shoulder-high grass is enough to keep our movements hidden. After Verena heals Akari, we'll travel through the night until we're well away from Havay.

"I've kept my side of the bargain," Akari reminds me the moment I set down my pack. "It is time to keep yours. Make the girl heal me."

"The *girl's* name is Verena," I snipe irritably. "And she'll heal you when she's ready." To Verena, I say, "Would you like something to eat first? I know it's been a long day."

Verena shakes her head, sucking her bottom lip into her mouth. "No. I want to get this over with and get as far away from *her* as possible."

Akari sneers and brushes a burned strand of hair from her face, her eyes darkening in a lethal gaze. "There is nowhere you can go that I won't find you, water-wielder. I hope you remember that."

"Really, Akari, have you learned nothing? It's pretty stupid to threaten the woman with the healing powers," Max says with an annoyed roll of her eyes. "Unless you'd like to die of infection, in which case, you're welcome to get on with it. One less mouth to feed."

Akari runs her tongue over her teeth and raises her chin to Verena. "Go on, then. And make sure you do it right. I have no wish to spend the rest of my days looking like him," she snaps, with a pointed nod to the patch covering my left eye.

I almost smile when Verena lifts her hands, because as clever as the queen is, she hasn't realized what's been obvious to the rest of us since Similis. Even if Verena was as powerful as Mirren, there is no restoring what's been lost. Anni was thorough in his ministrations, and while the wound can be knitted back together and the infection stopped, there is no creating something from nothing.

Akari Ilinka will never see out of that eye again.

Water rises from the canteen around Verena's neck, the droplets writhing in the air before sweeping gently across the witch-queen's face. She stiffens as they circle her mouth, no doubt as their wielder contemplates drowning Akari where she stands, but after a long moment, they veer up toward her injured eye. Verena's mouth twists in concentration, and as her eyes narrow, the jagged laceration slowly begins to close.

Verena's breathing comes in labored huffs as she struggles with the depth of the injury. Her lips press together so tightly they've turned white, and with one last concerted push, the last bit of the wound zips together. She takes an unsteady step backwards, teetering on her feet as the water trickles away from the queen's face and back toward her. Verena welcomes it with a shaky breath, coaxing it back inside the small canteen.

Akari raises a delicate hand to her face.

For a moment, everything is still as she runs her fingers up the length of the scar, bumping them over her still empty eye socket. There is no pretending this time that I don't enjoy her suffering: the harrowing realization that she is still disfigured, the rage at our betrayal. In a blink, she lunges at Verena, her fingers extended like claws. "*You,*" the witch-queen screams, half-deranged. "Pathetic, useless little bitch! I should have killed you the moment I laid eyes on you and saved the world from your existence."

Harlan pushes Helias behind him, and I grab at Akari's cloak in an attempt to yank her off Verena. I miss, grasping at air, but the water-wielder is surprisingly quick on her feet. With a guttural yelp, the water from the canteen leaps upward and wrestles with the witch-queen, wrapping around her mouth and nose until she's forced backward. Akari's claws turn to her own face, swiping desperately at the water to keep herself from drowning.

Verena paws at the ground and thrusts herself upward with a look of pure malice, coming to stand over where the queen flails desperately on the ground. Even with her diminutive size, Verena no longer looks like the mousy girl we first met. Her eyes bore into Akari Ilinka, feral anger honing her gaze into something deadly. "Your eye is but a fraction of the pain you've caused. You deserve to be marked with something ugly, outer proof of the soul that lives inside you. And every time it hurts, *Queen,* I hope you don't only remember the one who did it to you. I hope you remember *me.* I hope you remember me as you face your fate in Siralene, as you're met with the justice of every person you've ever wronged."

Ilinka rears back and the blood drains from her face as she realizes my intentions for her. That no matter how soft she thinks I am, I never intended to let her go free.

Verena isn't finished. "And if you somehow survive, I hope you remember *exactly* what my face looks like. Because the next time we meet, I don't care what it costs me. I'll kill you."

Verena spits at the queen's feet, but she waves her water off. Like an obedient pet, it splashes back inside its container, settling happily at her chest. She raises her eyes to mine and nods once. "Keep your word, Calloway. Or I'll make you regret breaking it."

I can do nothing but nod, as the water-wielder turns away and disappears over the hill. Back to her hovel in the city or to start new somewhere else, I suppose I'll never know. Perhaps she'll go find her family in Siralene.

Akari gasps and wheezes, desperately gulping down oxygen. She swipes at her hair, sodden tresses plastered to her chin and neck, but when she finally gathers herself and rises to her feet, it isn't the fury swirling in her eyes that has every muscle in me coiling in anticipation. It's the wild peal of laughter that erupts from her, the sharp sound ringing out over the silence of the plain. It raises goosebumps on my flesh and sends a shiver of dread skittering down my spine.

Because it isn't the laughter of a defeated woman, mad and desperate and wild.

It sounds like a battlefield, like blood-soaked mud and splayed corpses.

It sounds like victory.

And then, I feel it more than hear it. The soft tremble of the ground, the thick fall of hundreds of boots.

The queen's militia is on the move.

CHAPTER
TWENTY-FOUR

Mirren

The silence echoes across the moor, resounds against the walls of the cave, and reverberates in the hollow in my chest. There is no scream that can pierce it, no sob to abate its resonance.

Because in the hush is the lack of Easton.

I crawl toward where my brother lays still, having somehow fallen to my knees with no recollection of it. I don't feel the scrape of the rough shale skinning my shins, or the ache of my overexerted muscles. I no longer feel the stinging wounds on my back, or the bruises peppered over every inch of my skin.

I feel nothing but hollow quiet.

Anrai lunges at Avedis, his movements as quick as fire itself. Flames burst from his chest and line his limbs, casting his terrifying mask of fury in an odd configuration of shadows and blinding light. A ball of fire careens from his palms straight for Avedis' chest, but the wind-wielder is ready, and raises a wall of hard air between them. With a clap of his hands, the air howls and spears toward Anrai.

The clearing explodes as their powers collide with a boom that vibrates the mountains around us. Sparks and tree limbs alike rain down around me as I finally reach Easton, running my fingers over his skin, searching for his hand.

I weave my fingers through his, as I take in the emptiness in his eyes—an emptiness that pierces my chest like a giant blade. It is the Healing Center all over again, everything that makes Easton who he is having dissipated, leaving behind an empty shell I barely recognize. But now, there is no machine to breathe for him, no medicine to save him.

Death is no match for the power of my *other,* as I cannot create life where it does not exist.

My baby brother is gone.

Breaths come in painful wheezes in my lungs, strangled and gasping, like there will never again be enough oxygen. My hands shake violently as I reach towards Easton's cheek. And when I cannot bring myself to move further, to confirm the cold feel of death on his skin, my *other* threads through my fingers and washes gently over his face. It traces the delicate lines of his features and the smooth skin of his cheeks, touching and memorizing every part of him that I cannot. "I love you," I whisper into the night.

And though the words shake, barely more than a breath in the expanse of the Dark World, they are what finally breaks through the silence.

Tears pour down my cheeks as I rise. They slide over my mouth, the tangy taste of them, of salt and blood, grounding me to the present. Wind whips my hair in stinging strands against my face. I paw it away, squinting against the show of power snapping around me.

When Avedis and Shaw sparred in the manor dining

room, both men had kept their power curled inside them. But now, the entire moor vibrates with violent energy. Flames explode in sky high geysers and wind thrashes around me, the pressure in the air enough to steal my breath. Shaw hurtles ball after ball of molten flame, moving from behind a shield of fire so hot, all the oxygen is pulled from Avedis' air. It's the only thing keeping Shaw alive against the wind-wielder, from preventing the breath being stolen from him the same way it was stolen from Easton.

If Anrai has any reservations about killing our friend, it doesn't show. There is no hesitation in his movements, no restraint in the lethal explosions. He is fury made physical, his power fed by the darkest places inside of him, the bottommost pit of his shadows.

From this distance, I can't see Avedis' eyes. He is wrapped in wind, and the air shimmers around him with intensity as he bends the currents of the continent to his will.

He killed my brother. He is my friend. He once tried to kill me. He once saved my life.

The thoughts swirl as my *other* rises, but none settle. Contrasting currents, hot and cold, they clash against one another as I stand frozen, watching the battle unfold before me.

Shaw throws another tangle of flame at Avedis' head. The wind-wielder ducks and snarls, his hands waving in a circular motion as he's forced to direct his powerful current into staving off the firebomb. It's only a moment, a fraction of time, but it's all Anrai needs. Because he's already sent a small trail of flame licking behind the assassin, and now, fed by Avedis' own gust of wind, it explodes up the back of him.

A costly mistake, one uncharacteristic of the assassin.

Avedis is ruthlessly astute, learning everything he can about those around him. He *knows* Shaw, knows the strengths and weaknesses in his fighting style. He knows better than to give him even an inch of space in which to move, because Shaw will always take it.

The wind-wielder roars as flames lick up his clothes, hungrily devouring every bit of him they can. He flails his arms and stumbles back, desperately trying to pat out the flames, as his winds whip up around him, trying to snuff them out.

Shaw doesn't hesitate. He yanks two daggers from his bandolier, and leaps at Avedis' flaming silhouette. The flames flicker higher, wider, and Avedis howls in agony as Anrai pummels him to the ground.

The two currents of thought, of hate and sadness, crash inside me. But something softer laps against my heart at the sound of Avedis' misery. I don't want to give heed to it, because in softness lies everything about me that is breakable. But it's insistent as it trickles in my chest, cooling and soothing, even as the howl of anguish pricks at my brain.

Avedis would have known Shaw would trick him into using his own power against him. He should have seen it coming. But he didn't. Because the wind-wielder standing before me is not the man who helped me find Anrai against all odds. He is not the man who descended into the darkness below Similis to save Ferusa. He is not my friend who believed in me, gifted me with his faith.

The man before me is empty.

My *other* thrashes, my own currents demanding we let Anrai take what is owed, a life for a life. But my soul, bruised and beaten and entirely too gentle, won't allow it.

My limbs suddenly come to life beneath me. "Shaw,

don't kill him!" I stumble toward them, swiping at the tears on my cheeks. Anrai whips his head to me, dagger still pressed against Avedis' throat even as flames lick around them both, crawling over the wind-wielder's body.

There is nothing soft on Shaw's face, no sign of the man who only moments before held me so gently against his chest. The pale of his eyes flares and flickers, a wildfire poised to destroy everything in its path. It should scare me, the otherworldly rage possessed in that predatory gaze, but it only settles me further into myself. Because it's a power that sings to my own, that calls it to the surface to dance in vengeance.

"He's being controlled. Someone has his soul." Even as I speak the words, those currents lash inside me, demanding we take them back. That we let Shaw take from Avedis as he's taken from us.

Shaw's eyes widen fractionally as sudden understanding blooms on his face. Then, without question, he calls his flame back to him. The assassin has already gone unconscious, and I watch detachedly as they crawl from Avedis, up Anrai's arms to wreathe around his neck, before disappearing into his skin like he's absorbed them.

He pushes himself up and comes toward me, his face a clear contrast of rage and regret and angst. I look away, staring at the scorched earth around us with dizzying intensity.

Because if I see that he is back to Anrai, if I allow myself to feel his embrace, I will break down completely. I will lie down next to Easton and wait for the Covinus to come. I will give him my memories willingly, if only to spare myself from feeling the anguish to come.

So, instead of allowing myself comfort, I walk toward

Avedis' scorched body and kneel down beside him. The unscarred half of his face is now burned beyond recognition, his handsome features charred and mutilated in shades of red and black. I feel nothing as I examine them or as I press my hands to his still steaming chest. The emotions are there, so many they threaten to burst out of my very skin, but I don't allow them a moment of consideration before feeding them to my *other*. I wrangle their currents with ruthless precision and press them all into the wind-wielder.

Power floods my veins like a dam burst, before sweeping the familiar path through Avedis. When we were here before, he felt like a breeze over the ocean: powerful and sweetly edged. Now, there is only the bitter emptiness of an icy swell. Of howling caverns and empty pits.

When I finish healing every melted bit of him, and my breath comes in ragged gasps, I examine his unconscious form, hollowly noting the only scar remaining is the one across his eye. I've never before managed such a complete job, never before figured out how to smooth out every gnarl, every hurt. But somehow, I've perfected healing in the body of the man who murdered my brother.

Abruptly, I lean away from Avedis and heave violently, the few contents of my stomach pouring out of me in an acidic wave. Anrai, who's watched the display of power in silence, now comes to place a gentle hand on my back. I flinch away, even as I vomit again. Because his touch will make me feel my own skin, will remind me that I'm present even as my brother is not. That I am here, and he is gone.

"Lemming," Anrai says, and though his voice is soft, a hint of command lies in it. "We have to go. Now."

I don't look at him, don't look at anything but the frozen ground, and he doesn't force me to.

"Whoever has control of Avedis won't be far behind. And the militia will be coming for us now that they know where we are. We have to get him as far away from here as possible. The further we get, the less control they'll have."

His words echo in the logical part of my brain, the part that came alive the moment I stepped foot into the Dark World. The primal creature beneath my skin that forces me to move, to survive, even when I cannot fathom doing either.

"What about..." The name threatens to break me, so I don't say it. Only flick my eyes to where my brother lies still. *He is sleeping,* I tell myself. *Just like when he was little. Peaceful and happy.*

Anrai clears his throat as his gaze follows mine. "The ground is too frozen to bury him."

The rest of his statement goes unsaid because we both know. Even if the ground weren't solid, we can't spare the time. And I could never bear to leave him here in this forsaken land. He is too soft for this ruthless place, too good for its cruelty. "Burn him," I say, the words sounding as if they've been dragged unwillingly from my throat.

I feel Anrai's hesitation more than see it. When I finally turn to him, his face is anguished and unshed tears shine in his eyes. "Please." My voice cracks on the word, and it is this fracture that throws the stone mask down over Anrai's features.

Because he will always do what needs to be done, even if I'll hate him later for it. Even if he'll hate himself.

With a face of marble, he nods.

I crawl back to my brother, and lay myself beside him, feeling the familiar shape of him next to me one more time and committing it to memory. *Will you disappear, Mirri? Don't disappear like the rest of them.*

Then, I stand beside Anrai as he flicks his fingers.

And my brother is no more.

∽

Calloway

The approaching militia sounds like thunder rolling across the open plain, a sound that dives past my ears to vibrate against my chest. Foreboding and deep.

"Run!" I shout at Harlan, but he needs no prompting. His eyes are bright with fear, as he scoops up Helias and disappears into the tall grass, the boy bouncing against his chest. But even as they go, hopelessness flutters over me, the cadence of my heartbeat too fast and too slow all at once.

There is no cover here, nothing but miles of endless grassland. Our only hope is to draw the militia away from Helias, away from Harlan.

With a snarl of fury, Max tackles Akari Ilinka to the ground, her falchions flashing. "What have you done?" she barks just as she gets her fingers around the witch-queen's throat. But Ilinka is ready, ever the nimble warrior, and wraps her legs around Max's waist, leveraging her own weight to toss Max to the side and duck beneath her arms.

Akari hurtles at Max with a howl, and both women go tumbling through the grass. I notch an arrow, pulling the bow string tight as I level it at the witch-queen's back. But there's no need, as Max whirls up with a kick to the queen's jaw. And this time, when Max rises above Akari Ilinka, it's with her blade pressed firmly into the queen's throat. Because Ilinka has fought on battlefields longer than Max has been alive, but Max is a survivor. She follows no rules of engagement, no formula of technique

—she scraps, becoming whatever she needs to be to stay alive.

This time, it only took her one failed move to learn from her mistakes. To home in on the witch-queen's weakness. Anni's always said, *the art of death becomes you*, by which he means your weapon is an extension of your body, your instincts drilled so deeply, you're moving before your mind has had time to catch up. But Akari learned the arts with both eyes.

It's taken me months of practice, and my skills still aren't anywhere close to where they were before I lost my eye.

I take a few sharp intakes of breath as the sound of the militia grows closer. Keeping my bow strung and raised, I stalk toward the queen. Because Max could sever Ilinka's head from her body, and it wouldn't stop her army. Won't do anything to shield us in the open expanse of the plain. "Call them off," I tell her, my voice tight and lethal. "Or I swear to the Darkness, I will slit you from throat to belly before they ever get here."

Ilinka only smiles shrewdly, her eye flashing. "There is no calling them off. My militia is loyal only to me, and it is a loyalty that extends beyond my death."

A chill runs up my spine at her meaning. She has plans in place to punish those in her service if they were to ever betray her, plans set in motion by her death.

The witch-queen leans forward and bares her teeth savagely. "My wind-wielder alerted them to my presence as soon as we stepped into Havay. I stayed their hand until I could be healed. That pathetic little wretch of a water-wielder is probably already dead. And you're next Calloway Cabrera. Perhaps we'll burn you at the stake, a bit of poetic justice. You can die exactly as your family did."

The bow wavers in my hand, and the queen presses on. "And when your flesh is melted from your bones, I'll have a new prize in my collection."

Helias. She means Helias.

She intends to steal him away and break him as she broke Avedis; to twist him into something forever hers.

"Why don't you just put that bow down now, and surrender on your knees? You've already shown you're far too weak to split your soul, even to avenge your family." The witch-queen tilts her head, raven hair spilling in blunted edges over her jaw. "Though I will admit, I underestimated you. You may be too much of a coward to kill me, but handing me over to the Siralenis? You are far more ruthless than I imagined."

Max smacks the blunted side of her blade against the witch-queen's jaw, sending her sprawling to the ground. When she recovers, her hand clutched against a giant welt, she only laughs eerily. "I will go back to Siralene, of course. With my new earth-wielder. One of the four, I hear, and far stronger than any other. With him, I will annihilate all those who have dared to rise against their queen. I will raze the land and start anew."

"And what of me, Queen? How have you fooled yourself into thinking for one second I won't take your head right now and dance as your blood pours over my feet?" Max snarls.

Akari Ilinka laughs again. "Go ahead Maxwell of Nadjaa. Kill me and live to see what happens to your little earth-wielder. The Dead Prophecy will never come to pass after what my militia does to him."

As much as I hate it, the witch-queen is right. We could kill her and stand and fight, but two against a militia certainly won't keep them distracted long enough for

Harlan to escape with Helias, even with the head start. They'd be faster on horseback, but without the cover of the grass, they'd be leaving themselves wide open to archers.

The thunder of footsteps grows closer, and when I look to the north, a white cloud swarms over rolling grasses. The militia is here. And we're running out of time.

Max's eyes widen in horror as I meet her gaze, understanding me before I even open my mouth to speak. But I press on, because if I say the words aloud, if I commit myself to them, there will be no turning back.

I am many things: irreverent, forgiving, soft. But I'm also a man of my word.

"Get her to Siralene, no matter what it takes."

Max shakes her head, and I smile softly, even as tears fill her eyes. Max doesn't cry. I've done so many things wrong in this life, but in this moment, the fact that she finds me one of the few things worthy of her tears, makes up for most of them. "And I expect silks at my funeral," I tell her with a wet laugh as tears begin to blur my own vision. "*Silks*. Not satin. Or I will haunt you forever."

"Cal." My name is a soft plea, barely more than a whisper above the din of the oncoming army.

"We need Siralene. And those people need justice." The words serve as a reminder to her, but also to myself. The four may be the key to breaking the curse, but we'll all need to give something to end the Darkness. I've always prided myself on bringing light to the dark, levity to the unbearably heavy, and I'm able to do so now in my own way.

But Max must be the one to see it through. Alone.

She takes a step toward me, and a part of my heart breaks that I cannot embrace her, feel the familiar beat of her heart against my chest one more time. But she has a queen to steal away, and I have an army to distract. And there is no more time.

Shouldering my bow, I swing myself up onto the horse. "And please make sure Anni gets roaring drunk. I don't need his brooding ruining the festivities."

Max lets out a defeated laugh, and I memorize the sound, warmth blooming in my chest. "Love you," I tell her.

Without waiting for a response, I turn the horse toward the militia.

CHAPTER
TWENTY-FIVE

Shaw

My blood boils in my veins, thrumming past my ears and through my body like a rush of lava with nowhere to go. Rage and violence and sorrow pulse in time to my heart, and one thought burns in the back of my skull: *my soul never tore.*

I didn't notice in the clamor of the dungeon, in my anguish at seeing Mirren brought so low. The wound was lethal, and that's all I'd needed to know.

But when I stabbed the Covinus through the throat, my soul never fractured. Somehow, he lives. And because of my mistake, Easton is dead.

Shame presses down onto my shoulders, compresses my spine and curls through my veins like black sludge. It pushes me toward the edge of Darkness, but I refuse to fall. We aren't safe here, and if I give in to the chasm opening up inside me, the Covinus will come kill us all.

So I feed every bit of what I'm feeling to the abyss, and in turn, it rises to my call. It sparks at my fingertips and scorches every errant thought to ash. And deep in the ash is where I find that comforting calm, the primal single-mindedness that's saved my life so many times.

Mirren is still staring at the lone pile of ash. Her face is normally a painting of her thoughts, splashed with vibrant colors and luminous emotions, but now it's a blank canvas. White. Empty. She watches cinders trail into the wind with an unreadable expression, her body frozen as all that remains of her brother is carried away into the night sky.

I push the threads of my worry deep into my flame and turn away from where she sits.

We have to get off this moor. Now. Disappear into Ferusa long before the Covinus is healed enough to come after us. Because if he's truly alive and controlling Avedis, it won't be long before he follows. He sent Avedis alone to catch us by surprise: to kill me and drag Mirren back to the Castellium. My father never understood the ties of friendship, but the Covinus understands all too well, wielding his knowledge of the intimacies of love like a sword.

He did it for years in Similis, molding the Community's love and loyalty until it was his own personal shield. The Covinus never needed to descend to the savage level of warlords, always preferring a far neater method. Avedis is proof of that. The Covinus may be alive, but he's in no condition to mount an offense against us. So he sent Avedis, knowing we'd let him walk straight through our defenses. Knowing we would hesitate.

But the Covinus also miscalculated. Waking without a soul is immensely disorienting. There are no memories to tether you to who you were, to the body you reside in. And while Avedis' body is still a machine, his amnesia is a weakness. Physically, we're an even match, and the only way he could have held an advantage is using his knowledge of me.

Without it, he faced an unknown enemy, while I had known exactly who stood before me.

It's the only reason we're still alive.

I haul Avedis up by the armpits. His head lolls listlessly, as I curse the pure bulk of him. It makes no sense for someone supposedly as lithe as the wind to have muscles the size of boulders, and I grunt with exertion as I drag him slowly back toward the cave.

Luwei has already helped Sura up into the saddle of his mare, probably ready to run with her the moment the fight with Avedis began. But when he sees what I'm doing, he hurries down to help, grabbing the assassin's feet and helping me heave him backward with a strained sigh.

The Xamani boy proves to be surprisingly strong, and together, we manage to lug Avedis to the mouth of the cave and up onto the horse. I wrap a bedroll around his half-naked body and tie him to the saddle quickly, before linking the horse's reins to Dahiitii's. Luwei and I are both breathing heavily and swiping at the sweat beaded on our foreheads, when Mirren steps into the womb of the cave.

Luwei watches her warily, like she's liable to crumble at any moment. He's intimate with the fear of losing a sibling, of being helpless to stop it. But Mirren doesn't fall apart. Instead, she says in a blank tone, "It's the Covinus. Who's controlling him." She doesn't phrase it like a question, but I feel the urge to answer anyway.

Luwei's face pales as he swings his gaze back to me expectantly, waiting for me to contradict her. Instead, I nod. "My soul never tore. I didn't—I didn't notice until now, but...but the Covinus is alive."

I am bereft as the words leave me, as I admit to the other half of my soul that just as I hadn't protected her, I'd also failed to protect her brother. But Mirren doesn't react, only nods blankly. "If Avedis doesn't report back to him, he'll hunt us. All of us."

My mind whirls as I dig my nails into my palm. Torches of the militia flicker in the night, as they stream toward where we stand now. They saw my display of power, know we're on this mountainside. But I chose this spot for a reason, as the cave system that winds beneath the cragged rocks are infinite and deep. "We should split up," I finally say, having reached a decision.

Luwei begins stubbornly shaking his head. Mirren says nothing. "No," Luwei insists, shooting a worried look at Mirren. "What if they find you and steal your power as well, Fire-bringer? The continent will be done for."

"I won't let that happen," I practically snarl at the boy. "The Covinus is hunting Mirren, Avedis, and I. Not you. Sura's in more danger while she's with us. If you disappear, the militia won't bother to look for you. Not until they've found us first."

At the mention of his sister, Luwei's argument sputters weakly, just as I mean it to. As brave as he is, his love for her comes first. "What about the prophecy? If Sura doesn't tell it, the continent will be destroyed by the Darkness regardless of what happens with the Covinus."

I steel my gaze. "You're going to head south. Keep to the cliffs and get back to Nadjaa. Tell Denver what's happened here, about the coin and how the Covinus is controlling wielders' souls. Make sure he knows the threat Nadjaa faces." I heave a leveling breath. "Mirren and I will lead the militia through these mountains. We'll lose them in the tunnels and circle around through Yen Girene."

Luwei levels me with a grave look. "You trust your Chancellor to do the right thing? To not go after the coins himself?"

"I do." The words are out of my mouth before I can fully consider them—before I even know if they're true. But though hurt and betrayal still colors my feelings for Denver, I know who he is at his core. I watched him for so long. Every moment he thought no one was looking, I was, and because of it, I know what keeps his heart beating through the agony of living in the Darkness. "Denver won't condone more bloodshed to keep his power. He only does what he has to in order to keep the dream of Nadjaa alive. And that means it's the safest place on the continent right now."

Luwei hesitates, but then he nods. He hops up behind Sura, tucking his sister in close. She doesn't appear to have heard the exchange; her gaze fixed instead on Mirren. When her eyes flick back to me, they are haunted with shadows—of the dungeons, of the past. And even more terrifying, with shadows of the future only she can see. "Yen Girene is filled with spirits. So many souls split within the stone walls. Whoever enters there does not come out the same. You should avoid the city."

I nod, unease prickling at the back of my neck. I haven't been near the stone city since I lost my soul in its dungeons, but I know it isn't the spirits of the dead haunting its streets. Those are only rumors fed to the continent by my father; a way to protect the multitude of slaves he sent there to mine the abandoned Gireni riches. A faction of the Dark Militia oversees the work, and though the number is minimal compared to the might of Argentum, or even those that perished at my hand in Similis, it's still worrying. Especially if they answer to the Covinus.

The same unease strains Luwei's face. "The last time you told us to meet you in Nadjaa, you never showed. And that was before the spirit of the Darkness itself hunted you." The boy looks far older than his years as he stares down at me, his face lined with the horrors he's endured. The same ones we've all endured, toiling under the heft of the curse. "I pray the gods are merciful, and this time, you keep your word."

"The gods are gone, Luwei." It comes out as more of admonishment than a statement, but as I meet the boy's eyes, I don't take it back. "And the Covinus may have been the catalyst for the Darkness, but he's lived his life in the light. He doesn't understand the shadows the way we do."

Luwei doesn't respond. Only clicks his tongue and guides the black mare out of the cave mouth. Sura keeps her eyes trained on mine. Her normally shining hair is matted and dirty, her face skeletal and streaked with blood. But her voice is strong when she says, "Do not let her break, Shaw."

"Be safe," I reply. And with another click of Luwei's tongue, they're gone.

I gaze out at the white landscape, the city lights glowing in the far horizon. The previous night's snowstorm has softened the normally rugged landscape, but it has done nothing to soften my heart. My flame rises in my chest, licks up my throat, and for a moment I stand frozen, uncertain whether I will give in to its call and burn the entire northern territory to the ground.

I could do it. I could end it all.

A few months ago, even before the loss of my soul, I probably would have.

But my heart has torn and stretched and grown since then, and now, the moment is about more than my hate, more than my vengeance. Avedis gave up his soul so I wouldn't lose mine. I won't dishonor his sacrifice by giving it up willingly.

I clap my hands together and at the wave of my arms, a wall of flame as high as the walls of Argentum itself rises in front of the approaching militia. The fire flickers and ripples like a river, shades of red and orange and the palest blue undulating atop the snow. Heat radiates in great waves, and the snow melts in giant swaths, the water steaming up into the air.

I feed everything I've pushed down since Mirren was taken, everything I've refused to feel, and the wall rises higher. But it does not consume. It stays where it is, a glowing boundary between us and everything that seeks to destroy us. A barrier, and one that will be broken through by the water-wielders soon enough. But it will buy us some time. And it will lead them away from Sura and Luwei.

When I turn back toward the cave, I find Mirren watching me. Her arms are crossed protectively over her chest, like she's determined to keep pieces of herself from spilling into the dirt. Words bubble up and lodge in my throat, a weighted silence stretching between us. What words could possibly ease her heart in this moment? I've always found well-meaning sentiments to be hollow and dismissive, for words can't mend the gaping emptiness of loss; they cannot fill an aching void.

So without speaking, I wrap my fingers around her small waist and lift her onto Dahiitii. With practiced ease, I swing myself up behind her and pull her close to my chest, enveloping her thighs with mine.

Even now that I've released it, I can feel the wall of flame behind me as the militia begins to attack. Water cannons pierce the writhing heat, while winds whip frenetically from every direction in an attempt to suffocate it. I feel the attacks in my bones, in my abyss, a draining exertion.

Rather than acknowledge the exhaustion, I tuck my fingers gently under Mirren's chin and pull her gaze to mine. Something inside me cracks at her hollow eyes, and I'm not even sure whether it's her soul or mine. "I've got you," I whisper fervently. "Whatever the darkness, however far you need to fall into it, I've got you."

Mirren stares up at me with shining eyes, but beneath the stark echo of her grief, something sparks. A pinprick of light, a glimpse of the wild creature I saw in her the first night we met. The one who speaks to the most primal parts of myself. Its presence grounds me, assures me that though the world is crashing around her, she still has enough fight to survive. To make it through.

I kiss her forehead softly and tuck my cloak more tightly around her. Nudging Dahiitii forward, we begin our descent into the depths of the mountains.

The Xamani call the range Beh Ahti, meaning sharp rock, as the range doesn't rise gradually in elevation. Spires stick up straight from level ground, forming a natural sort of a prison to those unfortunate enough to be trapped in Argentum. But it isn't the mountains themselves that are unique. It's what lies beneath them: labyrinthine cave systems, carved by a millennium of erosion. Some wind and sprawl, while others are too narrow for even a child to fit through. Their path is mostly senseless, more often than not leading to caverns long caved in, but they're also our best option, so long as I can remember the way.

I used these tunnels as a boy often, hiding in the caves from my father until the shame of my violence abated enough for me to face him once more. I nursed injuries in the shelter of the rocks and used the passages as a quick route between the east and the west. South of here, it was in one of these very caves that Mirren and I discovered her penchant for nature-wielding. These caverns were as familiar to me as the Nemoran, but it's been years since I've used them to travel, and I'm sure the mountains have taken back many of the routes in my time away.

But as we ride into the darkness, the inky black passage lit only by the small flame I've conjured in my palm, I don't think of what will happen if we find ourselves blocked by a cave in. I have Mirren, and that's enough to ensure I don't fail.

~

We ride for a few hours, drawing deeper into the depths of the mountains. The stone is the same color as the Castellium, and I try not to pay attention to the way the water drips over the ridged surface. When we come to a fork in the tunnel, Mirren and I both dismount, leading Dahiitii by the reins into the narrowest passage. It veers sharply to the right, and then curves back toward Argentum, its path tracing much of the same ground we've already traveled. But the walls shrink so tightly around us, there is only room for one horse to move in a single file, which means there's no way an entire militia will be able to follow.

I lead us through four more sharp turns, before we begin southwest toward Yen Girene. We're now so deep in the earth, the world exists in muted silence, the only sound the echo of the horses feet and our own labored breathing. Avedis is still unconscious atop his horse, a blessing in a day of curses. He needs to be far away from Argentum, from the Covinus' control when he wakes. From this distance, he'll still feel the pull of the command tightening around his chest, but he should be able to ignore it long enough to listen.

That is, if he doesn't try to kill me the moment his eyes open, which is a distinct possibility.

Mirren hasn't spoken at all, and though I understand why, it only feeds the unease that's dug itself into the back of my mind. Even on our first journey to Nadjaa together, when I'd half-hated, half-loved her, her voice had been a welcome solace from my spiraling mind. And without it's grounding comfort, my thoughts now wander unbidden into dangerous places; places where light is an imagined entity.

I worry for Mirren; I ache for Cal and Max. I look back at Avedis' sleeping face and feel so much guilt, I think I'll vomit. And beneath all of it, regret for Easton, for the life he had just begun to build. More potential cut short by the Darkness, another soul swallowed by greed and power.

When we finally stop to rest in a small, hollowed out room, the air around me has begun to feel viscous, like my limbs are moving through mud. And when I help Mirren from Dahiitii, and she doesn't even muster the strength to snipe at me for it, the feeling only grows. I have no idea what time it is, as the dark is pervasive here no matter the hour, but the exhaustion in my body makes it feel like it's midnight in the middle of winter. Like the sun will never shine again.

Mirren sits against the cragged wall and tucks herself into the overlarge cloak, pulling her knees up to her chest and wrapping her arms around them, like she can make herself smaller than she already is. Like she can shrink enough to disappear into the stone.

I coax a small fire to life at the center of the room, and though we have no wood, it burns merrily. Pilfering what remains of our stores from Dahiitii's saddlebags, I hand some jerky and dried fruit to Mirren before settling beside her. I watch with furtive glances as she fiddles halfheartedly with the food, turning it over absently in her palm.

Grief has a way of stealing even the heartiest of appetites, but she's lost a visible amount of weight during her time in captivity.

"I'm afraid starving yourself still won't teach me a lesson," I say into the silence, intense relief washing over me as her eyes *finally* snap to mine. She's barely looked at me since I burned her brother's body, those emerald eyes perpetually downcast as she berates herself with all the ways she's to blame for his death. And I'm determined to spare her from as much of it as I can, even if it's by shouldering her anger. "Though if this is a campaign to buy you more of Evie's pastries, you may be on to something."

Mirren's mouth twists and her eyes flash as she decides whether she has the energy to respond. After a few long beats, she says, "I would have gotten myself kidnapped months ago if I knew it'd earn me more of those." Her voice is hardly more than a whisper, but she holds my gaze.

I let it smooth the restlessness in my skin, the prickling in my throat. Because there she is: not lost in the dungeons of the Castellium, or blown away by the wind along with her brother. Here. With me. And maybe, in this moment, she doesn't need poignant words. Maybe she just needs a distraction, something to hold onto. "It would have been easy, as you seem to have a penchant for it, Lemming. I think this is your fifth one."

"Fourth," she amends. "Avedis doesn't count. That was a murder attempt, not a kidnapping."

At her prim tone of voice and the absurdity of the sentiment—perhaps at the absurdity of life itself and the tangled mess of it—we both burst into laughter. Mildly crazed and desperate, it echoes off the damp rock of the cavern and out into the passage. When it reverberates back, the sound breaks something open in Mirren, and I can almost feel the crack in my own heart, as tears suddenly begin to pour down her cheeks.

Hot, fat droplets skim her skin and drip into her lap, disappearing into the thick fabric of the cloak. She doesn't acknowledge them, only swipes impatiently at her cheeks and burrows further into my side as I wrap my arm around her shoulders.

And then she eats. Tears falling, nose sniffling, she eats every bite.

When she's finished and her tears have dried, she's quiet for so long I think she's fallen asleep. Until she asks, "What are we going to do when he wakes up?"

I make a humming noise in the back of my throat, following her gaze to where Avedis' bulking form is still slumped over the saddle. "Could you heal him while he's unconscious, or does he need to be awake? Because I can tie him up, but bonds won't keep him from sucking the air from both our lungs."

Mirren stares at me. The sheen of tears magnifies her eyes, and as I study them, I'm reminded of the same sea that haunted my dreams as a soulless; as a child with a lethal fever.

I am still staring when she says, "Anrai." My name is a whispered hush, and though it wraps around me the way it always does when she says it, something cold settles against the base of my spine. Because I know.

Know what she will say, the truth of Avedis' condition. I want to cover my ears like a child. Shake my head and stomp my feet—anything to drown out the truth. But I keep my hands balled tightly in my lap and force myself to listen, because there are no falsities between Mirren and I. Even when the truth is unbearable.

"I can't heal Avedis." Mirren gasps, another sob ripping

from her. "I only managed to heal yours because you had a piece of my soul for me to hold onto. If I tried to do it with someone else..." She sucks in a breath, her cheeks shimmering with tears and firelight. "I think I'd be lost."

Her words are a physical blow to my sternum, and for a moment, I can't breathe. Avedis gave up his soul to save mine, and if there is no returning it—if it's truly gone forever—I have to accept the full responsibility. I have so much to hold up every day, all the lives I've taken and destroyed. I move with the weight of the world pressing down on my shoulders, wrapping around my heart, and some days, even moving my feet one step feels untenable.

I have not even learned to lift Nehuan's death, and now, I must take Avedis' ruin as well. Will his soul be the final brick? The one that breaks me entirely?

No. You do not break when others do. You do not relent while Mirren isn't safe.

You persist.

Abruptly, I stand up and stride toward Avedis. Staring at his prostrate form, I allow myself two deep breaths. And then I descend into the abyss, coaxing it up and through me, allowing it to take over. Erecting the ruthless assassin piece by marble piece, until there is nothing that can break through it.

I haul the wind-wielder off the horse. His head bobs like a sleeping child against my shoulder as I drag him to the back of the small cavern and shove him up against the wall in a sitting position. Fire flickers to life at my palm as I crouch in front of Avedis, and carefully wind the flame in a tight circle around his body.

When I look over my shoulder to Mirren, there's no outward sign of Anrai, no evidence of his soft and yearning heart. Only the assassin, the villain. "We still need him for the prophecy. And if we can't restore his soul, we'll have to think of other ways to force his compliance."

Mirren nods dutifully, but there is hesitation in her eyes. And I know it isn't hesitancy for the soulless man who murdered her brother—it's for me. For what I'll need to do to convince him.

She's right to be hesitant. Because for her, for her dream of light and hope for humanity, I would split the very fabric of the world. I would commit every atrocity imaginable, destroy every semblance of life, to ensure she never feels this way again.

Swallowing roughly, I wave my hand and allow a few scorching tendrils to lick at the edges of the bedroll wrapped around Avedis. It has it's intended effect: his entire body goes taut as the smell of smoke winds gently around him, a smell his body now recognizes as pain. His dark eyes snap open, zeroing in on me with the immediacy only a predator could manage. They are fathomless pits, the irises lined with the promise of death, of agony.

And in them, I recognize the ravening hunger, the madness that exists where a soul once resided.

I grin humorlessly, matching his insanity, as I say, "Hello, friend."

CHAPTER
TWENTY-SIX

Shaw

The first moments of waking after I lost my soul are still branded in my mind—trapped beneath the earth in the dungeons of the Castellium, enflamed with a power I didn't understand. My father's face above mine, calm and calculating as he watched me writhe and burn. I'd felt untethered by the pain and darkness, as there were no longer any pieces of myself I recognized. The feel of my own body was unfamiliar, consumed as it was. There was nothing to hold on to, and so I felt I would fall forever into the hollow, endlessly burning.

I don't know whether it was the loss of my memories or of the soul itself. Maybe it was my flame waking with nothing to sustain it. But when I opened my eyes in that dungeon, there was nothing human in me—there was only emptiness and a ravaging hunger.

As Avedis' studies me, the same madness radiates from him in waves.

The urge to consume, to hurt.

To fill what's lacking.

I've secured his wrists behind his back with a tendril of flame, and his ankles are bonded in front of him in the same manner. The ring of fire burns mere inches away from his skin, and while none of it hurts him now, the same won't be true if he tries to escape or summon his power.

He gazes furiously at me and shifts his hips slightly, the movement so surreptitious, it wouldn't be noticeable to anyone else. But I know Avedis, have watched him for months with the same level of detail I'd study any threat. He may not have his memories, but the sort of training we've both endured is carved into our bones, embedded in our muscles. He's testing his bonds. How far he can move before the pain immobilizes him.

Which means I'll need to talk quickly, before he figures his way out.

"You shall die for this." Though his words are soft, they're laced with the promise of death. If I release him right now, he'll suck the air from my lungs with no hesitation. As if reading my thoughts, his eyes darken and the air pressure of the cave drops.

"For which part?" I ask with an innocent tilt of my head, pointedly ignoring the way the air has begun to press in on my ears. "Tying you up or saving you from the Covinus' control?"

As I taunt him, I examine his reactions with a razor-sharp gaze. Losing a soul doesn't affect everyone the same way. It depends on who you were when you had one, what attributes were already buried deep when you lost it. Avedis could be rageful and explosive, like I was. Or he could be cool and cunning to get what he wants, a ruthless maneuverer. Only time will reveal his true machinations, but it'll help to know he won't murder us in our sleep simply because he feels like it.

The assassin narrows his eyes, and his face twists in malice. As he opens his mouth to reply, I wave him off indolently. "Save your energy. I already know...you want to disembowel me. Slit my throat. Suck the air from my lungs. Whatever." I roll my eyes. "All very predictable."

Avedis snarls, yanking at his flaming tethers with a hiss of pain. A harsh wind buffets through the small cave, and I crouch closer to the ground to avoid being blown over. "Ah, ah," I scold, feeding my flame to avoid it being snuffed out. "One more move like that, and she'll drown you where you stand." I jerk my head to Mirren. "And I don't think you have the power to take on both of us."

There is no spark of recognition as Avedis' hollow stare comes to rest on Mirren. He studies her with mild curiosity, his tongue swiping over his lower lip like he's considering drinking her power from the other side of the cave.

Mirren only stares back, unmoving.

Avedis sneers, his muscles coiling like his lungs recall what his memory cannot. His mind may not remember what Mirren is capable of, but his body certainly does. The wind dies down to little more than a whisper as Avedis calls it back to him. His raven hair flutters around his face, but for once, it does nothing to soften him. Somehow, it only accentuates his mania.

I try not to remember the call of that same madness, the way it clawed out of my skin, straining to consume everything around me. Pushing the memory aside, I swallow decisively. "I've kept you alive because I have a proposition for you, Wind-wielder."

A terrifying grin splits his face. "And why would I entertain an offer from a man daft enough to chain a wind-wielder? Water may not be snuffed out by wind, but I assure you, the air in her lungs answers to me the same as any."

The air begins to whip again in demonstration and his gaze is absolutely feral as it cuts back to Mirren. I grit my teeth in annoyance and dig my fingers into my palm to keep from tearing into him for daring to look at her like that. I should have known losing his soul would bring out Avedis' most irritating qualities, his penchant for arrogance and drama being the top among them. "Because I'm the only reason your sorry ass isn't a slave for the Covinus right now."

This snaps his attention back to me, and the air quiets.

"You can feel it even now...that tether wrapped around your chest. The one that squeezes until you bend to its call."

He doesn't reply, only presses his lips together.

"You awoke lost in the emptiness, his command in your head the only ledge to hold onto. And you followed it to make the pain stop, to fill the emptiness. But it will never do either of those things. There will always be another order. Your choices will never again be your own."

Avedis goes deathly still. Perhaps because of the truth imbuing my words, my own raw wound still apparent. Or perhaps his body not only remembers Mirren, but the time before. A time when his decisions, his sword, his body, had not been his own.

"The further away from him you are, the easier it is to ignore the commands. But when he finds you again, you'll have no power unless he wishes it so." The flame around him spurts and flickers wildly, writhing against the memory. "And you may not remember it now, assassin, but you have vowed never to be another's puppet again."

Avedis is silent for so long, I don't think he'll answer. His eyes bore into me, and I resist the urge to shiver. The color has always reminded me of a night sky over a city—dark, but never completely black. The pigment hasn't changed, but now, I am only reminded of a void, the vacuous space between the stars.

"How?" His voice slices through the silence.

"How what?"

"How did the Covinus take control of my soul?"

Dread slithers up my spine, coming to rest on my shoulders where guilt already weighs. But I only stare him down flatly. His mouth twists and he shakes his head with a scoff of disbelief. "As I thought. You profess to want to save me from his control, while it is *your* ineptitude that led me to it in the first place. And now, you hold me under threat of torture to plead for my help?"

The air between us grows so thick, I could slice it with a knife.

Avedis lets out another disbelieving laugh. "You're either truly idiotic or extremely brave, neither of which I have use for. So, which is it, Fire-bearer? Are you foolish enough to admit your weakness, or brave enough to exploit mine?"

"Avedis," Mirren's voice floats softly from behind me.

The assassin's gaze slides over my shoulder, fixing on the delicate mouth that spoke. The urge to jump in front of her, to protect her from that searing hunger, rises up so fiercely, I clamp my hands to my side. But Mirren doesn't flinch away from it. She doesn't move at all. Just stares and stares at Avedis as if she can see through what he is now, straight to the man he was. I don't tell her he's gone—that she may as well be appealing to a stone wall—because she knows better than most. How could she not, when she spent the last few months with the most depraved version of me?

Mirren stands, taking a few strides toward us. Her full lips turn down in a concentrated frown as she drinks in the lines of Avedis. Where they are the same, and where they diverge from the friend she knew. "Shaw told you to leave the city. He was going to sacrifice himself so we could all get out unharmed. But you chose to go back for him. You knew the risks and you chose it anyway, because that's the man you were."

Avedis' lip curls. "Well then, I most certainly deserve this soulless existence as punishment for being foolhardy enough to put my faith in other people. Especially the bastard Heir of the Praeceptor."

His eyes cloud and his words stop short, as if the memory of who I am has caught him off guard. With another shake of his head, the hesitation is gone, replaced by feral violence.

Mirren's jaw tightens and her eyes begin to churn. In them is the same determination that convinced her I was worth saving against all odds—determination that never wavered, even as the world sought to tear it apart.

But she said herself, this is different. There *is* no saving Avedis, no magical cure for his soullessness. This is what he will remain until he meets the Darkness' final calling.

"Mirren," I say softly, a warning as much for her as for myself. I cannot afford to hope now. Not when it could get us killed.

"You put your faith in us then because we were your friends. And if you don't have faith in us now, trust that we know you well enough to know you have no other choice than to come with us."

Avedis tsks, shifting against his bonds once more. The flame bites at the bare skin of his wrists, and he hisses angrily. "Ah, but that's the beauty of the Darkness, is it not,

Sea Witch? The way I see it, I have endless choices and none of them are encumbered by pesky little things like morals." His dark eyes glint in the firelight. "I'm free to murder to my empty heart's content. Free to destroy whatever I please, and *fuck* whomever I please." He cocks his head and runs his gaze from Mirren's head to her toes. "So tell me again about this *choice* I don't have."

Mirren doesn't falter. "You're going to come with us to Nadjaa. Because if you don't, you'll be running until the end of your days. The Covinus can't die, Avedis. You'll never know a moment's peace again."

"I know no peace now," he snarls, his voice like clashing steel.

"Maybe not." Mirren shrugs. "But you know true freedom. And you won't give it up so easily."

Avedis stares up at her hatefully from under his lashes, mulling over her words. When his eyes snap back to me, it's with barely concealed disdain. "You should have had her speak to me from the start. She's far more convincing than you."

I'm not even offended, as it's the truth. But then, the assassin's gaze shifts back to her, and his spite becomes something that edges appreciation. "Forgive me for not being able to remember our relationship, Ocean-wielder, but I must say, I find myself irrevocably drawn to your strength. We should ditch the barbaric hot head and find a bed in which to thoroughly *test* your resiliency." Avedis bites his lower lip lasciviously. "And perhaps mine as well."

There is no thought, nothing other than an explosion of flame around Avedis that mirrors the one in my chest. "Shaw," Mirren's exhausted voice freezes me where I am, "I don't have the energy for you going all feral and killing him."

I suck in a deep breath, drawing the flames back to their neat lines around the assassin's limbs. I don't dare open my mouth for fear of releasing the ones that lash on my tongue.

Avedis grins wickedly at having successfully bated me. His face is still filled with fervent hunger, but as I gather myself, I realize it isn't the same hunger that fills me when I touch Mirren—it isn't full and warm. It doesn't demand he pleasure her: it demands he *break* her.

"Ah yes, love. You don't need a savage fire-beast when your tastes are clearly far more...refined." His eyes slither to where I stand frozen, my lips mashed together, and victory lights his face. I curse myself for letting him get under my skin, for allowing him a crack to glimpse what's protected inside.

Avedis has always been an excellent read of character, a skill which has aided in keeping him alive and out of Akari Ilinka's hands for so long. But now, without his soul to ground the skill, he uses it to sow discord. To twist others and feed on their discomfort, and stupidly, I've played right into his hands.

Mirren fits the assassin with a sharp look. "If you call me 'love' ever again, I'll drown you where you stand." To me, she says, "Release him."

I gape at her. "Mirren..."

"He isn't going to kill us if he knows what's good for him. He's agreed to help."

Avedis raises a brow delicately. "Have I, then? I don't recall agreeing to any such thing."

Mirren throws a hand on her hip, stomping forward to glare down at the wind-wielder. He watches her right back, but as the moments draw on and she still says nothing, Avedis drops his eyes. I bite back laughter. Apparently,

Mirren's ability to assert authority over soulless assassins was not a one-time talent.

Avedis shifts primly, the habit so familiar to his soulful self, I have to blink against it. "You heard the lady then," he sighs, gesturing halfheartedly like he's about to be subjected to a Similian lecture. "Release me, you unbearable *prick* of a Fire-bringer, and I promise to listen. But that's all I'll promise."

With a wave of my hand, the fire at his wrists and ankles winks out. The circle around him crawls back to me in a slow line, before wrapping around my legs and spooling up my stomach to curl around my chest and neck. "Your promises mean nothing with no soul," is all I say.

"Well then you won't mind if I promise to murder you the next time a lick of your flame so much as brushes against me." Avedis pushes himself to standing, and the bed roll falls away, leaving only a few tatters of the remaining fabric of his clothes to cover his massive form.

But rather than being embarrassed by his nakedness, Avedis' face is incensed as he pinches at a particularly scorched section of what used to be his shirt. "This was Baakan stitched!" he cries, aghast, rounding on me with newfound fervor. "My soul is one thing—my clothes, absolutely another!"

Mirren steps deftly between us, plucking up the bedroll and shoving it into Avedis' arms. "I healed your skin, but I'm afraid sewing has never been my specialty."

Remembering himself, he dips his head irreverently to Mirren. "Many thanks for keeping my handsome looks intact, witch."

Mirren clenches her jaw, but she says nothing else. A part of me wants to wrap her in my arms and hide her from the sting of memory, to shield her from world's brutal ability to create more. But the primal part of me keeps me exactly where I am, which is safely between her and the wind-wielder. He's too unpredictable to let our guard down. He's already shown what happens when he's underestimated.

"Did you take the coin from my pocket? Before you threw me over the wall?"

Avedis narrows his eyes at my sudden change of subject. "Judging by your attire, I have far more coin than you could ever dream. What would I want with the paltry contents of your pockets?"

I push a sharp sigh through my nostrils. "The Covinus is stealing the souls of wielders and controlling them with two coins. That's how the Praeceptor controlled me, and it's how you're being held as well."

Avedis examines his nails and sighs, before blinking slowly at me. "As I've said, Fire-beast, I haven't all night for your tiresome tales. Get on with it."

Irritation prickles at the back of my neck. Avedis should thank the dead gods for the prophecy, because if he wasn't needed, I'd kill him right now to spare myself his unbearable snark. "The Dead Prophecy," I bite out, trying a different approach. "You're one of the four wielders needed to break the curse of Darkness."

Avedis lets out a noise somewhere between a laugh and a scoff. "And why would *I* be interested in breaking some silly curse?" He grins, his teeth gleaming white in the shadows of the cave. "I am the Darkness now and I kneel at the altar of depravity and sin." The way his lips wrap around the word 'sin' sends my flame sparking wildly up my arms. I dig my nails into my palms so hard, blood blooms beneath my nails.

The assassin continues, "I care not what happens to the

rest of Ferusa, so long as there's still a place for me to have my fun."

Mirren sighs as she comes to stand next to me, the sound strained with her exhaustion. "You care because the only way to break the Covinus' control over you is to break his power. And we can't do that while the curse is still feeding him souls."

Avedis makes a humming noise of neither agreement nor disagreement, but Mirren, as if reading his thoughts, presses on. "It's one thing to evade capture from one warlord, Avedis. It's quite another to have two hunting you. One who cannot die and controls your soul."

The wind-wielder's gaze shifts from irreverently disinterested into malevolence so dark, I wonder if Mirren's words have unintentionally unearthed a memory of the witch-queen. If so, Avedis gives no indication. He only shrugs and says, "I'll think on it and gift you my decision in the morning." Then he yawns dramatically. "As for now, I need my beauty sleep." He nods to the dark passageway. "And if you don't mind, I'll sleep in there to be sure neither of you decide to off me during the night."

With that, he strides out of the cave, wind billowing behind him. With a wave of his hand, the air between the two rooms blurs as he erects a hard shield to prevent us from following. I mutter a curse under my breath, and shoot a wall of flame at it, my own insurance he won't wake and decide to amuse himself by slitting our throats.

I lay out a bedroll and coax Mirren into it, before curling myself gently around her. I've never treated her delicately —there is no soft way to hold onto a current that pulls you home. There is only digging your fingers in and holding on for dear life, lest you lose it and find yourself adrift. But right now, she feels so fragile in my arms, I move gingerly.

Her tears have dried, but the hurt in her body resounds in our soul, a cold and metallic thing. It is not the same emptiness as being soulless; this one is full, almost *too* full, and it presses against her so roughly, one wrong move will shatter her and send all of it spilling through the cracks.

So, I am careful as I stroke her arm, her head, her hair, until finally both of us are lulled into a fitful sleep.

And when we wake in the morning, Avedis is gone.

Chapter
Twenty-Seven

Calloway

It's a fool's game really, to think I'll be able to distract an entire militia long enough for the others to escape, but no one has ever mistaken me for practical. My idealism is unfailing, fed by my faith in Max and Harlan, even as the grasses of the Breelyn Plain split like a stream around a rock and the witch-queen's forces march toward me.

I press my thighs together, steadying myself on top of the saddle. Letting go of the reins, I notch an arrow and line up my sights. And then I let my arrows sing. One right after another, they fly into the ranks.

My aim is not what it was before I lost my eye, but it's still far better than most, thanks to both my father and Anni's continued training. The witch-queen's militia has been weakened by their defeat in Similis, and it's only this disorganization that grants me the small reprieve of surprise. The front lines disintegrate into chaos as some of the arrows speckle the ground before them, while others stick straight into their shields.

A few soldiers fall, while others are trampled by their

panicking comrades. With all the magic flying around Ferusa, they think they're under the attack of a wielder, as no ordinary person would be stupid enough to ride head on into an approaching army. And though I'm only a momentary distraction, my chest is filled with heady light. Intoxicating, addicting, it's the same feeling as earning a bout of laughter from my serious little sister, or from lightening the load of Darkness Anni carries with a well-timed barb.

This will do the same: buy the people I love a breath of mercy, a glimpse of light in the ever-present Darkness of the continent.

Arrows whiz past me as I gallop toward the approaching army, drawing close enough to hear the barked orders of the commanders. I duck and weave on the saddle, but I don't slow even as the front lines begin to reform. As they realize I am not supernatural; I am nothing but a man with a bow.

The militia surges for me, but the sounds of the plain fade. I cannot hear the plod of hooves or the thunder of men. Even the winds whipping across the grass have fallen silent.

I only hear Vee's laughter.

And I let it ring through my veins, warming my chest and solidifying my spine into something stronger than steel.

Because with it, comes the realization it has never mattered that I never took revenge for their deaths. What matters is what I've done with their memory. Mama and Papa, Lila and Vee, taught me how to create a home, to love. And instead of acting in the hate borne of their last moments, I have lived in the love of every moment that came before.

And perhaps what would make them most proud, is I

have gifted it to others. The ones sacrificed and brutalized like Max and Anrai, the forgotten like Mirren, the shamed like Harlan. I've spent my days teaching them the same lessons my family instilled in me.

I can now see the glare of the soldier's teeth, the whites of their eyes, and when I grasp at my quiver, I find it empty. Three arrows fly toward me, two sailing well over my head, but the other landing true. Hot agony radiates from my shoulder, but I don't stop the horse. Bow in hand, I open up my arms and close my eyes. Ready for one last act of love.

Until my name rings out across the grasses. Thick, panicked, somehow carried over the din of battle. Like its speaker wills the word itself to be enough to pull me back, to halt the flow of time.

Panic surges up my throat, and when I whip my head toward the sound, it balloons into something pervasive that spears through every part of me. The golden hue of him is visible even in the growing dark, his hair windswept and wild as Harlan darts through the tall grass to my left. Similian rifle raised, he begins shooting, veering toward me.

Time warps and stretches as fear clamps over my chest, restricting my breathing. *Save yourself. Take what I give you.*

But I can tell by Harlan's demeanor, by his stubborn stance, he has no intention of turning around. His jaw is set in determination and there is no hesitation in his strides. And suddenly I understand: if I'm going to meet my end at the hands of this militia, Harlan will, too.

The realization is like waking up, and I swing my sword with my good arm at the soldiers clustered around my horse. My soul tears, but I hardly feel it over the emotion clogging my throat. Because in my most private moments, it hasn't been the cut of Harlan's waist or the irresistible pout of his lips against the slant of his hard jaw that I've imagined.

It's the look on his face now. The way it would look if a man like him—kind and faithful and brave—loved me.

And now that it's out in the open, vulnerable, and beautiful, a terror I've never felt settles over me. I've never been Anni with his unflappable bravery—I've been scared more times than I can remember. But in this moment, the fear is different. Sharper. One that slices deeper than my skin, past my heart and lungs.

Into my soul.

"Harlan, run! Save yourself!" I shout desperately, but my words are swallowed by the din of soldiers. And it's too late anyway, too late to keep him from harm, as he's caught their attention.

I'm helpless to do anything but watch them swarm toward him. Helpless, even as I yank the horse and dig my heels into her flanks, as I arc my sword toward throats and bellies. As another arrow slices my thigh.

I fight my way toward him with a desperation that muddies the world around me. Weapons flash and blood spurts, and somehow, I only see the space between us that never seems to shrink. There's no way to make it to him, and I want to scream at the unfairness of it. Both doomed to die a hundred feet apart.

Harlan zags, surprisingly nimble on his feet as arrows rain down around him. One skims his cheek, and he stumbles, just as a giant sword comes swinging at me from the side.

I'm thrown sideways off the horse, landing with a hard blow to the spine that knocks the wind from me. The horse bolts, and my palms scrape against loose dirt as I scramble to regrip my blade. Swinging it around with a roar, I slice through the soldier's stomach and shove myself to my feet, even as I'm swarmed by more swords. A jab to my shoulder, a cut to my forearm. They don't stop coming, a white wave of dread and weapons.

I lose sight of Harlan as he's swallowed by soldiers. I'm still yelling his name into the void, yelling it even as my own voice is drowned out.

Swords ring and blood pours and soldiers fall. My soul tears, once and then twice more, as I slice my way toward where Harlan disappeared under the throng of soldiers. *Too late. Always too late.*

And then, the world around us begins to shift.

I feel it in the air before anything happens, like the atmosphere itself shudders and twists. And then, soldiers begin to scream.

I slice through limbs, and kick out at bodies, trying to plow my way through. When I finally find an opening between bodies and grass and horses, I strain to see what's happening. Thirty feet away, where I last glimpsed Harlan before he was inundated, soldiers begin to collapse, though I can't see any weapon that fells them.

Their screams are harrowing, their unseen terror digging a hollow into my chest.

Then the soldiers around me begin to scream, and I no longer have any question as to the source of their fear. The golden grasses of the plain tremor and shake, their stalks splitting down to the roots. And from them, giant shoots burst from the ground. Thick, thorny tendrils wider than the streets of Nadjaa wrap around the witch-queen's militia, while smaller sprigs wind up the soldiers' legs, coiling until they are immobilized, and then pulling them waist deep into the ground.

I've forgotten how to breath as the ground around us

shudders and cracks. I dive sideways as a tree as large as the ones in the Nemoran shoots toward the sky, growing to full maturation in a matter of seconds. Green leaves dance and shimmer above me as I run, threading my way through the rapidly growing forest.

None of the vines touch me, even as I leap over soldiers stuck to varying degrees, all hollering desperately for help. I trip, my speed propelling me into the ground face first. My palms scrape against the dirt, and even as I scramble to my feet, the vibrations of the ever-moving earth send the pebbles skating across the ground like a river.

All around the world has turned into a writhing creature, the vines and trees its tentacles. The forest grows so thick, it blots out the moon, and for a moment, everything is shadowed in impenetrable night.

As quickly as it began, everything ceases. Eerie silence falls over the plain, it's echo made more apparent by how deafening the sound had been only moments before.

Panting, I climb to my feet, hardly daring to look behind me. When I finally do, all I can do is gape.

Moments earlier, an entire militia had crowded these plains. But now, there are no sign of any of the soldiers. Instead, looking as if it's stood for a thousand years rather than a few seconds, is the thickest forest I've ever seen. Wilder than the Nemoran, more dense than any in Baak. Towering trees line the border, and thick foliage fills in the space between them so fully, no light escapes the depths. Plants I don't recognize, or perhaps don't even exist, have trapped all of Akari Ilinka's forces within their grasp.

I am still staring up at its pure mass, attempting to make sense of what just happened, when a small voice behind me says, "Shaw told me to protect you."

I whirl around to see Helias, his dark eyes wide with

apprehension as he approaches me slowly. Like he'll be scolded. Words leave me entirely as I gape between the little earth-wielder and the giant forest, a condition which rarely besets me. Generally speaking, most circumstances only cause my words to come out faster and less filtered, but right now, I can find none of them.

Helias bites his lip and kicks at the dirt. "But I remembered what you said. I didn't kill them. Just trapped them a little bit."

"Helias, your power..." My words trail off, the wonder and horror of what the little boy just did mingling furiously in my stomach.

"I know it was bad," Helias sniffs, avoiding my eyes. And then, in a voice that sounds nothing like his own, but instead, eerily similar to the whispers of the Community he was born to, "Unnatural. Evil." Each word is a harsh snap of teeth. "Abomination, *wrong*—"

I don't allow him to finish as I snap him up into my arms and bury my face in his shoulder. I won't allow another drop of the Covinus' poison to spread through him, to make him hate who he is. His small body relaxes against me as he presses his nose into my collarbone and makes a little hiccupping noise. When I pull back, I force him to meet my gaze. "Nothing about what you just did was unnatural or evil."

The boy's face twists, like he may cry or laugh and hasn't decided which, but he masters it with an ability that breaks my heart all over again. "It was beautiful, Helias. Do you understand? Everything about you is beautiful. Don't you ever let anyone make you feel ashamed for who you are."

Helias' face smooths, and something in the depths of his eyes sparkles. And I realize now, Gislan was never the earth-wielder meant for the prophecy. While he possessed the power of the earth, he'd only been able to move it. Helias literally *commands* it; rules everything growing from its soil, nurtured in its womb.

"You are the true earth-wielder," I murmur to the boy, hugging him to me once more, "and you're perfect just the way you are." When I set him down, it's with a ruffle of his curls and a laugh of mingled relief and exhaled terror.

And when Harlan comes limping out from around a particularly gnarled tower of black-thorned vines, my laughter grows, a lightness I haven't felt since we were all together in Similis ballooning in my chest. And when his eyes meet mine, relieved and soft and shining, I swear, I can feel it in my bones.

I don't stop to think of everything tangled between us, the people and the traumas and the heartbreak—I only think of that feeling, of *him,* as I race toward him. To touch him and confirm the life thrumming through his veins; to drink it for my own and get high on the relief of surviving.

I stop just short of him, knowing the Similian discomfort with touch, but without hesitation, Harlan closes the remaining distance between us and steps into my space. So close he breathes my air, as I breathe his. "You can't ever do that to me again."

Words are my eternal companion, and though they usually flood from me in an uncontrollable wave, they leave me entirely for the second time in the expanse of ten minutes. "Okay," I answer stupidly.

"You can't," he says again, and this time, Harlan's voice cracks, and his unflappable calm cracks along with it. A fracture, hardly visible until it begins to break, the small fissures spidering across his skin and leaving his heart beneath wide open. His fingers flare wide at his sides before crumpling into a fist, like he can hold himself in place, together, if he doesn't move.

But he doesn't need to hold himself together. And neither do I. "Okay," I say again, this time, hardly more than a whisper.

His throat bobs and I follow the movement, somehow intriguingly masculine but cuttingly vulnerable at the same time.

"Calloway..." he pleads, and gods, I understand it in the depths of my soul. Understand it beyond the trappings of words or laughter, beyond anything tangible.

And it is in that understanding that I pull him to me and kiss him. His lips are deliciously soft and lush, but his body is hard against mine, solid and unwavering. And when we lean into each other and neither of us stumbles back, each of our bodies holding the other up, I think, *this is home built strong enough.*

CHAPTER
TWENTY-EIGHT

Mirren

The tunnel system below the mountains is a confusing maze of dead ends and cave ins. Some shafts veer off sharply and circle back toward Argentum, while others appear to go nowhere at all. A few lead straight down, and a distant part of me wonders if they lead to the pits of the Darkness itself. The occasional shout echoes through the passages, and though I'd been unnerved at first, I understand now the sounds are coming from miles away.

Sound travels differently here, suspended beneath the earth, and so do my thoughts. They stay frozen in stasis, suspended above me in a whirling cloud I can't seem to touch.

As I follow Anrai, I feel increasingly untethered. A part of me floats above my body, while the other, darker part threatens to drive me straight into the rock. Into the depths of the mountains below where I'll never find my way out again.

Only Anrai's hand in mine keeps me grounded to the tunnel as we walk. He's careful to keep stride beside me, and a part of me wishes he wouldn't—that he wouldn't consult me or keep me informed on where we're headed. A part of me wishes desperately to be treated as weak, to follow directions blindly. To be kept in numb oblivion rather than be rattled out of it by his faith in me.

But that's never been Anrai.

So, I walk beside him in silence for hours, the soothing clop of Dahiitii's hooves the only sound. My feet grow sore atop the hard ground, and my muscles, wasted as they are, protest as the miles pass slowly. The passage ceiling is too low to ride, but even if it wasn't, I'd keep walking. Even as pain begins to radiate up my spine, down the expanse of my back. Even as I shiver with what's surely fever, and sweat beads on my clammy forehead.

Because what is the pain of a whipping compared to death? I deserve this, deserve every bit of it for drawing my brother into my mess.

My determination to endure is for naught under Anrai's shrewd gaze. He takes in even the most minimal altering of my normal gait, and it's only a few moments later that he motions to a small cavern jutting off to the right of the main tunnel. "We'll stop here and rest. We'll make it out of the mountains by the middle of tomorrow."

He doesn't ask about the state of my back, or question why I healed my brother's killer, but not myself. But I feel his pervasive stare, the way it sinks beneath my skin to see everything beneath.

Ushering Dahiitii and I into the cavern, Anrai raises a wall of flame behind us, effectively sealing us off from the main tunnel. We are far too deep now for the militia to find us, but this is still the Dark World; there's always something lurking.

The fire bathes the shallow cave in golden light, and

shadows dance over the walls, illuminating the natural spring that drips softly down from the ceiling. I watch the water, momentarily hypnotized by the swirling hues of orange and red reflected from Anrai's flame.

He refills our canteens, and leads Dahiitii to drink from the spring, before coming to stand before me. His pale eyes reflect the flame like they themselves burn. But as he raises a finger and twists it in the air, I realize they only smolder softly, embers beneath the fire. He cocks a brow, daring me to disobey him.

On another day, I would, as one of my favorite places to be is under his skin. But today, I turn around with a huff and plop myself gracelessly on the cold floor. Pulling my legs up to my chest, I wrap my arms around my knees and curl into myself.

Anrai kneels behind me and gently peels off the top of my jumpsuit. A sharp breath hisses from him, almost like he doesn't quite mean it to. For a moment, everything in the cave seems to freeze as he takes in the state of my injuries. Of the once pristine skin, now shredded.

My muscles tense as his silence stretches on for long moments, as I wait for his horror, his pity—even for a snap of his rage. But somehow, he reins it in and instead, he leads me toward the trickling water. He peels off the rest of the jumpsuit and places me gently beneath the stream. It's icy cold against my scalp, but I lean into it with a moan, letting it run over my skin with a shiver.

Wash it away, I plead desperately. *Wash everything away.*

Anrai leaves me to it, turning to ruffle around in one of Dahiitii's saddlebags. By the time he's finished, and has tended to the horse herself, my teeth are chattering violently.

Taking my hand, he leads me toward the middle of the

cavern, the space having grown warm with his fire. Though most of my skin has gone numb, I leave the water reluctantly, its icy touch having soothed the fuzziness that's clouded my head most of the day. Anrai wraps his cloak around my naked body once more, and motions for me to sit. I do as I'm told, and stare mindlessly at the fire as he takes his turn beneath the water.

When he's finished, he comes to sit behind me, his powerful thighs squeezing mine between them. "This is going to sting," he warns. Liquid swishes, and the antiseptic smell of Similis fills my nose. Acid rises in my throat, because Similis, the Healing Center—all of it reminds me of Easton. And I've sworn not to think of my brother, because if I allow myself to ruminate on even the smallest memory of him, it'll crack the paltry wall I've built around my thoughts, and I'll drown.

Thankfully, the sharp current of pain that radiates from my back as Anrai begins to clean my wounds tugs me back from the edge. I focus on the pain, let it overwhelm all my senses until my breathing is labored. Anrai doesn't coddle me or ask if I need a break; he just works perfunctorily, starting at my shoulder and working his way down. And I am grateful for it, for the man he is—one who understands pain.

Moments of silence stretch around us, and when the burning in my back threatens to overwhelm me, and black begins to edge my vision, he says, "Do you think we'll ever see Avedis again? I really thought he was listening to you—as much as a soulless can listen, at least."

Shame surges in my stomach at the worry and guilt lining Anrai's words. When I woke to Avedis' absence, I was worried—but it had also been laced with relief. And rather than examine the maelstrom of emotions the assassin evokes in me, I'd shoved it all down into the recesses of myself along with everything else I'd frozen there. Even my *other* lies curled in a small pool at the center of my chest, a glacier too cold to touch.

It's as if I'm under the spell of the coins, but there is nothing magical about the barren numbness inside me.

"I don't know," I finally reply.

I release a sharp hiss through my teeth as Anrai moves on to the deepest laceration, a thin line that lashes from my right shoulder down to my left hip, the skin over my spine splayed open. My head swims as the disinfectant sinks into the wound. Anrai pauses as I catch my breath, and I want to scream at him to keep going—scream that I am floating into the Darkness, incorporeal and inhuman, and the pain is the only thing keeping me tethered to earth.

But instead, I bite down hard on my lip until I taste blood.

"I think you got through to him, Lemming," Anrai continues, moving on to a few of the smaller wounds. "And he has a habit of turning up when we least expect. Or...I guess when *I* least expect him," he says affectionately. It had only taken Avedis' dedication to me to win Anrai's respect, and I can't decide whether I love him or hate him for it.

When I don't respond, Anrai sets the cloth down beside me, the white fabric now red-stained and soiled. He's allowed me the comfort of a dropped gaze, of retreating so far into myself I can hardly see the world around me.

But now, he slides a finger beneath my jaw and slowly raises my chin until I'm forced to meet his eyes. His gaze is piercing, stealing things from all the places I've tried to hide them, and bringing them to the surface, like the skeletons of lost ships from the bottom of the sea. And as strong as the urge is to shove them back down, I don't look away.

Because he's the only person I trust to hold them.

"It's okay to be mad, Mirren."

"He wasn't himself. It wasn't him," I respond immediately, but my voice sounds rehearsed, like I'm reading a passage from a book.

Anrai dips his head in agreement, without taking his eyes from me. "It wasn't. But your feelings don't need to be rational right now. If you want to be angry, be angry. If you want to be sad, be sad—"

I brush his fingers away from my face and shake my head. "I don't want to *be* anything!" I glare at him fiercely. "I don't want to be angry or sad or hurt or destroyed. I don't want to *think*." My words grow wilder with each syllable, each one slapping against the rock of the cavern like a wave, and somehow, I've spun around to face him. My fists are tangled in his shirt, my fingers dug so tight in the fabric, the blood has leeched from them.

His eyes widen slightly, and his mouth parts.

"*Make* me not think," I growl at him, half-feral, tugging him roughly by the shirt until his face is touches mine, his breath hot against my mouth. Sweet mint and sharp spice fills my nostrils as I inhale deeply, allowing the scent to overwhelm me. If I breathe only him, I'll no longer have to be me.

My tongue swipes to wet my lower lip, and even as Anrai's eyes flare, tracking the movement with predatory focus, he holds himself entirely still. *Too* still.

And suddenly, the only thing that matters is unraveling that control—flaying through that calm façade to unleash the ravenous creature beneath. The animal as dark and primal as I am: who won't hesitate to take everything from me to sate its own demanding hunger, and then give it all back, until all I can remember is the pleasure of *him*. Can only beg for it, reduced to nothing more than a needy body, my mind left somewhere far behind.

"Erase my thoughts, Anrai," I challenge darkly. "Give me something other than pain."

He hesitates, his face lined with worry, and I want to erase that too. I slide into his lap, the overlarge cloak pooling around me, but doing little to hide anything. His breath hitches as I wind my legs around his waist, pressing myself down onto the already hardening length of him. I feel his restraint in his tense muscles, in the heated temperature of his skin, and when I meet his eyes, he looks agonized. Desperate. Ravenous.

"I'm so cold, I'm numb," I tell him, the words barely more than a pleading whisper against his lips. "I don't want to be numb anymore."

Anrai searches my face for another tortuous beat. A tormented noise sounds from the back of his throat, and finally, *finally*, he tangles his fingers in the hair at the nape of my neck, and gently tilts my head to his. His mouth is reverent, his tongue gently massaging my lower lip before sweeping inside to run along mine. His free hand trails down my side, and even as his fingers grip my hip, there is a careful awareness to his touch.

Heat blooms at the surface of my skin and pools at the center of me. I writhe in slow circles on top of him, as he moves his mouth over my jaw to flick the sensitive spot behind my ear. He runs his lips down the side of my throat, his mouth infuriatingly light even as I press closer to him. "Tell me what you want from me, Mirren," he breathes, his words sending sparks shooting through my belly, contrasting currents of heat and ice.

He trails his tongue lightly over the spot where my neck and shoulder meet, before he bites at it so gently, I feel as though I'll come out of my skin. But even as insistent heat burgeons deep within me, and flutters over my cheeks and breasts, it isn't enough. I'm still aware of the cave around us, and the world beyond that, and I *need* Anrai to take it all away—to forget everything but his name, his words, his command.

A needy whimper escapes my mouth as I try to grind down harder, to force him to relieve the growing ache, but his hands at my hip and hair keep me in place as his mouth continues to move leisurely across my collarbone. "Tell me, Mirren. Tell me what you need."

Suddenly, I hate him. I hate his infuriatingly talented mouth, and the way a few strokes of his fingers is all it takes to set me ablaze. Hate how much he sees and his gentle care of it.

I wrench myself abruptly out of his arms and to the other side of the cave, even as my body protests. I rake my fingers through my hair, but it does nothing to soothe the incessant burn, or the throbbing want. When I turn back to Shaw, he's frozen in place, watching me warily. Despite the mussed state of his hair—his swollen lips and scorching gaze that sets the flame in me burning anew—he makes no move to come after me. Because a part of him is still tethered to his worry, still existing somewhere thought and restraint rule. And I won't have that.

I want him as undone as I am.

Tilting my head, I look down at him through hooded eyes, latching on to the hunger in his gaze, as I unclasp the cloak and let it drop to pool at my feet. A thrill shoots through me as I stand bare before him, as his eyes go dark and hooded. He licks at his lips, like he can taste me already. My breasts heave as Anrai runs a greedy gaze down my body, drinking in every curve; worshipping it in the same lascivious manner he would if he used his hands.

But he keeps still, his fingers clenched into fists at the side of him, like he can keep himself anchored through pure will.

Without breaking his gaze, I slowly lower to my knees. And then even more slowly onto all fours. His eyes flare with that fire I crave, unbridled and volatile. When I begin to crawl toward him, my movements lithe and agonizingly slow, the very air around us sparks with heat, and flame shoots from his fingers, scorching handprints into the rock.

Abruptly, he rises to his feet, like the distance will grant him his sanity, but he can't tear his eyes away. His face is sharply cut and beautiful, and when I stop just short of him, gazing up at him from where I kneel, it is absolutely feral. Dangerous.

"Ask me again," I rasp, tilting my head and wetting my lips.

Anrai follows the movement with rapture. "What do you need from me?" The words are hoarse, guttural, and a heady power radiates through me at how easily this powerful man comes undone for me. I'm the one on my knees, but there's no weakness in it. Only addictive power. Control.

"I want you to wreck me," I growl at him, moving to hook my fingers around the waistband of his pants and shimmying them down. And with a noise of pure satisfaction, I swipe my tongue over the tip of his straining erection.

His entire body shudders, tightening and releasing in turn, and he moans as I taste him. Ever so slowly, I run my lips down the steel length of Anrai, wet and slow and teasing. His heat rolls over my tongue and his taste drives into my brain as I follow the trail of my mouth with my hand. My grip is as light as his had been in the moments before, and I revel in the exploration of him, in the feel of silken skin stretched over the hard ridges.

My lashes flutter as I gaze up at him, and another thrall of power sparks low in my stomach at the sight. His shoulders rise and fall rapidly with labored breaths as he digs his teeth into his lush bottom lip. His bronze skin is vibrantly flushed, and thick tendrils of raven hair spill over his forehead to frame his face.

And those eyes. Pupils flared so wide, only a sliver of the glacial blue is visible, as something dark and heated sparks in the depths of them. Anrai's beauty has always been sharp and lethal, but desire has edged it into something careless and wanton, every bit the wicked heir.

Warmth pools insistently between my thighs, and I press them together to relieve the ache, as I lick and suck around the base of his cock, before slowly moving my mouth and hand back up. But even with the whole of his predatory gaze focused entirely on me—even with the way his eyes flash like he's considering all the ways he'll devour me—he keeps his fingers fisted at his sides, nails digging into his palms.

His small tether to reality. He still holds himself back, still keeps a stranglehold on his baser instincts, out of worry.

I smile wickedly, and then wrap my mouth tightly around the length of him. The last tether of his self-control pulls taut. And when I take him deeper, working him with my tongue and lips until he bumps the back of my throat, the tether snaps completely.

He groans and fists his fingers in my hair, the tips

digging deliciously into my scalp as he thrusts his hips. The broad tip of him bumps the back of my throat again, and this time, I relax and moan around the wide length of him. Anrai fills me just as I needed to be filled, the taste and scent of him overwhelming me, until I drive forward again and again, squirming and moaning as I take him deeper.

Anrai bucks his hips again, harder this time as he loses control, and as I watch him from beneath my lowered lashes, I swear I'll come apart right here. *This* is what I needed. To be taken out of myself completely and inundated in him. I flatten my tongue and round my lips as he thrust again, my moans of pleasure lewdly muffled by his thick length. Wanton heat slides down my thighs as I meet him stroke for stroke, bobbing forward and taking him deeper down my throat.

Anrai groans, and flame skitters from his fingers to wreathe around my neck and body, sparking wildly until I don't know whether the burn comes from inside or outside me. His entire body shudders, the rigid muscles of his abdomen contracting, and I smile around him and work my tongue along the underside, driving him further toward the edge.

He's so close; to giving in, to coming apart. But instead, his eyes flash and his flame tightens around me, pulling me backward like tethers of silken rope. They press me into the ground, coiling around my wrists and positioning them above my head. The wounds on my back smart, but the edge of pain only sharpens the heat of pleasure as Anrai arranges me before him like his own personal feast.

I writhe as he kneels between my legs, arrogant in the slow measure of his movements. He's enjoying the sight of me squirming beneath him, desperate for any bit of friction to sooth the blooming ache at my core. He presses a finger to my lips, testing, and I suck it greedily into my mouth. His lashes flicker as my tongue works, reminding us both what it felt like for him to take my mouth.

Anrai runs his glistening finger down my chin and throat, a trail of soft embers blooming in its wake. I thrust my breasts toward him, their peaks taut, but he only smiles and deliberately runs his finger between them. Down my belly, to circle each of my hip bones. "So needy," he rasps, as I press my hips up and bare myself to him in offering. *Take me. Make me yours.*

His eyes light on my glistening center, but rather than taking what I so desperately offer, he begins moving his fingers again, maddeningly slow. They trail down my upper thigh, so close to where I need him, but never touching it. "Anrai," I beg, my voice a small echo in the cavern.

He tilts his head with a vicious grin, drinking in the shudder of my body as he finally brushes his finger over that bundle of nerves, so swollen I could cry. The touch is so light, so delicious, that my legs go weak. I strain at the bonds of fire, to claw at his smile or consume it whole, I don't even know.

"Yes, Lemming?" Anrai asks, his voice unbearably casual, even as he draws his finger once more over my clit.

I buck and my hips lift off the stone floor, but he's already stolen his touch away with a dark laugh. He waits until I settle once more, until I'm entirely still but for the needy whimper in my throat, before he brings it back, pressing ever so lightly down. Then he leans over me, his voice a shadowed whisper against my throat. "There is more than one way to be wrecked, Mirren. Now open for me."

Without thought, I do as he commands, spreading my legs wide and baring myself entirely to him. His body slides slowly over mine, the friction of his stubble so maddeningly light and delicious over my skin, I nearly come undone. "Good girl," his voice rumbles over me, through me.

Anrai leans back on his heels, gaze transfixed on the most intimate part of me as he brings his fingers back and draws a small circle through the wet heat, before bringing them to his mouth and sucking the taste of me from them. I whimper again, but that only furthers his sinful smile, as he begins to work me slowly. Languorously. He brings me right to the edge as he continuously brushes up against the place I need him most, but never more than a light touch, so fleeting, I'm driven mad with it.

I writhe before him as heat unfurls deep in my stomach, radiating to my skin in scorching waves, until I'm a panting, wild creature. Anrai watches that too, his tongue darting out to wet his bottom lip as I lose my humanity entirely and become only a vessel of pleasure. Tears of anger and desire sting my eyes, as he denies me over and over again. "Anrai, please." I'm not even sure what I plead for, only that the want is painful, sharp-edged, and desperate. Every thought has emptied from my head beyond my need for more of him. For *more*.

For him, I will crawl, I will beg—anything to soothe the blazing need inside me.

"There are those manners," Anrai says with a satisfied smile that only feeds the burning flame. So devastatingly handsome, his beauty only fed by his wickedness, carved by that sinful intent. He pulls his shirt over his head, and the bronze of his skin seems to hold the warmth of the flame behind him. His own arousal strains against my thigh, hard and pulsing hot, and another electric thrill runs through me at how much pleasure he takes in my ruination.

When he finally circles the pad of his finger decisively

over my clit, tears of relief well in my eyes as I scream out. I throw my head back, riding wave after wave of cruelly edged pleasure, the rush of it nearly unbearable. And though an ocean-wielder cannot drown, in this moment, I want to. To be overwhelmed by his current, to never surface from his depths.

He showers kisses over my breasts and stomach and pushes two fingers deep inside me. My hips buck off the ground and the wounds at my back sting with the movement, razor-edged pain honing the decadence of the pleasure into something beyond words. He licks at the sweat beading along my feverish skin, the rhythm of his fingers still far too slow.

And when he lowers his head and begins to massage me with his deft tongue, I lose all sense of myself. I scream and writhe, straining against the tethers of fire still wrapped around my wrists. Because still, it is not enough. I want him to take me between his teeth, to lick at me and tear me apart, until I can do nothing more than tremble.

"That's it," he smiles against the center of me, the movement nearly sending me tumbling over the edge. "You look so good like this." He pumps his fingers faster, curling them up and pressing against the spot that makes the world narrow and then explode. "So good spread open for me." He sucks me into his mouth, laps at me with his tongue like only my flesh will satiate him. "So beautiful when you shed that Similian skin and become the wild, desperate thing I know you are."

With his words, the hot wave of my climax crests over me once more. I buck and thrash against his mouth, but before it can crash, Anrai pulls away, leaving satisfaction dangling above me.

I cry out, desperate and hot and furious as his low, dark

laugh skitters over my fevered skin. He sheds his pants fully and kneels once more before me, running his hard length against the spot his mouth abandoned. A moan slips from my lips as he coats himself in my pleasure, the bundle of nerves now so sensitive, it almost hurts. I thrust my hips upward, trying to soothe the ragged edge of agony his tongue left behind.

"Anrai, please, I need—" I gasp out in a half-sob.

"Look at me, Mirren." His voice is brutal, and my body's response is more of a reflex than a conscious decision. Like it lives to be commanded by him and him alone. "I know *exactly* what you need."

I nod desperately, writhing beneath him, my body moving of its own accord, driving after the pleasure it needs; the pain it demands. And of course Anrai knows exactly what I need; he's always seen the parts of me I haven't even been able to acknowledge myself.

He nudges my entrance with the head of his cock, and I shudder as a fresh wave of need barrels through my veins. When he begins to slide in, thick and full and agonizingly slow, my eyes roll closed and another deep moan sounds from my throat. "Look at me, Mirren," he says again. "You wanna come apart? You want to forget everything but pleasure? Then so be it, but you won't forget who gives it to you."

I snap my eyes open. His eyes are no longer smoldering embers, but an untamed inferno. His gaze lashes over my skin as he slides himself in so slowly, my heart and lungs feel like they'll burst. The ridges of his abdomen coil with the movement, the scars spread over his skin like stars in the sky pulling taut and then loose. The muscles of his arms ripple as he digs his fingers into my skin, gripping my hips and holding me still. I drink all of him in greedily, my head swimming as he moves further into me.

He releases my wrists, calling the flame back to him. It wreathes around his chest like twined armor, reflecting in his eyes and against his skin. Anrai looks inhuman, the embodiment of flame itself, every bit the villain the rest of the continent sees him as—Fire-bringer, death incarnate—but I feel no fear. Because I know I could crumble before him, thoroughly destroyed, and he's the only one strong enough to hold the pieces together. To melt and meld them until they're whole once more.

When he's seated fully within me, he breathes deeply. And though he is the beautiful one, the one that looks like an avenging god, the way he stares down at me leaves me breathless. Reverent, hungry. Like he could watch me forever and never get enough.

He moves inside me, and there is no more languishing, no more unhurried touches. Now there is only desperation, as he pulls out and slams back in, hitting the spot deep within me that causes stars to explode behind my eyes. I clench around him, moaning wildly. The wounds on my back sting with every thrust, every wave of pleasure edged with pain.

But he doesn't ease his rhythm, doesn't change positions. Because Anrai knows—knows I *need* the agony along with the bliss. To be punished and rewarded, to forget and remember all at once.

In seeking to undo Anrai, I've unraveled completely. I was delusional to believe getting lost in him would somehow distance me from myself. Because the way he moves inside me only grounds me further into my soul, our soul. He is more part of me than the breath in my lungs, than the beat of my heart.

His eyes burn as he lays himself bare before me, everything he's held in since we were torn apart, and as he thrusts into me, harder, deeper, *more,* I come back to myself. To us.

The numb ice encasing my soul melts, and everything I've kept buried washes over me in a deluge. "Anrai," I cry out, digging my nails into his backside, as the fullness—the pleasure and the pain and everything in between stretches me to my limits, pressing against my ribs, my bones, my skin. My *other* unfreezes, lapping against my heart in soft waves. "Anrai," I cry again, as electric sparks burst behind my eyes and deep in my belly.

It is too much, and it is not enough. It's everything at once.

"I know Mirren," he whispers against my throat, "I've got you."

And because he has me—because he *always* has me—I allow myself to let go. To fly apart at the seams. Dropping into the depths of pleasure and pain, I scream out as my climax finally crashes over me, more powerful than any ocean wave, than any wildfire. Because it is the two elements combined, exploding through me in a rush of ice and heat, of dark and light.

As the heat of my body contracts around him, gripping him tightly, Anrai tugs me up to his chest. With one more powerful thrust, he tumbles over his own edge. A moan at his lips, flame bursts from his skin, buffeting the air around us with his power. It radiates through the cavern, sparks through the air. All the terror, the rage, the sorrow—all of it explodes, before dissipating into wisps of smoke.

Anrai holds me until our breathing evens, the sweat-slick skin of our chests still pressed together. And after, when the pleasure has receded and my body is spent, he lays out a bedroll and curls me into the cradle of his body. His hands run softly along my scalp, his touch sending tingles down to my toes. I lean into him with a groan, stretching like a cat.

"You're mine, Mirren," he whispers into the damp lengths of my hair. "Whatever you need, no matter how dark, I'll give you without question. I only ask one thing in return."

I shift to meet his gaze over my shoulder. He is devastating in the shadows of the firelight, all sharp angles, and strong lines. His face is still raw and vulnerable, his stone mask having crumbled between us, and when he speaks, his voice is both tender and earnest. "Don't leave me. Don't go where I can't follow. Let me into the Darkness with you."

My throat heats, and my vision grows watery, but I manage a nod.

Because somehow, I've found an eternal warrior. A man strong enough never to balk at the horrific depths of me, but to join me in them. And though the world rages around us, and my heart still tears itself apart in my chest, Anrai is enough to make me believe I'll make it out the other side.

CHAPTER
TWENTY-NINE

Shaw

I wake entangled in Mirren. Her legs are woven between mine, lushly soft flesh pressed against hard ridges, and her small hands are curled against my chest. Her lips are slightly parted, deep breaths of her sleep tickling in humid puffs at my throat. As I watch her lashes flutter in the midst of a dream, I realize this is the first time since she was taken, I've awoken without a tight knot of dread stuffed behind my ribs.

It had been there after our escape into the tunnels, fed by the loss of Easton, the guilt of Avedis' sacrifice and by Mirren's own detachment. We'd escaped the Dark Militia, but we weren't safe from the weight of everything that had happened. I could hardly breathe beyond my worry for her: what if she broke and I couldn't hold together the pieces? What if she fit them back as something she no longer recognized?

So, when she'd begged me for oblivion last night, I hadn't been able to resist her. It had been both selfless and selfish, in that I gave her exactly what she craved, while also taking it for myself. To bury myself in the woman I knew, to feel her soul and mine, and remind myself with every touch that she is not lost. *You love her but she has not been lost. She loves you, and she will always be yours.*

With every thrust, I'd punished us both for ever doubting. With every touch, I'd led her back to herself and found myself there too. Stripped, bare, and utterly raw.

And today—today my mind is finally clear, but not in the way of the killing calm where every thought burns away in service of violence. It's now clear in the sense I am a man who knows exactly who I am in the world, and where I stand. What I am capable of, and what still needs to be done.

I am the Heir, scourge of the continent. And I am Firebringer, savior of Similis. I can be both. I *have* to be both. Because despite our loss, our heartbreak, there is still so much to do.

I tug Mirren to my chest, and she makes a small sound of contentment that draws a smile to my face. I spent the first few weeks after we met learning the vibrant emotions that splash over her face, and I've spent the past few learning her sounds. Of frustration, of happiness, of pleasure. She has so many, and I'd happily spend the rest of my days discovering the sonance of each one.

"Lemming," I whisper, nuzzling into her skin, my stubble scraping softly against her throat. Her eyelids flutter and her lips open wider, and for a moment, I consider moving between her legs and watching how her lashes move then. Only the thought of escaping the mountains keeps me from it. We may have lost the militia for now, but that doesn't mean they haven't sent assassins after us.

Until we make it to the other side of the mountains, we aren't entirely safe.

I brush my lips gently over her forehead and whisper her name again. This time, she shivers against me and her eyes blink open, that stunning green sparkling in the light of my fire. She blinks again, and I witness the memories of the past few days come back to her, agony and ecstasy washing over her in turn. Her body tenses, but when she finds my gaze, the worry smooths from her face and the ghost of a smile tugs at her mouth. "Hi," she whispers, her voice laced with sleep. "I was dreaming."

"Of what?"

The shadows that flicker in her eyes send a hot spike of rage through me. "The Covinus," she answers wearily.

A selfish, twisted part of me is thankful the man survived my sword through his throat, because it hadn't been enough. He isn't deserving of a quick death—he deserves something far more depraved, and I'm just the person to grant it to him.

"Even before I was taken, I dreamed of him," Mirren admits softly. "I didn't realize it, but it was his memories I was seeing. Memories of the time before the curse."

I furrow my brow as I digest her confession. "What kind of memories?"

Mirren's tongue darts out and swipes over her bottom lip as she considers. "They're disjointed and faded, almost like an old video." She shakes her head, realizing I've never seen a video. "I mean, tattered like an old photograph. But —he was in Nadjaa. It looked different than it does now because it was electric. And there were the flying machines from your stories."

I stare it her in shock. Nehuan had been the first to tell me about the machines that hung in the air, that flew over oceans and to the end of the earth. I'd been enamored with the idea of being able to escape, to fly to a place no one could ever find you again, and after that, I'd hoarded stories of the machines like precious jewels. But I'd never truly thought they were real.

"And he was in love with a woman. Iara. I—I think she might have been the first queen the stories talk about. She was a water-wielder, like me."

I swallow down the possessive flame that shoots up my throat.

"And she had a brother who was a fire-wielder. The Covinus used one of the coins to steal her brother's power. He wanted to be Iara's equal, but she was horrified by it."

My anxiety spikes, remembering how Mirren trembled as she recounted what the Covinus had tried to take from her in the Castellium. I hadn't pressed for more as she'd been so close to breaking and I haven't asked since. I don't know whether it's kindness or cowardice. Because though I don't have an exact answer to how *much* he took from Mirren, the fact that she hasn't healed is answer enough.

I swear under my breath. "That's why he tried to steal your power," At Mirren's curious look, I clarify, "Because he was never Iara's equal. In his mind, stealing the most powerful water-wielder's power would have finally made him worthy of her."

Mirren frowns, and her forehead crinkles. "You'd think he would have learned. Something went wrong when he stole fire. Like something rotted inside him."

I caress her bare arm with my fingers, enjoying the way she squirms beneath my touch as I mull over her words. "The stories say only a certain kind of soul can withstand the creation of fire. If the Covinus wasn't one of them, maybe the power broke something in him. Twisted or burned it somehow."

"Or maybe it illuminated what was already broken," she says slowly. "I don't understand. If he has so many wielders in his control, why *steal* power? It seemed like it took as much out of him as it did from me."

My jaw tightens. "Men like him will never be satisfied with others being more powerful than themselves. They'll always take everything until no one else can stand before them. You're one of the four, more powerful than anyone else on the continent. If he was going to siphon someone's power, you were the only person that would be worthy."

Flame skitters from my fingers, drawing goosebumps to Mirren's skin. "I'll tear him limb from limb for touching you, Mirren, I swear to the dead gods. For taking your mother and brother, I'll make him pay every bit of blood he owes you."

Mirren swallows roughly. "The curse keeps him alive, Anrai. Iara cursed him for losing his humanity, but I think somehow his mortality got wrapped up into it. It's the only explanation for why he's alive after such a grievous injury. And it also explains why he doesn't want the curse broken, even though it was meant for him. He has no interest in being mortal again."

She nestles closer, gazing up into my eyes. And gods, I want to pull the blanket up over our heads, to cocoon ourselves away from the rest of the world, so she never again has to think of warlords or darkness or death. "He's going to come for Nadjaa. It's where Iara cursed him, and I think—I think the Dead Prophecy is connected to the valley somehow. It began there...it makes sense it would end there."

Her words bury themselves beneath my heart. I've

never allowed myself to claim Nadjaa as home. I thought I didn't deserve a place so bright when my soul was so dark, something Denver only reinforced when he took me prisoner.

But despite my resistance, the city and everything it stands for is embedded in me, melded into bone and muscles. It's why, deep down, I understand why Denver did what he did—why, even though it broke me, I don't entirely hate him for it.

Because I would do exactly the same thing to protect the dream of the free city.

"Then we go back to Nadjaa. And we do whatever we have to do to complete the Dead Prophecy. We'll return the Covinus' mortality and show him exactly what Dark World retribution looks like for a mortal."

Mirren's face crumples as grief washes over her once more. "What about—what about my father?"

There are so many layers to the question, I'm not even sure where to begin. *What about my father's betrayal of us? What of our betrayal of him?*

And the worst of them all—*How do we tell him of his son's fate?*

I don't answer any of them. Instead, I press my lips to hers, softly breathing in her scent of salt and sea. "Our friends are going to Nadjaa. We'll meet them, and figure it out together."

Mirren nods, and in spite of my resolve to leave early, when her mouth opens for me, I sweep my tongue along hers. And when her moan vibrates through my soul, I take her beneath me and worship every inch of her body until she is trembling. It's softer than the night before, an echo of the tender ache of my heart every time I wake beside her.

And when she comes apart, I devour her sounds and imprint them in my memory, in my bones.

You love her. Don't let her be taken from you.

Not by the Covinus or the Darkness. And not by her own grief.

I won't allow it. We are permanent, a monument of stone against the ocean of time. There is nothing strong enough to sweep us out to sea, nothing to erode the foundation, and I'll make damn sure of it.

After, we dress and eat, we lead Dahiitii through the tunnels. We climb upward, until our muscles burn, and the passages widen.

And when we emerge into Gireni territory and feel the heat of the sun for the first time in days, I lift my face to absorb the rays. They feel like hope, warm and soft, because at least, for the moment, we've emerged from the darkness.

∼

Calloway

The next few days are filled with hard travel and little talking, as we head south toward Siralene. We avoid the trees of Baak, choosing to skirt around the coast of the Tyrilian sea instead to attract less attention. Of the few travelers we do meet, none comment on the Akari's gag or the fact she's now tied to a horse. With the disheveled state of her clothes and shorn hair, along with the new scar running from her forehead to her ear, no one would recognize her as the once proud warlord, but I'm still grateful for the Ferusian propensity to look away from other's troubles: sometimes, your own is all you're able to carry.

Harlan walks ahead with Helias. The little earth-wielder has been passing the time by shooting trees and flowers up from the earth, and then bending in half with laughter when Akari Ilinka's horse startles and rears. The sound of his merriment is a welcome change from his solemn silence, but even as it brings me joy, my gaze remains on Harlan.

Always Harlan. I'm greedy for the swing of his hips as he walks, and the way his stride seems to eat up the space not only in front of him, but around him, carving the shape of him into the landscape. I consume his shy smiles in the firelight and get drunk on the cadence of his soft laughter that comes every time he has to help Helias up after tripping over his own plants.

We haven't spoken of the battle, nor of the terror that sluiced through me when the militia overwhelmed him; nor of the moments after, when that same terror drove me to take what I've imagined since the moment we met.

Max follows my gaze and raises her eyebrows in an obnoxiously knowing manner. When she opens her mouth, I cut her off with a sharp huff. "I know," I mutter in response to her haughty look. And when she opens her mouth again, I repeat more forcefully, "*I know.*"

"Do you?" she bites back, undeterred. "Because it seems to me, we're in the middle of the end times, the curse is coming to a head, you've almost died *twice* in the past few weeks, and for some reason, you're still dawdling around like you have all the time in the world."

I glare at her. "So what? The world ending doesn't change the fact that he's Similian or in love with someone else." I kick obstinately at the dirt. "People kiss people all the time when they think they're about to die. It's just adrenaline. It doesn't mean anything."

"I thought we were all going to die, and *I* didn't kiss you," she points out in a maddening sing-song voice.

"Real shame for you, as I'm a fantastic kisser."

Max laughs, and my dour mood lightens, even as the keen spark in her eye grows sharper. She won't be letting this go. I roll my neck, my skin beginning to feel uncomfortably tight as she stares at me expectantly. She says nothing more, only watches me as the silence stretches on, digging into my bones just as she intends it to. Max knows how much I despise silence, how quickly I'll fold just to make some noise.

With a sharp exhale of frustration, I do just that. "What do you expect me to do? Tackle him right now, and rip his clothes off?"

"You could at least wait until Helias is out of earshot," she deadpans, before rolling her eyes slowly to the sky like I'm the greatest test of her patience. "I expect you to grow up and have a conversation. You've heard of those, haven't you?"

I grimace like I've swallowed something unpleasant. "Sure haven't. Sounds terribly boring."

Max gives a resigned shake of her head. "If Anni were here, he would kick your ass for being such a coward."

My mouth drops open, and I whip to her indignantly. "I am *not* a coward! I'm…judicious."

She makes a humming noise of disbelief. "A fancy word for coward. The least you could do is talk to the man. How do you even know he's still in love with Easton if you haven't asked?"

"The tongue down each other's throats was a pretty big indicator."

"You just said kissing doesn't mean anything."

"*In time of life or death, Max,*" I wheeze in exasperation. "I swear, you're determined never to listen to anything I say."

But despite myself, I grin broadly at her. The journey from Similis has been rough on us all, and Max's appearance has begun to reflect it. Her clothes are coated in a thick layer of dust, and holes have worn through both the knees and elbows. The hem of her cloak is tattered and frayed, and smudges of exhaustion stain the skin beneath her eyes.

She looks as tired as I feel. And still, she's not once questioned my decision to take Akari Ilinka alive to Siralene, because Max understands the *why* of me. I don't need to tell her that I can't sacrifice a piece of my soul to kill the queen, but I still need to make my family's death mean something.

"You should talk to Harlan tonight. Before we go to Siralene in the morning," she says, as though I've cast my thoughts aloud. "It's going to be hard, Cal. Going back... handing her over alive." For a moment Max's gaze grows distant, and I know she's suddenly far from here. Somewhere the surf crashes and though the sun shines all year, plagues Max in shadows of Darkness.

She shakes her head as if remembering herself. "You deserve to have someone with you through that. To hold your hand. To ground you."

"I have you," I respond immediately, without considering my words. Because I don't need to, not really. Max and Anni are my family, and they've always been enough. I've never needed anything else, never needed more. I've loved them freely and without restraint. I've given my whole self to them without question because I *know* life is short and love makes it worth it.

But Harlan is different. Allowing myself to love someone like him feels akin to throwing myself off a cliff: I could fly, or I could hit the ground and break everything in me.

Anni really would call me a coward if he were here, especially with the lectures I'd subjected him to after he met Mirren. Is this how he'd felt? Like if he gave his heart to her, there was a chance it would be ruined entirely? That *he* would be ruined entirely?

And did the thought of it both terrify and intrigue him, like the horror of it was what made it tantalizing?

I clear my throat, wrapping my thoughts of Harlan up tightly and storing them for later. "Do you think Anni's alright?"

If Max is surprised by the abrupt change of topic, she doesn't show it. Perhaps because it's been on the forefront of her thoughts as well, in the smaller moments when we haven't been scraping to survive. "I don't know. It worries me that we haven't heard from Avedis. He should have sent word by now."

"There are wind-wielders all over the place. Maybe he doesn't want to risk the message being intercepted by the Covinus." I grin at Max, and add brightly, "Maybe the Covinus is dead, and Anni has taken over Argentum and has been too busy ordering people about to send word."

Max nods, but she knows I'm convincing myself as much as her. "Shaw will save Mirren. We know that much. The rest we can only guess."

Anxiety prickles at the back of my neck, as I remember the shadow's on Anni's face in the bowels of Yen Girene; the determination in his eyes when he brought down the entire Boundary only a few months ago. Anni will persevere through things that would kill most others, and that was before he was driven by love. Now, there's nothing in this world that will stop him.

The thought isn't as comforting as it should be.

WAVE OF LIGHT

~

We make camp at the edge of the lush forest bordering Siralene. The city's beauty glows against the crashing horizon of the Storven sea, the verdant plants splashed against the crisp curve of the ivory buildings. I haven't considered the stain a rebellion would leave, or the way it would run through the streets like a visible scar. The white pavers no longer gleam under the lantern light, some buckled in places and littered in others. The fighting appears to have been concentrated near the palace, as a few of the turrets are damaged, while others have fallen completely.

The smell of it is the same though, and as I take in the wounds, the disrepair only heartens me. I've learned a lot about healing in the past month, enough to know that sometimes it looks like this: messy, ravaged, a work in progress.

As we make camp, the ocean below begins to crash furiously against the rocks as a storm blows in from the south. Max and I do our best to construct a few small shelters from palm leaves and branches, stacking boughs as icy rain lashes at our skin. We tie the queen to a tree, ignoring her furious threats as we bury her beneath branches.

After dinner, Max wraps a bedroll around Helias and huddles against him. Despite the roar of the storm, it isn't long before exhaustion overtakes them both.

I pull the hood of my cloak over my head and volunteer to take first watch, leaving Harlan in the warmth of the lean-to. The hood doesn't do much good, as the wind blows the rain sideways, whipping it furiously across the cliffs. I huddle against a tree, bow in hand, and stare out as lightning streaks across the sky, reflecting in the dark water below. Rain beads on my lashes and streams down my cheeks, and I'm muttering a fervent curse at what has surely become of my hair, when Harlan comes to sit beside me.

He pulls up the hood of his own coat, shivering as he blinks rain from his eyes. My heart somehow stops and jerks right up into my throat at the same time as his warmth fills the space between us. Which is ridiculous. It's wet and freezing, and there's no way I should be able to feel any of his body heat.

But I do. And I want to draw closer, instinctively, and desperately, like there's a magnet beneath my skin and his.

Instead, I keep my eyes trained on the trees and concentrate on keeping my heart from leaping out of my mouth. "You can sleep," I tell him. "I've got watch for a while."

Harlan doesn't respond. I feel his eyes on my skin, the heat of that warm gaze. The pull of it grows more insistent, until I finally turn my head to look at him. When I do, it feels like I've been punched in the stomach. His own lashes have darkened with rain and beaded into clumps. Rivulets of water run down his cheeks and jaw; they sparkle on his lips. And suddenly, I can think of nothing but what they felt like beneath mine.

Strong and steady. His whole body had felt so solid.

What would it be like to have something like that to hold onto, something that never wavers even as I crash against him?

The urge to get up, to move, to do *something* pulses inside of me, but I keep my limbs frozen at my sides, lest they do something they can't take back.

"How are you?" he asks, his voice soft even above the rain.

"I've had far better hair days, that's for sure."

A ghost of a smile pulls at Harlan's lips, and I drink it like wine. Maybe it's the Similian in him, but Harlan never smiles unless he wants to. Never just because someone else expects it. And I love that, love that when his smiles do come, they're well-earned. Genuine.

"I meant how are you feeling about handing the queen over tomorrow?" He inclines his head to where the queen sleeps. "It has to be hard…giving her up after what she's done to you."

"Ah." I sweep the palms of my hands over my face, the heat of my skin feeling like fever. "I'm already planning my outfit for the parade the Siralenis are sure to throw for me."

Harlan shakes his head and exhales softly, something entirely too close to disappointment lacing the small sound. "By the Covinus, Cal, is everything funny to you? A passing amusement?"

I furrow my brow, confused by his sudden frustration as my own unspools hotly. "This is the Dark World, Harlan, so yeah. You'll forgive me if I'm a little flippant about life or death when it's been looming over my head since I was born."

Harlan nods. "Okay," he concedes, sounding oddly defeated when I hadn't even known he was fighting. "I understand." He swallows roughly and makes to push himself off the ground. And even though I told him to, the thought of him leaving is suddenly unbearable. "You have to be irreverent about everything to survive here."

"No, you *don't* understand. Not everything," I admit, my voice low as I catch his wrist softly. His eyes snap to where my fingers wrap around his bare skin and then slowly rise to mine, a myriad of emotion swirling in their depths.

"Life is short, Harlan, and I live for each moment as they come. I flit from one thing to the next because I never want to lose a moment to boredom. I laugh when things are serious, and I usually leave before things can get that way." His face twists and his shoulders are still, like he's stopped breathing entirely. Like he hangs on my every word. "I am careless and casual."

I see his hesitation along with his hurt and as he presses his lips together, a desperate fear threads through me. That he'll walk away and never know the truth of me. That he'll stay and learn every ugly bit of it. But I don't allow it to take root as the rest of the words tumble from me. "But not with people. Never people."

His eyes flare as I gather the rest of my courage, because Max was right. Time is fleeting; and if there's a chance for a small bit of golden light in the expanse of the darkness, a pinprick of happiness, being afraid of it is senseless. So, I exhale my terror, and tell Harlan the truth. "Never...never *you*. I will always be careful with you, Harlan."

Harlan's eyes shine. I drop his wrist gently, only to run my fingers lightly over the sensitive inner skin. His eyes drop to the movement, and his body goes still as a statue.

"I never meant to make you feel otherwise. Like you were just a distraction, or a momentary amusement. But you have to know, it was out of fear."

A line forms between Harlan's brows. "Of what?"

He's drawn closer, his upper body tipping forward in anticipation, and it sends a shockwave of pleasure sizzling down my spine. "Of you," I reply breathlessly. "I know there are pieces that can never be mine, Harlan. And I didn't think I could live with that." Harlan's skin is soft beneath my fingers, the heat of it radiating from him and into my bones. "I only know how to love in wholes."

For a moment, it feels like the entire world has stalled around us. I don't hear the heavy beat of the rain or the howl of the wind. I don't see the damp forest, or the trickle of droplets pouring down from the leaves. I only see Harlan, suspended in front of me like a painting, frozen and beautiful. His face is so close, his breath is mine. Heavy and ragged, like he's just run up a mountain. The desperate sound of it ratchets my own to a dizzying level.

The feeling only grows as his tongue darts out to lick at the droplets gathered on his lips. His eyes grow dark as he stares at me, like he's imagining doing the same thing to my mouth.

His voice is a low growl when he replies, "I'll give you whatever pieces you want," and then crushes his mouth to mine. And gods, his lips are just as soft as I remember. He opens to me, and I plunder his mouth with my tongue, devouring his surprised exhale of pleasure.

I tangle my hands in his golden strands and his fingers dig into my shoulders, grappling at each other as we collide. Each of us pulling, tugging, clawing. *Closer, closer, closer.* And neither of us gives an inch, our bodies only locking tighter as we roll back onto the carpet of decayed leaves. He tastes of rain and mint, and it spikes straight through my brain; sparks beneath my skin like the electricity of Similis, and suddenly, I can think of nothing but driving further against him. Because Harlan is solid, steady, every part of his body rock hard against mine, and I know he won't break beneath me.

It's like a sparring match, with tongues and teeth and hands, as we both crash against one another. But neither one of us cedes. And the rightness of it has me yanking at his pants, licking at his skin, moaning into his mouth.

Harlan catches the sound greedily, laps it up with his tongue, swallows it until its only his. His fingers skim over my chest, pull at my shirt, rake through my hair. I sweep my tongue along his throat and grind my hips roughly into his until he moans, too. Loud and uninhibited. And it is even better than earning his smiles or his laughter; headier than any alcohol I've ever imbibed.

And in that moment, I know I was right to be afraid.

Because there will be no coming back from this.

CHAPTER
THIRTY

Mirren

Time warps around us as we ride toward Yen Girene, like the past and present overlap in diaphanous layers, sheathing everything in a surreal film. Tucked into Shaw's warmth, it is easy to pretend the last week never happened. His voice whispers stories against my ear to pass the time, just as he did when we first met. I try to lose myself in the dreamy lilt of his voice, the magic of his tales. I pretend this journey is that first one, when hope for my brother still burned brightly in my heart.

But even the pretending leaves a bitter taste in my mouth. It only reminds me that while leaving Easton in the Healing Center all those months ago left me feeling empty, it's nothing to what echoes in my chest now. Jagged, bleeding, and shaped like the curve of one of his rare smiles. The numb shock of trauma broke against Anrai, and since, almost every bit of me *feels*.

Sometimes it's anger that blazes through my veins, bright and hot, while other times I'm bereft, and the grief crashes down on me so powerfully, I can't speak through the sobs. Anrai holds me through it all.

When we stop to make camp for the night, tucked into a small clearing set inside towering ruins of a civilization long past, I build a fire while Anrai hunts. Though he could light one with half a thought, I appreciate having something to do with my hands, and I concentrate far harder than needed as I arrange the sticks. The supplies he came with have dwindled to nearly nothing, so when he returns with a rabbit, my stomach growls loudly.

He prepares it quickly and sets it to cook over the now blazing fire, before coming to check my back.

The infection has cleared, and itchy scabs have begun to form on most of the wounds. Anrai still hasn't asked why I haven't healed myself properly. He only peels back the bandages and cleans each laceration carefully, before wrapping them back up. Tonight, he gently pulls my shirt back down and scoops me into the cradle of his arms. And for the thousandth time, I thank the dead gods for him.

That he somehow senses not to press me, senses that I haven't even been brave enough to examine the reason for my power's stagnancy myself. I don't know whether my *other* is as heartbroken as I am by my brother's death, or if the Covinus broke something irrevocable when he siphoned it from me.

I can't bear the knowledge that one more thing has been permanently stolen, so I keep the thoughts buried deep and try to look forward. To Nadjaa. To restoring the Covinus' humanity and sparing Ferusa from the Darkness.

I cannot forget the slimy feel of his greed, the unquenchable thirst for power, and I know I'll do whatever I have to in order to keep it from reaching Nadjaa's borders. From poisoning everything light and good. The Covinus' tenure in Similis, where he ruled over our thoughts and emotions and stole our autonomy, hadn't been enough to soothe that malevolent hunger. It was only a temporary salve on a gaping wound, and in bringing down the Boundary, we've ripped it back open, letting it free to bleed into the land.

And now, we have no choice but to stop it.

I stare at the fire, watching the flames lick cheerfully up the logs. Shadows flicker over the crumbling stone around us, and smoke curls up into the night sky. "Do you think our memories make us who we are?"

Anrai tilts his head down to look at me, furrowing his brow as he thinks over the question. He knows better than anyone what it feels like to lose your memories, how severing the ties that held you to yourself sets you adrift. He knows what it is to question the validity of the ones left, to be unable to understand their importance, to fill in the blanks. To know you've lost *something* and drive yourself crazy trying to name what it is.

"In a way," he finally replies. "But I think some things are carved so deeply into our bones they can't help but shape who we are, even if the mist of the memory has faded."

He sweeps his fingers through my hair absently, and a shadow darkens his face though the sun has not yet set. It is the shadow of a different sort, made in the worst places of humanity. "What are you thinking of? Avedis?"

For a moment, I regret saying anything. Anrai has always seen to the bones of me, whether I wished him to or not, and this will only feed what he probably already suspects. But I force myself to go on, because if I cannot give it to him, it will poison me. "A little. But more just memory as it exists. Avedis doesn't remember who he is without them and neither did you. The Covinus tried to take who I was through stealing my memories. And I've just been wondering how they shape us. If I'm—well, if I'm the same person I was before I went into the dungeon."

"Even in the darkest depths of soullessness, you were there, Mirren. My father tried to take everything that made me who I was, but there was no way he could ever go deep enough, because you were embedded in every piece of me." He searches my face. "The Covinus took your brother, and some of your memories, but he can never take what matters. You loved Easton and that won't leave you. Take comfort in the pain, because it means you'll always feel what he meant to you."

Take comfort in the pain.

I repeat Anrai's words in my head throughout the next few days, their rhythm weaving through every thought. They thread through my grief and flow through my *other*. Because Anrai is right. I deserve the pain, a punishment for the ways I've failed. But I am also lucky to feel it, to have had something that makes the agony of loss so acute; lucky to be alive and well enough to be honed by its sharp edge.

And so, I live on without Easton, driven by the deep ache of his loss. I use it to sharpen my resolve and steady my hand, more determined than ever to learn the Dead Prophecy and make it come true. Once powered by my belief in people, in their inherent goodness, my intent is now stained with darkness. Because now, I don't want to break the curse only to save Ferusa.

I want to break it to destroy the Covinus and everything he's worked for. Destroy him so thoroughly, he'll regret the day he ever decided to take Easton from me.

And maybe I should be wary of the burgeoning darkness—the way it slips through the fractures in my soul and spills into the crevices of my heart left by Easton's death—but I'm not. I feed it to my *other,* allowing it to build inside me until the pressure is almost unbearable. Deep and abiding, it presses against my lungs until I can't breathe. It squirms under my skin, searching for a release. But I keep it wound tight, adding to my agony.

When we grow close to Yen Girene, Anrai suggests we scout the city to put a rest to the rumors once and for all. And though even the name spoken aloud sends shivers of dread skittering into my stomach, I see the wisdom in it. Yen Girene is the closest city to Nadjaa, and if the Covinus has a faction of the militia stationed there, we need to know about it.

We leave Dahiitii grazing in a small meadow hidden in a thick copse of trees, and go the rest of the way on foot. The path is just as cragged and impassable as I remember, though this time, we aren't aiming for the city gates. Instead, we keep to the trees and swing west, keeping out of sight of the top of the towering wall. I mimic Shaw's lithe steps, placing my feet in the imprint of his, but his strides are far too wide and after only a few moments, I give up, resigning myself to tripping the rest of the way.

Crows circle the gray sky, their caw slicing through the quiet and my stomach turns unpleasantly. Do the bodies of the Gireni citizens still rot in the streets, torn apart by scavengers?

I get my answer soon enough, as we reach to the highest vantage point. The gates are swung wide, the entrance to the city gaping like a hungry maw. No guards patrol along the top of the obscene wall, and no one moves in or out. Though the majority of the city is shrouded from view, it's clear there's no life inside it. The only thing changed since our last time here is a hole nudged up against the mountain Yen Girene is built into. By the looks of it, it's been freshly dug and then covered with a haphazard pile of pale rocks.

Anrai's gone still beside me, his fingers resting on his bandolier.

Bile fills my mouth as I stare at the hole, and realize it isn't rocks piled inside it.

It's bodies.

Anrai mutters something in Xamani under his breath, an exclamation that sounds both like a curse and a prayer. Then his eyes sharpen, that predator's edge honing the fire within. "It must have taken an army to move all of them. And yet, there's no movement. No battlements, no mining. There isn't even a damned supplies delivery."

Even without the advantage of his keen senses, I know he's right. There is no movement at the top of the towering walls, and no sign of life beyond the city gates. No sounds echo except the sound of the birds, which I now realize with a sickening punch to the gut, gather to feast on the grave.

"Should we try to get closer?" I ask uncertainly.

Anrai's mouth twists, his eyes scanning the landscape. His restlessness made me uneasy when we first met, the way he always seemed poised for an attack, but now, it settles the blood in my veins. "No. It might not seem like it, but the city is definitely guarded. My father *told* me it was protected. And if it weren't, there'd be warlords lined up at the gates to murder each other over the gems in those mines."

He narrows his eyes. "Something's here. I just can't figure out what."

"What about your power?"

He glances at me sidelong. "What do you mean?"

"Well, we can't go in, but your power can. What if you

just send a bit of it in and see what happens? We're hidden well enough up here."

A wicked smile tugs at his mouth as he gazes at me approvingly. "Like poking a beehive?" He shudders. "I did that once as a child in the gardens of Argentum. I can't say it ended well." Even so, excitement shines in his eyes.

"And I'm sure you learned no lessons."

He grins in response, and despite the pain at my back and the one boiling beneath my skin, I can't help but return it. "Let's poke and see what comes out."

Anrai tilts his head and swipes his tongue across his bottom lip. "Though it's extremely inconvenient at times and frustrates me to no end, I gotta admit, Lemming...there is something alluring as hell about your reckless streak."

"I'm inconvenient?" I arch a brow.

Anrai's smile only grows wider. "Unbelievably."

"Well, you've been a thorn in my side since we first met."

He leans in close to my ear, his soft laughter trailing over my throat. "I live to crawl under your skin. To get inside you and stay there."

My toes curl at his tone, but I only fit him with a haughty look. "Let's see that power, Fire-bringer."

Anrai's mouth twists at the name, but he doesn't object. Just pushes his hands out before him as flames spark at his palm. They dance merrily, a collage of oranges and yellows and reds. But none of the pale blue of his eyes, the most destructive of colors.

The flames leap from his hands to the ground, and a tiny ball of light trails delicately down the mountain side as if led by an invisible candle wick. At my questioning look, he explains, "There's no reason to raze the city square first thing." And then, in that familiar commanding tone that sends heat to my skin, "Be ready to run."

I hold my breath as the fire trails down the hill, snaking between jagged rocks and unwieldy boulders, unsure what I'm even waiting for as anxiety unspools in my chest. Everything is still, the eerie quiet lodging beneath my skin like shards of ice.

Anrai directs the fire between the two open gates and for a long moment, nothing happens as the flame sparks and crackles in the shadow of the entrance to Yen Girene. I push out a relieved breath, laughter balancing on the tip of my tongue, when suddenly, noise explodes.

It swells in the air and ricochets off the mountains, and it takes me a protracted moment to determine its source. Then, all at once, black-clad soldiers swarm from the gates. They move like a singular organism, a dark wave swallowing the steep landscape. They circle around where Shaw's small flame burns, shrouding it in an impenetrable swath of black.

For a moment, all is quiet again as the militia goes eerily still. Anrai glances at me hesitantly, his confusion a mirror to mine. With a lazy flick of his wrist, he urges the tiny ball of fire higher. It doesn't touch the soldiers, only sparks and spools upward toward the sky in a spiral of light.

As one, the militia raise Similian-issued rifles and begin firing at the flame. Indiscriminate and ceaseless, gunshots crack through the silence, sounding like rain pounding on the roof of the quarterage.

"What in the Darkness?" Anrai whispers slowly, brow crinkling as he watches the militia unload thousands of rounds at the flame. It makes no sense to shoot at fire, no sense to waste the expensive ammunition.

And still, more soldiers stream from the gates, pouring onto the steep path leading into the city. Hundreds, if not a thousand of them. None appear to be wielders, as no one steps forward to douse the flame. Instead, they surround it, the mass of bodies so thick it absconds the light behind their marching feet.

Something tugs at the corner of my mind. *Their feet.*

"They're marching in unison," I whisper in horror.

Not the unison of a well-trained militia, with a step slightly off-kilter every so often. Each footstep of every one of the soldiers falls with precise rhythm, not one of the thousand boots missing a beat. It's unnatural, that not one would stumble or trip on the jagged road leading out of Yen Girene.

"We have to go," Anrai says as the militia begins to spread over the path, snaking up the trail. Without waiting for my response, he hauls me up and sets me in front of him, hastily ushering me back toward where we left Dahiitii. He steadies me as my feet slip on the loose shale, and my heart begins to thump uncomfortably in my chest at what we just witnessed. What it means for Nadjaa.

We run until we lose sight of the soldiers, slipping deep into the trees and to the clearing where Dahiitii chomps happily on some clover. "Shaw—" I start, panic squeezing the words from my throat. *What was that? What does it mean?*

A part of me is grateful Anrai doesn't answer as he lifts me on to Dahiitii's back, because deep down, I know exactly what that was. There's only one thing that would cause someone to move so unnaturally: like they're attached to strings, no longer human, but warped puppets subject to another's whims.

The power and time it would take to control an army

this size—it seems impossible, even for the Covinus. How did he do it while he was holed up in Argentum with me?

My thoughts spiral as Anrai swings himself up behind me. He gathers the reins, but before he can usher Dahiitii into a gallop, I feel him freeze around me.

Standing directly in our path of escape is a little girl. Hardly bigger than Helias, with a spill of yellow curls, her blue eyes blink up at us slowly. They contain none of the mischievous spark inherent to children, none of the merriment. Her face is blank, the hollow expression so eerily out of place amongst her delicate features that it forces something slimy beneath my ribs.

It takes another horrible moment for me to realize the girl is dressed in the same black as the Gireni militia. And holds the same high-powered rifle, its sleek, Similian lines gleaming in the setting sun.

The girl raises the gun. "You are trespassing," she says, her voice robotic beneath its childish cadence.

Anrai has dropped one of the reins to raise his hand, and my stomach roils as the pressure behind my eyes rises. I want to throw myself at the girl; to grab her and take her far away from here. It isn't fair, to have another life cut short so early, to have all the promises of a future stolen from her.

But Anrai knows me too well, the direction of my thoughts and the feel of my horror, and before I can throw myself off the horse, he drops the other rein and wraps his free arm around me in a steel lock. I squirm and shout in protest, but my words are lost as the little girl pulls the trigger.

Anrai raises a wall of flame so hot, the bullet slows and melts on contact. A scream lodges in my throat, of horror, of devastation, as he yanks the reins. And though I try, when I look back, I cannot see the child beyond the rage of fire.

~

Calloway

By morning, the storm has relented, leaving the air heavy and cloying as Harlan and I approach Siralene. The emerald roof of the palace sparkles on the road above us, and beyond that are glimpses of the Storven, its waters a calm swirl of greens and blues. It's days like today Lila and I would paddle a canoe out, swearing we could see all the way to the floor below. The thought doesn't sting as much as it normally does as I walk through the same streets we'd run through to the docks.

Because though the city remains, change is apparent in its disrepair. The streets no longer gleam, and half the planters we walk past have become overgrown, spilling over the pavers and spidering over steps and railings. Children with black bands tattooed around their small throats chase each other up the street, and though their clothes are still little more than tatters of fabric, their bodies beneath look nourished and well.

Harlan is quiet beside me as I drink in the changes of the city. Healing is a messy business, and Siralene is proof. Its pristine exterior has been upended to dig out the rot that festered beneath, and I think Papa would be so proud.

When we reach the palace, it is no longer guarded by men in white regalia, but people in an assortment of different clothing, armed with a variety of weapons. The woman nearest to the door eyes us warily as we approach, her fingers tightening fractionally on the handle of her axe.

She is older than us, her weather-tanned skin crinkled

at the corners of her eyes and mouth, but her body is strong, like she doesn't keep the axe around simply for decoration.

"We'd like to speak to who's in charge," I tell her, holding my hands up peacefully. Harlan does the same, but the woman has already noted the position of his rifle, and my sword. Her eyes narrow on the bow slung over my shoulder, and then skate to my hair where they hesitate.

Then she bows subtly, motioning for us to follow her into the palace.

I glance at Harlan, but I realize immediately it's a mistake. I've never been good at resisting the pleasures in life and watching him is pure pleasure. One I certainly don't have time for if I'm to keep alert. But as his fingers tighten at his sides, I remember how deftly they touched me. So soft, only the barest hint of callouses on his wide palms.

Harlan gives the guard a patient smile, and I think of how it felt to upend that unwavering calm. To break through it until he was just as wild as I was, just as hungry.

I clear my throat pointedly and duck inside the large archway of the palace, following the guard's long strides. She leads us through the wide corridors, and though I've never been in the palace, I'm positive it didn't look anything like it does now when Akari lived here. The roof's been partially demolished, leaving the ivory rooms open to the elements. The floor is still slick with yesterday's rain, and it's only my inherent grace that keeps me balanced on my feet.

After a few moments, the guard stops, motioning to wide balcony that juts out over the sea. "Am I right to assume you're a Cabrera?" She eyes me curiously as I jerk to a halt, like some invisible tether has been yanked.

It feels like a lie to say I am, to claim a name I've done

my best to ignore for the past five years. But whether it's witnessing the change in the city, or Harlan's calming presence beside me, I find the courage to nod. To take my past and meld it with the man I've become. "Yes."

The guard looks at me with a mixture of pity and respect, and I find it doesn't ache like it used to. "Welcome home," she says simply, before stepping back to allow us entrance.

The balcony is shaded by climbing vines and plump fruit trees, and a soft breeze tickles my hair as we step out onto it. I'm not sure what I imagined when I thought of the leader of the Siraleni rebellion, but it is not the diminutive woman leaning against the marble railing. Her ebony skin glows against the crisp white silk of her draped dress, and her feet are bare as she stares out at the sea. When she turns to us with a warm smile, I stare at her for a full minute before remembering my manners and returning it.

It's odd, to be greeted in a palace by warmth. By trust. But the way the woman approaches us demonstrates both. Her golden bangles clink at her wrists as she envelops Harlan in a hug. Incredulous surprise has lifted his brows and widened his eyes, but he returns the embrace. "Shina, I didn't—I had no idea..."

I watch the exchange with confusion, wondering what it is about the woman that's jumbled his normally smooth words. Then he shakes his head with a laugh. "You're the one who overthrew the witch-queen?"

Shina smiles demurely, and her eyes sparkle. "I am the only one she let close enough to discover her weaknesses."

Realization washes over me. Shina was the woman the witch-queen loved. The one Max and Mirren saved from the Anni. As if following my thoughts, Shina says lightly,

"Love is not always the remedy. Just as often it can be the poison itself."

I nod dumbly, even as Shina laughs, the sound of her merriment tinkling around the balcony. She nods for us to sit, plopping herself into a deep cushioned chair. "Have you come on behalf of the Ocean-wielder?" she asks, pulling her legs up and draping her dress over her feet. The chair seems to swallow her whole and with her delicate features, she appears almost childlike. Certainly not someone with the stomach to overthrow a violent warlord.

"Actually, Shina, it's Calloway who wanted a word with you. He's Siraleni, you see, and…he's brought you a gift."

Shina's eyes slide to where I'm still trying to adjust myself in the cavernous cushion, without toppling onto the floor. I freeze in place, and sit up straighter, smoothing my hair nervously. "I have."

Though her face doesn't change, something sharpens in the depths of Shina's gaze. Something that tells me her soft exterior hides a cleverly sharp mind. "A gift? Or a means of coercion? Mr…"

"Calloway. Calloway Cabrera. You can call me Cal."

"Cal," Shina amends. "I have lived in the Darkness long enough to know there is rarely a gift freely offered. Let's be open, shall we? I know you are close with the Chancellor of Nadjaa, and I also know the circumstances in the north. You are here to gain my alliance, and though I would not be averse to such a thing in the future, I won't be offering up Siraleni help any time soon." Though her words are kind, there is an air of finality about them.

"War is coming, Shina. And though it may come to Nadjaa first, Siralene is not an island unto itself. Your home will be next unless we do what we can to break the curse and destroy the Darkness."

Shina looks thoughtful. "You know the prophecy, then?"

"Not in its entirety, but I know enough of the Covinus to understand he won't rest. Not until he has the entire continent in his power."

Shina leans back, stretching her legs out in front of her and dancing her toes on the floor. "I have sympathy for your plight," she says, appearing entirely genuine. "But I'm afraid we are stretched thin as it is, and I will not sacrifice the health of my people for someone else's war. We will continue to heal and rebuild here. I am not Akari. I refuse to send any of them to die for a cause that isn't theirs."

I hate her words, but I understand them. It's the way of Ferusa, of the Darkness, to look out for yourself above all else. When I glance at Harlan, his face is one of resignation. Clearing my throat, I push myself to standing. "Be that as it may, I would still offer you a gift."

Shina cocks her head, like I've truly surprised her for the first time. "Why?"

"Because the first step of breaking the curse is to not let the Darkness make every one of our decisions. To rise above self-preservation and help others, even when it does nothing for ourselves."

"Is this Harlan's Similian influence rubbing off on you, Calloway?"

I laugh lightly and shake my head. "No. It's what my father and my mother taught me, and it's what I live by."

Shina smiles, before giving me a nod of respect. "You are always welcome to come home. We could use more of that sort of thinking here. I'm afraid it will take years before we are able to erase the stain of fear and blood Akari left behind."

Harlan's eyes gleam as he watches me, and a sudden

restlessness overcomes me. To hand the witch-queen off and get back to Nadjaa. To let go of what's tethered me to guilt and shame. To move on to the lightness of Harlan's embrace, of Anni's laugh. Max's faith, and Mirren's soft trust. "I think I have a way to help the process. To bring justice to the grieving and the wronged."

I take a deep breath and exhale the past. And when I inhale again, the Siraleni air feels fresher than it ever has before. There is no smoke, no blood. Only the sea. "I'll bring you to the witch-queen."

CHAPTER
THIRTY-ONE

Shaw

The forces of Yen Girene don't follow us beyond the Girennia range, whatever control the Covinus employs keeping them trapped in the valley. For now. It's only a matter of time before the Covinus comes and directs them to attack Nadjaa from the north.

But Nadjaa's vulnerability isn't why nausea surges up my throat a full hour later; isn't why my ribs feel as though they're being squeezed by an iron vice, a moment away from cracking.

By the time we reach a safe copse of trees and boulders, I think I'll scratch right out of my own skin. I leap from Dahiitii like her saddle is on fire and stumble toward a thick pine, just as my stomach contracts and I heave violently. My fingernails find purchase in the rough trunk of the tree, and they're the only thing that keep me on my feet as I bend in half beneath the unbearably heavy weight of my soul.

I can't breathe beneath it. *I'm going to drown. I'm going to drown.*

Soft fingers touch the back of my neck. Hesitant at first, but then more decisively as they press into my aching muscles. Mirren strokes slowly as I expel everything in me. And then after, when my empty stomach still clenches violently and I can only stand there, trembling and gasping for air.

Finally, I claw my way to standing, swiping at my mouth. Breaths come painfully short, like there isn't enough oxygen to save me from suffocation. When I finally gather the courage to turn to Mirren, I almost flinch, expecting to see my own disgust mirrored back to me. But there is none on her face, no sign swirling in those emerald irises. There is no pity either, none of the condescending sympathy I've come to despise from people. The kind that feigns empathy, while truly thinking, *is this not what you deserve, Heir?*

Mirren only continues massaging the tense muscles of my neck, waiting patiently. And for a moment, I wobble and consider falling to my knees to thank her for it. For her capacity to simply *be* with me. To not try to assuage the horror or the guilt, but to stand with me through it until I manage to shoulder it again.

When my breathing finally slows, she asks softly, "Did you—"

I cut her off with a shake of my head. "No, I raised a shield between us, but she didn't pass through it. The girl's alive."

Mirren furrows her brow. "Then, why..."

I swear loudly, raking my fingers through my hair until it stands on end and squeezing my eyes shut. Even now, when I have nothing left in me to expel, my soul still presses down on my shoulders, drives violently against my chest. And I am so tired, I want to curl up and let it crush me to nothing.

But instead, I dig the heel of my palms into my eyes until stars bloom and breathe until I can finally manage to speak. "Because *I* did that to her." The words are rough, ragged, and though whispered, they slice through the air like a blade.

Mirren's confusion only grows. And still, her fingers work soothingly over my skin, her touch so kind and so soft that I shrug it off. Because for the first time since she healed my soul, I can't bear it.

Hurt flashes in her eyes, and I swear again. *Ruin. You only ruin.*

"I recognized that little girl," I finally admit in a rush of words. "She's from a small village near Baak."

Mirren stills. She is never still, not truly, but she is now. And I've done that. My atrocities, my darkness, it's finally become too much to endure. But I force myself to keep going, to trust in Mirren when I don't trust myself. "I tested her whole family. She wasn't a wielder, but the rest of them were. The militia rounded them up and sent them to Argentum, and she was left alone. I made her an orphan."

I meet Mirren's eyes and will her to understand. "None of those people in Yen Girene were wielders. But the Covinus is controlling all of them." I moisten my lips and swallow roughly, attempting to cool the burning at the back of my throat. "I think...Gods, Mirren—I think I took their souls."

She stares at me, her thoughts whirling across her face. "But...but you have to kill to lose your soul. Are you saying all of those people, including that little girl, have killed enough people to lose their souls?"

I shake my head, and the world tilts around me. For a moment, I'm sure I'll be sick again. "No. I think it's those coins. I sent my power into them, testing and prodding and pulling, but I was following a command...I didn't understand the magic I was using, and I didn't care to because it felt *good*." I shudder, remembering the call of the coin. The way it crawled through my veins. "It felt old and foreign. Like the dead gods' chamber beneath the Boundary, and now—well now, I think all those souls belong to the Covinus. Every person I tested. Whether they were wielders or not."

Realization washes over Mirren's face. The number of people I tested. The amount of souls under our enemy's control.

Bile rushes up my throat, and I bend in half as I retch again. But even as my body rebels violently, my stomach clenching and my throat scraping, I know there will be no peace after. There will only be more of it, more of the pain and the heaviness and the consequences. It will never be easier, never lighter. It will always be waiting to pull me beneath the depths, drown me in darkness.

I fall to my knees and bow my head against the cool grass. *Why are you still fighting it?*

Mirren curls her body around mine and scrapes her fingers in gentle circles along my scalp. Immense shame overwhelms me at being weak enough to allow the thought purchase. After everything she sacrificed, everything she gave, it's disrespectful. It's spineless and pathetic to consider giving up, even for a moment. I don't deserve her sacrifices or her sympathy.

We sit like that for a long while, surrounded by the chirping melody of the forest. Its familiar song settles my heartbeat, my breath, and after a while, my skin stops itching. I'm able to calm the swirling thoughts and hone them into straighter lines. To focus on Mirren's gentle touch and not hate myself for allowing it.

"We have to warn Denver. I tested most of the continent, save for Siralene and Nadjaa. Which means you're right. The Covinus will come for Nadjaa next. And we have to be ready when he does."

Mirren nods, her small body still curved around mine, her face pressed into my back. I meet her gaze over my shoulder. "I'm sorry—for the outburst."

Mirren rears back slightly, tilting her head in confusion. "Why are you sorry? That's a lot to process."

I press my lips together, drinking in the tilt of her mouth, the slant of her nose. Even with the strain of everything she's been through, the smudges of exhaustion beneath her eyes and the matted state of her hair, she's the most radiant thing I've ever seen. Like the sun after a storm, shimmering over calm waves.

Shame washes over me again. "I just feel like—like every time things get too heavy, I'm failing you somehow. That I'm not appreciating what you gave me, that I'm not worthy of it. But gods, Mirren. Sometimes...sometimes I get so tired."

Determination lines her eyes. And I find I can't look away from it, drawn like a moth to flame, just as I was when we first met. "Shaw, you aren't failing me because you struggle. Every day, every moment you choose to fight, you make me proud." She circles around and settles herself in my lap, winding her legs around my waist. She draws her face so close to mine, the different shades of green swirling in her irises are crystal clear.

They churn like waves against a shore, and they hypnotize me just the same.

"Don't ever think that I don't see you. People think you're strong because of your power or your weapons, but I know better. You're strong because of what you carry every day. Because of your strength of will, and your refusal to let it overcome you." Mirren holds my jaw gently in her fingers, soft palms brushing against rough stubble. "I see you, Anrai Shaw. And I am so proud to call you mine."

For a long moment, I just stare at her, unsure whether I want to cry or scream or pull her beneath me. Because gods, if there's one thing that makes everything feel lighter—my soul, the world, the darkness—it's Mirren. My equal who never balks, who never looks away.

I swallow roughly. "I see you too, Lemming. Always."

∽

Calloway

Akari Ilinka is right where we left her, though now in addition to the ropes binding her wrists, a hot pink gag has been stuffed into her mouth. I suppress a smile as we approach and Max rises to greet us. She looks entirely unapologetic, giving a casual shrug in the queen's direction. "I warned her to shut up. Apparently she isn't as adept at following orders as she is at giving them."

Before I can reply, Max notices Shina peeking out from behind the two guards chosen to accompany her, one of them being the older woman who recognized me earlier. Max's brows draw close together, and her mouth parts in disbelief. "Shina?"

Max turns to me, like I'll confirm she's seeing things, but I only smile. "Max, meet the woman who organized

Siralene's awakening," I introduce, ruffling Shina's hair. We may not agree on the best way to approach Ferusa's problems, but I like the rebel leader anyway. Anyone who outwitted the witch-queen, and was able to maintain her good humor, is a person I want to know.

"It's good to see you again, Maxwell," Shina replies.

Max takes in the woman with newfound appreciation. "You're far more savage than you look."

"I get that a lot," Shina admits, sharing an intimate smile with her guards. "But I find it helps to be underestimated."

Max makes a humming noise of agreement, as Shina gestures to the queen. "Untie her, please."

Max hesitates, but I give her a reassuring nod, and she does as Shina asks. With a disgusted glare at the queen, she slices through the ropes holding Akari's wrists and then pulls the gag from her mouth.

Shina steps forward and the air thickens with tension. The queen's eyes widen, and I grip my sword, expecting the heat of her rage—for her to attack the way she did with Verena—but what I see instead shocks me into silence.

Hurt. Raw and vulnerable *hurt*.

I never thought the queen capable of something so tender. As long as I've been alive, she's been wrapped in spiked armor, untouchable and dangerous. To see her stripped of it now feels wrong, like peeling back layers to reveal places never meant to be seen. I want to turn away from it, to see her only as the inhuman monster I know her to be, but something keeps me frozen in place.

Akari Ilinka rises to gracefully to her feet. "Shina—" The name is a gasp on her lips, ragged and pained.

Now I understand her true fear in being returned to

Siralene. It wasn't facing the justice of her people that terrified her; it was facing the failings of her own heart.

Shina walks toward the queen, her steps slow and measured. "Yes, Akari?" she whispers softly as she comes to stand directly in front of her. Akari Ilinka towers over the small woman, but Shina does not look at all inferior. Her chin is held high, and there is no shame to be found on her face as she stares down the witch-queen.

Akari's face is agonized for one more brief moment, before it twists with fury. In an instant, her humanity dissipates, leaving only the power-hungry warlord. "I *loved* you," she hisses through her teeth.

For the first time, Shina's face is not kind. It's like the queen's presence has sharpened every angle of her. Her eyes flash, and her mouth draws into a hard line. "You don't know what love is, Akari."

"I gave you the world!" Akari shouts, taking one furious step toward her. Max raises her falchion, but Shina waves her off without taking her eyes from the queen.

"You *stole* my world," Shina says, taking her own charged step forward. The queen's eyes widen at her nerve, at the steel of Shina's spine. "You murdered my family and stripped me of my identity, carved everything I cared about away until I was the shape *you* wanted." Another step forward, and this time, the queen relents. Steps back. "You loved that I served you. That I became exactly what you wanted. That is not love, Akari. That is madness. I was only ever a vessel to you. Another way to stake your control, to expand your power."

Though Shina's words are soft, there is nothing of the same in her face. She is all strength as she stares down one of the most powerful warlords of Ferusa.

"You traitorous little whore—"

Now, Shina smiles. "You deserved everything I did to you and more. And now that you've faced my justice, you will face the rest of the Siralenis as well. Every person you enslaved, every family you murdered. Every son or daughter sent to the workhouses. All of them will have their chance to speak."

Akari Ilinka howls in rage as Shina motions her guards forward. They've just reached the queen when both suddenly collapse where they stand.

More instinct than decision, I step in front of Shina just as a dark shadow darts out from the trees. I'm knocked to the ground by a blur of dark hair and clothing, the force of the impact driving the air from my lungs as I grapple with the anonymous attacker.

My fingers dig into flesh, and I leverage my feet around their waist, swinging myself up. Without pausing, I drive my fist into a rock-hard abdomen, even as wind roars past my ears, drowning out the sound of everything around me. I'm thrown sideways, and my spine collides with a tree trunk hard enough to crack something near my ribs. Stars bloom behind my eyes and my skull rattles, as I blink furiously, trying to gather my bearings and make sense of the scene before me.

A storm whips through camp, its power far rivaling the gale of last night. And at the center, a familiar shaved head.

"Avedis, what the fuck?!" I shout furiously, running at the assassin. He is terrifying standing over the witch-queen, a wraith spawned in the pits of the Darkness. His face glints with delighted malice as the wind howls around us, a harrowing, lonely sound. Max and Shina have both fallen to the ground, Max's arm around the rebel leader, like she can keep her from being blown away entirely. Harlan's grabbed Helias and dragged him behind a fallen trunk, only visible by the boy's curls wildly whipping in the wind.

Akari Ilinka writhes on the ground, clawing desperately at her throat, her nails dragging red lines down her own skin. Avedis laughs loudly, his delight ringing hollowly in the storm, like he's never had so much fun in his life.

He doesn't appear to notice anyone but her. As enamored as he is with her suffering, almost hypnotized by it, he doesn't have time to react when I hurtle myself at him. Hitting Avedis is like crashing headfirst into a tree, and I swear, my bones rattle in my body, as we go down in a tangle of fists and feet.

My knuckles crack against his jaw. His head snaps sideways and he snarls, wrapping his giant legs around my waist and flipping us both over. "Avedis!" I shout again, even as I squirm from beneath his weight, and aim my boot at his knee. I'm well-trained, but the assassin is different. He's bred like Anni—not just trained in violence, but *grown* in it. I have no hope of beating him—I just need to somehow stay alive long enough to talk some godsdamn sense into whatever madness has overcome him.

He pins me to the ground, and I pound my fists against his chest. The assassin doesn't even bother to look at me as he wraps his large hand around my throat and begins to squeeze. His eyes are still on Akari Ilinka, his gaze weirdly trancelike. I chop my forearm down hard against his, and his fingers loosen enough for me to bellow, "What in the Darkness is wrong with you?!"

Avedis finally slides his gaze to me, and though his hand squeezes my windpipe, horror somehow squeezes it tighter. There is nothing I recognize in that gaze, none of the clever curiosity I've come to appreciate in Avedis.

There is nothing at all.

"I'm Cal," I explain desperately, realizing the wind-wielder may not have any recollection of me at all. As far as he's concerned, I'm only an obstacle, standing between him and the witch-queen. "We're friends! Well...maybe not *friends*, but we're acquaintances!"

Avedis snarls and I yelp out, "Very good acquaintances! The best acquaintances you can be!"

The wind-wielder freezes above me, but it isn't my words that have stayed his hand. It's Max's swords: one at his throat and one at his spine. The witch-queen coughs and gasps on the ground, as Shina rises behind us.

"You have three seconds to remove your swords, Princess," Avedis rumbles. "Or you'll find yourself without breath." His tone is almost casual, but there is nothing relaxed about the way the wind-wielder stares at Max. The dark irises are fathomless, an endless pit that crawls and writhes.

Max only tilts her head and sharpens her gaze. "Call me Princess one more time, and you'll find yourself without a tongue."

Something like interest gleams on the assassin's face. "Ah. What a shame it would be to relieve me of my tongue before I could bless you with its many talents."

My eyebrows shoot up in surprise, as Max's face twists in disgust. "Ugh. Spare me, assassin."

"Are you so self-flagellant as to request I spare you from pure pleasure, Princess?"

"What in godsnames happened in Argentum?!" I interrupt hotly, wiggling out from under Avedis and shoving him bodily. "Where is everyone else?"

Avedis' gaze slowly crawls from Max to me, and I immediately wish it didn't. It digs beneath my skin, scratches at my lungs, like his eyes are made of Darkness itself. "Is it not obvious, Calloway?" He drawls my name in the same way he always does, proof he has his memory. "I went into Argentum with a soul and came out missing one."

"Where's Shaw and Mirren?" Max bites out.

"I'm sure the fire-bastard is off somewhere torturing himself, and the Ocean-wielder..." Avedis grins widely and it sends fresh dread skittering down the back of my neck. His eyes flash to where Harlan listens a few feet away. "The Ocean-wielder is probably thanking the dead gods I relieved her of the burden of a brother that cared nothing for her."

A soft gasp escapes me. "You...you killed Easton?"

Avedis only smiles wider as he watches Harlan's face drain of color. And I swear, the colors around him drain away, too, as his heart breaks in front of us all. For a wild moment, I consider tackling Avedis again, pummeling his face over and over for the way he drinks in Harlan's pain; for causing it in the first place.

"I murdered the boy, and I will murder you all if you do not hand over the queen."

"Why haven't you murdered us already?" I ask before I can fully consider the wisdom of the question.

Avedis examines his nails in boredom. "I may be soulless but I'm also pragmatic. No use wasting energy on murder when there's no need. Your pain will do nothing to satisfy me. It is hers I demand."

At the very least, soulless Avedis appears far more reasonable than soulless Anni, which doesn't come as a surprise. While the wind-wielder has always been murderous, he's never contained the innate anger of my brother.

"You do not have the sole claim to her pain," Shina says, and everyone turns to stare at her. She stands next to Akari Ilinka, her hands held out toward the queen. It takes me a protracted moment to understand, to realize what's caused Avedis' face to suddenly go even more feral.

Water swirls a hairsbreadth away from the witch-queen's mouth. Shina is a water-wielder.

"Shina," Avedis says with an exaggerated nod of his head, just as the queen's eye widens in recognition and she hisses, "*You!*"

Avedis smirks. "You'll forgive me if I don't bow." Then his eyes narrow as he truly takes in the queen's appearance for the first time. He goes completely still as he takes in the mutilated pull of the new scar, the way it runs from her hairline, through her cheek and to her other ear, in a perfect imitation of his own. His whisper is deadly. "Who did that to you?"

Ilinka says nothing, her face flushed with rage as her eyes flicker from Shina to Avedis.

"Shaw did it," Max answers, as the space between us all goes taut. Like one spark will cause everything to explode.

Still, Avedis doesn't move. "Why." It isn't so much a question as a demand.

"To honor you the way he knows how," I reply softly.

"I cannot imagine that unbearable prick honoring anything but his own ego."

"Well, he's not great with the words—or the emotions—" I admit affectionately. "—but he is great with the violence part of friendship. If you need revenge, Anni's your guy."

Avedis makes a disbelieving noise in the back of his throat, and then shifts on his feet, like the entire conversation has unbalanced something in him. I ready myself to leap at him, as he prowls toward Shina, but she proves her bravery once more and doesn't flinch back. I now see how she overthrew the witch-queen's reign. The woman is fearless.

But I suppose living your life entirely in fear relieves it of its meaning eventually. The same way one grows accustomed to the cold.

"I know what she did to you, Wind-wielder. I know what she took and the hollow it carved. The pain you demand."

Avedis tilts his head. "You are not soulless. What could you know of any of it?"

"A soul does not need to be lost for it to be ruined," Shina replies simply. "We are the same, you and me. But where you only see your own hurt, I see everyone's. The queen will answer to her people."

The wind whips more furiously and leaves swirl in the air.

"If you do not stay your hand, I will drown Akari where she stands, and you will have none of the vengeance you seek."

Avedis is a tempest given form as he stares at the small rebel leader. But his wind dies down and the trees around us quiet until we can once again hear the distant crash of the sea.

"The wind-wielders of Siralene have heard the whispers of you, Avedis. Your spirit is ancient, the depth of its storm born in the beginning of time, when there was nothing but air and dust. Go to Nadjaa and make peace with the Fire-bringer and Ocean-wielder. Break the curse. And you have my word, that when I am finished with Akari, I will give you your vengeance."

Avedis' mouth twists in disgust, like he can't imagine anything worse. "If you break your oath, I will get my fill of pain from you, Shina. Small as you are, I imagine you would be quite the feast."

Shina simply raises her chin and looks at me. "I cannot gift you an army, Calloway, but consider this my offer of friendship," she says to me with a pointed nod. "What happens after is up to you."

CHAPTER
THIRTY-TWO

Shaw

I turn my face toward the sun, its warmth soaking through the thick fabric of my cloak and into my skin beneath. Sweat beads on my brow, and I swipe at it absently as I take in the valley. Winter hasn't yet settled in Nadjaa the way it has in the northern part of the continent, and a part of me wishes to avoid the city entirely and go straight to the black cliffs near the manor. To stretch out by the pond with Mirren in my arms and let the rays melt every part of me that's been encased in ice since Argentum.

But unfortunately for my daydreams, the entirety of the Nadjaan guard is on alert for anyone traveling over the passes, and most especially, for Mirren and I. We're relegated to the same small footpath we escaped on, one I've never made Denver or his guard aware of, but even then, the Chancellor will know of our arrival. Since magic's return, he certainly has wielders in his employ to keep him apprised of every traveler.

When the city comes into view, my breath catches just as Mirren lets out a small sound of pleasure beside me. The

Averitbas mountains stand tall in the distance, and the colors of Nadjaa spill down the cliffs like a splashing rainbow, the shades made all the more vibrant against the black of the bay.

I haven't been here since my soul was restored, and though I've thought about it more times than I can count, somehow, I'm still unprepared for the way the sight of it grabs hold of me. Of the feel of being here once more.

Warm. And not simply because of the sun, but because I've arrived home. Why was I never willing to claim it before, to anoint it with the name?

My gaze travels to the center of the city, toward the towering Council House. Even from here, the bustle of activity is visible, rebuilding what Mirren destroyed only a few months ago. I imagine Denver in his office on the topmost floor, hunched over his books, pushing his glasses back up his nose as they repeatedly slide back down.

Was it Denver that kept me from considering Nadjaa home? Had I somehow sensed the wall that existed in him, the one built to keep others from ever truly knowing him? Or was it simply the fear of claiming something that could be taken from me, the fear I'd never recover from its inevitable loss?

It didn't matter in the end. Nadjaa was stolen from me, and I'd survived it. Survived it by finding true home. One that can't be burned or flooded.

Together, we descend into the city, keeping to the quieter streets as we make our way toward Aggie's cabin. We discussed going to Evie's first to learn how Denver reacted to Luwei's news, and what he's been doing since. Mirren had suggested finding Asa to hear the prophecy, but in the end, our need to know if Max and Cal have arrived safely with Helias won over everything else.

As we grow closer to the cabin, anxiety spools through me. It had been suppressed by survival until now, but these streets smell like Max, and they sound like Cal, and now my mind spirals unbidden through everything that could have befallen them during our separation. What if the Similians couldn't heal Cal's wound? What if the witch-queen escaped her bonds and got her revenge against me by hurting them?

By the time Aggie's cabin comes into view between the trees, adrenaline courses through my veins. The small cabin's ramshackle appearance has only grown in eccentricity in my time away, with the addition of a plethora of wind chimes now strung up around the porch, bleached white and tinkling in the light breeze. The woman herself stands in the threshold with her weathered hands on her hips and a vaguely annoyed look on her face, as if she expected us and we're somehow late.

When I pull Dahiitii to a stop at the foot of the steps, Aggie's irritation dissipates and her face crinkles in a gap-toothed smile. "Anrai Shaw," she says, as I swing myself to the ground. "You kept your promise."

I offer Mirren a hand, which she promptly ignores, throwing herself off the horse despite her injuries. She sways wildly, but miraculously manages to keep to her feet, and my mouth twists somewhere between a grimace and a smile. As much as I adore it, sometimes I think Mirren's independence will be the death of me.

"What promise is that?" I ask Aggie, just as my gaze snags on the chimes and I realize they are not made of clay, but rather, small bones. I avert my eyes hastily, deciding I'd rather not know. Like most things with Aggie, there is usually a price to knowledge.

"You always promised to come visit, even after you'd

been consumed. And here you are, just in time for the moon festival."

I stare at her, doing a quick calculation in my head. We've been on the run for so long, I hadn't realized it was that time again, but in three days, the moon will be at its fullest above the Averitbas and all of Nadjaa will be celebrating in the streets. Dancing and laughing, like the entire continent isn't gathering to destroy everything they hold dear.

"I'll always come back to you, Aggie," I reply affectionately, moving up the rickety porch stairs to hug the old woman. Her bones are delicately light in my embrace, like the bones of a bird, and she cackles with delight.

Her unseeing eyes move to Mirren behind me. "And you, little bird. You spread your wings and flew away, and yet, here you are once again. I do hope this time you remember how to swim."

Mirren's mouth flattens in annoyance, and I resist the urge to laugh. "Birds don't swim, Aggie," she says with no small amount of exasperation. "But it's good to see you, too."

Aggie makes a humming sound, and then laughs loudly as though Mirren's made a hilarious joke. She waves a hand in the air, ushering us inside. "Come in, come in. You can get cleaned up before you tell this old woman of your adventures. I'm afraid these knees aren't what they once were, so my only choice is to live vicariously through you."

Mirren follows Aggie inside the cramped cabin, and I duck in behind them. The air is thick with the smell of herbs, and I nearly run straight into a dangling bunch of what looks suspiciously like aconite. "Planning on poisoning someone, Aggie?" I brush the plant aside and close the door behind me.

The old woman merely laughs as she shuffles toward the small woodstove. "Perhaps," she replies airily. She motions toward a large pot of water already warming on the top of the stove. "Carry this into the corner so your little bird has privacy to wash."

I do as the woman says, hauling the pot to the only corner of the cabin that isn't stuffed to the brim with odds and ends. A small stool is set against the wall, and Aggie unties a multicolored curtain from the ceiling, and sweeps the thick fabric around it.

"Throw those filthy clothes on the floor and I'll see to getting them washed. Until then, you can wear this." Aggie hands Mirren a long, emerald colored robe. She accepts it gratefully and disappears behind the curtain.

"Tea?" Aggie asks me innocently.

I glance at the aconite, before shaking my head. "I'm fine, thank you."

Aggie shuffles into the kitchen anyway, pulling herbs from various bundles as she goes. "You should know, Denver is having this house watched by wind-wielders. He'll already know you're here."

I push a sigh through my teeth. I'd figured as much, but hearing it confirmed unsettles me anyway. "I'm not ready to see him, yet." I glance at the heavy curtain. "Neither is she."

Aggie nods. "Then you will not," she promises.

"Thank you," I tell her genuinely, suddenly feeling wearier than I can ever remember. My bones ache and my muscles are heavy. Perhaps it's the warmth of this cabin, or finally being somewhere my body recognizes as safe, but I know if I close my eyes, I could sleep for an entire week. But then, I remember Cal and Max and my entire body tenses again.

Before I can get the question out, Aggie sets me with a milky stare. "They have not been here, boy. Not since you all left together."

The abyss rises in my chest, a conflagration of anger and terror and denial. Because Max and Cal should have arrived long before Mirren and me. Their trip from Similis to Nadjaa was far shorter than the one from Argentum. And if they aren't here, and haven't sent word, it can only mean something terrible happened.

And Helias. I'd promised him he'd always be safe. Where is he now? Have I failed him too? I force my panic down. "And Asa?"

"In the weeks after you left, the Kashan and his little apprentice were here most every day. We listened to the whispers of the earth and to the stories of the past, and eventually, he found the right one. It wasn't easy, but the Kashan is not a man that spooks easily." Aggie lets out another menacing cackle. "He was persistent in unearthing what the Darkness wished to bury."

"You've heard the prophecy?" I ask in alarm.

Aggie shakes her head. "I'm afraid not, boy, not in its entirety as its meant to be heard. It was not to me the story spoke. And before we could discuss it further, our Chancellor put the Xamani under constant watch, trying to ferret out the words for himself. Asa and I thought it best not to meet any longer. I have not seen the Kashan in over a month."

Mirren ducks her head out from behind the curtain. While it wasn't a true bath, she's washed away the thick layer of travel dust and muck, and her cheeks shine a rosy pink against the layers of emerald fabric wrapped around her.

She comes to sit beside me, and unable to help myself, I

reach for her hand, winding my fingers between hers. The feel of her skin ebbs the tension in my muscles, and my thoughts calm. Though Mirren's touch no longer physically tethers me to my soul, I find myself constantly seeking out the reassurance of her skin against mine.

"I think I should go to Evie's. See what I can learn about what Denver's goals are. Then we can prepare for how you want to approach this."

Mirren nods, understanding I mean to go alone. I'll need to be invisible to walk through the city without Denver finding out, and though Mirren has many skills, keeping quiet is not one she excels at. "Okay," she agrees with an ease that surprises me. Mirren is rarely agreeable, and even less often is she easily convinced not to come at something with every bit of her fortitude.

I narrow my eyes suspiciously. "Are you feeling okay?"

She glares at me and shoves her shoulder into mine. "Very funny," she mutters. "I want to stay and talk to Aggie. About..." She hesitates, and the hurt that exists within the confines of that pause makes me wish the Covinus were standing in this cabin, so I could melt his skin from his bones. "About what happened in Argentum."

I don't know whether she means what happened to her in the dungeons, or what happened to Easton afterward, but it doesn't matter. I only feel relief that Mirren is willing to talk to someone about it, even if that someone isn't me. I have yet to see a glimpse of her power since she healed Avedis, and the fact that she hasn't healed herself fills me with dread.

Did she use the only remaining bit on the man who killed her brother? Is there now only emptiness where her water should reside? Desert where there should be an ocean?

She hasn't said, and though I will always press Mirren to a point, I'll never force her over the edge of breaking. And this time, that edge has remained stubbornly out of my view.

"Alright," I say, though I'm not at all certain it is. "I'll be quick."

Mirren nods and accepts tea from Aggie far too eagerly. I twist my mouth in disgust, before turning to the old woman. "Can you keep her hidden from Denver until I get back?"

Aggie smiles, her weathered face crinkling in delight. "The guard is far too scared of this house to step one toe out of the woods."

"Probably because you curse everyone who does with death by inanimate object," I point out with a half laugh. "And poison the others."

Mirren coughs, choking on the sip of tea she just imbibed. Aggie just shrugs, unperturbed.

"Be quick about it, boy. The Darkness moves swiftly."

◠

Mirren

The door has barely closed behind Anrai when Aggie turns her cratered stare in my direction. "Up!" she barks impatiently.

I jerk in surprise and stare at her in confusion, even as she rounds the table and thwacks me on the arm. "Up," she yelps again.

Throwing my arms over my head to protect my ears from a direct hit, I do as I'm told with a harried sigh. "By the gods, Aggie, I'm going!"

The old woman points to the threadbare sofa centered

in front of the woodstove. The cushions are wrinkled and worn, their color a very unappetizing shade of brown I'm certain was not the shade originally intended. The entire thing looks like a frog, with the legs oddly squatted and the middle sagging almost to the floor.

"Lay down," Aggie instructs. "Unless you'd rather have more tea."

I don't truly think Aggie would ever harm me, but I'm also not absolutely certain, and it's enough to goad me into doing what I'm told, even as I shoot her an obstinate glare.

Without waiting for permission, Aggie pulls the soft robe aside, exposing the wounds on my back. The skin has ceased to feel like skin at all, now all itch and sting and pull; one giant scab. Aggie makes a noise of approval. "Well at least the boy isn't entirely daft. These don't appear to be infected. But they could use a good *brijaa* salve, to speed the healing."

She disappears into the kitchen for a long while, and I shift irritably on the couch. It smells strongly of herbs and woodsmoke, and while it isn't entirely unpleasant, I'd rather it not smell like anything at all. Finally, she comes back, the sofa somehow sinking further to the ground as she arranges herself next to me.

"Is it a Xamani salve?" I ask, my curiosity itching just as surely as my wounds.

Aggie tuts. "Ferusa existed before the Darkness, child. And some things, like this salve, are older than even the continent."

I furrow my brow, chiding myself for expecting a simple answer to a simple question.

"Speak while I work, little bird. I can feel your questions scratching their way out of your skin from here and keeping them in will only rub you raw."

I stare at the murky brown cushion for a long moment, as Aggie begins to press the cool salve into my wounds. Her gnarled hands are calloused and rough, but she touches me gently. The concoction stings, but it isn't unbearable, and after a moment, the burning itch begins to cool slightly.

There are so many things I need to ask. But questions bring answers, and I don't know if I'm strong enough for some of them. I settle on something that has nothing to do with me at all. "When we first met, you said you knew my mother. What did you mean?"

I know now Azurra never made it out of the Boundary. Aggie couldn't possibly have known her, unless the old woman somehow traveled to Similis and breached the wall long before Shaw did.

"You know the earth speaks to me. Your mother spoke to me, too."

It's an answer and not an answer at all, but by now, I'm used to the roundabout way Aggie speaks. She will always answer my questions, but it may not be the way I want or a way I can understand, and it's something that cannot be changed. Just abided by. "How?"

"Perhaps it was the will of the old gods, an echo of their power that sent her voice to me. Who can truly know?" I shiver, as she applies a fresh glop of the substance to my shoulder. "In her final moments, perhaps she believed so strongly in a better world, she tied herself to it and I heard the threads of her heart in the earth itself. Her heart is what drew her to your father, and also why she never followed him into the Dark World. She couldn't leave the rest of her people to their fate."

I mull over Aggie's words, both pride and heartbreak wending through me.

"Your parents bonded over such a strong belief in

change. A world of lightness for you to live in. But ultimately, it is what tore them apart."

"Does—does Denver know about this? That you saw my mother's final days?"

"Denver knew something was different about our meeting, but I never said, and he never asked."

Frustration heats my cheeks, and I shift uncomfortably on the couch. "Why didn't you tell him what you knew? That's not fair to keep such a secret from him. He spent his life believing my mother was alive and Easton and I were cared for. If you had told him—"

"If I had told him, it may have broken him entirely," Aggie interrupts sharply. "I am not arrogant enough to presume another person's limits, and if Denver needed to hide the truth from himself in order to keep whole, it was not my place to violate his peace."

I fall silent, scolded. Because Aggie is right. There is so much about my father's life I remain ignorant of, but of one thing I'm sure: he loved my mother. And it had broken him. Perhaps stubbornly holding on to the hope she was alive was the only thing that had kept Denver from falling into the depths of despair. From giving up entirely.

"Aggie, the Covinus tried to steal my *other*—my power —in that dungeon. I don't know if he succeeded."

Aggie finishes with the salve. She sets the clay bowl on the floor and helps me up to sitting. Despite her frail appearance, her arms are far sturdier than they look. She sets me with that eerie gaze, and for the first time, I don't feel like squirming beneath its power. I let her see beneath my skin, through my heart and lungs, to the depths of what resides in me. Finally, she says, "Do *you* think he succeeded, little bird?"

I bite my lip. "I don't feel powerful anymore. I feel broken—and weak."

Aggie stares at me so long, for a moment, I expect that horrible low voice to speak once again from her lips. But it's only her that says, "You feel human, girl, which is why your spirit chose you. The elements could have bonded to any other species on any other world, but do you know why they chose ours?"

I shake my head, my throat thick with emotion.

"Because we have such high highs and such low lows, but we do not break. We *bend*. We change shape. We become something new." She grips my fingers in her hands, and I stare down at them. Dark skin against light. Gnarled and paper thin against young and spry. "We endure, Mirren. And you, my dear girl... you are more capable of endurance than most."

A hot tear rolls down my cheek. "What if I can't do it this time? What if it's finally too much? What if he took everything that made me who I am?"

I don't know if I speak of my power or my brother, but Aggie answers anyway. "Then you dig deeper. To what is immutable about you. To what cannot be stolen. You find the new edges of yourself, and you fit them into what makes you." Aggie gazes at me fiercely. "And then, you press on."

CHAPTER
THIRTY-THREE

Shaw

The city buzzes with preparations for the lunar celebration as I make my way to Evie's bakery. Delicious scents waft from open windows, sweet sugars and tangy spices mingling on the fresh sea breeze. I've always loved the variety of food Nadjaa offers: the aromatic herbs of Baak, the powdered sweets of Dauphine, and even a few of the delicacies from Tahi Ohua have made their way to the Nadjaan markets.

A pang of regret tugs at me as I realize Mirren's never had the opportunity to remain here long enough to experience everything the city has to offer, always pulled in another direction. And now is hardly the time while at odds with her father and hunted by the Covinus. But gods, I'd love to take her to every street stand in the city and watch her face as the tastes bloom in her mouth.

I keep to the shadows and alleyways, sure to avoid any establishment Denver has a stake in or any tavern Cal and Max have dragged me to over the years. When I arrive in the market district, I scale the side of a flower shop, and then travel the rest of the way by roof, leaping nimbly from one to the next until I reach Evie's. The smell of the sea swirls in my nose, and this close to the bay, the sounds of the water lapping up against the docks is unmistakable.

The sound reverberates in my chest, and then somewhere deeper in the back of my brain. I tense as anxiety spools through me, along with a hot rush of rage. Because though the Praeceptor is gone, the stain of his influence remains. And I despise him for it—for the way he took something so sacred, a piece of Mirren, and twisted it into something so malevolent. When will I be able to hear the sound of water, and not think of the dungeon?

When will I only think of her? Of her beauty, and her strength?

"You look like an overgrown bat up there," a voice says from the topmost window of the boarding house, startling me so fully from my thoughts, I nearly tumble backward off the roof. "An overgrown, *brooding,* miserably handsome, bat. Really, Anni, would a little color in your wardrobe kill you? It's the middle of the day, and you're dressed like you're on your way to haunt unsuspecting travelers."

Relief explodes in a cool wave as I regain my footing and lean to peer over the side of the shingled roof. Calloway's copper head hangs out of the window. His freckles have disappeared behind an impressive sunburn, but he looks decidedly alive as he grins up at me with shining white teeth. "Hey, brother."

My throat grows thick as he ducks back, allowing me space to swing down and climb inside. My eyes can't move fast enough as I take him in, running from his head to his toes in search of any sign of hurt. When I finally determine he is whole and healed, every horrible thing I've imagined in our time apart comes racing to the surface of my skin just as something hot settles in my stomach, and I punch him in the arm.

"Hey!" he shouts with an injured look. "What was that f—"

"Where in the Darkness have you been!?" I shout, the words bursting from me in a loud jumble. "I thought you were dead!" I hit him again, and this time, instead of rocking back on his heels, Calloway swings and punches me in the shoulder.

"Well, I'd say we're even, you bastard! You didn't even bother to send word you were alive—"

"—I *couldn't* send word—and I haven't heard a peep from you—"

"—you burn me alive and then... *nothing*!"

"You were bleeding out, you son of a bitch!"

"Boys!" Max interrupts loudly, stepping lithely in between the two of us. Her voice rattles me from my panic long enough that all the other feelings—the softer, more vulnerable ones—overwhelm me. With far more violence than intended, I grab them both and yank them to me. I bury my head in Cal's shoulder, ball my hands into fists in Max's cloak. She lets out a strangled noise of relief as both of their arms come around me, and I inhale them as I would oxygen.

And when I release them, I feel like I can properly breathe for the first time in a month. I meet Cal's gaze sheepishly. "You're okay?"

He smiles at me, and it smooths away the jagged remains of my fear. "Better than okay." He stretches down to touch his toes in demonstration, and then rises with a wiggle of his brows. "We've got a hell of a story for you."

Max rolls her eyes, the motion as loud as if it were a sound. "By hell of a story, he means he decided to channel your stupid ass, and take on an entire militia by *himself*."

"It wasn't as foolish as she makes it sound—" Cal snipes back with a shake of his head, but for the moment, I don't even care. My friends, the foundations on which I rebuilt myself, are here. Alive. Whole.

"As much as I'd *love* to listen to more of this nauseating display of friendship," a familiar voice drawls, "are we not in this city for a reason?"

Avedis leans against the threshold with his arms crossed over his chest. A smug smile crawls across his face as he stares at me. His dark hair has been shaved to his skull once more, and if I'm dressed like an overgrown bat, so is he, the dark leather of his gear pristinely shined.

More reflex than thought, I push Max and Cal behind me, and send a dagger flying for the wind-wielder's heart.

He brushes it off midflight with a lazy flick of his wrist, and the knife clatters loudly to the floor. Flame rises at my fingertips, the flicker of light reflecting in the soulless pool of his eyes, but the assassin doesn't move. Only cocks his head. "Good gods, Fire-beast, have you no control? Do you truly intend to take out this quaint little bakery and half a city block, just to soothe your ego?"

He peels himself off the doorway and stalks forward, his movements serpentine and lethal. "Your paramour isn't even here, and still, you growl like a Ditya protecting a carcass."

"Shaw..." Max warns, but I don't dare take my eyes from Avedis as he saunters right up to me.

He flicks his wrist again, and the flame at my palm blows out. "I've considered your offer."

I narrow my eyes warily. "Is that what you call running away like a coward? Considering?"

Avedis' lips thin as he runs his eyes over me distastefully. "Now, now. That's no way to talk to a man whose help you so desperately need."

"I don't need anything from you," I reply through clenched teeth.

Avedis only grins more widely, stepping so close his chest brushes mine, and it takes everything in me to hold still and not rise to the taunt. He hums cheerfully, drinking in my frustration. "If only that were true. Where is that sweet little Ocean-wielder of yours? Perhaps I should ask *her* what she needs from me." He runs his tongue over his teeth lewdly, and his dark eyes glint with maniacal excitement as he devours my reaction.

Flame shoots up my throat and rolls over my tongue, but I'm saved from responding, as Max swears loudly and roughly pushes Avedis, apparently not at all intimidated by his soulless state. He stumbles sideways in a decidedly ungraceful manner, and shoots Max an annoyed look. "For the gods' sake," she huffs. "Can none of you use your words?"

"That's rich, coming from you," Calloway mutters, before pressing his lips together under Max's hot glare.

"Avedis has agreed to help with the prophecy," Max explains in an exaggeratedly slow tone, like she's explaining something to children. "Shaw, you need him for that."

"I gave him the chance, and he ran. He doesn't have a soul, how are we supposed to trust him now?"

She sets me with a pointed look. "As I recall, he extended *you* the same chance not so long ago."

I scoff. "As *I* recall, he punched me in the jaw."

"You started it, Fire-beast, but I will always finish it."

Max throws her hands in the air, and snaps, "If you

don't quit trying to murder each other, I will murder you both."

"I do love when you get bossy, Maxwell," Avedis purrs, and Max responds by pushing him again, knocking him into the nearest wall.

"Why?" I ask, failing to ignore the feral way the assassin now stares at Max. Like he's never seen anyone so engaging. Like he's imagining how playing with her would feed his emptiness, at least for a short while. "Why now? You had no interest in helping us when you left the mountains. You were content to spend the rest of your life on the run, just like you always have."

Avedis sniffs. "Things change," is all he says. And then, under Max's furious look, he sighs loudly and adds, "My memories began to come back quite quickly after we spoke, and I was driven to seek out my own revenge before I attempted to untangle the mess *you've* put me in, beast."

Realizing who Avedis refers to and how he must have crossed paths with Cal and Max, I glance at Cal. "Is she dead?"

A tangle of emotions flits across Cal's face, but before I can determine what they are, the assassin answers for him. "Let's just say a mutual friend of ours showed me of the wisdom of allowing our queen to suffer before she meets her final end. The witch-queen lives. For the moment, anyway." Avedis grins wickedly and cocks his head. "I must admit, I did appreciate your homage to our former friendship, twisted as it was."

For an absurd moment, I feel like smiling back. Because though I'd done it for someone different than the man that now stands before me, I have no regrets. For everything Avedis has done for Mirren, for me, he deserved that and more. "Where is she now?"

"The people of Siralene have revolted," Cal replies. "I gave the queen to their rebel leader to face the justice of her people."

There is clearly more to the story, but Avedis chooses that moment to loudly interrupt, "Well. As horrendously *touching* as this reunion has been, I find myself out of my mind with boredom. I'm sure you'll understand my taking leave in order to find the company of someone more...entertaining." He waves irreverently, before dipping into a sardonic bow at my feet.

When he rises, he swings a cloak around his shoulders and stops in front of Max, that same devilish grin adorning his face. "Care to join me, Maxwell? I think you'll find me far more enamoring company than these two."

Max shudders in disgust, her face twisting. "Please take this exactly how it sounds—I would, quite literally, rather die."

Avedis smiles wider, not at all put off by Max's disgust, but seemingly encouraged by it. "Oh, we will have such fun together, my murderous darling."

And with that, he leaves the room with a flourish, slamming the door behind him.

I let out something between a breath and a curse. I should be thankful that Avedis' brand of soullessness is far less angry than mine was, even if his idea of fun is pissing everyone off. But I don't trust that writhing pit of emptiness I know to be inside him. He's been sated for now, but that won't remain so for long.

"You gave Ilinka to the Siraleni?" I ask Cal, my voice a mixture of admiration and disbelief. Because it isn't at all what I would have chosen, but it's a choice that defines what I've always loved about Cal. Unselfish and honest, he didn't hoard revenge for his own, but shared it with others.

As if reading my mind, Cal gives me a sheepish smile. "It wasn't entirely an unselfish decision."

"What do you mean?"

He dances on the spot, like he's been holding in this secret the entire time and it's been clawing its way out of him. "It was a gesture of goodwill. I turned over Akari Ilinka and asked that, when the time comes, they'll send aid to Nadjaa. Shina refused, but I'm hoping she changes her mind after she has time to think it over."

"Shina?" I repeat in surprise.

"Yes, Shina." Cal waves me off exasperatedly, like the revelation the queen's lover is also the organizer of her downfall is old news. "And as the rest of Akari's forces are trapped inside the magical terror forest—" At my growing confusion, he shakes his head as if to say he'll explain *that* later, and hurries on, "—the Siralenis have a good chance of making the change stick."

He sucks in a breath. "She's the reason Avedis is helping us. She promised she'd give the queen to him after she's faced justice if he helps us to break the curse."

I furrow my brow. "Does Avedis know they'll most likely kill her? If he loses his revenge, it's going to be a problem for all of us."

"I'll worry about keeping him leashed. You worry about the prophecy itself."

I'm about to reply when the door bursts open once more, and a small bundle of curls shoots into the room. The air rushes from my lungs as Helias collides full speed into my stomach, his hands clabbering for purchase as he scrambles to climb my legs like branches of a tree. I laugh, lifting the boy up, his body so wonderfully light in my arms.

He buries his head in the crook of my neck and the silk of his hair tickles the stubble on my chin. "I protected them for you," Helias whispers with pride. "All of them." My breath catches, but when I lean back, I see the little earth-wielder's deep brown eyes are not shattered with the weight of death—instead, they sparkle in the first smile I've ever seen from him.

"You did good, hellion," I tell him, my throat thick once more as I ruffle his hair and set him gently on his feet.

"Yeah, remember that terror forest Cal mentioned?" Max says, curling a hand over Helias' shoulder affectionately.

Helias nods enthusiastically. "I growed it right there in the middle of the field."

I glance at Max in shock, but she only shrugs. "I guess it's true what Asa said about the four original wielders. You're all more powerful."

"I could show you right now, Shaw!" Helias volunteers, and the building begins to shudder beneath us. I grab the boy and toss him into the air, his giggle tinkling like a bell.

"Maybe later." I return him to the ground. "Away from civilization."

Helias giggles again, and it rings in my chest like a chime. He curls his small hand in mine, his palm sweaty and warm, and somehow, wonderful. I stare dumbly down at the gesture, at the boy's faith in my goodness.

Feeling unsettled and happy at once, I glance around the room. One person is still missing. "Where's Harlan?"

At the golden boy's name, Calloway visibly stills and it's enough to send a new wave of unease through me as Cal is rarely ever still. "He needed air," he replies stiffly.

I shoot a glance at Max, but she doesn't meet it, instead, watching Cal with an unreadable look. Tilting my head, I set Cal with the same look he reserves for me, one that says

I'll sit here all night if I have to in order to ferret the truth out of him.

He bristles and rolls his eyes, pushing an impatient huff between his teeth. "Avedis is a bastard."

"Not new information."

"He told us about Easton. About what he did to him... and he certainly wasn't delicate about it."

Of course, Harlan would be upset by Easton's death, but there is something more to it, an edge underlying Cal's words. But he only shifts on his feet, avoiding my gaze so spectacularly, his eyes hardly land before they bounce to the next thing.

Max plops herself ungracefully into an armchair and curls her legs up beneath her. "Harlan and Cal had a thing," she announces perfunctorily to Cal's complete horror. "*Before* the news."

"It wasn't a *thing*," Cal hisses indignantly, before whipping his head back to me. "It wasn't a thing! It was—" He interrupts himself with a loud curse, and I have to work to keep my laughter from spilling out. "Well, I don't know what it was, but clearly, he needs space and I'm giving it to him."

Cal nods enthusiastically, and begins pacing, like he's convincing himself as much as me. "Yeah, space. It's normal. Healthy, even."

"Healthy, is it?" Max muses acerbically, and this time, I can't help the low chuckle that rolls out of me.

Cal spins around and narrows his eyes. "Don't you dare laugh. You've spent the better part of your relationship with Mirren sulking in some forest."

I laugh, raising my hands in peace. "Can't I just enjoy that for once, it isn't my ineptitude being discussed?" I look to Max conspiratorially. "Please tell me there were moonlit trysts."

Max grins in wicked delight. "Even better...*rain.*"

Cal scoffs in irritation, shaking his head, even as his sunburn brightens to a tomato red and his neck flushes.

My mouth drops open in feigned shock. "Calloway Cabrera... is that—are you...are you *blushing?*" I grab his face, pretending to examine him for a mysterious malady. "The man who once walked naked through the business district is *blushing?*"

He punches me in the arm, but there's no fight behind it. "You two are the absolute worst," he proclaims. "I don't know why I subject myself to this. Surely, with my good looks and charming personality, I'd be able to attract less obnoxious friends."

"Less obnoxious, maybe," Max agrees. "But certainly less fun."

Cal concedes with a sheepish grin.

"I'm happy for you, brother," I tell him sincerely. "Whether it's a thing or not a thing, you deserve someone as good as you are."

Calloway swallows roughly, before sniffing and gathering his thoughts. "Speaking of which, how's Mirren?"

Max sits up, suddenly far more alert.

There are a million ways to answer that question, and I'm still not sure any of them would fit. *She's destroyed. She's resilient. She's broken. She endures.* After a long pause, I settle on, "She's alive."

They wait for me to gather my thoughts. I bite my lip, wondering where to even begin. "She's been through a lot. The Covinus tortured her, terrorized her with memories. And then he tried to take her power for his own." Familiar rage claws at my chest, and I try to tamp it down. To save it for when it's useful. "I don't want to press her to relive her trauma, but I'm beginning to wonder if he succeeded. She hasn't been able to heal herself since Argentum. Not fully."

And then, settling myself on my bed, I recount everything that's happened. And though it is painful, speaking of the terror and horror, as the story spills out of me, the weight of my soul begins to lighten. The tension in my shoulders ease, breaths come easier in my chest. Because my friends listen without comment, without judgement, and share in lifting the burden.

CHAPTER
THIRTY-FOUR

Mirren

Time inches on in the cramped cabin as I sit with Aggie's words and wait for Anrai to return. I wash my clothes and hang them to dry, wondering how I'm ever to endure when the world is so sharp. It doesn't seem feasible, to endure with the hole carved in my chest by Easton's loss, to live around the gaping wound where my memories used to exist.

Aggie said loss reshapes us, but there is no shape to me now. I am scattered lines and fuzzy dots, a jumbled mess of sharp edges and unfinished strokes. And I'm not sure I see a point in gathering them, not when the world will shatter me again as soon as I'm whole.

I've taken to wandering restlessly around Aggie's cabin, fingering each of her trinkets without truly seeing them, by the time Anrai appears at the edge of the forest. My heart leaps into my throat when I see who he's brought with him, and I'm immediately up, tearing out of the cabin like it's on fire. Bare feet, hair a half-dried mess, robes tangling around my ankles, I race across the small clearing toward the trees.

When I reach them, I leap at Max, tears clouding my vision as I throw my arms around her neck with a sob. Her own eyes are lined with silver as she hugs me back tightly. Words elude me entirely, but I find they aren't needed as we hold each other. She pulls back with a wet laugh, and I hurtle into Cal with the same enthusiasm. He laughs brightly as I collide into his chest and wraps his arms around me. Helias bounces around our feet, and I scoop him up, dragging him into our hug.

"You gave us quite a scare," Cal says softly, hugging me tighter.

"I missed you," I whisper into his shirt.

When I finally pull away, it's to find a pair of golden eyes watching me sadly. Harlan stands a few feet behind the others, hands in his pockets. A sob rips from my throat as for once, Harlan is not calm or serene: his lower lip trembles, and the torment on his face breaks wide open in as he takes a hesitant step toward me. And it is all I need, to see my own grief reflected on another's face, to send me crashing into him.

He fists the back of my robe tightly, burying his head against my shoulder, his tears and mine mingling. "I'm so sorry," I gasp. Harlan's shoulders shake with silent sobs as we hold each other. "I'm so sorry, Harlan," I say again. "He should never have come for me."

Harlan raises his head, his eyes shining, and his cheeks splotched in shades of red. He wipes at them impatiently, staring down at me. "Yes, he should have," he says, and though his fingers shake when he weaves them with mine, his voice is steady. "Easton did what he needed to make amends, Mirren. To finally allow himself to truly love. And now, we're able to grieve someone who was worthy of it."

"But Harlan—I took him from you. I can't imagine what

you're going through. If—if I lost Anrai, I don't—" My words trail off, as the sentiment is too horrible to consider. "And I didn't protect him. I should have done better at protecting him."

Harlan searches my face earnestly. "You and me, Mirren, we're bound, and not just by the ceremony. We're bound in the way we've always fought for love, together and apart. We can't regret Easton giving himself over to the very thing we fight for. He deserved to feel its warmth, even if it was in his last moments."

I swipe at my wet cheeks, swallowing roughly. Harlan puts his arm around me, squeezing me to his side as we turn to join the others who've already gone ahead to the cabin. And for a moment, I allow myself to be thankful that Harlan and I made it out of Similis—that in the expanse of the Dark World, we have space to feel, to grieve, however we need to. And that my brother had the honor of experiencing Harlan's true heart, even if it was only for a short while.

Cal climbs the porch steps to where Aggie stands in the doorway. He claps her heartily on the back. "I've gotta say, Aggie, I'm disappointed in you. All this nonsense about bricks, where was the warning about tree limbs?"

Aggie cocks her head, her blind eyes twinkling with merriment. "I thought you smarter than that, Calloway. One must always be careful of trees and their most ancient of magic." She turns and disappears into the dim cabin.

Cal furrows his brow and charges after her. "Are there any other innocuous things I should be wary of?"

"Well, obviously the sweet cakes, Calloway."

Cal's mouth drops open in appropriate horror. "What?! You can't be serious."

"It took death to make you a believer, did it, boy?"

"I'd say more of a 'healthy skeptic' than believer," he replies, rubbing the side of his abdomen absently. "But I'll probably be avoiding brick walls in the near future."

Aggie laughs again as we shuffle behind her into the heat of the cabin. Max hands me a fresh pair of clothes, and I smile at her gratefully before ducking behind the multicolored curtain to get rid of the infernal robe. When I emerge, everyone has situated themselves around the scrubbed kitchen table. Helias is perched on Anrai's lap, the little earth-wielder gazing up at him like he holds the sun.

And I suppose in a way, to Helias at least, Anrai does.

Anrai catches me watching him, his mouth tilting in a small smile as he beckons me over. I squeeze into the chair between him and Max, the warmth of their presence sinking beneath my skin even as anxiety prickles at the back of my neck.

"Alright, Lemming. Denver definitely knows we're here by now. What do you want to do next?"

I press my lips together, hesitating. I need to warn my father, but the thought of seeing him wraps my ribs in a furiously tangled web of dread. Because seeing Denver will not only involve making a battle strategy: it means confronting both of our worst failings.

I'm not ready—not ready to face it yet. Not without knowing exactly where I stand.

"We need to see Asa. But we need to do it alone, and I don't see how we're going to manage that without my father finding out."

Anrai grins, arrogant and wicked, the pale of his eyes sparking. "If you want Asa alone, alone is what you'll get."

∽

"You ready?"

Night has fallen, and though the moon festival is still a few days away, the silver orb hangs large in the sky, casting the Xamani camp in ethereal light. Shadows cast by the tents shift and sway in the soft breeze, and Shaw watches them all with a sharp gaze. He's sunk into a crouch beside me, the dark leather of his gear wrapped around his body like the sheath of a weapon. His black bandolier is crossed over his chest, and I run my fingers around the supple leather of my own, buckled over my borrowed dress.

"You look entirely too excited about this."

He grins, his eyes nearly colorless in the moonlight. "Stealth, plotting, a little violence…what's not to love?" He twirls a dagger deftly between his fingers. "Besides, Aggie's cabin is too stuffy. It makes me want to crawl out of my skin."

I roll my eyes, wondering if there's a place Anrai doesn't feel restless. He'd hated the gray monotony of Similis, but would he feel at peace here in Nadjaa? Somewhere open and airy on the edge of the sea, filled with books. Or would he be happier wandering to the edges of the world, finding something new every day?

Both appealed to me at one time, but now, the dreamy thoughts are sharply edged. Because there may be no home, no world to explore, if we don't stop the Covinus from taking it all for himself.

Anrai happily swipes another dagger from his bandolier, the black of the blade seeming to devour the moonlight. "It's just like old times together, Lemming," he says with a suggestive wiggle of his brow.

I pull my own knife, running my index finger reverently over the ornate carvings. "Let's hope for less stabbing this time, shall we?"

He tsks. "Where's the fun in that?"

And with that, he springs into action, stalking through the shadows toward the first two Nadjaan guards. And though I've watched him a million times, the ease and silence with which he prowls still manages to stun me. Graceful like a cat, and far more dangerous, Shaw wraps his arm around the first guard's throat while the other's back is turned, and savagely squeezes his windpipe. The man doesn't even have the chance to scream before he's slumped at Anrai's feet. In a flash, the second guard joins him.

When both lie in an unconscious heap, Anrai grins back at me, a hint of flame leaping in his eyes. He motions the others forward from where they were hidden, and then flips the first guard over to disarm him.

Avedis saunters forward with a bored look, undeterred by the heat of Anrai's glare. "Thanks for the help," Anrai mutters, piling two swords and a few daggers on the ground next to him.

"I've been told my brand of help is not acceptable within the confines of the city," Avedis simpers sarcastically. "Don't blame me for the terribly dull company you keep."

Cal comes up behind him with a roll of his eyes. "I've been accused of being many things, Avedis, but *boring* has never been one of them." He toes one of the unconscious men with something like amusement. "Poor Rocher," he says. "Always at the wrong place at the wrong time."

Anrai, having disarmed both guards, stands up, and thrusts a lantern into Cal's arms. "Max and Harlan will signal when they make it to the next guard, signal back every ten minutes if everything is calm. If you see trouble, it's three flickers and a long flame."

Cal nods. "Got it."

"And you," Anrai barks at Avedis. "Send a message to Mirren and I if there's trouble. And don't kill anyone unless it's necessary."

Avedis tilts his head innocently. "We may have different definitions of necessary, Fire-bastard."

Anrai ignores the assassin, motioning to me with a mischievous grin. "Come on, Lemming."

While we'd been silent sneaking up on the Nadjaan guard, we purposely make noise as we approach the Xamani camp. The Chancellor may keep them under his watchful eye, but the Xamani have their own warriors protecting the more vulnerable of the tribes housed within. We sheathe our daggers and raise our hands, moving slowly as we approach. But as we grow closer, the two Xamani don't raise their bows, instead acknowledging us with smiles. "Very nice work with the guards," one laughs. "Nice enough men, but too nosy for their own good."

The other guard nods his head to the camp behind him. "The Kashan has been expecting you."

We thank them and walk quickly through the quiet pathways between tents. The day's fires have burned to little more than embers, and though most have long retired to bed, the camp still feels inviting. Animals rustle in the distance, and the smell of warm spices and leather still hangs in the air. Weariness washes over me, and for a moment, I desperately wish to lay down in a pile of furs and sleep for days.

My father knows we're in Nadjaa; he'll guess that eventually we'd come to see Asa, which means we must move quickly.

When we reach Asa's tent, I breathe a sigh of relief, as I'd half expected the Chancellor to be waiting for me. But it is only Asa's personal guard, motioning us forward. "That went a lot more smoothly than I thought it would."

Anrai shrugs irreverently. "Less stabbing. Less screaming. But also, less fun."

I roll my eyes with a smile, just as Asa pokes his head through the tent flap. "Come in, come in." We've barely stepped inside, before he wraps me in a warm hug. Some of the tension ebbs from my shoulders, as Asa embraces me as I imagine a father would. Allows me to lean against him, and ease the burden of weight I carry, if only for a moment.

When he pulls back, his hands are soft in mine and his eyes shine with both pride and sadness.

"Sura?" I blurt out. "Is she okay?"

Anrai sent them ahead to keep them safe, but so many things could have befallen them between the wastes of Argentum and Nadjaa. And Sura had been so weakened by the dungeons, she would have been in no condition to fight, leaving Luwei alone in protecting them. To my relief, Asa nods, and squeezes my hands. "Luwei and Sura made it back safely, and my little Kashan is recovering well." At my wandering look, he adds, "You will not find her here. She is in the city proper tonight."

Asa turns to Anrai. "You have come home, *zaabi*," he says simply.

For a moment, Anrai appears speechless. I wait for him to deny it, to rebuff the word and all it implies like he usually does. But he says, "In more ways than one, Kashan."

Asa's handsome face crinkles in a bright smile, and the two men embrace each other.

When they pull apart, Asa ushers us further into the tent. A fire burns cheerfully in the center, its smoke curling upward toward a small slice of the night sky peeking through the very top. The ground is covered in thick furs and brightly woven blankets, and a small kettle bubbles on a grate over the fire. "We have much to discuss, and our time alone is limited. I'm afraid your father has ears everywhere, even in the heart of our home."

Anrai shifts uncomfortably. He used to be the one gathering information for Denver, and though he rarely speaks about falling out of my father's favor, I know the betrayal still stings.

"Why is Sura in the city?"

"She was determined to find the wind-wielder."

Anrai's eyes widen. "Asa, Avedis is soulless—she shouldn't go anywhere near him, it's not safe..."

The Kashan nods, but he doesn't appear surprised by the news. "Sura holds much guilt in her heart for what happened in Similis." Asa's eyes flicker to me. "And in the Castellium. She believes she owes the wind-wielder a life debt and is determined to pay it."

When I open my mouth to protest, to insist Sura has nothing to atone for, he shakes his head sadly. "It is not up to us to decide what burdens another's soul. If Sura's feels too heavy to carry, she must do what she must in order to lighten it."

I swallow roughly, feeling at once seen and chagrined. Because isn't that exactly how my own soul feels? It was shattered in the Castellium, yes, but it disintegrated above ground with the death of Easton. And without him here, there is no one to tithe to, no one to fix the debt, and I am left floundering.

Asa motions for us to sit. I plop myself down on one of the furs, curling my legs beneath me as Anrai sits beside me.

"The story I am about to tell did not come easily. It was dragged from the depths of time, from the pits of the Darkness that ensnares it. The Darkness wished to keep it buried, hidden for eternity, so that nothing would know of the way to destroy it. It takes much of my strength to tell it, so after you hear it, you must promise me you'll leave immediately. I may not be in much of a state to help you, should your father or another council member come for you."

Anrai reaches for me, his rough callouses scraping the tender skin of my palm. His other hand flutters at his side before he snaps his fingers shut. He appears uncharacteristically nervous as he watches Asa, like he's poised to attack the story the moment it comes out. His anxiety heightens my own, threading through the bond of our souls and burrowing into me.

Asa closes his eyes and breathes in deeply. Anrai fidgets more.

We sit in silence for a few long moments, the only sounds being Asa's breathing and the merry crackle of the small fire. And then, the Kashan begins to speak, and we both tumble into the magic of his words.

Once, there was a queen.

Her name was Iara, and she was not a queen by birth or title, but anointed so by the love of her people. She was kind to all she met and gave away all she was given. The nature spirits danced around her in joy, and one in particular, a wild spirit of the ocean, bonded with her fully.

For a time, all was well, and the land flourished beneath the First Queen's care.

But it would not always be so. For one of Iara's dearest friends, a man who hid the darkness of his heart behind proclamations of love, was determined to possess her. Not born to coexist with nature, he set out to change his fate in order to earn the queen's affection.

The man traveled for many years, following the tales of worshippers and doubters alike, until one day, he came upon a god. One of the youngest and still naïve in nature, the god traveled alone. The man begged the young god to give him that which he lacked, to gift him with the company of a nature spirit.

But despite the god's youth, the being sensed the growing darkness in the man's heart and refused his request. The man insisted the god was wrong, and that the shadows of his heart did not matter, as there were plenty of malevolent wielders.

But the god understood far better than the man how delicate balance was; knew because he had seen the gods' own world destroyed by its upset. So, he refused the man once more.

The man grew angry and slayed the god with his dagger. Because though the gods were all-powerful, they could still bleed. The life seeped from the young god, coating everything around him in shades of gold, including the human coin he carried in his pocket.

The man stole the coin, now imbued with the young god's life force, and with it, he learned the secrets of the Darkness. Secrets not meant for malleable human hearts.

The man stole what was not his, and with it, poisoned the sacred places of the earth to fuel his unending greed. But the wealth did not sate him, and the darkness in his soul only grew.

The man took and took, stealing more and more, and the darkness speared out from his soul and seeped into the world, nurtured by violence and greed. It spread to those the man touched, to those he hurt, until it was an unstoppable blight on the land.

Iara pleaded with the gods to stop him—to take back what had been stolen from them. Feeling the queen's love mirrored their own for this world, they gave Iara a coin—the twin to the one the man had stolen years before. If the queen threaded her power through it, she would be capable of returning everything taken.

Iara met the man in his home by the sea, a city of moonlight and splendor, and when she saw him, her breath caught in her throat. Because in spite of his many evils, he had not changed. He was handsome, her dearest friend—and the same love that convinced the old gods to give Iara the coin, also caused her to hesitate.

Because when the man realized he would never possess Iara as he possessed all things, he killed her for the remaining coin. And with her dying breath, Iara spoke the words that would curse the land for a millennium to come:

Those who doom others will in turn doom themselves.

The last of her power threaded through both coins, and when she passed, the man's soul was torn apart by the loss. It shattered into a thousand pieces and fell in shards across the continents. His soul embedded in the valleys and rivers, in the mountains and plains, cursing everywhere they landed with darkness.

The man had finally gained the power he sought in the possession of two coins, but his love for the queen had shattered him.

Wars broke out and famines plagued even the most fertile of land as the Darkness spread. Man fought over resources and chaos descended where there was once joy. As more and more lost their souls and doomed themselves to the Darkness, the thicker it became. The spirits were hunted to the point of extinction and the old gods lay down in a cave to give their final words.

They knew the only way to stop the Darkness, to restore the souls of the human race, was to restore balance. To give back what had been taken. The curse was borne of selfishness and possessive greed, and only a selfless love would put it right.

Asa shudders, contracting and contorting like he fights against a phantom evil. And when he speaks again, his voice is resonant and deep, beyond anything I've ever heard. Like all the beauty and tragedy of the story has settled in his mouth, waiting to be spoken by his tongue.

Eyes of sea and heart of light will forge the darkness
To meet destruction in the soul of flame
Conscience of air and flight must be heartened
And blood of the earth shall be tamed.
When the spirits awaken in the expanse of night
Where the land walks into the sky
So what was taken must now be given
Or the Darkness' final calling is nigh.

For a moment, none of us move, the depths of Asa's words still winding between us like a living thing. Then, the Kashan shivers violently, and crumples next to the fire in an enervated heap. He tugs one of the furs up to his chin, before finally opening his eyes. The story drained him, and as the firelight bathes his face in shadows, he appears far older than he did only a few moments ago.

Like when I first met him, and survival had demanded everything he had.

As if broken from a trance, Anrai steals his hand hastily out of mine, folding it away into his lap and staring at it like he would a dangerous weapon. My heart tugs, already following the dark path of his thoughts. "Shaw—"

He shakes his head. "I'm not a skeptic anymore, Lemming. If the actual, *original,* Dead Prophecy tells me I'm going to destroy you, we should listen."

With no small amount of ferocity, I grab his hand back and yank it into my lap. Though Anrai unclenches his fist and allows me to weave my fingers between his, he is still wary as he watches me from beneath his lashes.

"Do you remember what I said to you in the Council House?"

Anrai's eyes flash, the tender memory still edged with hurt and sacrifice. Hesitantly, he nods.

"I meant it. Aggie told me the first night what would happen if I let you in. I've never gone into this blind."

Anrai's eyebrows climb into his hairline, before falling deeply over his eyes. "What do you mean 'she told you'? What exactly did she say?"

I fit him with a haughty gaze. "That you were the Darkness and the Darkness changes all those it touches, especially me."

Anrai blinks. Runs his fingers through his hair. Let's out a rough laugh. "You're telling me that Aggie *prophesied* to you I would destroy you, and you *still* didn't run away?"

"If you make one comment about my lack of common sense—"

Anrai cuts my words off with a kiss. When he pulls away, his eyes are like a shattered mirror, reflecting both light and shadows. "Not your lack of common sense. Your soft heart. Your bravery. I've been in awe of them both since they day we met."

I stare at him, momentarily speechless. Because what is there to say when the thing Anrai loves about me, is the exact thing I don't want to be anymore? I don't want to be soft, vulnerable to every sharp thing in the world. I don't want to be malleable, to change shape and endure. I want to be impenetrable, so when the weapons of the world come for me, they find nothing soft to pierce. Only armor.

"You're beautiful, Mirren, inside and out. And if I have to thank the dead gods every single day for that infernal prophecy—if that's what led me to you—I'll get down on my knees and do it."

Anrai kisses my forehead before standing to go to the small kettle by the fire. He pours a steaming cup, and hands it to Asa. The Kashan accepts it with a grateful look, sipping on it slowly. When the color begins to return to his face, Anrai asks, "What did it mean? 'That which was taken must now be given'. A lot of things were taken in that story. Power, lives, souls. Which does the prophecy demand?"

The Kashan sips at the tea, watching the tendrils of flame leap and flicker. He looks smaller than he is, diminished somehow by sadness and exhaustion. For a moment, I worry the story took too much.

There is a long pause in which the only sound is the crackle of flame. Then Asa raises his gaze to mine, the warm brown eyes full of warning.

"They are all the same thing."

Chapter
THIRTY-FIVE

Calloway

"You're late," Avedis muses, as I raise the lantern, signaling to Max and Harlan.

"By, like, two seconds," I mutter, my irritation prickling hotly.

The assassin only shrugs, and links his hands behind his head, stretching himself out on the cool grass. He turns his head, eyeing Rocher's unconscious form with appreciation. I wrinkle my nose in disgust, dousing the fire in the lantern as Max and Harlan raise theirs in return, signaling all is well. "He's a nice guy. Leave him be," I snap with far more vitriol than intended. It's been a long night, made longer by the wind-wielder's infuriating company.

"Are you the only one here allowed to appreciate a pleasing form?" Avedis muses.

I curse inwardly for my brief show of emotion. Avedis with a soul was devastatingly clever, but aside from the occasional murder-for-hire, he'd generally used his powers of observation for good. But soulless, Avedis is a virus: searching for any opening, any vulnerability, and using it to worm his way inside. He feeds on reactions, on the human emotions he can no longer feel.

"Until two weeks ago, I didn't think you appreciated *any* form," I reply carefully.

Avedis shrugs, leaning his head back into his hands and closing his eyes with an arrogant smirk. "On the contrary, Calloway. I appreciate beauty in all aspects."

Though my curiosity rises, I tamp it down and mash my lips together to keep from questioning him further. *Don't ask questions you don't want the answer to,* my mama used to say, and the dark hole in Avedis is surely filled with things I don't want to know.

Avedis shares no such hesitancy. "I couldn't help but notice an odd tension between you and the Similian," he says, the innocence of his voice sending a fresh spike of annoyance through me.

"Couldn't help but notice?" I repeat in a mocking tone. "Or caused the tension and want to continue to exploit it until my head implodes?"

He peeks open one eye. "Perhaps both." Now, the other opens and I steel myself against the way his hollow gaze grates against my skin. Despite the fact we've traveled together for a while, for some reason I still expect his eyes to be the dark of a summer night, warm and breezy and full.

But they're as cold as the space between stars.

Unsettled, I open my mouth simply to fill the void. "You could have broken the news far gentler."

Avedis tsks, his scar pulling tight and then releasing with the movement. "The way I see it, I did you a favor. How pitiful to go around thinking your relationship is something strong enough to withstand the Darkness, when really, it's feeble enough to fall apart at the first test. Thanks to me, you know now what it truly is." He shimmies slightly, his handsome face so arrogant that I have to clench my fist at my side to keep from hitting him. "You're welcome."

I plop on the ground next to him with an irritable sigh, laying my sword beside me. "Not everything needs to be Darkness tested. Some things are better off nurtured."

"Is that what you're doing then? *Nurturing?* Is that why you volunteered to be with me instead of with him on watch?"

"I volunteered to be with you because if you had been with Max, you would absolutely not be breathing by now."

Avedis lets out a swoony sigh, like he can't imagine anything more romantic than Max slitting his throat. I swallow down my repulsion with a shake of my head, ignoring the seed of truth in Avedis' sentiments. Papa always scolded me for jumping headfirst into everything without bothering to look, but he'd always said it with a laugh and a wink. I hadn't considered it could be something detrimental until I was older, something that could be dangerous.

Now, I know the risks. I try to think before I jump. But once I leap over the edge, I'm right back to the same little boy I was: the one who closes his eyes and enjoys the surprise and joy that climb his throat every time he falls into the unknown.

And that's exactly what I've done with Harlan. I leapt, and there is no climbing back up this time. There is only surviving the fall.

He hasn't touched me since he learned of Easton's fate, and I haven't pressed the issue. Because I am in it now, and I'll be here after he figures out what he needs. Even if what he needs isn't me.

Avedis sits up abruptly, and his mouth twists in a feral

grimace as he grabs his sword and leaps to his feet. "There is someone in the camp," he explains with narrow eyes. I've already grabbed my bow and stood up beside him to raise a different signal to Max and Harlan. One that means, *help*.

Avedis listens to his wind for another long moment, and then lets out a delighted laugh that sounds far more harrowing in the night air than it should. "It's that sniveling wretch of a politician. Jayan."

∾

Shaw

As I stare at Asa, there's a moment I am all flame. There is no air, no calm—only heat. I can't speak, lest it explode from me the way it did in Similis, reducing this tent and everything in it to ash.

Mirren swallows, and though I try to focus on the delicate bob of her throat, the world is awash in shades of red. Because I don't care what the godsdamn prophecy says: I'll burn the whole world before I let anyone take her from me again.

I wait for her to argue, for her usual unending barrage of questions, but neither come. Swallowing down fire, my voice rasps as I ask, "What are you saying, Kashan? I lost my soul and still lived. We've lost our power before and didn't die. It—it doesn't have to be all or nothing."

Asa, who still looks mildly ill, nods to Mirren. "Tell him, brave one. Tell him of what you experienced."

How in godsnames Asa knows what Mirren went through in the dungeon, I have no idea, but right now, it doesn't matter. I look to Mirren, to her hands still clutched in mine. And just like in Argentum, she suddenly appears small. Fragile. And it makes me want to let my fire spear from me, to stop trying to tamp it down or control it, and let it ravage every person that's ever hurt her.

"When we were in Yen Girene, or behind the Boundary, our power wasn't gone, it was only suppressed. But Anrai—I *saw* what happened after the Covinus stole the first spirit. The wielder died. He and his power were so intertwined, when it was torn from him, the wound was too great to survive. There wasn't enough left of either of them."

I shake my head fiercely. "No." It comes out as a command, but in reality, it's a wish. A wish to have been born somewhere far from this cursed continent, to have lived somewhere where there was no Darkness, and it didn't demand everything my soul-bonded and I have to give. "I refuse to believe that after everything, we're just supposed to, what..." I exhale sharply, the adrenaline pulsing through me making me shaky. "...lay down on some funeral pyre and die?"

My control slips and flame spears from my palms, lighting one of Asa's rugs on fire. The Kashan rises calmly and picks up the kettle, dousing the flame with the leftover tea. When he looks back at me, he doesn't appear at all upset. Only tired. "The Dead Prophecy was spoken in the tongue of the Old Gods, and then passed down from generation to generation. Stories change and grow, until only their bones remain the same. Do not lose hope, *zaabi,* for the strength in which you carry it may be exactly why you were chosen."

I resist the urge to laugh out loud. If I was chosen for my hope, the spirits were sorely mistaken. I have never operated within the confines of hope, in the imagined goodness of dreams. Instead, I've toiled away in the Darkness, and only relied on what I could claw out with my own hands.

My fire rises again, and I rake my fingers through my

hair, the scrape of my nails against my scalp the only thing keeping me from exploding entirely.

Asa comes beside me, his eyes shining with the exact hope he speaks of. I want to smother it, to tell him I'm not worthy of that hope, and this time, I'm not even sorry. Because if it comes to sacrificing Mirren or Helias to save Ferusa from Darkness, there is no choice to make—I'll damn the whole continent.

"We can't know exactly what the prophecy demands, but we do know *where*," Asa says.

"And when," Mirren adds softly.

I turn toward her, head tilted.

"*Where the land walks into the sky*. You said it to me on our first journey to Nadjaa. The lunar celebration."

The knowledge settles into me with a rightness I immediately shy from. Nothing about this can be right. But in my heart, other words beat: *You've always known the Darkness demands all of you. Is this not a fitting end?*

I push the thought away savagely, just as footsteps sound outside the tent. "Is that your guard?"

Asa hasn't even finished shaking his head when Jayan ducks into the tent. I pull two daggers from my bandolier and move in front of Mirren, who's already leapt to her feet, eyes wary on the slimy politician as he straightens his tunic primly. He moves his watery gaze in narrowed distaste around the Asa's tent, before they finally settle on the Kashan himself.

"I told Denver you couldn't be trusted," he says victoriously, "but even with your backward ways staining our city, the fool would not be persuaded."

Asa watches Jayan, but beneath the composed set of his face lies something sharp. Something made of steel and fire, honed by Darkness. Because the Xamani may be peaceful, but they are also warriors when they need to be. And Asa knows exactly what kind of person he'll need to be around someone like Jayan.

"You are trespassing, Councilman."

"This is Nadjaan land, Asa. I am never a trespasser in my own city." I bristle at the lack of respect in his voice, the use of Asa's given name. Jayan is not a friend and should not be greeting the storyteller like one.

"According to our agreement with Denver—"

Jayan interrupts with a humorless laugh, and dread spears through me. "Any agreement you have with Denver will be void after tonight. A new Chancellor is on the horizon."

At our looks of confusion, Jayan smiles wider. "I suppose you wouldn't have heard, but there's been a special election. Results will be announced at the lunar celebration."

"By law, a special election can only happen if the current Chancellor has put Nadjaa in danger. What prompted this?" I demand, my mind spiraling. Despite Denver's shortcomings, he cannot lose his seat to someone like Jayan. Not when the fate of the Dark World rests on Nadjaa remaining strong.

Jayan's grin is serpentine. "Why, *you* did, Fire-bringer." He spits the name with disgust. "You and the Chancellor's unnatural spawn." His gaze snaps to Mirren, and it takes everything in me not to lunge at him, to dig my dagger into his flesh and slice that look right off his face. "You ravaged half the continent and then escaped imprisonment. The citizens of Nadjaa have been calling for your blood, and I intend to give it to them."

"You're under arrest, Shaw. And you, too, Asa, for harboring a fugitive." He runs his tongue over his teeth.

"Securing the Praeceptor's Heir and ridding the continent of your evil will prove to the voters that I am the only one who cares for their safety. That I am the only one capable of making the hard decisions that will keep Nadjaa secure."

"Shaw never once threatened Nadjaa. *I* was the one who blew up the Council House." Mirren snarls, her body vibrating with rage. "I should be the only one under arrest."

"Unfortunately, your father has seen to it to grant you immunity, Ocean-wielder. But know this...if you remain in Nadjaa after the election, it'll be to your own detriment. I'll hang you right beside him."

The air pressure in the tent drops, and as Mirren stares down the councilman, the tea Asa poured over my accidental fire rises behind Jayan. The droplets sparkle in the air like a curtain of diamonds, casting oddly writhing shadows in the firelight. Relief floods through me as I take in the determined set of Mirren's mouth, the fight in her eyes, the beautiful show of her power. I haven't seen an inkling of it since she healed Avedis and feared there would be no recovering what the Covinus stole.

She fists her hands at her sides, and the tea falls lifeless to the floor once more, and suddenly, I understand with overwhelming clarity.

Mirren is still as powerful as ever. It isn't that she can't use it—it's that she *won't*.

Jayan, who's noticed none of this, beckons to me. "Come quietly, Fire-bearer. And I'll see to it you get a fair trial. Though I have to say, your peers will not be kind to you."

An inappropriate laugh erupts from me. As if everything isn't bad enough, Nadjaa itself is on the brink of being led by a power-hungry imbecile, who's stupid enough to believe I'll come quietly to my own death. Flame sparks at my fingertips as I stare down Jayan. "I'm not going anywhere with you, Jayan. And I think you're smart enough to know what will happen if you so much as look at *her*."

"I thought you'd hold onto such sentiments. I came accompanied with half the guard and a water cannon," Jayan replies snidely. "And though you may be able to eventually burn through us all, I've heard you have a new soul. Do you truly want to be the first man to lose *two*?"

Flames wind their way up my arms and settle over my chest, begging to be unleashed, but before I can, there's a loud crash outside the tent. I laugh again at the way Jayan jumps, his paranoia no doubt a result of being a two-faced piece of shit. I feed the fire, readying it at my palms to meet Jayan's guard, but when it's Max's head that ducks through the tent, I call them back into myself with a sigh of relief.

Jayan backs as far away from Max's twin swords as he can manage, shouting for his guard even as he stumbles. Max crowds him with a look of pure fury, stalking forward until his toe catches and he sprawls backward, landing on his ass in an ungraceful heap.

"Your guard is otherwise occupied at the moment," Max informs him with a chilling smile, tipping the blade of her falchion to his throat.

Jayan's face flushes a cherry red as he struggles to push himself back upright amid the weight of his finery. "You would do well to reconsider your company, Maxwell. After tonight, you'll no longer have the protection of the Chancellor."

Max's mouth twitches, and I have no idea whether she's refraining from smiling or snarling. Her eyes flash and for a terrifying moment, I think she might actually take off Jayan's head. As much as I despise the man, he certainly doesn't deserve a piece of her soul. But Max reins herself in, even as her eyes narrow dangerously. "You'd do well to realize I need the protection of no man, Chancellor or otherwise."

Jayan's face pales and he rears back in panic at what he sees on Max's face; what I've always seen in her: her will to survive. His eyes flash in a silent plea to Asa, to Mirren, and finally to me, as if one of us will save him from Max. When none of us move to intervene, the councilman swallows roughly and bows his head to grovel.

Max makes a disgusted noise, and nods to me. "You better go. Cal and Avedis are outside, but Cal is spending most of his energy keeping Avedis from murdering the whole of the guard."

"I'll have my *ahtan* escort the councilman out of camp," Asa says, referring to his Xamani guard.

"If they so much as lay a finger on me, I will consider it an act of war, Asa," Jayan sneers, even as Max digs the tip of her blade in. "As soon as I'm Chancellor, I will banish you from these lands and your tribes will be homeless once again."

Asa only smiles wearily. "If standing up for what is right is an act of war, Councilman, then you may consider me a warrior. I can only hope the rest of Nadjaa are warriors as well. *Ahtan!*"

The Xamani warriors stream into the tent, having never left their post, even as the fighting broke out. Asa nods to me, and I take Mirren's hand and lead her into the night.

The camp around us has descended into pure chaos. Muffled shouts and loud crashes echo through the dark, and a lonely wind howls between the tents, leaving a path of thick dust floating in the air. Regret shoots through me at having brought our fight to the Xaman doorstep, but when Asa steps out into the night behind me, he claps his hand over my shoulder reassuringly. "You are well versed in our stories, *zaabi*. You know no land is our home. Our tribes are, and they are the home we protect."

I nod reluctantly, remembering the home the Kashan offered to a soulless wretch. Now knowing the prophecy, the idea seems more distant than ever, the point of a horizon I'm damned to reach for eternally, but never grasp. But I won't forget the feeling of being offered one.

Asa hugs Mirren, and when he pulls back, he cups her face between his brown hands, his eyes shining with pride. "Keep your hope, brave one. It takes strength to remain soft in a world so cruel. Nurture that softness. It is why the spirits chose you and what will save you in the end."

Mirren doesn't respond, but as she hugs the Kashan one last time, I don't miss the way she digs her teeth into her lower lip. Like if she doesn't, a scream will escape her mouth.

We trace the outskirts of camp, before ducking back into the wood to find Dahiitii grazing where we left her. Mirren's body settles against mine, warm and lush even through our clothing, and though I should be grateful for our escape, I can only think of her small show of power in that tent and wonder what else she holds back.

CHAPTER
THIRTY-SIX

Mirren

Keep hope. Stay soft.

As we ride away from the Xamani camp and around the outskirts of the city, Asa's words pulse through me. Anrai's body rocks against mine in time with Dahiitii's powerful strides, but even as I nestle into the ridges of his chest, I hardly feel his warmth. I only feel the rising pressure of my power, pressing against my skin, my lungs, my ribs. It is hot and icy, the convergence of currents creating a violent storm threatening to rupture.

Since Argentum, I have kept my *other* close, curled near my heart, but now, there is no holding on as it feeds on my rage. I can't think around it, can feel nothing but unending fury. My grief is swallowed by it, an ocean rising up to take back the land, sweeping everything away and leaving only devastation behind.

It began as a small anger at Jayan, at his demand for Anrai, but it was a trickle that burst a dam. Now, the rage spreads. At Jayan. At the Covinus. At the world for being so unfair. The rage spirals, raising shipwrecks from the deepest depths of my soul. Rage at my father for leaving me always alone. At the Darkness for demanding so much from me. At the universe for stealing away anything I love, and then expecting me to sacrifice what's left to save it.

I don't even realize where Anrai has taken us until we turn up the trail to the manor. The last time I was here, the moor smelled of smoke and ash, but now, there's only the sweet tang of ocean air lingering on the crisp breeze trailing in off the Storven. Dahiitii has barely come to a stop when I leap from her. My feet smart as they hit the ground, and I nearly fall over as I scrabble back upright. The pressure is unbearable, and tears sting my eyes as I turn away from the manor and run. There's no thought other than to get away before I combust; before I ruin everything around me.

My breaths saw in my lungs and sweat plasters my hair to my forehead as I stumble down the path toward the cliff pond. Acid rises in my throat, and for a moment, I don't know whether I'm going to be sick, or level the entire bluff.

Stay soft. How can anyone stay soft in a world so hard, a world determined to slice at your skin until you bleed all you have into the Darkness? The only way to survive is to be sharper—to cut through the world before it cuts through you. To keep everything inside where nothing can hurt it. Anrai told me that when we first met, and I'd refused to believe it. That refusal has cost me everything.

When I reach the pond, the cerulean water is calm and sparkling, and the eaves of the surrounding trees sway softly in the breeze. I shed my shoes and wade into the pond, splashing around the side until I reach the edge where the water pours into the Storven below.

I watch the waves crash, feeling them in the marrow of my bones. Angry and dark, my rage undulates like the sea, no longer content to break against the shore, but wishing to *consume* it. To punish everyone and everything that demands something of me, that takes when I have no more left to give.

The Darkness stole my parents, and then Easton, and now it would steal the small amount of happiness I've carved out for myself in this world. It demands I give all of myself, and gives nothing in return.

The air around me heats, and despite his silent feet, I know Anrai is here. He doesn't speak, only sheds his boots and comes to stand beside me, his pants logged with water and his gaze fixed on the white caps of the sea. Normally, his presence is a calming force, but right now, my *other* lashes so wildly, the call of his magic only furthers the untenable pressure. My ears ring with it, my heartbeat painful in my chest.

So what was taken must now be given.

I won't give up another piece to this world. They don't deserve to be freed from the Darkness, not when half of them want us dead and the other half would do anything to steal our power for themselves.

"Do you want the world to burn, Lemming?"

When I whip my head to him, I find nothing but determination in his gaze. No judgement. No pity. And certainly, no calm.

My *other* howls in approval, the strength of its storm growing stronger, a relentless ache that now pierces through my skull. I squeeze my hands into fists and dig my teeth into my lip, as my body begins to shake with the strain of holding on.

"Say the word, and I will raze the entire continent for you. Wash it clean of everything that would hurt us, until there's nothing left."

My heart leaps into my throat, and for a moment, I'm

unable to speak. Because Anrai is intimate with rage, with the price the world demands, and he'll do exactly as he says if I ask. He'll punish them all.

He's always understood the blackest parts of me, the twisted depths everyone else would shy away from. The parts that hold onto things so tightly, they leave claw marks. And he will never ask me to change them, to be anything other than what I am, even if what I am is messy and shattered. He's only ever asked me to show him the pieces, to let him join me in my darkness.

If I want revenge, if I want to destroy Ferusa in the name of my pain, Anrai won't stop me. He'll do whatever he can to empower me, to make my wishes a reality.

"We'll watch the flames together," he says softly.

The breadth of his acceptance settles beneath my skin, in my lungs and bones, as I stare at him. The world has always wished me less, but Anrai—he has always wanted *more*. So instead of shoving down my anger, my despair— instead of fighting to hold onto my power and my rage, I give it to him.

My *other* bursts from my skin, leaping for him like it intends to devour him whole. Anrai doesn't break my gaze as he welcomes it to him, his eyes burning like a signal fire. In the shadows of the trees, my power skirting up and down his body, he looks like an otherworldly illusion, a terrifying reminder that though he is human, he is also something different.

I raise my chin. "I want them all dead."

Anrai's gaze darkens as my power runs up his arms and tangles in his hair. Then, he smiles wickedly. "Then we'll make it so."

My *other* shivers around him, and then flows in rippling tendrils toward me as I step closer, winding around both our limbs, like it draws and binds us together. "I want everyone to pay for what the world has taken from me. They don't deserve our sacrifice."

Anrai keeps his hands pinned to his sides as he bows his head and stares up at me through a curtain of dark lashes, his gaze positively vicious. My warrior, who knows every strain of the Darkness' song, the tempting resonance of its call. "I would punish them all for you, Mirren."

And in this moment, I understand the nature of Iara's curse. Because reason has no place in the Darkness; you allow it to unthread slowly, and its tenor is so sensuously alluring, you have no choice but to allow an inch more. Just another small taste.

But a taste is never enough, is it?

Not when the world is so harsh. Not when everything is pain, and the only relief is the pain of another.

And gods, what I wouldn't give for some relief.

As if sensing the direction of my thoughts, Anrai narrows his eyes and tilts his head, that arrogant grin pulling at the corner of his mouth. "Show me your rage, Lemming." Flames roar to life in his open palms as he backs away slowly. Coming to a stop on the shoreline, he plants his feet, readying himself for a fight. "Show me the creature that claws your chest, that roars her fury."

He beckons me forward, as my body trembles more furiously. "It isn't gone. It's right here. *Feel* it."

Perhaps it's the creature he speaks of, the one made of shadows and abandonment, that snaps its jaws. Or maybe it's my grief, cutting like a whip against my ribs. Whatever it is, I set it free, and it explodes from my skin, from my soul, a detonation of everything I've tried so hard to hide away.

Mingling with my *other,* the creature takes the form of a

hurricane of fury that barrels directly for Anrai. He doesn't miss a beat, raising a wall of fire so hot, my whirlwind evaporates against it with a violent hiss of steam. Snarling, I summon another wave from the pond and send it crashing toward him, and the monster in my chest howls in approval. *Uncage me.*

Anrai laughs, and the sound skitters across my skin as he sends a fireball careening for my head. I duck with a sharp curse, energy zapping through my veins like my body has awoken alongside the beast. I've held myself back, afraid of what's been lost, of what is left—but now, I allow myself to truly feel for the first time since the Castellium. To unleash everything I've tamped down. I let out a sigh of pleasure. Of relief.

The Storven calls to me, its dark depths fusing with my own, until I am ancient and fathomless. I hold the same rage of the waves, the same grief of the lost, and when I sing to the sea, it answers with fervor. A wall of water rises behind Anrai, the pure mass of it shadowing the entire cliff in watery darkness. The sound of its fury is deafening, an ancient rumble that reverberates in my blood.

Anyone else would cower beneath the ocean's fury, but Anrai doesn't even glance at the wave poised above him. Instead, his pale eyes glimmer, positively feral in the moonlight as they fix on me. He runs his tongue slowly over his lips, and then, with a fury too bright to witness, my soul bonded bursts into pure fire.

I shield my eyes against the blinding blaze of energy, and the wave crashes down on top of both of us as my concentration falters. The pressure steals the breath from my lungs, and though the world turns upside down for a moment, my soul is righted. Despite the fractures, despite the stains, for the first time since I left that dungeon, I feel like myself. The Covinus didn't break me. I am not less. Why have I been cowering?

I swipe impatiently at my eyes as the water recedes back into the Storven. Anrai is still entirely dry, kept that way by his fire, and with another grin, he beckons me forward with two fingers.

Sopping hair plastered to my neck and shoulders, clothes sodden and clinging, I leap for him. Power all but forgotten, all that matters to the creature in my chest is that I do not cage it back in, do not keep it bound with the chains of society. So I don't.

I let it control me, giving myself over to its primal need and feral hunger. I yank at Anrai's shirt, and claw at his chest, biting his lip until the taste of iron mingles along our tongues. And if I was expecting mercy, I find none in his hands, as he wraps his long fingers around my throat and squeezes, forcing my mouth open wider against his plundering tongue.

A wave of molten heat pools between my legs, as I tear down his pants and dig my fingers into his muscled backside, hard enough to bruise. He laughs into my mouth, that arrogant, swaggering laugh, that sends a fresh wave of fury and desire sparking through me like electricity. We stumble to the ground, a tangle of bare skin and greedy limbs. He pulls me on top of him and groans as I nip at his chest, my hands gripping the hard ridge of his cock.

Tongue sweeping at the seam of my lips, he yanks at my dress until my breasts spill into the open air. I cry out as he buries his face between them, licking and biting in turn. Then, he grips me by the bottom, hiking me up until my legs straddle the sides of his head.

Anrai's teeth dig into the bottom of his lip as he yanks my underwear aside, and I nearly come undone at the sight of him between my thighs. He keeps his gaze fixed on mine, not giving me a chance to hesitate as he pulls me to his mouth, his tongue like velvet as he sweeps it hungrily over my entire core.

A loud moan escapes me, and my legs shake as I struggle to hold myself aloft. But Anrai is having none of it. Holding back has never been how our game is played.

"If you're going to drown me, Lemming, this is how I want to go," he growls into me. And then, he scrapes the most sensitive, aching, part of me with his teeth. I scream out, in both surprise and pleasure, and my legs give out beneath me as pain mingles with decadent bliss. He eats me with fervor, like he's starved and I'm his only nourishment. Each long lick only serves to further unravel me, until I lose all sense of hesitation and cry out to the open sky as I grind down on his tongue.

I swivel my hips, and Anrai growls in approval as I become the wild, dark creature Anrai has set free. *I am not less. I am not less.* I clutch my legs on either side of him as I ride his face, the vibration of his groan against my sex sending me tumbling wildly over the edge.

But Anrai doesn't allow me a moment. He lifts me off of him and bends me over. My climax is still ripping through me as he sheaths himself inside of me in one swift thrust. I cry out, gripping a tree as he thrusts into me hard and fast, and as my body struggles to adjust, the edges of pleasure blur into each other until I can hardly think.

He tangles his fingers in my hair and tugs me up against his chest, the slight sting of pain only heightening the decadent warmth that's spread to every part of my body. He wraps his other hand around my throat as he pounds into me, his rhythm unrelenting even as he tilts my head back enough to look at him. "Do not make yourself less than you are," he growls against my ear, the primal command in his voice heightening each thrust, driving me further toward the edge. I clench around the thick length of him, and still, he doesn't relent. "You will not hide any of what is mine," he says, his hand at my throat all that keeps me to my feet as my eyes roll back into my head.

"Feral. Dark. Powerful." He accentuates each word with a rough thrust. "You will not cage any part of yourself in service of those weaker."

Keeping his hand at my throat, he pulls out of me, only to flip me around against the tree and bury himself inside me once more. His power snakes down my stomach, the warmth almost unbearable as it comes to rest at the apex of my legs. "Look at us, Lemming. Look at the perfect way we fit."

I follow his command, nearly coming apart at the sight of the way he takes me. The way he owns me, just as I own him. "You're made for *me*. Mine. And you will not pretend to be anything *less*." His flame weaves tendrils around my core and throat and breasts, until I no longer feel my body, just molten heat and primal need.

He pounds into me with a fury that feels like punishment, a resounding retribution against any who would try to cut me down, try to leash what lives inside me. As pleasure and heat build, I moan loudly, feeling every edge of my body just as Anrai has demanded. Every part I've tamped down, every part I've ignored, I free them for the first time in my life. Because Anrai is a wildfire, and no cage will ever hold him back—not even one I've constructed for myself.

Our eyes locked, Anrai thrusts once more, and I tumble over the edge as pleasure consumes me, spreading outward from my chest to every inch of my body. Every bit of my skin burns, with desire and freedom, as he spills into me with his own groan of pleasure.

When we part, Anrai kneels before me once more. Spreading my knees apart, he uses his shirt to tenderly clean the inside of my thighs, punctuating each swipe with a deferent kiss. When he's finished, he gazes up at me, the fierce fire of earlier now burned to embers.

Emotion climbs my throat, and I don't know whether I want to burst into tears or laughter. I settle on some combination of the two, a rough scraping sound that contains everything I've just released. And though the world still rages around us, I feel immensely lighter, a weight lifted. As I watch Anrai, gratitude floods through me. The Darkness has taken so much, but it gifted me *him*. A man who knows my soul better than I do, who brings me back to myself when I am lost.

Who doesn't let me cower in my brokenness but lifts me up in my strength.

"I don't want the world to burn," I finally say, lowering myself to kneel beside him.

Anrai smiles softly and nods, his fingers still splayed over my thighs. "I know."

I bite my lip. "Is it ridiculous that after everything, I still want to save it?"

Anrai pulls me into his lap and gathers me to his chest. His warmth seeps into my bare skin, and as I breathe in his scent, of open air and smoke and spice, I realize I can move without the pull of scabs. There is no more itch, no more unbearable sting of pain. My back has healed.

"It's not ridiculous, Mirren. Your heart won't be defeated, even when it's been shattered. It's a power I envy." He kisses me gently. "A power I love."

I thread my fingers through the silky tendrils of his hair,

before bringing them to cup his face. He watches me with the same intensity he always has, the gaze that makes me feel like I could burn inside it. "What if it means dying?"

Shadows of smoke sweep across his face, but he doesn't waver. "Asa told us to keep hope. So we believe we can save Ferusa without having to give our lives."

I raise a brow. "You don't believe in hope. You're the most cynical man on the planet."

Anrai cedes a small smile. "I am," he agrees, his expression growing oddly earnest. "But you *are* hope, Lemming. And I've always believed in you."

CHAPTER
THIRTY-SEVEN

Shaw

We bathe in the pond and then dress, the silence lingering between us no longer a strained divide. It's now a warmth that ties us together, a place we both reside comfortably, and when Mirren takes my hand, that comfort swells. Because just as Mirren has always seen me, through the Darkness and self-hate and horror, I see her.

I once thought the only thing I was good at was killing—destruction—but maybe that was only because I hadn't met her yet. Because if I know one thing, it's that I was made to love her. To show her the way back to herself when she's gotten lost, to hold a mirror up when she's gone blind. It's as natural as breathing, not so much a choice as an inevitability.

Hand in hand, we walk the path back to the manor, and though I know as soon as we emerge from the trees, we'll be stepping back into reality, I no longer feel sick with apprehension. Whatever we face, we face together.

Mirren's breath hitches beside me, and as caught up as I am in thoughts of her, it takes me a moment to realize why.

I follow her frozen gaze to a familiar shadow darkening the scorched doorway of the manor. I halt in place as Mirren releases a measured breath through her teeth.

Reality has found us sooner than expected.

"Do you think there's still time to run away?" I whisper out the side of my mouth, only half joking. I scan the clifftop for Denver's guard, and though there's no movement, I can't help but run my fingers along my bandolier, an old habit. Because as much as I still love the man who found me in the Nemoran all those years ago, who educated me and gave me a better life, I don't trust the man standing on the porch.

Because he's still Chancellor, at least until tonight. He'll do whatever he needs to in order to protect his city.

Including arresting Mirren and I to win an election.

Denver steps off through the threshold, his descent down the front steps hobbled by his pronounced limp, a permanent remnant of my father. In that way, Denver and I are similar, both bearing lasting scars of the Praeceptor, but Denver has yet to acknowledge our shared wounds. He sees me as the same monster the rest of the continent knows me to be, and there is no bonding with a monster.

Mirren doesn't move, watching as her father slowly makes his way toward us, her emotions splashed vibrantly across her face. Distrust. Dread. Hope. When Denver draws close enough that I can see my own reflection in the lenses of his glasses, I've the absurd urge to throw myself in front of Mirren. To protect her from whatever her father is about to say, from whatever hurt he may cause.

But I keep still, even as he stops a foot away and drinks in her wild appearance. Mirren has never needed me to fight her battles for her—she needs me by her side.

The space between us grows viscous and electric.

Denver's knuckles are white on the top of his cane, and I'm still staring at his hands when he says, "You've come home."

Ridiculously, I almost flinch against the word, until I remind myself he isn't speaking to me. It's to his daughter he speaks, not to the violent orphan who went against everything he believes in and destroyed innocent people. But when I flick my gaze upward, it's to find Denver staring at us both.

Mirren stiffens beside me, apparently just as averse to the word in her father's mouth, and her power rises to her skin. The droplets sparkle in the rising sun, and pride radiates in my chest. Because in her eyes is the same spark that called to me when we first met as my heart recognized its equal. And my soul-bonded will no longer let anyone diminish her, break her.

Denver watches the display with mild curiosity, even as Mirren widens her stance, like she's readying herself for an attack. Of words, or weapons, it doesn't seem to matter when it comes to her father. The damage is the same.

"If you're waiting for an apology, you'll be waiting awhile," she bites out.

A small smile tugs at the corner of Denver's mouth. "Mirri, you may be grown now, but I know you well enough to know I'd be better off waiting for rain in a desert."

Mirren only stares at her father, her face sharp. "If you're here to arrest Shaw, I swear to the Darkness, you'll regret it. I don't care if it's to win some stupid election or to save the entire world, you won't take him again."

Something flickers across Denver's face, rising and receding so quickly I have trouble placing it. Anger? Sadness? Regret?

Chancellors and warlords do not regret what they've

done to keep their seat of power. They move through the world with no thought of who they hurt, only what they've gained.

But once—once Denver was full of regret. When he found me in the Nemoran, he'd told me that saving Max and I was his penance. I hadn't understood it at the time, but now, I realize he was at the Boundary to gaze upon his failures. To punish himself with them, flay himself open with memories of the children and wife he'd abandoned, the city he couldn't save.

"Winning the election no longer matters," Denver says softly.

Mirren's brow wrinkles, as alarm and dread ring through me. If Denver is ceding the city to Jayan, things must be worse than we thought.

"Come." Denver motions toward the manor, which only furthers my confusion. There's no way it's been repaired already, no way the old house is fit to inhabit. "We have much to talk about."

With a hesitant glance at me, Mirren follows her father toward the house.

I rock on the balls of my feet, torn between following or staying, when, without looking over his shoulder, Denver says, "You too, Shaw."

Now, the dread slithers in my stomach like an iron snake, chains around my ribs and squeezes. Perhaps Denver's guard is waiting in the manor, an ambush to arrest us both. Only the thought of what Mirren did to Denver's last water cannon keeps my feet moving forward up the steps.

I gaze up at the ruins. The last time I was here, it had been both the best and worst day of my life. Because I'd claimed Mirren as mine, but in doing so, had also claimed the weight of my soul. The breadth of my destruction and the horror of my actions. The day is dissected in my mind as a thick black line, a tear in the fabric of my heart, holding both the most beautiful and terrible things in my life.

When I duck through the threshold, I am still expecting the foyer to be covered in ash and debris, but instead, the cracked marble shines through where it has been singed. The fragments of glass have been swept away, the shattered doors and chunks of plaster all cleared from the room. I glance down the hall to see evidence of new drywall, and instead of the smell of smoke, the scent of new paint clings to the air.

There is no militia waiting, only an eerie stillness, an abandoned air where there was once so much life.

I turn to find Denver watching me with an unreadable look, and beneath it, a myriad of emotions claw at my ribs. I thought the manor was lost, and though I hadn't actually been the one to set it on fire, I caused it all the same. Cal always thought I was being dramatic when I said my relationship with the Praeceptor would destroy everything I loved, but it had in the end, hadn't it? It stained and tore and mutilated everything good, down to the only place I've ever felt safe.

"You're...you're rebuilding?" My voice cracks slightly. As Chancellor, Denver has his choice of residences, both in the city and on the peninsula, most far more elegant than the shabby manor. "Why?"

His face doesn't change, but again something flickers in the green of his eyes. "Because it's our home," he answers simply, before turning down the hall toward his office. Feeling more confused by the moment, I follow him, Mirren's hand in mine.

Our. He said *our.*

Before, I would have said I had no right to it.

But now, in the marrow of my bones, I feel the truth of the words. The manor is my home, Nadjaa is my home. And in spite of everything, Denver is the man who gave me that. Maybe part of the reason my soul recognized Mirren as home was that she holds only the best parts of her father, the ones that shielded and loved me.

When we reach Denver's office, it's to find the room entirely repaired. A new desk made from thick oak sits in the center, the surface scattered with various missives and pens. New shelves line the back wall, and it appears Denver wasted no time in filling them with books. A strong part of me wants to head directly toward it, to peruse through the titles and discuss which ones are worth reading like we used to.

But instead, I sit in one of the two overstuffed armchairs positioned across from the desk. Mirren perches on the arm, and though Denver takes note of her choice not to sit in the remaining chair, he only purses his lips and lowers himself slowly into his seat.

When he notices the way I continuously scan the room, he says, "I have granted you both immunity. The guard will not touch you again so long as I am Chancellor." He folds his hands on the desk in front of him, seeming to consider his next words.

"Similis has fallen." The sentiment echoes through the room, before settling squarely over my chest. "Word arrived this morning. The Dark Militia invaded two days ago and lay the city to ruins."

Two days. Which means the Covinus hadn't even waited a full twenty-four hours after I stabbed him through the throat to mount his next offense. To be sure that when he meets Mirren and I here in Nadjaa, nothing will be able to stop him.

Denver pushes his glasses up his nose. "They now move toward Nadjaa with the entirety of the Similian weapons armory."

Mirren swallows audibly, but she doesn't cower from the news. Only straightens her spine, lifts her chin, and stares at her father. "You sent no help and left Similis with no one to protect them from the Dark World. Or from themselves."

Denver presses his lips into a thin line, before hefting a soft breath and pushing forward. "Stories of what happened at the Boundary have been abundant in your absence, Mirri, and I took them to heart. I've been fortifying our borders and strengthening our guard ever since learning the true nature of the Covinus. But I did not anticipate the Covinus moving so quickly, or him winning the alliance of every warlord. I still don't understand how he's gained command of so many armies, how he's won them so easily to his side. He's finishing what the Praeceptor started. He comes for this city, for the freedom we represent."

My stomach surges up somewhere near my heart. *You destroy.*

"He comes for more than that," Mirren replies. "The Covinus is *from* Nadjaa. It was called something different that long ago, but he holds this place in high regard. And because of that, it's where the Dead Prophecy is going to come to pass."

Denver's gaze narrows, and then relaxes in realization. "I should have known Asa would tell you the prophecy. You've always had a way of earning loyalty. A character trait I've long admired."

Mirren shifts, as if uncertain what to do with the compliment. Uncertain whether it's a compliment *at all* coming from a man who's sacrificed such tender things in order to keep peace. She clears her throat. "He didn't gain the loyalty of the warlords of Ferusa, he *stole* it. He controls the souls of thousands of people, and because of the curse, he can't die. But if we can complete the prophecy, it'll break his control. He'll be mortal again."

Denver pales, and shame winds up my throat, its tentacles black and viscous. They squeeze the air from my lungs, the blood from my heart. They squeeze until my ribs crack beneath them, and my vision goes blurry. I did that. *I* stole those souls, built an undefeatable army for an immortal monster.

"He grows closer to Nadjaa," Denver finally says, but I hardly hear it as the Darkness of the abyss surges. "Two, maybe three days away at the most."

You love and so it will be taken from you.

I do not build homes, I take them.

And I have stolen this one from not only myself, but from everyone I love. From Mirren, from Max and Cal and Helias. Nadjaa, the light of the Dark World, is going to be annihilated because of me. Suddenly I can't even bring myself to look at Mirren or Denver. I fold up and curl in, as my soul presses down onto my spine.

And then, Denver asks softly, "Where is your brother?"

His voice is a soft plead, but it may as well be the steel edge of a sword the way it tears through me. I jump to my feet, the world swaying and shrinking around me, as I stumble toward the door. Acid surges into my mouth, choking me as I attempt to swallow it down.

"Where is your brother, Mirri?" Denver asks again, as I careen into the hallway. Because Denver gave me a second chance at life, and how have I repaid it? By destroying his home and failing to protect his true son.

For the first time in my life, I run away. Away from Denver, from Mirren, from myself. And I am still running when Denver's howl of anguish echoes behind me.

∽

Calloway

"Oh no you don't," I shout huffily, grabbing at the collar of Avedis' cloak and pulling him away from a disheveled-looking barmaid.

A gust of wind buffets my face even though we're inside of Seesa's and should presumably be safe from such things. I swat at my hair and at Avedis' cloak as the fabric billows up into my face. With a muttered curse, I grab a hold of the tree trunk mass of his upper arm and yank him backward. The barmaid in question makes a little squeak of protest, her eyes lidded and the flush of her skin matching the color of the brick wall she's pushed up against. "Trust me, darling. You'll thank me later."

Avedis whips around, his dagger pointed at my throat. The stubble on his face is still speckled with dried blood from the fight at the Xaman camp, and matching dark stains coat the blade. "You are truly a murderer of all things fun, Calloway."

I swat the dagger aside. "That is the rudest thing you've ever said to me," I retort, pushing him away from the barmaid and toward where Max, Harlan, and Sura sit in a corner booth. The place is mostly empty as it's still early morning, but the hour hardly ever matters at Seesa's. There are always drinks to be imbibed and music to listen to, and though none of us have slept, I was hoping the distraction would keep Avedis from giving in to his darker predilections.

"You deserve that and worse," the assassin insists ruefully, finally giving in and allowing me to steer him into a chair like a sulking, over-large child.

"We both know I am the epitome of fun, Avedis. *Hardly* a fun killer. A fun birther, if you will."

Avedis wrinkles his nose in disgust and throws himself impatiently into the booth, knocking shoulders with an alarmed looking Harlan. The assassin narrows his eyes on Harlan, before they cut to me, his annoyance replaced by newfound mischief that sparkles darkly. "And I suppose you've never searched for company at a tavern before?" he challenges.

"I'm not a saint," I retort hotly. "But I also didn't leave them bleeding out on the floor afterward, unable to recover from the experience."

Avedis looks unapologetic. "Then I stand by my sentiments. A true stick in the mud."

Sura's face twists in devastation and I know she's remembering the wind-wielder only a few hours before, tearing into Jayan's guard with unrelenting cruelty. Avedis with a soul had been efficiently brutal, but Avedis without —well, it is something else entirely.

He'd taken pure pleasure in the pain, like it awoke something primal and lascivious inside him. He'd licked his lips as his victims gasped; he'd laughed as the blood gurgled from their mouth. It had taken both Harlan and I to restrain him even the least bit, but it had been Sura, who'd arrived just in time, who'd finally been able to rein him in.

And now, by the way she stares at him, I understand it's because she feels responsible for the state of him. He gave up his soul to protect her, and she is trying to repay the favor in her own way—by attempting to stay his hand, to minimize the devastation he causes.

I don't know how much longer the situation is tenable, how much longer we can keep him from destroying everything around him. But we have no choice until the prophecy is complete.

And after—I don't want to think about what comes after. A reckoning, I suppose.

"We told you, no hurting anyone in Nadjaa that isn't a willing, *knowing,* participant." Max sips at her drink, a fruity pink concoction that makes my head hurt just looking at it.

Avedis crosses his arms obstinately, even as he raises an inviting brow. "Are you volunteering, Maxwell?"

Max only sets him with a steel glare, before downing the rest of her drink. She pushes out of the booth, and announces, "I'm getting another round. Harlan, come help me."

Harlan gives her an obliging smile, and even though he would probably rather die than drink spirits at nine in the morning, follows her toward where Seesa's golden curls lean over the bar.

Avedis lifts his ale to his mouth, downing the amber liquid in one swift gulp before plunking it back on the table. He crosses his arms over his chest and glares at me sulkily. "As I have no soul to lose, I don't know why I should be subject to your insipid rules. It isn't fair."

I resist rolling my eyes. "Life isn't fair. And you heard Shina. If you want the witch-queen, you'll abide by the rules until we can complete the prophecy."

"It isn't as if you're friends with that barmaid. What's it to you if she meets her end tonight? I'm not a *selfish* sort of monster...I promise she'd enjoy her last moments greatly."

He runs his tongue along his teeth, like he can taste her skin.

A soft noise of horror escapes Sura and her deep brown eyes go wide as she sets them on Avedis. "You say such horrible things, Wind-whisperer," she says sadly. "Have you no hope for the state of your soul when it returns to you? You've seen the way Shaw struggles. Do you not see we are trying to keep you from the same?"

Dread grips me at the hope in Sura's words. She thinks Avedis can still be saved.

Avedis' dark gaze turns savage, the thick scar pulling taut with his grimace as an icy wind whips over the table. For a moment, I half-expect him to burst into a storm of fury and destroy the entire tavern, but the wind quiets just as quickly as it began. "This is not a fairy tale where love conquers all, little Kashan. Life is not a Xamani legend where magic wins the day. This is the Darkness, where magic is the beast that consumes. Your tribe was slaughtered and taken captive, surely you know the nature of our world better than most."

He tilts his head, running an assessing gaze over Sura as her eyes fill with tears. Ferreting out each weakness, every small fissure to dig his fingers into. I tense, ready to jump in between them, but Avedis only says softly, "There is no saving my soul, sweet Sura."

Sura gnaws at her lip, staring back at the assassin with brimming eyes. But no tears fall as she lifts her chin. "You arrogant *paasji*," she snaps harshly, the Xamani word for 'outsider'. "You have been alive only a quarter century, and yet you claim to know every mystery this world holds. Shame on your ignorant conceit!"

An angry flush has risen to Sura's cheeks, and she bats furiously at her cloud of dark hair as she leans in toward

Avedis. The wind-wielder has the good sense to look properly scolded, eyeing the little Kashan like she'll spit fire at any moment. Instead, she lashes out amotion, a slice of her small hand through the air and then a curve of her fingers. A curse and a dismissal.

Avedis' shocked gaze trails after her as she stalks off to join Harlan and Max at the bar. I let out a low whistle. "Well, you sure pissed her off."

Avedis glares at me, his lips thinning. "Cuttingly observed, Calloway," he says, voice dripping with sarcasm. "I suppose you, too, expect me to keep sinless and pure for some silly dream? It can't be helped you all blame yourselves for the state of me, but rest assured, I intend to make the most of it if only you'd loosen the leash."

I finish off the dregs of my drink and drop the empty glass onto the sticky table with a small *clink*. "Sinless and pure? Is that really how you'd describe your mercenary ways pre-soullessness?" Licking my lips, I settle back in my chair. "Just don't murder anyone while we're here. The Nadjaan guard loyal to Jayan is already trying to arrest us, and we don't need any more trouble."

Avedis' only reply is setting me with a dead glare that I promptly look away from, if only to avoid having to once again see the shattered depths contained within. Instead, I let my eyes drift to the bar, where Max has goaded Harlan into trying a sip of her drink. He eyes the pink liquid like it may jump out of the glass and bite him, but hesitantly picks up the glass between two fingers.

He puts his lips to the drink, and for an absurd moment, I find myself jealous of a dingy tavern glass. Harlan squeezes his eyes shut and takes a brave swig, to the beat of Max's resounding cheer. His face crumples in disgust as his eyes snap open again, and he coughs repeatedly as Max laughs.

I startle in my seat, tearing my eyes abruptly away from the scene, as I realize how long I've been staring. How oddly enamoring even the simplest things can be when done by someone who's burrowed inside your heart, body.

I cough in embarrassment, waiting for Avedis' biting comment. If I'd planned on giving him no ammunition, this was a terrible lapse in judgement.

But when I turn my head, the wind-wielder is gone.

CHAPTER
THIRTY-EIGHT

Mirren

When I was small, my father was the rock I held onto during the tides of my anger. Whenever the world veered out of control, he always knew how to set it right. The right words, a soft hug, a smile. Nothing shook him, not even when everything seemed hopeless.

But now, I watch him crumple before me. I watch him curl into himself as the light in his eyes dims. I watch as he gives up hope. I watch as he breaks.

If I was a better daughter, I'd go to him. I would put my arms around him and share in his pain, so that maybe, between the two of us, it wouldn't feel so heavy. Instead, a vicious part of me drinks in his torment. Devours the way the echoing ache of Easton's death expands from Denver's chest and into his face; the way hope empties from his eyes like water down a drain.

I do not blame my father for Easton's death, but his grief is not mine; mine is intimate. His is grief for what could have been—the son he never got the chance to know. It isn't made up of smiles and conversations; of pudgy hands carved into strong ones; of soft moments and painful ones.

When he looks up at me, his eyes shine with tears behind his spectacles. I know better than to expect an apology, so I'm not disappointed when he doesn't offer one. Instead, he clears his throat and sucks in a harrowing breath. "Will you tell me about him, Mirri?"

His request is humble and soft, and that same vicious part of me considers tearing into it. Shredding through that softness with talons to punish him for his weakness. But Easton would have been kind, and so in his memory, I am too. "For a long time, I could only see what the Keys took from me," I begin, repeating my brother's words to me, "But Easton was the good in them. He shone with patience, with kindness. He was not allowed to use the word, but Easton loved his Community, and always wanted the best for them. For me."

My voice cracks and a tear slips down my cheek, but I force myself to press on. To speak of the good and the bad. The easy parts of Easton and the hard. But mostly, I speak of the way we loved each other. The way he nestled into my heart as a toddler and fit himself there so well, he could never be taken from me, not truly. Not even now.

And despite all my father's mistakes, he's the one who gifted us that. The Covinus stole important memories of Denver, but there are so many others that remain, so many small moments where the fierceness with which my father loved is clear. Denver loved my mother and blessed Easton and I with witnessing what true devotion looked like: the sacrifice, the selfless beauty. And it had imprinted somewhere deep within our souls as something rare. Something to hold on to, no matter what.

When I'm finished, breaths ragged and tears sticky on

both our cheeks, my father bows his head to me in gratitude. And maybe because of this rare vulnerability, the cracked open state of him, I have the courage to request something for myself. "Will you tell me about Mom?"

Denver's eyes widen, and his shoulders rise with another silent sob. He's quiet so long, I'm sure he'll refuse me, but then, the calming sonance of his voice fills the room. "Similians do not want, because we have enough. Food, warmth, Community. There is nothing more we could desire."

He tangles his fingers together in front of him, staring at them for another long moment. And when he looks back up to me, his eyes have changed: they are no longer docile and calm, but flare with a ravening strength, like the mere memory of my mother is enough to revert him back to the man he used to be. "But when I saw Azurra stand to walk toward the stage at our Binding, I *wanted*. I wanted her more than anything in my entire life."

"I tried to fight against it, as I was determined not to be a weak Community member. Determined not to go against the Keys. But the longer we were together, the more I was around her, that want only grew. And when I realized she returned my feelings, the want exploded until it was a fire that burned us both."

He swallows roughly. "I didn't know—I was young, naïve, and I—I didn't know what it would cost us. I just knew how it felt, like a burst of electricity had been sparked in my soul. I felt more alive every time I touched her than I'd been my whole life."

Something in me gapes open at his words, at the raw ache in them. Because I know exactly what he speaks of, the shape and feel of it all.

"At first, we were content to keep our love a secret, but

then we had you and Easton." Denver gazes at me sadly. "And, by the Covinus, seeing you was like seeing love embodied. So beautiful, so full of hope. We realized we couldn't allow Similis to dim your hope as it had ours, couldn't deny you the chance to feel what we did. To love and be loved in return. So, we began to plan."

Now, Denver looks through me, suddenly somewhere far away from Nadjaa. Somewhere lost in memory and tinged in pain. "Your mother was assigned to the Covinus building, and so whenever she was able, she researched as much as she could about the Dark World. We decided that I would go first, build something safe for our family, and then I'd come back for her. I was giddy with our plans, and my head was in the clouds, and I got sloppy. I kissed her outside on the street."

He frowns. "Someone saw and told the Covinus. I was Outcast the same day." Denver laughs ruefully. "But even that didn't dim my hope. I did exactly as I told Azurra I would. I built a place that was beautiful, that was free, that was peaceful. And I came back to the Boundary every year and gave our signal through the trees." Denver heaves a shaky sigh and pulls his glasses off his face to rub his eyes. "She never came. Eventually I accepted she never would."

My father's heart leaks through his words, and I find myself enamored by the rare glimpse of it. The part of himself he's hidden away, the pieces who made up the man I used to worship. "But you never blamed her. You were upset when I spoke ill of her."

He smiles softly. "Because I knew your mother, all the spaces of her heart. If she didn't meet me, she had a good reason. And I had to respect that, even as I was trapped on the other side of the Boundary forever. Away from her, away from you. I loved Azurra enough to trust she knew best."

I consider the man before me: a construct of broken pieces, the shards bleeding out from beneath his cultured exterior. "She wanted to come."

His eyes snap to mine, and for a moment, I consider denying him: hurting him like he's hurt me. But I've come so far in my journey from Similis: I understand now that my dark spaces are nothing to be ashamed of, but neither are my soft ones. And there is no honor in slaughtering an already wounded man.

"When the Covinus held me hostage, he tried to steal my memories and my power with two coins." Denver's face pales, and I force myself to press on. "And in fighting back, I somehow dove into his mind. I saw Mom. I think—I think in her research, she realized what those coins were capable of. That they were made with the old gods' power. Even in her last breaths, she wouldn't tell the Covinus where she'd hidden one of them and he killed her for it. She didn't want to leave you. She wanted to come. She hid the coin with Easton. Mom gave me the way to find you."

Denver looks as if I've shredded through his skin, horrified, and sated at once. And I understand it, the way it would feel to know my mother never stopped loving him, but also know there's nothing he can do to change her fate. To save her.

"Are you giving up on Nadjaa?" I finally ask. "Is that why you no longer care about the election?"

Denver's eyes shutter. "Nadjaa is lost. Even with the mountains and our militia—even with *you*—there is no winning against the Covinus' forces. He is too powerful."

"You aren't even going to try? You love this city. And he

deserves to suffer for what he did to Mom. For what he did to Easton."

My father pushes back in his chair, his spine stiffening. "You just heard what happens when you make decisions with your heart, Mirri. And gods know, you've sacrificed far too much in service of them. It's best if we cut our losses, sail somewhere else. Somewhere far from the Darkness."

"We can't leave Nadjaa unprotected. If Nadjaa falls, everything falls. You'll leave the continent to eternal Darkness. To misery and suffering."

Denver's jaw hardens. "That is sentiment speaking. Have you not already lost enough to sentiment and loyalty? Your brother is gone, your home is gone, you've given up your soul." A hot spike of anger pierces my heart, even as Denver presses on. "I will not allow my life to be derailed once more by emotion over logic, and I no longer make my decisions based on nostalgia. And I would encourage you to start doing the same before you're completely destroyed by it."

"That isn't true."

"What?" he replies, startled by the cutting calm of my words.

"You say you haven't made any decisions based on love and sentiment since Mom, but that *isn't* true."

Denver stares at me in bewilderment, and though a strong part of me wishes to run from this room, to leave my father alone with his stone heart, something keeps me planted in my seat. "Seven years ago, you allowed your heart to make a decision." My father's mouth parts, but I don't wait for him to speak. "Shaw and Max."

He shakes his head and shifts uncomfortably. "That wasn't—anyone with a soul would have saved *children*."

"You had an entire city to run, the continent was at war,

and maybe you're right that any decent person would have saved them. But you didn't just bring them to safety, did you? You brought them home and loved them. You instilled your dreams and values in them. Your heart *changed* them. And in doing so, you changed the tide of the Darkness."

Denver is eerily still as my words wash over him.

"If you'd handed Shaw and Max off to someone else, if you'd washed your hands clean of them, they wouldn't be who they are today. Max wouldn't have extended me friendship and protection, and Shaw—his soul would have been overcome with Darkness and he never would have escaped it. Without your love, he never would have tried to save you. He wouldn't have been at the Boundary. I would have died the moment I stepped over it and the Dead Prophecy, the promise of balance, would have been over forever."

I rise, my muscles aching with exertion as I set my eyes on my father. "So, you can say all you want that logic is stronger than love, but it isn't. And you taught us all that. It's time you remember."

∼

Shaw

The waves of the Storven crash against the black cliffs, the surf driving upward in a foam of white before receding back into the clear blue depths. My heart pounds in my chest, driving upward toward the gnarled scar above it with every beat. I run my fingers over it lightly as shame winds around me.

"Contemplating jumping?" an unbearably smooth voice asks from behind me. I curse inwardly, not bothering to turn to Avedis. "Shall I help? I did so enjoy the last time I got to throw you off a cliff. Your head bobbled like a macabre ragdoll. Very undignified for the Heir."

"Shouldn't you be off terrorizing innocent civilians? Or at the very least, hiding in the wind like the coward you are?"

When I turn toward Avedis, his smile is serpentine as he slides his gaze pointedly toward the manor. "Hmm. It doesn't seem as if I'm the coward here, does it, Firebreather?"

I curl my nails into the crescent of my palm to keep from hitting the snide look off the assassin's face. But even as my anger rises, I can't deny he's right. I shouldn't have left Mirren alone, should never have torn from Denver's office. I am the Heir of the Praeceptor, and I never run. But today, I had. And I can only hope Mirren forgives me for the weakness—for being unable to bear the agony on Denver's face, agony I've caused.

Because it hasn't seemed to matter that Denver's own actions are also partially responsible. All I can see is his face when he saved me, his soft hands, his gentle expression—he made me his son and in return, I've ruined everything he loves. His true son, his city. And worst of all, his daughter.

Avedis sits, swinging his legs so that they dangle over the edge of the cliff. And because I have nowhere else to go, I sit down beside him.

"The Covinus has taken Similis. His army marches toward Nadjaa as we speak," I say into the silence.

Avedis' answering purr sends shivers up my spine. "As far as I'm concerned, they can't arrive soon enough. I may very much die of boredom in this godsforsaken city, and I'd appreciate a break in the monotony."

Death. Pain. That's what will soothe Avedis' boredom—his emptiness. Another casualty of Anrai Shaw. "Thank you," I tell him. The sudden change of subject has him whipping his head toward me in disbelief. "I...I never said thank you for what you did, but I'm so grateful, Avedis. For coming with me to Argentum in the first place. For—for saving me. There's no way I'll ever be able to repay the life debt, and I just...I hope you know how thankful I am."

Avedis' face wrinkles in distaste. "I don't know why you're bothering to tell me this now as I have no heart to appeal to."

I shrug listlessly. "Because it makes me feel better."

Avedis scoffs. "Am I just to be a sounding board for all you soul-ridden?" he says irritably. "This is truly a fate worse than death."

He's right. Avedis is the last person in Nadjaa I should be confiding in, the only one who won't care at all about the dire circumstances we face. But it's for this same reason, the words slide easily from my mouth. I can't bear another look of devastation, and Avedis only looks bored. "He's controlling most the of the population of the continent. Every person I tested while I was under my father's hand. And the prophecy is demanding everything we have to give."

The assassin yawns, stretching his arms above his head and extending his neck from side to side in an unconcerned manner. "Prophecies tend to do that, nasty little things. Everyone talks about the old gods like they were some wonderful entities, but they were just as selfish as the rest of us."

I stare at him. "They gave their lives to break the curse."

"Well, they didn't do a very good job, did they? And perhaps, if they hadn't hidden in a cave until things were abysmal and it was entirely too late, we wouldn't be in this mess." A muscle flickers in his jaw. "Of course, they demand we give up everything we have to fix their mess. Just like you gave up everything to fix your father's, and I gave up everything to fix yours."

An inappropriate laugh threatens to escape my mouth, but I tamp it down with a press of my lips. "Will you give up your power to save Ferusa? If that's what the prophecy demands?"

"No." The wind-wielder's reply is immediate. "But I would give it up for revenge on the Covinus for taking what was not his." He sighs again. "My power has brought me nothing but trouble my entire life, the wrong sort of attention. I'd gladly hand it over if it meant the Covinus' death." His gaze sharpens, suddenly like the edge of a blade. "As I need no power to carve my penance from the witch-queen."

I'm saved from responding by Cal and Max crashing through the foliage on the manor path, Cal looking harried and Max, extremely annoyed. "Good gods, Avedis," Cal shouts, bending over with his hands on his thighs to catch his breath, "I told you to stay!"

"And yet, I am not a dog, Calloway, nor a particularly well-trained human, so you'll excuse me if I took the opportunity to save myself from your incessant and pathetic mooning over the Similian."

"We thought you were murdering your way through half the city!"

Avedis grins. "All in good time, friend."

Max pushes past the assassin, her eyes on me. The corner of her lips turns down as she takes in my appearance. I've never been able to hide from Max and have never truly tried. In her, I found a kindred spirit that night in the Castellium, and there has never been any point in pretending anything otherwise. I wait for her remark, but instead, she kneels beside me and pulls me into a hug.

Relief settles in my body, as her heart beats in time with mine. And when she pulls back, her face is positively feral, ready to cut through anything that would hurt us. "What's wrong?"

"Oh Maxwell," Avedis interjects with a dramatic air, "it's more of the same. The world is on the precipice of total annihilation and our brooding beast of a fire-wielder has once again managed to make it all about *him*."

Calloway guffaws, before shooting me an apologetic look. "I mean, you do have that tendency, Anni," he explains with a sheepish shrug. Schooling his face into seriousness, he asks, "What's going on?"

I explain what's happened with the prophecy, with Denver, with the Covinus, doing my best to ignore Avedis' dramatic sighs and loud exclamations of boredom. When I'm finished, they're silent for a long beat, the only sound the crashing of waves and the distant buzz of insects. I steel myself, half-expecting them to fall to my feet and decry it all hopeless. Denver's already given up hope; why wouldn't they as well?

But when I dare a glance in their direction, Max's expression is one of fierce determination, while Cal's is calmly calculating. It's everything I wouldn't have dared hope for.

And it's Max—the woman who guards her hope behind a wall of fire and brimstone—who says, "We'll figure it out. We keep hope."

Cal glances at her sidelong, his face an appropriate mixture of pride and incredulity, but she presses on, "Hope that Nadjaa won't break beneath the Covinus' forces. Hope the prophecy won't take everything you have to give. Hope for a better world."

Mirren appears behind Max, her curls a wild halo

around her head. "Hope," she repeats, hugging Max, her face illuminated by a radiant smile.

Max grins, before looking to me once more, a challenge dancing in her eyes. "You once gave me hope for a better world, Shaw. You told me we could be something different. Something better. Even when there was no hope of it, you believed. We can do it again."

Emotion lodges thickly in my throat as the past and present layer on top of one another, but I manage a small nod. Max is right. The world has crashed around all of us before, everything we thought we knew tumbling down and burying us alive. And we all fought our way free. Together, we can do it again.

Cal claps me on the back, with a delighted laugh. It lights my chest as he wraps Max around the neck and pulls all of us into a tangled hug. Even Avedis, who appears mildly embarrassed by the entire display, allows himself to be caught up in the snare of arms.

I breathe in the breaths of those I love—the ones brave enough to pick up their broken pieces and use them to fight for something better—and take heart we're strong enough to face whatever comes.

"So, what's the plan?" Cal asks.

I can't stop the smile that slides across my lips. "First, we go celebrate hope." Cal whoops as he realizes what I mean. "Tonight, we dance."

CHAPTER
THIRTY-NINE

Mirren

"I don't know how many times I have to say it, Mirren," Max chides as she rakes a comb through my hair, "put your hair up when you sleep. Some of these tangles are going to take an hour to undo."

I wince as she yanks on one in painful demonstration. "I've been a bit busy," I reply hotly. "What with being kidnapped and the continent about to fall into total darkness."

"Continental destruction is no reason not to look good," Max replies as she deftly undoes another knot.

"Here, here!" Calloway chirps from the corner, raising his already half-empty wine glass to cheers the air.

As most of the manor still isn't fit for inhabitants, we've been relegated to using a room at Evie's to get ready for the lunar celebration. Cal propped a window open when we arrived, and the energetic pulse of Nadjaa, along with the delicious scent of Evie's pastries, has been drifting in and out of the room. Skiffs and boats have already begun to gather on the Bay of Reflection, their music pulsing over the water in cheerful bursts. The merchant square and docks have been hung with tapestries and lanterns, and though still unlit, the pale shimmer of the fabrics is ethereal in the setting sun. Neighbors duck in and out of shops and houses, helping each other with preparations, and laughter rings between the buildings in melodic swells.

I breathe it all in, feeling happy and bereft at once. Whatever happens after tonight, I am so thankful to be here, in this place, with my friends. My family. But a part of me still aches for my brother—will always ache—for the things he'll never have the chance to experience.

Max pins a few tresses in place, an assortment of other pins pinched between her lips. When her eyes meet mine in the mirror, she spits them into her hand, freeing her to speak. "Are you thinking of Easton?"

His name hurts in the open air, but there is also a sense of relief in hearing someone say it. Not skirting around his loss or avoiding the discomfort of the topic. Not letting his memory fade because it hurts too much to speak of.

"I was thinking he'd probably hate all of this, but I wish he'd gotten the chance to see it anyway."

Max smiles gently, as her attention moves back to my hair.

Cal takes another gulp of his drink, and nods in agreement. "He definitely would have hated the debauchery—"

"—and how loud it is," I add.

"And the amount of people," Max laughs.

Cal raises his glass with a smile and a wink. "I bet we could have gotten him to dance, though. I'm very persuasive."

I laugh, the sound surprising me as it bubbles up. Soft and unused, but still there. I haven't forgotten how to do it, how to allow lightness into my chest. "Now I'm sorry I'll never get to witness my brother trying to dance. Could you imagine?"

We all dissolve into laughter at the thought of Easton, so stick straight, attempting any sort of fluidity, and my heart tugs again. I wish he had the chance to experience *this* —laughter, friendship.

Max presses the final pin in place and throws her hands on her hips as she stands back to survey her work. "What do you think?"

"Ravishing," Cal offers helpfully from his sprawled position on the settee. He brushes invisible lint off his own suit, a piece perfectly cut to fit his lithe form, the emerald-green color complimenting his freckled complexion and making the copper of his hair glow.

I stand, staring at myself in the mirror. Max has done immaculate work as usual, taming the tangled bird's nest of my hair into soft curls that pour down my back. She's pinned the front back, accentuating the rosy flush of my cheeks and my kohl-darkened eyes. Max grins at my reflection, and I blush when she announces, "You're a knockout."

The dress arrived on the doorstep of the boarding house only a half hour prior, a gift from Anrai. I have no idea how he found or paid for it such last minute, but it's the most beautiful thing I've ever seen. The bodice is modest but fitted, intricately beaded in whorls of cerulean gems, the pattern reminding me of the brightest sea, but it is the train that truly makes the gown devastating. Dark spills of midnight blue silk trail from the waist, tumbling down like a waterfall itself. Somehow, Anrai has managed to dress me in the armor of my power.

"I love it, all of it," I answer honestly, wondering at how far I've come. The last time I stared into a mirror like this, I felt embarrassed to look beautiful. Now, I am settled in my skin, my strength. "Thank you, Max."

She pulls me in for a hug, and then shoos me gently from the mirror. "Now, I have to fix my own face," she laughs.

Her face needs absolutely no fixing, as she looks stunning in her own red gown, but I don't point this out. Instead, I plop myself ungracefully next to Cal on the settee, where he happily offers me his wine. I take a large gulp and resist the urge to wipe my mouth with the back of my hand and ruining Max's hard work.

"Anni better not have spent all his time looking for your dress," Cal muses, tugging the glass back to take his own swig. "He swore he wouldn't show up looking like death come to call."

"I don't know if a suit is enough to change that," I reply honestly to Cal's guffaw of laughter. Cal left Anrai and Harlan to Avedis' care, as apparently an eye for fashion is not something that disappears upon the removal of one's soul. Cal insisted it was only because he was ready so much earlier than the rest of the men, but I get the impression it has more to do with avoiding Harlan.

Since their return to Nadjaa, something between them has clearly shifted. An electricity exists in the space between them that hadn't been there before, a magnetic pulse that both pulls them together and forces them apart. I haven't broached the topic with either of them, as I didn't want to press into an already tender wound.

But I think of Harlan's devastation at Easton's loss, and of the expression on Cal's face as he watched him unravel. And before, Harlan's heartbreak when he realized Easton would never choose him, never love him as he deserved. Strings of love and hurt, all tangled together so furiously, it's impossible to sort the bitter from the beautiful. It's a fact of love that no longer scares me—its ability to ruin you just as easily as it lifts you up—because now I understand the sharp edge is what makes it so beautiful.

"Hey, Cal?" He bumps my shoulder gently with his in response, and wordlessly passes me the glass. I take another small sip and lower it into my lap. "I hope you know how wonderful you are. And how much goodness you deserve."

Cal flicks his eyes to mine curiously, his face as open and exuberant as the first time we met. "Why Mirren, are you trying to make me blush?"

"I hesitate to know what it would take to make you blush," I laugh, handing him the wine and tangling my fingers in my lap. I've never been practiced at putting emotion into words—never been good at wrapping up the way someone can feel like the sun itself and shaping it into something tangible. But after tonight, the world may tip on its axis, life as we know it shaken off into space.

So, in spite of my clumsiness, I try anyway. "I just hope you know how much I love you. Both of you."

Max pauses the reapplication of her lipstick to incline her head toward me, an acceptance and a return. Cal smiles brightly and hugs me into his side, swiping at his eyes with his free hand. "Ya know, I think Anni may have rubbed off entirely too much on all of us. Since when have we become so broody?"

"Speak for yourselves," Max replies, running a soft finger over the corner of her scarlet painted lips. "I never brood."

"You just wait, Max. Your time will come," Cal says, wiggling his fingers ominously in her direction.

As more laughter spills around the room, the air

suddenly sparks and heats. Anticipation thrums through me, and I whip my head to find Anrai leaning against the threshold, watching the three of us with an uncharacteristically dreamy look.

And gods, his presence steals the air from the room as his mouth quirks into a half smile, his pale gaze glimmering in contrast with the dim light of the hall. His ink black hair has been combed into submission and the bronze of his skin is beautifully warm against the open collar of his black shirt. Matching black pants hug his muscular legs, but it's the deep crimson of his velvet coat, cut perfectly to taper in at just the right place, that has me digging my teeth into my lip, as he drawls, "Hello, Lemming."

Anrai kept his promise to Cal. He doesn't look like death. He looks like pure flame, blindingly bright and devastatingly ruthless.

"You're wearing color!" Cal gushes as he leaps up to examine the seams on the velvet coat. "And you didn't burst into flame! I'm so proud of you, I might actually cry," he exclaims affectionately, running his hands over the buttons even as Anrai shoos him off.

"Get off me, Calloway," he says with a laugh, shrugging off the attention as his eyes meet mine again. They spark when I stand and run down the length of me, lingering on each place the gown hugs. And then longer on the places left bare. And just like the first time he brought me to the lunar ceremony, heat rushes to the surface of my skin, the heady sweetness of his approval far more intoxicating than the wine.

Anrai holds a hand out with a devilish grin. I take it, stepping into the warmth of him as he leads me down the hallway.

"You two kids have fun!" Cal calls after us. "Try not to ruin any long-standing Ferusian relics while you're out!"

We're both laughing as we make our way down the stairs and through the bakery, where Evie is piling trays of sweets into her husband Berik's patiently waiting arms. She gives us a quick wave, before urging Berik out the door and into the street. The bell on the door tinkles behind us as we follow them out, but before I have the chance to take in the beauty of the market, Anrai tugs me into the darkness of the alleyway between the bakery and a book shop.

His body presses me into the rough bricks as he brings his mouth down on mine. His hands are restlessly insatiable, skimming the beaded bodice, tracing the hourglass shape of my waist and hips, dipping beneath the slit to caress the smooth skin of my inner thigh. I reach up and wind my arms around his neck, pulling him closer, tangling my tongue with his until I'm breathless.

Just like that, I forget entirely about the lunar ceremony, about the dress, about the hundreds of people milling about a few feet away. All I remember is the feel of him, the heated hunger that pulses through me, the sparks that light up my chest and behind my eyes. And I want more. More of everything about him. I want to get drunk on it, to consume every piece of him.

Anrai pulls back slightly with a strained laugh. "Max will kill me if I smear your lipstick," he mutters against my throat.

I fist my fingers in the velvet of the coat and yank him back toward me. My blood pulses as I breathe against his mouth, "It's been a good life. Worth the risk."

His laugh is sweet along my tongue as he kisses me again. This time when he pulls back, it's to run his eyes from my head to my toes, drinking me in. His breathing is uneven and flame sparks at his fingertips wildly, like he doesn't mean it to. He shakes his head with another rough laugh, his eyes hooded and hungry. "You're so godsdamn beautiful, I swear, it hurts to breathe. All I wanted all day was to see you in that dress..." Anrai leans in and runs his tongue lightly over my skin, like he's tasting me in small sips. "...and now all I want to do is tear if off of you."

I smile broadly. "I promise you can tear the whole thing in half later. Though it seems pretty well constructed. I don't know if you'll be able to manage."

Anrai nips at the juncture of my throat, and growls, "Haven't you learned not to challenge me, Lemming?" But even as he laughs, a shadow flickers in his eyes.

And I understand it. 'Later' is something the Darkness might steal. 'Later' may never come.

Unless we fight. Unless we keep hope against all odds. Unless we tear through the Darkness with our teeth and flood it with light.

I stand up straighter, taking in the crimson of his jacket, the cerulean of my dress. The black of his clothes and the night-sky blue of my train. *You are the light and the dark, just as I am the dark and the light.* We are not one or the other, but both fire and water, in synchronicity and it is this, the acceptance of balance, that will change the world.

"Let's go dance," I say, tugging him toward the square. "Let's go be with our family."

∽

Shaw

Perhaps it's because I've been away for so long, but the market district is more stunning than usual. Everything is draped in sheaths of silver and white, but rather than feeling colorless, it only magnifies the natural colors of the world around us. Midnight blues and blacks of the bay, deep verdant greens of the climbing plants and trees, coral and tangerine streaks of the setting sun, all reflect in a shimmering riot.

Shrieks of delight echo from the water, answered by the resounding laughter of the market. Though most Nadjaans don't usually venture to the celebration until well after sunset, it seems everyone has made an exception tonight, as hundreds of people already swarm the streets and bay. Whether it's the special election, or the rumors of the impending invasion, the air sparks with energy and the feel of it brings a smile to my face.

Because whatever Denver is now, he built this. A place determined to celebrate the beautiful things in life, even when horror lurks at the edges. A city that can somehow come together even when we're all so different. Nature wielders, politicians, farmers. Mothers, fathers, sisters, brothers. From different parts of the continent but all wishing for the same thing: a better life.

I sip slowly at a glass of cherry wine, the sour-sweet taste puckering my mouth, as I watch Cal spin Mirren around. Her laugh settles in my chest even from this distance, and I can't help but smile more broadly as Cal dips her low in his arms, before lifting her up and spinning her to Harlan.

The Similian blushes furiously as he catches her stiffly around the waist. Mirren giggles again, and breaks into the strangest dance I've ever seen, all while maintaining eye contact with Harlan. Her joy is contagious as he finally cracks, laughing shyly, and begins to move his body. Max holds Helias in her arms, whirling the boy around in wild circles, the shimmer of his answering smile luminous.

Avedis has abandoned his quest to defile the citizens of Nadjaa, at least for the night, and appears content to lead Sura around in a very pretentious-looking waltz.

Months ago, I stood on the fringes of this very dance floor, greedily watching what I thought I could never have.

Something beautiful. Something soft. Both had seemed so far out of my reach.

You love and so it shall be taken from you.

But maybe the fear—the edge of terror honed by life's fleeting nature—is what makes it so sweet. It doesn't matter how long I have it; it matters how I savor it while I do.

Mirren's eyes light on me, her emerald gaze sharpening mischievously as she beckons me forward with one small finger. My body instantly tightens in anticipation, the abyss flaring outward as I follow the invisible tether toward her, the pull of our souls. Her teeth dig into the pillow of her lush bottom lip as she runs her gaze from my face to my chest. And then further down.

"Warrior," she whispers, half-mocking, as she shimmies into the cradle of my arms. Luscious, rolling curves against sharp-hewn edges. "I believe our last dance got interrupted."

"I cannot be blamed for my always impeccable timing," Avedis pipes up as he and Sura waltz by. He's shaved his hair down to the skull once more, and though his wind is invisible, his mere presence brings with it the smell of a storm. Of wild air and soft breezes.

Ignoring the assassin, I take Mirren's hand in mine, pressing my other against the small of her back and pulling her even closer against me. Until I can feel the shape of her beneath her clothes, smell the ocean on her skin. Leaning down to her ear, I rasp, "That shall have to be remedied."

Together, we sweep around the dance floor, our movements fluid and surprisingly graceful for the catastrophe of a woman I hold. Unlike her first dance—her first venture into Ferusa—she no longer fights against herself. She flows freely, her power emanating from every part of her, until she shines brighter than the rapidly rising moon.

Emotion rises in my throat as I hold her closer, as we spin and whirl.

She is too much.

Mirren has always been told she doesn't fit, is too bright, too loud, too *everything*. So I steal the sentiment back, strip it of its jealousy and anger, and hold it up as something new: Mirren is too much. Too much to be struck down by some curse, to be defeated by someone like the Covinus who is only filled with emptiness.

Maybe this is the hope Asa spoke of—not borne of thinking the best of the world, but thinking the world of one person. Because my hope is planted in her heart, its vines tethered into her soul. Whatever the prophecy demands of her, she will give it, but she won't be left empty by it.

Security in this hope is what keeps me dancing, even as the moon begins to peek up from behind the Averitbas range, the silvery orb glowing against the black mountains. Hope that keeps me laughing, even when the danger outside the city grows closer. What keeps me from stealing Mirren and hiding her away and letting the world burn.

Because no one else would be enough to save it.

The hope is fed by the family of misfits we've somehow tethered together. A lost princess. A hopeful farmer. A soulless assassin. A steady Similian. An orphan boy. All brought together by fate and forged in the Darkness.

We dance even as Jayan's win of the Chancellor seat is

announced. Even as the absence of Denver stretches wide over the ceremony. We laugh until our stomachs are sore, and then we laugh some more. Mirren makes water animals dance in the air over a group of children, Helias at the forefront, their shrieks of delight ringing warmly through the night air. Cal does an impeccable impression of Avedis' stuffy waltz, which the assassin takes as a personal affront, demanding a trial by dance. They only make it halfway through the first song, before the two of them are wrestling on the floor like brothers scuffling over the last piece of candy.

Harlan wades between them with an amiable smile, and it isn't long before Avedis and Cal give up the fight in order to join forces to convince the Similian to drink more wine.

Max twirls Mirren around, both of them clinging to each other as they trip over the hems of their dresses and careen sideways into me, dissolving into fits of giggles.

I keep the hope in my heart, a warm hearth, a signal home, even when a sudden hush descends over the livening crowd. The music comes to an abrupt stop, and it's only then, I see Denver standing on the dais. He's shaved and changed into finer clothes since we saw him at the manor, and his eyes are hidden behind the silver reflection of the moonlight on his spectacles.

He clears his throat softly, and all of Nadjaa stills. He has no need of yelling, no need of force. Because when Denver speaks, people listen.

"The Covinus' army is halfway across the Breelyn Plain," he says. "They are coming."

CHAPTER
FORTY

Mirren

"You had no right!" Jayan shouts, storming hotly into the meeting room of the Council House, his black cloak billowing behind him like a black cloud. "Nadjaa is *mine* now! I am Chancellor and you had no business causing a panic."

Council members swarm in after us, their voices just as loud as Jayan's, the feel of their fear filling the room more surely than water.

My father is the only one who appears calm. Even though he leans on his cane, his face is unflappable as he makes his way decisively to the ornate chair at the head of the table. The Chancellor's seat. Jayan practically growls, his hand twitching like he's considering drawing a sword in the middle of the council chambers.

"According to law, I remain Chancellor until midnight," Denver reminds him in a low voice. "And I will act as such. I will not leave my people in ignorance to be destroyed. They deserve to know what's coming and to have time to prepare for it."

Without waiting for Jayan's reply, my father settles himself in the chair. Folding his hands before him, he stares at each Council member in turn. All fall silent and take their seats without argument, leaving only Anrai and me standing awkwardly near the door. Upon hearing my father's speech—his love for his people woven into his words, in the care he took to answer each of their questions and assuage their fears—he'd immediately taken a skiff to the Council House, and we'd gone after him.

When I left my father in the manor, he'd been determined to ignore his heart, to allow cruel logic to win out once again over love. But in showing up to the lunar ceremony, in laying his heart on the line for his city, some of the gnarled scar tissue left by his calloused choices were smoothed.

And when he meets my eyes now, I know he means to stay. To fight for his city. To see his dream to the end. And the pride in my father that had pulsed through me as a child reawakens.

Denver nods to me, and then to Anrai. "Mirren. Shaw. As long as you intend to stay in the city, please sit. Your powers will be useful to the defense of the mountain passes."

As Anrai and I take our seats, Jayan rounds on Denver, apoplectic. His eyes bulge, and his face turns an alarming shade of scarlet. "These two are under arrest! They should be dragged to the square and hanged this instant! You cannot possibly mean to include them in the defense of the city. They are just as likely to use the information to destroy us all."

Denver's voice remains quiet, but firm. "As I said Jayan, this is *my* city for the next five hours. And as such, I will see to it that it is properly defended."

"By traitors?!"

My father eyes the councilman from behind his glasses. "Are you able to flood an entire mountain pass? Turn a cliffside to ice?"

Jayan stutters in response.

Denver only raises an eyebrow mildly. "Create a boundary of fire to burn through an army?" Jayan's mouth opens and closes, reminiscent of a large-mouth bass. My father hums. "I thought not. Now, if you would do us all a favor and take a seat, we'll begin. You've wasted enough time."

Jayan's face twists in rage, but when he finds no allies in the other council members, he crosses his arms and drops sullenly into the chair at Denver's right.

"Shaw," my father begins. Anrai's eyes widen at the direct address, and he digs his fingers into his palm beneath the table. "Tell me what your strategy would be."

Anrai blinks, slightly shellshocked at my father's request. He shifts uncomfortably as everyone's stare pivots in his direction. Some with distrust, others with outright hatred. Only Evie watches Shaw with something like faith. Anrai clears his throat. "Denver, I don't think—I mean, no one wants to follow my leadership."

I open my mouth to argue, but my father gets to it first. "You are intimate with the inner workings of the Dark Militia, as well as the nature of the soulless. Your wielding skills are not limited to the resources around you, and you are the most capable and well-trained soldier in all of Nadjaa. I think you are exactly who we should be following into battle."

For a moment, Anrai is speechless, staring at Denver with a look I've rarely seen adorn the handsome angles of his face. *Hope.* Then he shifts, his body stilling as he becomes the man he was trained to be—born to be. The one who will tear through the world to protect what is his. And Nadjaa is his.

"We need to flood every pass and block every foot trail. Avedis and Mirren can make quick work of it. The militia has their own wielders and will blast their way through eventually, but it will slow them down and give us enough time to organize our forces." His voice brooks no room for argument, its deep tenor lulling even the most stubborn of council members into a quiet respect.

"If we block all the passes, surely the Covinus will give up," a dark-skinned man says from a few seats down the table. "The Dark Militia has no ships. There is no other way to get to the city."

Anrai stands, gesturing to the intricately painted map of Ferusa hung behind the Chancellor's seat. He points to Baak, to Dauphine, to Yen Girene. He points to Ashlaa, Kin Rylene, and dozens of other smaller territories. "The Covinus controls all these forces. Which means he has use of their ships. Their wielders." He stares at the map with a frown, his mind visibly whirling.

Denver watches him patiently, even as Jayan jumps once more to his feet. "This is ridiculous. Does it matter how many forces we have when we have wielders that would be able to destroy them all? Burn them. Sink their ships. Good riddance."

"It may come to that, but these people..." Anrai shakes his head. "These people are innocent. They're being controlled by the Covinus. They don't deserve to die."

"Not our problem," Jayan snaps.

"It should be," Denver interjects. "Do you think we should win a war that destroys everything but Nadjaa?

There will be no one left. And I will not have my daughter and son lose their soul to win you a war."

Jayan sneers, even as warmth settles in my chest. *This* is the man I idolized, the one whose arms were safe and whose head was full of dreams. Who was willing to risk everything he knew to give his children the chance at love he never had.

"In four hours, Denver, that will no longer be your decision. They can either lose their souls defending this city, or they will hang in its square. Seems an obvious choice to me."

Anrai ignores Jayan, his eyes finding my father's. So much passes between them in a fraction of a moment, it's hard to grasp a single one. "We should put out a call for any wielders who would volunteer. Earth-shakers should take the north, water-wielders to the south. Wind-wielders split evenly between them."

"And you, Fire-bringer?" Jayan snarls the title like it's offensive. "Where will *you* be?"

Now, when Anrai turns to the councilman, nothing remains of the calm advisor he just was. Though his body is entirely still, the room around him seems to vibrate with energy. Each cut of his body appears somehow sharper, and his eyes—they *blaze*. Untethered, wild, they rage with unrivaled power. Jayan has the good sense to take a step back, even as Anrai's whispered voice says, "I will be waiting, Jayan. I am who they will call when every line has broken, when every militia has fallen. Because I am the harbinger of destruction." He lowers his chin, staring so fiercely at Jayan, for a moment I worry the councilman might burst into flame where he stands.

But Anrai leashes himself, smiling humorlessly. "I am

the last line of defense, because if you call upon me, there will be nothing left."

Eerie quiet settles over the room as everyone watches Anrai, but he needs no approval. Because now they know, they only exist on his mercy. He could destroy them all with barely a thought, and it's only his goodness that keeps him from it. A shiver runs up my spine, but it isn't fear. It's anticipation, pride, my *other* pressing against my skin, dancing in my chest to the primal call of his.

"It's settled then. The Covinus will arrive at the base of the Shadiil range by hour's end. Rocher is already organizing the guard, but more preparations will need to be made. Mirren, you will take care of the passes. Shaw, you will be in charge of gathering wielders." To the People's Council, he says, "Each of you will need to alert your districts and get them to safety. Get the weakest to this House as soon as you can. The rest can head for the fields at the base of the Averitbas. It's the farthest away from where the militia invades, and the safest place we can offer."

Without argument, the Council stands, nervous chatter breaking out once more as they stream from the room. Jayan storms out as furiously as he came in, and dread sinks into my stomach, as I doubt the councilman will be following orders.

Anrai presses his lips together as he watches Jayan's cloak disappear down the corridor. "Denver," he starts softly, the name on his lips both hopeful and desperate.

My father nods, his eyes shining behind his spectacles. "I know, boy," he says softly. "I know we cannot win. But my daughter has reminded me there is grace in the fight. Strength in the faith." He pushes his chair away from the table and rises, forgoing his cane as he stands before Anrai. "Somewhere along the way, the dream became more important than who it was for, more important than *why* we were building it."

He tilts his head to me with a sad smile. "It was all for you, Mirri. I wanted a better world for you and Easton, a place where you could ask whatever questions were in your head and have them answered. A place for your soft heart to grow, to be protected. None of it means anything without you."

Denver heaves a shaky breath, and I realize with alarm his eyes are lined with tears. For a moment, I sit frozen, uncertain whether to go to my father or stay where I am.

"And you, Shaw," he says softly, "the boy who appeared out of the Darkness to save me."

Anrai goes completely still. "You're the one who saved me," he replies deferentially, but Denver shakes his head.

"No. It has always been the other way around. You found me when I was alone, when the Darkness had stolen my reasons for living. Watching you grow, watching you learn...it reminded me that even though I failed my family, didn't mean I had to keep failing. *You* are the reason Nadjaa exists as it does, the reason *I* exist." My father limps slowly toward him and reaches his hand toward Anrai's shoulder.

He hesitates, as if fearing Anrai's reaction, and for a long beat, we all stare at his hand frozen in midair. "The man you are today has nothing to do with me. You were always that man, always the same pure soul. Forgive me for allowing my desperation to overcome me. Forgive me for ever allowing myself to forget who you are."

Anrai's expression tears wide open, and every desperate, lonely thought bubbles through the gash. Shaking slightly, he wraps his fingers around Denver's outstretched hand and places it on his own shoulder.

Denver's throat bobs. "There are so many ways to lose

your soul," he whispers, his eyes flashing to mine. "I am sorry I lost mine."

My own emotions rise like a flood, a deluge of every horrible and hopeful thing I've felt since my father left all those years ago. For a brief moment, I am breathless as my *other* thrashes wildly, fed by the torrent. But there's no time —no time to sort out the places that have been mended and the ones that still hurt—so instead, I say, "We aren't beaten yet. We can still stop him."

I glance at Anrai uncertainly, and he gives me an encouraging nod. A sign he'll follow where I lead, even if that means giving up everything. "The Dead Prophecy. It says, *so what was given must now be taken*. We can make him human again. Break the control he holds so he can be defeated."

Anrai narrows his eyes thoughtfully. "You think if we break the curse, it'll return the souls he controls?"

"It might. We have to try."

Anrai swallows roughly, but nods, standing straighter as he runs through strategies in his head. "Then we need to figure out where we need to be when the moon rises fully. Aggie might have an idea." He meets my gaze. "And we're going to need to get close enough to the Dark Militia to steal one of those coins."

The idea of Anrai being anywhere near the Covinus sends a bolt of panic through me. "Anrai, he—he can't be killed. You can't fight him alone."

The answering grin on Anrai's face is terrifying. "I'm not going to be, Lemming. If I were the Covinus, I would want to suppress the opposing forces' wielders, but I would *also* stay toward the back of my army in command. So I'd keep one coin with me, and one..."

Realization dawns on me. "And one at the front!"

As Anrai grins, Denver watches us with an unreadable look. "Mirri, the wording of the old gods is far too vague. What if—what if it demands everything of you?"

"It won't," Anrai snaps back, before remembering himself. He inhales sharply, scraping his fingers through his hair. "I only mean...Denver, you know your daughter. She is so full...of life, of hope, of rage, of strength. I have faith she can break the curse, faith that she was chosen because she is the only one who can do it and survive."

"And you, Shaw?" Denver challenges. "Are you full enough to survive? I've already lost one son; I refuse to give up another."

Anrai blinks. Then quietly, "I've sworn to spend my life trying to be worthy of Mirren. If I die trying, then so be it. It will be for us. For our dream. For something better."

Denver looks like he wants to continue arguing. Like he's considering throwing his cane to the side and tackling us both to keep us from it. But he reins himself in, and says fiercely, "Then we fight."

CHAPTER
FORTY-ONE

Shaw

The mountain rumbles beneath my feet, and my stomach surges into my throat as the ground begins to roll, collapsing in on itself with a deafening roar. Beside me, Helias claps excitedly, bouncing on his toes. His dark eyes shine as a boulder the size of the Council House tumbles down from one of the cliffs, crashing through trees and rock alike. "This is so much fun!" he says with a grin.

I ruffle his curls, even as a sharp pang of regret slashes through me. An eight-year-old should not find preparing a city for war 'fun', should not ever have to face the horror of what's to come. Especially Helias, who has already suffered so much loss in his short life. I wish I could steal him away from here, somewhere he could live happily and never have to give anything else up.

Because as much as I'm ready to sacrifice everything, Helias shouldn't have to.

"Can we do another?" he asks eagerly, swatting impatiently at an errant ringlet.

"Three passes weren't enough for you?" Cal asks,

coming to stand beside us with his hands on his hips, surveying Helias' handiwork with affection. We've all changed out of our finery, and Cal has traded his emerald green suit for far more muted leather gear. "Two terror forests and a rockslide are probably enough for today. We need to get you back to the Council House."

Helias wrinkles his nose and pouts his lower lip. "I don't want to go where the *babies* go."

I chuckle. "Children, Helias. Not babies. And it doesn't matter how many mountains you can move, you're still a child."

For the moment. When the moon meets the Averitbas Mountains, he'll be asked to be so much more. And it isn't fair, but I've found no way around it, no other way to break the curse, and give the Nadjaan's a fighting chance.

Helias glares at me, kicking sullenly at the dirt. With a small laugh, I relent. "How about the field with Harlan? You can help him and Asa protect the others."

He considers my words for a long moment, before deciding it's an acceptable compromise.

"Aggie, you should go, too," Cal suggests, adjusting the imprinted leather strap of his bow. "I can take you there before I head over to Shadiil Pass."

Aggie, who's idea of helping Nadjaa prepare for invasion has been whacking the earth and wind wielders with her walking stick whenever their power wanes, glares at Calloway. "Do not purport to speak to me like a child, Calloway. I shall stay here where I am useful."

Cal arches a brow skeptically. "How is terrorizing the few wielders who've volunteered to help us useful?"

To his point, Aggie thwacks a young wind-wielder in the leg. The girl, who can't be more than twenty, yelps and shoots the old witch an injured look. Aggie stares back unapologetically, and with a sniff, the girl squeezes her eyes shut, refocusing on the tree limbs she'd dropped while trying to construct a blockade.

"This is a battle. You don't even have shoes on, let alone armor," Cal tries again, looking to me for help. I shrug, knowing better than to try to tell Aggie anything.

She points a gnarled finger in Cal's direction. "If you don't quit condescending to me, I will curse you and your first born." Though Aggie speaks in the same eerie singsong voice she always does, Cal has the good sense to look perturbed, raising his palms in peace, as she adds, "And how could I hear the earth if I wore shoes?"

Cal wrinkles his brow, opening his mouth and then decisively closing it, like he doesn't even know where to begin. I clap him on the back with a laugh. "Leave it alone, there will be no convincing her of anything. Will you take Helias to the Council House on your way?"

Helias and the other earth-wielders have made the west side of the city nearly impassable, which means we'll be able to focus our forces on the Shadiil pass and the sea. Cal will go meet the archers manning the clifftop at the gap, while Mirren and Avedis will be stationed on the bluffs overlooking the Storven once they're finished blocking all routes over the mountains.

Harlan volunteered to help with the evacuation of citizens, and then to stand guard with Asa and the Xaman tribes in the fields at the base of the Averitbas. And Max and I will be near the bottom of the pass, where we'll try to infiltrate an army as large as the Breelyn Plain itself to find an infernal coin, and try not to lose our souls in the process.

We'll all be apart as the might of the Covinus breaks against the mountains, scattered to different points of the city, and after everything, it feels wrong—even if it's only temporary.

Only until the moon rises, when we will have to escape from beneath Jayan's hand and make our way to the topmost street in Nadjaa, where the land walks into the moon. And after...after is still unknown.

"Of course," Cal replies, drawing me from my thoughts. "But aren't you heading the same way?"

I nod, anxiety unspooling like barbed wire at the base of my spine. "Yeah, but Max and I need to get a head start to hide before the militia arrives." My eyes stray to Max, who has been bent over her swords for the better part of an hour meticulously sharpening their blades, and for the thousandth time, I wish I was going alone.

But as my power will be stolen by the coin, and I'll be far weaker than normal armed with only shadows, I need someone who won't be affected by its power. I'm thankful to have Max's skill covering my back, but the protective side of me wants to tie her to a tree and keep her far away from the Covinus.

Cal nods, his russet eyes growing uncharacteristically serious. "Anni—"

"Don't, Calloway," I interrupt in a sudden panic, certain whatever he means to say will slice through my shoddily erected calm façade. "Don't get sappy on me. This isn't the end, and we aren't going to talk like it is."

Cal shoves my shoulder, and I rock backward. "I will get as sappy as I please, and you will love and endure every minute of it," he snaps hotly, his glare daring me to argue. I press my lips shut, as he heaves an annoyed sigh. "I just wanted to say, whatever happens tonight—or any night, for that matter—I'm grateful I chose you."

The words settle over my heart like a warm blanket,

filling in the places that had been stuffed with dread only a second earlier. Like usual, Calloway somehow knows exactly what to say. *I didn't drag my friends to the edge of the abyss; they accompanied me here, hand in hand. And it makes all the difference in the world.*

And he's right. Cal chose me when I was all snarling madness and made me his, and I am a far better man for it. It is something I've always envied about him, the ability to choose something and never second guess it. To jump without fear, to *love* without fear—once Calloway decides someone is worth loving, he simply does.

"I love you, brother," I tell him, pulling him into a rough hug.

"It's amazing what emotions imminent death will shake loose," his muffled voice says into my shoulder.

I shove him heartily, laughter ringing through me even as I shake my head. As a boy, I was eternally alone, and thought I always would be. But somehow, I've not only found my soul-bonded, but my soul*mates.* In Cal, who still laughs in the face of death. In Max, whose stubbornness and loyalty are the reason I still breathe. Even in Avedis, that soulless bastard who understands the worst parts of my life and never leaves me to waste away in the memory of them.

When I watch Cal leave, Helias' hand in his, I memorize the shape of his stride, the heft of his shoulders, the copper sheen of his hair. And instead of fear or dread, I only feel thankful.

When I turn back to Aggie, it's to find her now demonstrating an odd sort of a dance to a horrified looking earth-wielder. "Aggie, I have a question before we leave."

The old woman stops mid-dance, her arms still stretched into the sky and her legs planted at odd angles.

The earth-wielder shoots me a grateful look, taking Aggie's momentary distraction to slink away. "What is it, boy?"

"Where the land walks into the sky...does that mean anything to you?"

Aggie eyes sparkle, and she pushes herself up to standing, before hobbling toward me with a happy smile. "Anrai Shaw, it seems you have finally climbed out of the Darkness long enough to see the world around you clearly."

I stare at her dumbly, wondering if that's her answer, but to my relief, she goes on. "The dead gods brought me to Nadjaa a very long time ago."

She reads the skepticism on my face, even as I try to hide it and thwacks me with her stick. "Even now, when your entire world has been shaped by them, you doubt."

I shrug. "How do beings that are dead speak?"

Aggie smiles, a gaping, toothless thing. "The gods were never mortal, which means they could not die a mortal's death. Their essence is weak and fractured, but it still exists in the earth as surely as the Darkness does. I was blessed with the ability to listen."

Max sheathes her falchions in an 'X' at her back, and comes to stand beside me, listening intently as Aggie continues. "When I was young, the gods pulled me away from my home and toward this place. It was a sacred space, the last place the darkness would consume. I built my house there and promised to always keep watch." Aggie laughs heartily at our confusion and grips my hands in her gnarled fingers. "Oh boy, how I will miss the blade of your soul, as pure as steel."

Max and I exchange another dumbfounded look, but Aggie doesn't seem to mind. She just laughs again and squeezes my hand. "I have protected the sacred space where the land walks into the sky for a very long time, stood watch against the Darkness as the world changed around me. Civilizations fell and new ones were built in their place, but I have always endured, fed by the magic of the moon. Of the light."

I stare at her, my mind whirling.

"And now, my job is done. Good luck, Anrai Shaw. And remember the Darkness is devious...do not allow it an inch of space in your heart."

With that Aggie gives Max and I a wink and turns her attention back to the wielders. I feel the goodbye in her words, though I don't entirely understand why.

Feeling unbalanced, I climb onto my horse. A black mare from the manor stables, as I'd given Dahiitii to Mirren. Max mounts her own steed, and together, we ride up into the Shadiil Mountains.

As we climb higher, weaving through trees and over rocks, I gaze behind me at the sprawl of the city. Nadjaa's colors sparkle, a rainbow even in the depths of night. The moon has risen more than halfway above the peaks, the silver curve of it casting the range into shadow.

"After all these years, its beauty still takes my breath away," Max says, her voice slightly dreamy as she gazes down at the place we found home. "I don't think I'll ever get used to the view."

I smile in agreement. We tie the horses to a tree and ascend the rest of the way on foot, the path treacherously steep, loose gravel slipping beneath our feet and showering down the cliff edge. When we crest the peak, the other side of Ferusa expands before us. The wind whips at my face, and the mountain trembles as I squint at the Breelyn Plain in the distance.

The abyss writhes furiously, lashing at my throat, and

radiating to the tips of my fingers. The deep burn of pain, of love, of power.

Because spread across the amber grasses of the plain, as far as the eye can see, are the Covinus' forces.

Moving as a singular organism, a writhing black wave, the army comes.

CHAPTER
FORTY-TWO

Mirren

They attack from all sides.

As our wielders battle the Covinus' wielders from where they're stationed atop the peaks, wind and rain begins to whip through the Shadiil mountains. The bulk of the army has gathered at the base of the largest pass, rallying their forces to begin blasting through the blockade. The ground trembles, even on the opposite side of the city where Avedis and I now stand overlooking the Storven, and the power of so many elements combined reverberates in my chest.

My breath hitches, as we watch what looks like a menacing cloud gather on the horizon. But the night sky is entirely clear, and I know it's no storm darkening the sea. It's an armada of ships.

Anrai was right. The Covinus has control of every resource of every territory.

And now, they all come for Nadjaa.

Panic winds around my throat, squeezes my windpipe. Fear, that, even with the aid of three other water-wielders and Avedis, I won't be strong enough to prevent that many ships from landing on our shores; won't be able to keep them from sweeping through our bay and then up into the city.

"Are you ready to have some fun, Sea-witch?" Avedis asks with a sparkling grin. His dark gaze grates against my skin, the promise of storm and pain. But I don't shy away from it like I have every time he's looked at me since he lost his soul; now, I let it bolster my resolve. Because as horrible as it is, Avedis has nothing to lose in this fight. He'll gorge himself on the pain of his enemies, on their blood and suffering, and won't relent until none of them are left standing.

His gaze sharpens on me like I've cast my thoughts to him. "It's why I gave my soul for you," he says with relish, "because I knew."

Surprise wends through me. Avedis hasn't spoken of that day in Argentum, and I've been too afraid to ask. Too afraid to find out what made him sacrifice everything, what small spark began the events that ended in him murdering my brother. "Knew what?"

He grins again, but there's no humor in it. It's the dark edge of a cliff. "Knew you are the only one capable of taking *his*. Don't let my sacrifice be in vain. They attack what is yours. Now isn't the time to be merciful."

I examine the gnarled pull of Avedis' scar, the mismatched way it knits together his left brow. I trace it down over his cheekbone, to the shaved shine of his skull and the full set of his lips, and I think how wrong he is. As I drink in the face of my brother's killer, of *my* would-be assassin, my heart is filled with mercy.

Because his is also the face of my friend. The man who helped me when he had no reason to, who sacrificed his soul without hesitation because he believed in me. His is the face of a man I once trusted not only with my life, but the delicate things that made it worth living. I raise my chin. "Together then, Avedis."

Letting out a delighted laugh, he turns to the sea. He raises his arms above his head and claps them together in one decisive beat, before slowly pulling them back apart. A hurricane bursts to life between his palms, hot and cold currents whipping between his fingers. With another laugh, Avedis pushes the storm to sea.

Closing my eyes, I burrow deep into my *other*, and feel for the power of the Storven below. It lashes up at the sky, agitated by Avedis' wind, and its dark depths roil beneath the surface. Waves rise to our call, the ageless rage of the ocean mingling with my own, as Anrai's words echo in my mind. *Do you want the world to burn, Lemming?*

Yes, my *other* replies, the voice ancient and depthless. *Our flood will renew. Erase everything from the depths of time and begin again.*

I snap my eyes open and watch my waves roll toward the ships. It is not the soft roll of a quiet day, but those of a monsoon, giant, undulating mountains of water that roar. Their peaks meet the power of Avedis' wind, and sky melds into sea. The horizon becomes impossible to see as the sky turns black with menacing clouds, and a curtain of heavy water shrouds the ships from the rest of the world. It's impossible to tell which droplets rain down and which climb upward, as the gale force winds whip them in every direction.

With a peal of wild laughter, Avedis rips the clouds open, and the ocean begins to churn beneath the current of his wind. There are no screams above the sound of the sea's fury, as the ships pitch sideways and succumb to the storm. Masts crack and sails fall into the murky depths. Hulls splinter as they're carried on the waves, smashing into each other. Sailors dive from the sinking wreckage, only to be swallowed beneath the frothing waves.

Agony radiates through me and I'm breathless as my soul tears once, then again.

Then again.

I'd been so far gone when I'd killed those soldiers in Argentum, I'd hardly felt the wound in my soul, but now every nerve in my body burns with torment, and my ribs ache so fiercely, for a moment, I'm sure they'll crack. Avedis places a soft hand on my shoulder, and I turn to him as a clammy sweat breaks out on my forehead. "Allow me, Lady."

There is nothing kind about his words, only the thinly veiled frenzy of his ravaging hunger as he breathes in deeply. His exhale is soft, satiated, and I shiver as I realize he's drinking in the sailors' fear. The pain of their deaths. The hopelessness of their horror. Avedis' shoulders rise and fall calmly with another satisfied breath as more and more ships collide, meeting their end in the bottomless depths of the Storven.

From behind the wreckage, ships skirt around the churning waters, sailing toward the southern cliffs nearer to the manor. The two water-wielders stationed there work together to pull the currents toward the rocks. I feel for the strength of the waves, for the other wielders' power, so different from mine in its warmth, yet alike in the base nature. Like theirs is a sunbaked shallow pond and mine... mine is the icy depths of the ocean itself.

Together, we raise the wave high, pulling the ships on the current and sending them careening toward the cliffs. Two splinter against the rocks, while another manages to keep itself afloat by turning sharply and racing backward.

Rain pelts my face, and plasters my hair in sodden ropes to my shoulders and back. I raise my hands to the sky, dancing in the essence of my *other*. The current swirls beneath me, around me, pulling me with it toward the depths of myself.

But this time, there is no fear of the dark that lives at the bottom, no hesitation as I leap and freefall into them. It is all me, the wild black of the deep and the cerulean of the surface. Both rise up to the call of my soul, both feed my *other,* whole, and ancient, and new at once.

The sea churns and more boats fall beneath the onslaught of Avedis' storm. But there is no rest, no victory.

Because still, more come.

~

Shaw

The Covinus' army is endless. A black blight spreading over the amber grasses of the Breelyn Plain. Max and I have snuck around the destroyed pass, up along the cliffs of the Shadiil, and from here, we have a clear view of the never-ending wave of people and weapons; of the robotic way they move, arranged neatly in companies and platoons.

To the untrained eye, it would simply appear like a well-trained army, but I don't mistake them for soldiers. They are people. People *I* damned to this soulless existence.

Max crawls on her belly next to me, a knife gripped in her hand, her falchions strapped securely to her back. Her eyes narrow as she watches the enemy's movements. "They have wielders at the front lines," she says slowly. "Which means the coin can't be near them."

"They'll keep it close."

"How do you know?"

As if in demonstration, the mountain around us, which hasn't stopped shaking for over an hour goes still. Screams echo through the range as the power is ripped from the Nadjaan wielders stationed at the mouth of the pass, the sound of their pain ricocheting off the rocks off the pass and the trees. I grimace. "Because that's what I would do."

I climb to my feet, before helping her to hers. "Ready, Maxi?"

She hesitates but nods, and I know it's because she doesn't like all the unknown variables in the plan, everything that could go wrong in the blink of an eye. I don't like it either, but I purposefully don't think of all the ways we can fail, because I don't fail. And I'm certainly not going to start now when all of Nadjaa is on the line.

I'll do whatever I need to in order to protect what's mine. Even if it means slaughtering the very people I damned and losing my soul. Even if I'll never be able to live with it afterward.

For my family, I'll do it.

Max whispers under her breath and touches her heart, a prayer to the Tahi goddess of death she's always revered. And when she turns to me, dark braids haloed around her head and eyes shining with fervor, Max could be the warrior goddess herself, come to punish. "I'm always ready."

Max and I once changed the tides of the world. Together, we can do it again.

"Don't reveal yourself until we're sure who holds the coin. No matter what's happening to me. We're only going to get one chance at this."

She nods solemnly before disappearing into the shadows of the trees. Fire sparks at my fingertips, and tendrils of white-hot flame spill from my palms and trails down the mountainside, where it conflagrates in an explosion of light and heat. The front lines of wielders—water, wind, and earth alike—scatter as my wildfire tears between the ranks, bursting in unpredictable eruptions.

The smell of ash fills the air and the sky flickers, the reflection of flame in the smoke turning the night an eerie shade of orange. The ranks reform as the soldiers push three water cannons to the front lines, to the edge of my burning boundary. Three figures move forward in unison, their hands raised as they feed the water from the earth into the cannons.

They aren't as powerful as Mirren, unable to match my flame on their own, but with the force of the cannons, they begin to blast a hole. The killing calm settles over me, and the abyss burns. I've never fought a war before as my father always preferred to send me alone as an invisible weapon. But my entire life *was* war before I escaped him, and I'm well practiced at the degradations one must sink to in order to survive.

I plunge deep into the abyss, the place I've tried so hard never to allow myself to fall back into again. My heart flames and my chest burns as I weave three burning spears from the raging inferno and thrust them straight through the wielders' hearts.

My soul tears as they fall dead, and I welcome the familiar agony. An old satisfaction threads through me at their deaths, at defeating my enemy, but it's lined with different things than before. When I was a boy, each kill had given me a chance to please my father. Now, it's my own pleasure, twisted in the depths of darkness, at the annihilation of anything that threatens what's mine.

The water cannons die instantly, but there's no victory

in it, even as I begin to weave fire through the rest of the infantry, scattering them before they can break against the Nadjaan blockades. I watch as some of the soldiers throw themselves at the flame, the sight eerily reminiscent of when I faced my father months ago. Acid rises in my throat, because unlike when Cullen ruled, now it isn't loyalty or fear that drives the soldiers to their death. They have no choice.

Another soldier lights up like a torch, and I yell in frustration. The Covinus is betting on my humanity, on the inherent goodness that will keep me from burning through his forces. He knows I feel their pain, empathize with the sick feeling of watching yourself commit horrors and being unable to stop. Unlike my father, who never understood the power of emotion, the Covinus was created in them. Born in jealousy and hatred, forged in obsessive love. He's always known their strength, and it's why he used them to control Similis.

If they didn't love, they'd have nothing to fight for. Nothing but him.

"Fuck," I mutter again, glancing up at the moon as my soul tears again. Moonrise is still over three hours away. Enough time to steal a coin, but far too long to keep the forces from the city without losing all our souls in the process.

My heart pounds in my chest, as the minutes drag on, and I'm just considering damning the entire plan to throw myself headfirst into the army, when I feel it.

A pulse of Darkness, an otherworldly call of power spearing out toward mine. As it draws closer, I do nothing to hide, only coax my flame higher and higher. My breath saws in my lungs and blood pumps through my veins like fiery magma. Disgust curls my lip as the forest around me buzzes. The movements are silent, but the air of the forest sparks with tension as I draw my daggers.

The call of the coin grows louder, a blaring pulse of white noise that drowns out even the sounds of battle. It tugs at my flame, presses into my chest, searching for a way inside my soul.

I know the feel of this soul, it seems to say. *Come back to us, Fire-bringer.*

Pain rips through my skull as the coin-wielder appears between the trees, her blonde hair seeming to glow in the dim shadows. The little girl from Yen Girene. My nerves sizzle and spark as the coin rips my power away, and the wall of flame recedes into me, its path dying to nothing more than smoking embers. Frigid ice encases my heart, my bones, each bit of me feeling a moment away from shattering.

I only manage to keep to my feet by holding onto the rage that pulses through me, watching as the little girl's hands bleed freely over the coin. As I see the blank stare in her eyes, the unnatural way she moves toward me, cocking her head and watching me blankly.

I feed the rage by imagining Mirren enduring this pain for so long, trapped in the Covinus' dungeons. I dig my nails into my wrath with a snarl, clutching it until I, too, bleed. And when the black edging my vision begins to recede, I see the girl through tear-stung eyes.

And somehow, the sight of her only deepens the cold. Grief washes over me, pouring down my throat. I drown in guilt, in what I've done to the girl—in the pain I've caused not only her, but the entire continent. The ice pulses through me, and shards dig into my lungs.

End it, Fire-bringer.

The coin's power threads from the girl's blood and

into me, digging for any bit of pain it can feed from, any bit of agony to steal. Its hunger is ravening, and it rakes through me with claws. She moves toward me slowly, and the closer she draws, the deeper the agony. I'm inundated in it; lost in the punishment I've craved since I was a child.

The Darkness' final calling brings with it the pain you deserve.

I writhe on the ground as my brain tears itself apart, and knives dig into my skull, into my soul. And still the coin pulls, siphons my fire, grows stronger on my agony. There is no abyss, no voice to keep me alive.

Only me and my own darkness.

The girl stands over me, a blade in her hand. She slices shallowly at my forearms, meticulous and clean, and my own daggers drop to the ground. Blood pours over my arms, and I have no power to assist in cauterizing the wound. Gritting my teeth, I spin, kicking out my legs even as my teeth clack in my skull.

But it's too late. I know the rhythm of battle like Mirren knows the waves, so all I can do is close my eyes and brace for the blow.

It never comes.

I peek my eyes open to see Max standing behind the young girl. Her face is twisted in panic and horror, one blade pointed at the girls' throat, the other at her belly. Max's eyes flick to me, and her fingers tighten imperceptibly on the pommel of the sword.

The determined look in Max's eyes grounds me back into my own soul. I scrabble for my daggers. It isn't self-flagellation that drives me to me my feet, but something far purer. Something forged between Max and I the moment I stabbed my father, something that solidified in our bones.

It cannot be dug out, cannot be broken, infallible and unyielding.

Guilt and self-hatred do not wrap my fingers around my knives. It's love for my friend that guides the blades through the child's throat, and then deeper. Blood sprays in a crimson torrent, as I whisper, "I'm so sorry. May you find peace in the Darkness."

The girl collapses on top of me and her eyes bulge and blink once. A fraction of a moment stretches between us, a fragment of time between life and death, where the girl is herself once more, like her soul has returned to accompany her to the afterlife. And in that moment, her eyes find mine, and I let out a sob as she gazes at me in gratitude. In relief. "Thank you," her small voice rasps.

When she goes still in my arms, I think my heart has shattered, that my organs will spill through the crack in my chest.

Tears pour down my face as my power rushes back into me, tendrils of flame licking over my skin and imbuing strength once more in my bones, the coin's hold broken with the girl's death. But as I stare down at her face, now innocently still, ice crackles over my heart once more.

Because when I finally glance up at the trees, it's to find hundreds of soldiers staring back.

CHAPTER
FORTY-THREE

Calloway

The world around the Moon City trembles.

The mountains below my feet quake with fury, as the earth-wielders send pieces of rock tumbling down cliffs. The sky churns above me as the wind-wielders and water-wielders work. Lightning streaks across the night in disorienting flashes, and crashes of thunder echo, so powerful, they shake buildings in the distance. Rain pours down in an icy deluge, and the droplets feel like tiny blades as they are whipped by wrathful currents.

Smoke has wreathed the moon in shades of orange and blood red, turning the beacon of hope into a harbinger of the death to come. I lost sight of Anni and Max as soon as my brother's fire died, and though it was expected, the sense of disconnect is no less harrowing. I hate being the one to stand behind the lines—to not be close enough to cover their backs, to protect them from any threat. Including themselves.

The army is so large I can't see its end, and even as it surges forward, I am torn—torn between where my feet stand on this mountain, and where my heart faces an oncoming militia on the Breelyn Plain; where it stands at the base of the Averitbas with a sword, a barrier between the innocent and those who seek to hurt them; where it commands the weight of the ocean, and tries not to drown beneath the responsibility.

And there is nothing for me to do but wait. Nothing to be done but to regrip my bow and watch as Mirren and Avedis face an entire armada of ships, as Shaw and Max try to steal a coin that renders one of them powerless and weak.

Enveloped between two wind-wielders, one an old fisherman who has spent his life in the Barrow, the other a teenaged girl with pockmarked cheeks and wild blonde hair, I watch them work. From this distance, our bows would normally be rendered useless, but at the wielders' urging, our arrows soar through the air, and rain down effortlessly on our targets below. Denver has ordered our forces to wound, not kill, an order that will expire at midnight when Jayan takes the Chancellor seat.

I can feel his beady gaze from here, even though he stands a few hundred yards back. He's made it clear that once he leads Nadjaa, the wielders and guard will all be ordered to sacrifice their souls. Ordered to slaughter the thousands of innocent lives below.

Unless Anni steals the coin and Mirren figures out how to break the curse, the Darkness will finally do what it's threatened my whole life. We'll destroy each other, and the only thing remaining will be the Covinus.

No more love. Only greed. Only power.

There's been no sign of Shina or the Siraleni forces. Perhaps I should have been more forceful, demanded she to agree to send help. It's too late for regret now. There's only room for hope, but as the earth rents apart around me, the more slippery the thought of hope becomes.

Despite the flurry of arrows, the front lines reach the mouth of the pass. Avedis' blockade towers higher than the Council House, dwarfing the Covinus forces that line up in front of it—huge trees piled high, their trunks sticking up from the ground like giant javelins. The earth-wielders collapsed the steep cliffs that once lined the wide route, and now, it's an obstacle course of giant boulders and sharp rocks, made more treacherous by the newly formed quagmire of waist deep mud, courtesy of Mirren.

I make a quick count of enemy wielders as the earth shudders violently, and in one smooth motion, every single boulder blocking the pass lifts into the sky.

And then careen into where our forces lay in wait. Screams rent the night and the Nadjaan guard scatter beneath the onslaught, as carnage rains down around them. I toss my bow over my shoulder and scramble to my feet, barely managing to keep from tumbling backward from the ledge as the mountain trembles again.

Denver stands a few feet from Jayan, huddled over a barrel that's been repurposed as a table, examining the maps and schematics spread out in front of him. He traces a finger from one end to another, before shaking his head and muttering something indecipherable. I've seen this look on Denver's face many times, one that indicates his mind is somewhere far from here as it calculates things I can't possibly keep up with.

I hope it's something to turn the tide of this battle, because things are about to get so much worse.

"Denver, he didn't kill them," I say by way of greeting, my words sandwiched in between exhausted breaths.

Denver raises his eyes to mine, and it takes a full

moment for the impact of my words to overcome him. His brow furrows as he waits for me to go on.

"The Praeceptor...he never killed the wielders Shaw tested. He must have kept them all prisoner in Argentum."

Denver's face drains of color, and he slowly licks his lips as the implications weigh down between us. "And now, the Covinus controls them all."

I nod, even as dread and panic slither up my spine and then around my chest, squeezing my ribs until I think I may suffocate. "They may not be as powerful as our wielders, but with so many of them, they're going to make it through the passes far faster than we thought. Our wielders are outnumbered a twenty to one."

Jayan saunters forward, flanked by two guards I don't recognize. "If you are apprising the Chancellor of battle progress, you are speaking to the wrong man, Mr. Cabrera," he says, his watery blue eyes narrowed shrewdly as he adjusts his finery.

The councilman is dressed for an evening in the arts district, rather than for getting his hands dirty in battle, which means one thing: he has no plans to assist the people he leads. He'll send them all to their soul-deaths, or their *true* deaths, without batting an eye. I twist my mouth in disgust and raise my chin, feeling the uncharacteristic urge to snarl at the pompous ass.

But instead, I turn back toward Denver, eyes shining. "I know exactly who my Chancellor is, Jayan." Jayan bristles at the disrespect in my tone, bares his teeth. "And it's the man who's trying to save his people, not sacrifice them for his own gain."

Denver's mouth lifts in the ghost of a smile, his approval clear. I've never seen him in the fatherly way Anni does, as I've always had the memories of my own papa to keep me steady. But Denver has always been exactly what I needed him to be—my friend. Someone to lean on, someone who cares. His friendship kept me tethered through my most wild urges, a reminder that there is always someone who expects me home.

"Pull back and reinforce the north line," Denver says, his voice brooking no room for argument. The guard beside Jayan nods once, and spins on his heel to carry out the order. To the other, Denver says, "Make sure the earth-wielders are well stocked. It's going to be a long night."

The man salutes Denver despite Jayan's clear disapproval. His face has turned an unappetizing shade of puce, and I stiffen as his fingers wander to his blade like he's considering putting it through Denver's chest and taking the Chancellorship early. But he reins himself in, and snarls, "An hour and a half, Denver. Then, the militia is mine."

Denver doesn't rise to the bait. He only sets Jayan with a pitying gaze, like he's dealing with a tantruming toddler rather than his rival. "Ninety minutes is a lifetime when it comes to changing the world, Jayan."

The councilman sneers and stalks off, leaving us alone, but Denver doesn't look at me. His gaze is on the northern horizon, where Max and Anni fight an endless enemy alone. "I had faith in them before, and they changed my world. Let's keep the same faith they will do it again."

∼

Shaw

We run like hell.

Hundreds of soldiers dart from the shadows and shoot between the trees. I hurtle balls of flame behind me, and smoke fills the air as pine needles crackle and spark. The fire spreads, and my soul fractures as we tear up the mountain. Waterfalls of loose shale pour down the steep incline around us with every rumble of the peak, and our feet slip as the earth moves beneath us like a wave.

When I dare a look over my shoulder, it's to find the soldiers have nearly caught up, despite how fast we run. My breath is painful in my lungs, and my muscles burn with exertion and still, they grow closer. Because the soldiers aren't in charge of their own bodies. They'll run them ragged, even to death, to honor the Covinus' command.

Fire blazes up behind us, but my flame is far weaker than usual. The abyss hasn't fully recovered from the effects of the coin, and it still feels like shards of ice are embedded in my heart.

My blood rushes in my veins like acid as Max cries out beside me. She stumbles sideways and claws at her throat, her mouth open in a silent gasp as she reaches toward me in desperation. I grab her by the arm, pulling her up onto a limestone ledge and shoving her behind me. The militia is only a few steps behind, and I scan them furiously, trying to determine which of them is the wind-wielder.

The coin burns in my palm, and my own air is stolen from my chest. I gasp, trying not to pass out even as black edges my vision. The cool calm of determination settles over me as I run my thumb over the imprint in the metal. The mountains and moon above a wild sea. The home that runs in my blood.

I cough and my vision swims as I pull a dagger weakly from my bandolier, and without hesitation, slice through my own palm. The iron tang of blood fills my nostrils as I squeeze my hand into a fist. *Blood magic.*

It's desperate. Delusional. But it's the only hope we

have of escaping without losing our souls. When I open my hand once more, the coin sparkles, its metal immaculate. My blood is gone, like it's absorbed into the metal. I stare down at it in shock, as the coin pulses darkly and an intoxicating wave of power threads through me, even as my own fire is ripped away.

Despite the agonizing cold, air fills my lungs, and my vision clears. Max sucks in greedy breaths beside me, her hands clutched to her chest as she attempts to slow the wild beat of her heart. Still clutching the coin, I roll to my side with a wheezing cough. My head swims as I come to my feet, but the dagger in my hand is steady.

The nearest wielders have collapsed, clawing at the ground and moaning in pain, but others glare at us from behind the invisible boundary of the coin's power. Three of them raise their hands in unison, and together, they raise water from the ground.

"Run, Max!" I bellow, pulling her to her feet and pushing her in front of me.

We scramble up the sharp rock, digging our fingers into the slippery surface, made even slicker as water pelts us from behind, and then crests over our heads in a giant wave. My vision goes blurry as it crashes down, inundating us both, and I try desperately not to breathe in as it wraps around my mouth.

Max's foot slips, and she skids backward into me with a desperate cry, almost sending us both tumbling back down the sharp rock. My fingers slip as I wrap them around hers, trying and failing to steady us both.

"Shaw," she shouts, equal parts terror and fury on her face, as she claws her way back up the ledge.

And I know it isn't terror of what we face—it's the fear of what I need to do for us to survive. Burn the chasing army to ash. Kill them all. Save our lives and damn my soul.

"Get behind me," I tell her calmly, pushing in front of her even as she pounds at my chest in furious protest.

"Shaw, you can't—"

The words die in her throat as I meet her gaze. What she sees there, I can't begin to name, but it's enough to widen her eyes. To terrify the woman who's afraid of nothing. "Maxi, I need you to make sure I find Mirren afterward. I don't care if you have to tie me up and drag me to Aggie's cabin, make sure I complete that prophecy. Okay?"

Max swallows audibly, and tears spill down her cheeks as I hand her the coin. But she nods.

The world pulses around me as I pull away from the coin's power, slowly untangling myself from the darkly woven web. More water begins to flood our feet, and as it rushes around our ankles, the strength of the current pulls us toward the edge.

I plant myself more firmly and close my eyes, feeling the abyss rise in my chest. The wildness of flame, a blaze to incinerate anything that would try to touch us. It consumes everything inside me, my rage, my love, every shattered part of myself.

It was easier, last time, not knowing what waited for me on the other side. But now, I remember the aching hollow, the unrelenting hunger—the incessant pain and rage. I know every intimate part of what awaits, and still, I burrow further into the abyss.

Flame spirals up inside me, building and building, and I let one small breath escape my lips as I prepare to let it all go.

But then, the mountain beneath us shudders violently, and the immensity of the earthquake throws both Max and

I to the ground. The current rushes around us, sending us both catapulting toward the edge, choking and sputtering. Max screams as my feet slip from the cliffside. I grunt, my fingernails cracking as I dig them into the rock. Anchoring myself with a groan, I claw my way back up.

I've barely managed to catch my breath when the spectacle beneath us steals it again. The world around us trembles, and the mountains groan, an ancient sound that reverberates through my chest. Soldiers and wielders alike begin to scream as the ground opens up beneath them. Like a gaping mouth, the earth swallows them whole until no one is left.

Hundreds of lives. Gone in an instant.

Max is shellshocked, frozen in place as the earth shifts once more, and dirt moves to cover the hole. And then everything goes eerily quiet.

I scan the mountain around us, my eyes landing on a ledge only a few feet from ours. Crouched up against the rock is a familiar earth-wielder. One whose name I never learned before I granted her mercy all those weeks ago outside Similis. Mercy even as the abyss demanded her blood.

She gives me a subtle nod. Through it an understanding passes, one woven in the depths of the Darkness. A life debt, paid.

The earth-wielder goes stiff and collapses to the ground, and for a moment, time seems to stretch unnaturally around us. Even the sounds of the army blasting through the mountains fade away, as Max and I watch the earth-wielder's soul leave her.

Max's yelp startles me from my horror, and when I turn to her, the coin spills from her hand. We both watch it clatter and roll across the ledge, before coming to a stop in a small divot. And when Max unfurls her palm, there is an imprint of the coin burned into her skin. Nadjaa, but upside down and reversed, just like the underworld of Max's goddess, Kehena.

Hope replaces dread. Because of the earth-wielder, because of the kindness Denver and Mirren instilled in me —because of Max and her loyal soul—we still have a chance of reversing the tide of war. "Her soul is safe with us," I tell, pressing three fingers to my lips and extending them outward, in the salute of the islands. "Let's go make sure it wasn't given in vain."

~

Mirren

The Storven churns, waves like mountains rising from the deep and then crashing down with violent fury. The wind has calmed, if only for the moment, because Avedis has gone still beside me, long legs curled beneath him as he listens to the world around us. He's been frozen like this for almost half an hour, and with each moment that passes, my anxiety grows.

We've heard nothing from Anrai and Max, nothing from Cal. Harlan and Helias are safe in the meadow near Aggie's cabin, but they're only protected so long as Nadjaa's borders hold until we break the curse.

I feed the worry to my *other*. My anger, my grief, my love —all of it bursts forth from me in waves. Beautiful. Deadly. I dig into the deepest parts of myself, the dark corners of my heart, the lost spaces of my mind, and I savor every moment of it. It's taken losing everything to find myself, to accept each part as it is. To break apart and rebuild, to grow even when it hurts.

The waves rise to my call, and a lump forms in my throat: regret that it took me so long to embrace the power that has always resided in me, so long to understand the beauty in being unencumbered by other's expectations. Because in less than an hour's time, it will be gone.

So what was taken must now be given.

And I will give it. All of it. To bring forth a dream of light, to spark hope in the heart of the continent.

Avedis' eyes flick open, and when they find mine, the hollow depths claw through my chest. "They have the coin."

My *other* laps at the edges of my heart, our relief a soothing rhythm that both calms me and strengthens my resolve. "Then let's go."

Avedis tilts his head, and something about the way his eyes sharpen is eerily inhuman. "Are you sure that's what you wish, Lady of the Depths?" His smile is cutting, and unsettling in its knowledge. Like the black crevasse of his gaze somehow sees past my skin, down into my most selfish thoughts. The ones that wish to hold on to my power, to give nothing up for a world that has never done the same for me.

"If we give up the line, the armada will invade. And maybe breaking the curse will be enough, or maybe Nadjaa will burn." He examines his nails, even as his voice takes on an ominous edge. "Or perhaps you and I should get on one of those ships and leave Ferusa to the pits of Darkness they've well earned? Go rule some foreign land where they worship our power."

For a moment, I hate the wind-wielder. His grin grows wider as he devours every miniscule reaction, and then wider still as he realizes I've actually considered it, however briefly. But even as shame colors my cheeks, I think of my father. He's proof, one is never the whole of their actions. One mistake, one moment of weakness should not doom you to a lifetime of Darkness.

I straighten my spine, and manage to look down my nose at Avedis, though his bulky frame towers over mine. "We're breaking that curse. And then we're going to kill the Covinus. And I don't care if I have to drown you and drag you kicking and screaming, you're going to help me."

The white fangs of his teeth gleam in the moonlight, as he gives me not so much a smile as a feral snarl. He bows his head fractionally. "Then lead the way, Lady."

∽

By the time Avedis and I make it to Aggie's cabin, the moon has almost fully risen above the peaks, its silver orb arching majestically over the sky. The evacuees that were able have made camp in the meadows, nestled safely in the shadows of the mountains. Even the Xamani have come to protect the innocent, the *ahtan* interspersed between the Nadjaan guard.

Harlan's golden hair looks almost silver in the moonlight, its odd hue made more noticeable beside the dark hair of the Xamani Kashan. Helias clings to Asa's neck with impressive strength, even as the Kashan appears deep in discussion with Harlan and a few of his men.

When we approach, Harlan gives me a shy smile. The Similian style rifle is tucked beneath his arm and a sword is sheathed in a scabbard at his hip. His sun-darkened skin glows against the crisp white uniform of the Nadjaa guard, and despite everything around us, I smile back. I'm not the only one who's settled into themselves in the past few

WAVE OF LIGHT

months, and though Easton's loss will always be an ache between us, Harlan appears at peace.

"Avedis and I scattered the armada. But it's only a matter of time before they regroup and attack the bay," I tell him and Asa hurriedly, the words coming in a harried flood, "And if I—if we don't come back—"

Harlan pulls me into his chest, his heartbeat steady against my cheek as he wraps his arms around me. For a moment, I relax against him, allowing its rhythm to lull me into a sense of calm. "You'll come back. And we'll hold the city until you do." He leans back to examine my face, his expression earnest. "We're Bound, Mirren. Where you go, I go. You won't go anywhere I can't follow."

Harlan says it like it's the simplest thing in the world, like our fate hasn't been twisted by magic, and darkness, and old gods. He's always had a way of stripping the most complicated things down to their bones, has always exposed the roots of what matters. And he doesn't have to say the rest, or remind me what we fight for, because Harlan has always known. He knew in Similis long before I did, knew the things worth dying for.

Helias scrambles down from Asa. "Is it time?" he asks eagerly. When I nod, his eyes narrow in suspicion. "You won't make me wear a cloak, will you?"

I laugh, as a deep voice behind me says, "You don't have to wear a cloak, hellion."

I whirl around with a yelp and throw myself into his Anrai's arms. He catches me around the waist with a pained grunt, but he doesn't let go, only buries his face in my hair. I pull away, searching him for signs of injury, but he waves me away impatiently. "I'm fine, Lemming. Just some shallow cuts."

When he notices me searching behind him, he

hurriedly assures me, "Max is okay, too. She went to find Cal on the front." His glance slides to the moon behind me, the glacial blue of his eyes appearing almost colorless in the silver light. "We don't have much time. And the Covinus has thousands of wielders under his control. It won't be long before they reach the city."

"We will do our best to protect the people, *zaabi*," Asa says, his own bow slung over his shoulder and an assortment of axes sheathed at his hips. "Good luck."

Anrai takes my hand with one of his, wrapping his other around Helias', and with Avedis next to me, we make our way through the crowd. Mothers and fathers holding their children, siblings racing between fires and tents. Thousands of lives who've never had the chance to live in light; to find balance; to forgive themselves for a moment of weakness.

Together, we pass Aggie's cabin. The small windows are dark, and the bone chimes clink softly in the breeze that follows Avedis. Rounding the little house, we find the path Aggie spoke of. Forgotten by everyone but the old woman who hears fragments of the dead gods, who faithfully walked it before every lunar celebration to thank the moon for her light.

The trail appears to once have been paved in the same white cobblestone as Nadjaa's main streets, but now, they've been desecrated by time. Roots slither beneath them, upending them in parts and crumbling them entirely in others. Green weeds shoot up between the bricks, and wildflowers spread over them like a thick carpet.

As is nature's way, it reclaims what was once stolen. Balance.

We keep a hurried pace as the moon lingers before us, the path nearly as light as if it was daytime. When the way becomes too cratered, climbing upward into the Averitbas peaks, Anrai scoops Helias onto his back. None of us speak, like the silence of the trail has settled beneath our skin.

We climb higher and higher, but rather than thinning with the altitude, the greenery becomes steadily thicker, until it nearly obscures the moon. Twigs and branches tug at our clothes and snag in our hair, until finally Avedis unsheathes his sword to hack through the vegetation and clear a path.

When the forest has nearly strangled every bit of light from the sky, the foliage suddenly opens wide, revealing a place of such beauty, it steals my breath.

The circular clearing is carpeted in plants and flowers of every color, the like of which I've never seen before. The aubergine of Aggie's robes, the green of my father's eyes. The red of the metropolis square. The blue of the Storven Sea. Every color imaginable ripples over the ground in vibrant waves, like the entire clearing is a pond made only of rainbow and if we take one step forward, we'd be able to dip our toes into the vivid hues. A stream runs through the center, the water so clear it reflects the color around it to near perfection, its presence only given away in the cheerful trickle of droplets over smooth stones.

In the middle of the stream is a small dais, the arch of which overlooks the majesty of the surrounding mountain range.

Similar to the Nadjaan marriage custom but much larger, the dais is carved from two differing materials, though neither is wood. One is made of marble, the pure, sparkling white of Nadjaa. And the other is crafted from obsidian, the color of Argentum. Woven together and delicately carved, the dais perfectly frames the moon, its light spilling into its curves, climbing its pillars, and pouring over the carpet of color.

Even Avedis is silent as we take in the astral beauty of the clearing, breathless and enamored. Because somehow, this small space between the mountains is the beginning and the end, both the birth and death of light and dark.

We wade through the shallow stream, stepping up onto the dais. Ethereal light glows all around us, like we've stepped into the moon itself.

When I look at Anrai, any remaining air leaves me entirely. Bathed in shades of shadow and silver, flames wreath his body and flicker in his eyes. They burn along the edge of each of his muscles, wreath his hair in a fiery halo. He's no longer a fire-wielder—he *is* flame. And by the way he's staring at me—like he's been bewitched—the power of the dais must also be bringing my *other* to the surface.

Indeed, when I glance at Avedis, he doesn't just hold the storm. He is the eye itself, uncatchable, uncontainable. And Helias, beautiful little boy that he is, looks like every rich color of nature has come to rest along the surface of his skin.

Anrai pulls a small wad of fabric from his pocket, unwrapping it slowly like he expects it to detonate at any moment. The tarnished copper of the coin gleams as he sets it gently in the center of us. The call of it is stronger here than I've ever felt, it's pull nearly rocking me from my feet. Reminiscent of the Boundary, it tugs at my hair, prickles the back of my neck, scrapes across my skin.

It searches for what was taken.

Soon, I tell the coin, the gods, the Darkness. *Soon what is yours will be returned to you.*

Anrai weaves his fingers through mine. I take Avedis' hand in my other, and together we form a small circle.

Closing my eyes, I breathe in deeply. What began as a journey to save my brother will end in so much more. More than Easton, more than me.

Let the Darkness end in love.

With one last breath, I prepare to give up everything.

Until the resounding click of a bullet being loaded into a barrel rips through the calm of the night.

CHAPTER
FORTY-FOUR

Calloway

The moment the Covinus army breaks through the Shadiil pass feels like an eternity, the minutes warping and stretching around Max and I. It steals the noise from the air, the breath from my lungs, as we watch Nadjaa's barrier of safety come crumbling down.

The pass itself is now only wide enough for two carts to travel comfortably side by side, so the enemy is forced to slow as they begin to funnel into the range. Wind and water-wielders lead the charge, drowning our soldiers and choking the air from them. Arrows rain down from all sides, and I throw up my shield as I charge forward with Max and Rocher at my side.

I whirl, slashing tendons and skewering through muscle. Blood spatters my vision, clings to my lashes, as I lash out with a feral roar.

But the militia keeps coming.

Soldiers walk on shattered legs, crawl over rocks until there is no more skin on their shins. Some of their skulls have been partially caved in by falling debris, and still, they stumble forward. The sight is unsettling, this army that does not stop because of human pain—who *cannot* stop.

The Covinus' command ushers them ever forward, no matter that their bodies can no longer keep up.

Nausea surges up my throat, and I swallow it down as I lunge forward into a crowd of water-wielders. The sound is deafening, clanging metal and severed flesh and the agonized screams of the injured, but it is nothing to the smell.

Of blood. Of death.

Max bumps her shoulder into mine. She's dressed in the armor of the guard, same as me, pilfered from some old supplies in the dungeons of the Council House, but while mine fits oddly, Max's looks like it was made just for her. And maybe this *is* what Max was born for—facing down the Darkness itself, channeling her fury to righting the injustices of the world.

I flash her a cheeky grin, because there's no one else I'd rather have by my side to face down a possessed army. "Remember, *silks*."

"We just need to give Shaw and Mirren time," she says, planting her feet and running her blade through a water-wielder's thigh. Max yanks it out with a sickening squelch, already ducking beneath a particularly fierce looking wind-wielder and slamming her fist up into his jaw.

"Right." I land another kick with a winded breath. "Hold off a continental army of the living dead. No big deal," I shout, as the soldiers and guard edge us forward in a sea of bodies. "I swear to the dead gods, those two had better not expect a wedding present after this. Destroyed Council Houses, ruined creepy magical walls, and never satisfied."

Max laughs as we break into a run, and it's the last

thing I hear before the sound of violence overwhelms everything around me.

We fight at the other's back, guarding each other's blind side as we always have. Blood and gore spray everywhere, and my vision goes a hazy shade of crimson that I've no time to wipe away as the enemy keeps coming. My muscles scream and a sickening heat courses through my veins as the soldiers cease to be human, reduced only to limbs to cut, stomachs to slash.

No amount of training could ever have prepared me for the realities of true war.

Max charges forward, her face deadly calm in comparison with the world around us. She's a whirlwind of steel and power, and whoever she meets falls at her feet. I slash and whirl, elbow a jaw and crunch a knee beneath my boot, and still cannot manage to keep up with the force of her fury. She doesn't seem to tire, only pushes forward with an animalistic snarl.

The Nadjaan guard, who'd been breaking beneath the pure onslaught of Covinus-fueled bodies, find renewed strength in Max's determination. Those she fights beside become as fierce as she is, despite the sheer numbers of the enemy cresting over them.

And then, the order comes up the line. Yelled desperately from all the way up the mountain, where Jayan stands watch.

Fight to kill.

The air seems to spark, the desperation and violence igniting into an uncontainable firestorm. The wielders on the cliffs begin aiming to crush entire flanks, and the men and women of the Nadjaan guard begin slicing at arteries, disemboweling stomachs, slitting throats.

Now, when the soldiers fall, they do not get back up.

And it is both a relief, that with each slash, we cut down some of his power, and a horror: because with every slash, a Nadjaan loses a fraction of his soul. Allows a bit of the Darkness in.

And the Darkness spreads, seeps like spilled ink through every fissure. Until things that once seemed horrible are now appealing. Things once evil, now only practical. Things like the horror of war.

I've felt the seep of it myself, from that first wind-wielder in Nadjaa. Felt it as my heart pumped through my veins, urging me to take Akari Ilinka's life. To drink her suffering. I'd been able to overcome it, but how long until I'm not? The Darkness will only grow stronger with every kill, and in turn, the Covinus too will grow more powerful as every soul that's lost will be fed to him.

Suddenly I understand with a horrifying clarity why there's been no sign of the Covinus. He has no intention of winning this war. He *wants* us to destroy each other. To collect and control every Nadjaan soul.

"PULL BACK!" I scream, yanking at the nearest soldier and pushing him behind me. The man ogles me like I've lost my mind, and maybe I have, as I start pushing my way through the lines, yelling until my throat is hoarse. "Pull back! Don't kill them! There'll be no one left to protect the city!"

As I scream, the guard beside me slits the throat of a Covinus soldier. And when the soldier falls, the guard's eyes flash black. He turns, setting his sights on the nearest Nadjaan and lifts his sword. I stab the guard through the throat before his blade can land. His sword clatters to the ground and blood gurgles from the wound as fresh agony rips through me. I stumble through it, clutching at my chest, searching through the fray for anyone in charge.

When I reach Rocher, I grab him by the collar. Once a crisp white, it's now stained dark with blood and gore, and the sight of it on the once peaceful man is enough to send fresh acid careening through my stomach. "We have to pull back," I shout at him. "The Covinus wants us here fighting."

"How do you know that?" he shouts back, impaling his sword inside the belly of a young boy, only a few years older than Helias.

"Because if we all lose our souls in this pass, *he* will devour them. We have to pull back!"

Rocher shrugs my hand from his shoulder, whirling around to block a blade aimed straight for my neck. "If we pull back, Nadjaa is gone, Calloway. If we have to lose a few souls to protect our home, then so be it."

Fear and desperation grip me, winding around my throat. I spin and the world tilts as I take in the carnage in every direction. Already so many lay still. Already, so many tear through their former comrades, now possessed by the Covinus' command.

And I'm helpless to do anything about it. "Pull back!" I shout again, but my voice is carried away by the wind, lost in the fervor of violence.

"All will be well, Calloway." Aggie's sing song voice at my ear in the center of the battlefield is so unexpected, I rock back on my heels and nearly fall over. Regaining my footing gracelessly, I whirl to see the old woman standing less than a foot behind me. She is barefooted as usual, her dark aubergine robes contrasting against the long white ringlets of hair that hang to her waist. Her cratered eyes pierce right through me.

I stare at her with my mouth open, mystified that though the war rages around her and blood sprays in every

WAVE OF LIGHT

direction, none of it touches Aggie. Though I see no shield, every arrow, every blade—none of them touch her.

I shake my head wildly, trying to clear the cloud of confusion and fear. "Aggie, we have to get you out of here—"

The words die in my throat as she begins to move toward me, her normally labored gait suddenly smooth and youthful. I freeze as she reaches a gnarled hand out and brushes her knuckles gently over my cheek. "He is not here," she says, the familiar sing-song quality of her voice entirely gone. Now, she speaks in layers. Inhuman depths, folded in on one another until it is the incomprehensible sound of her voice.

"Who—who isn't here?"

Aggie stares and stares. "He is not here, Calloway, but all will be well. The Darkness changes all those it touches, but so does the light." The calloused tips of her fingers dig painfully into my cheek, and I'm struck with the urge to pull away. *"That which was taken will now be given.* And all will be well."

A blade slashes entirely too close to the old woman, but she doesn't spare it a glance. Aggie only smiles, and then removes her hand from my skin. She turns away from me, toward the oncoming slaughter of soldiers, and drops the draping robe to the ground. Bare skinned, white hair gleaming in the moonlight, she begins to walk through our forces.

The path in front of her parts like it's been sliced through with a knife, and as she passes Max at the front line, her intentions become horrifyingly clear.

"Aggie!" I scream, wrestling my way through the bodies that separate us. I collide with shoulders, punch out at stomachs and knees alike, no matter that it's our own forces. Whatever the foolish old woman means to do by standing unarmed and barefoot in front of an enemy army, I won't let her do it.

Max does a double take and lunges for Aggie, but Max, who has impeccable aim, who I've never seen miss *anything* at such close range, somehow does.

Max's face pales eyes in horror as Aggie walks straight into the middle of the fighting. I'm still reaching for the old woman, still inundated in a sea of bodies when the Covinus forces lunge for her. Their weapons flash, and as gunshots ring out, terror renders me momentarily immobile as Aggie disappears from view, obstructed by the mass of soldiers.

A horrified sob rips from me when suddenly, from the place the old woman disappeared, a light begins to glow.

Not the yellow light of the sun, or the sterile illumination of Similis—but a pinprick of pure gold. It's hardly visible beneath the onslaught of the enemy, but its shimmer is so bright, I have to shield my eyes against it, as understanding and grief rush through me in equal measure. *The Darkness changes all those it touches, but so does the light.*

And who better than to channel the light than the woman who worshipped its existence her entire life, who understood better than anyone the power of listening. The gold light surges and radiates, and as I'm still staring in shock, everyone within its sphere turns to mist.

"PULL BACK!" I scream, yanking at Max's shoulder. She's frozen in place with her sword still raised halfway up, staring at the place where Aggie disappeared. "PULL BACK!"

Whether it's the help of the old gods themselves, I'll never know, but somehow, the Nadjaan guard hears my message. We surge backward, toward the mouth of the pass, running frantically toward the city. Behind us, the golden light's power grows, bathing the cliffsides in shimmering hues of the heavens. Every person who meets it disappears inside its power, vaporized where they stand.

The otherworldly power reverberates, and Max and I are slammed to the ground by the explosion. My eardrums ring and my jaw clacks as I hit the dirt hard enough to push the air painfully from my lungs.

I cradle my body over Max's, shielding her the best I can, as more reverberations echo, radiant, deadly, waves of godly power. And as I lay there in the ruins of what was once the front lines of Covinus forces, I realize that Aggie, the woman everyone deemed a fraud, a lunatic, a witch, truly was a conduit of the old gods.

A seer who spoke the words others would never hear. A power in her own right, trusted with a weight most mortals would never be able to hold. The power of knowledge. Of faith.

When the waves finally stop, and I manage to push myself up to squint through the dust, there are no more soldiers in the pass. And Aggie is gone.

CHAPTER
FORTY-FIVE

Shaw

The fire in my veins turns to ice.

Or maybe, it burns so hot it has gone cold, like the flame of the underworld from Max's stories.

Avedis has Helias by the throat, a small pistol nudged up against the little boy's temple.

"Avedis," Mirren whispers, her plead ringing through the clear night air. But the assassin doesn't acknowledge it. There is no charming humor on his face, no deprecating smirk.

As he wraps his arm more tightly around Helias' neck, there is nothing at all.

I shake my head fractionally, moving to stand between him and Mirren. "It isn't him," I breathe, planting my feet. The last time Avedis and I fought, we'd nearly levelled a city. I'd only won by the slight advantage of him having no memory of my fighting technique. But now, the assassin is well-versed in my strategy.

Helias' lower lip trembles and he squeezes his eyes shut, like he can block out what's happening. My abyss flares, wildly trying to spear from me, to destroy any who would harm the boy, but I keep it wrapped around my heart, and scan the clearing around us.

Because soul or not, if Avedis has a gun to the little earth-wielder's head, it's because someone is forcing him to do it. The man who stole his soul. But there's no sign of the Covinus, no sign of anyone. I remember the painful tether under my ribs that flared whenever my father bent me to his will. He didn't need to stand right beside me to control me, only somewhere nearby.

Mirren ducks beneath my arm, her own power wreathed along the bare skin of her arms. "Avedis, you don't want to kill him," she begins, raising her hands like she's placating a wild animal. And truly, Avedis isn't far off. "You want the curse broken. The Covinus is controlling you right now, making you do things you don't want to do. You have to fight it if you want your freedom."

I remember the tortuous flare in my brain, a divide made of glass and fire that rent through every rational thought in the gods' chamber last spring. There had been the agonizing command of my father, wrapped around my heart, my ribs—and then there had been the part of me that still existed. It had clawed at my skin, at my brain. Tried to chew its way through my muscle. Fighting against my father's steel arm of control, grounded in the steady light of Mirren's soul.

But Avedis has nothing left to battle with. So when he slides his dark eyes to Mirren, it may as well be the Covinus staring out.

"Oh, I do think I want to kill him," Avedis purrs. Helias whimpers as Avedis tugs him closer, the ghost of a demented smile on his face. "What better way to fill the void than watching you tear yourself apart with the guilt of being unable to save him. Pain is satisfying, but yours—" he shudders in pleasure, momentarily closing his eyes. "*Yours* is so luscious. So *deep*."

The fire in my heart sputters, and Avedis tilts his head like he can see straight through my skin. "You see everything you were denied in this boy, and everything you never got to have. And it's going to be so much fun making you watch him endure the same torture you did. Forcing you to relive every bit of your trauma. I think even a soulless wretch such as myself might be satiated with *that* pain."

He runs his tongue over his teeth, and begins to drag Helias backward, through the stream and toward the edge of the clearing where the moon is so close, it looks like you can dip a hand straight into the molten silver.

Toward where the Covinus must be hiding. It would make sense he knew of this clearing, knew of the place the Dead Prophecy would need to take place to break the curse. "Mirren," I say from the corner of my mouth, my voice full of warning, but she needs no prompting, her sharp mind already miles ahead of me.

"If you touch your power, I'll shoot the boy in the head," Avedis warns with relish. Helias bites his lip, his brave determination not to cry out tugging at my heart. "Allow us to leave with the coin, and perhaps he'll even survive."

There is no survival if Avedis makes it to the Covinus. Not for any of us. There's nothing but Darkness and slavery and destruction. Mirren doesn't look at me, but I don't need her to.

I know her heart as she knows mine.

And we'll both die before we leave the world to sink into the dark.

I burrow down into flame, thanking the dead gods for its versatility. For when flame burns, sometimes it is a magnificent show of light and power, while other times, it remains invisible, an unseen entity eating silently away.

Avedis snarls as the revolver in his hand goes red hot, and Mirren and I lunge. Her, for the path behind the assassin, and me, for Helias.

I grab the boy and shove him behind me, as wind begins to roar through the clearing. It slams against Helias and I with the force of brick wall, buffeting us farther from the dais. The sound of it is a scream against my ears, and the pressure presses against my sternum so hard I can't breathe.

The water from the stream rises to Mirren's call, turning to shards of ice that she sends flying toward Avedis. He halts them with a lazy flick of his wrist, before spinning them in midair and sending them shooting back toward her.

She ducks, raising a wall of water as a shield, and I use his momentary distraction to send spears of flame spiraling for his throat. Avedis laughs wickedly, dousing the spears with another wave of his hand.

I grit my teeth against the current of wind. We're wasting too much time. We have to get Avedis back under the dais or all the souls in the valley below will belong to the Covinus.

The ground begins to shake, the multitude of flowers rustling like they've suddenly come alive. And then, they begin to grow, spearing like vines to climb Avedis's legs. They wrap around his shins, and thread tight around his ankles, like the plants intend to pull him into the earth. Cursing, Avedis kicks out at them, slicing at their roots with his sword, but it only causes the plants to ensnare him faster.

Helias drops to the ground behind me, choking and

clutching at his throat as Avedis squeezes the air from his lungs with a wild snarl. The vines go lifeless, falling away from Avedis and curling up in dead stalks at his feet. He levels a terrifying gaze on Helias. Baring my teeth, I step in front of the boy and lower into a crouch.

"Enough," a sniveling voice says from behind me.

Avedis' wind instantly dies as the man who commands him steps into view behind me. The Covinus' white-blonde hair looks silver in the moonlight, his face pale and waxlike. He's no longer dressed in the odd navy jumpsuit of Similis, nor the regalia of the Dark Militia. Instead, he wears white robes, befitting a god of the old stories.

The garb's cleanliness is so disconcerting against the landscape of terror and fear he's sown, the blood being spilled in the valley below at his hand, that it takes me another full moment of staring at it before I notice who stands beside him.

Jayan. The councilman cocks his head dangerously, his watery blue eyes lit with fervor as if he's already imagining me on my knees before him. When he looks to the Covinus, there is no fear or reverence. "You can have the girl and the wind-wielder, but I want the boy," he says, nodding to Helias. Rage pools in my chest. Jayan sold out his city, his people, to lap at the crumbs of power around the Covinus. "And I want *him* dead," he snarls toward me.

It's all I need to snap out of my surprise. With lightning speed, I pull two daggers and send them flying toward him, racing after my knives with a bellow of rage.

But fury clouds my reasoning. *Emotion on a battlefield is death.* In my determination to punish the man who hurt Mirren, to end the threat against Nadjaa, I turn my back on Avedis.

Mirren screams, a harrowing, desperate sound, and the

world seems to blur around me—everything goes fuzzy except for the crack of Avedis' shot, spinning directly toward Helias' heart. And there's nothing I can do, no time to throw myself in front of it, to knock it off course.

Jayan's furious shout echoes somewhere in the fray, the prize he was so close to having in his possession, stolen from him. My breath freezes in horror as I whirl, helpless to do anything but watch another innocent be sacrificed to the Darkness.

A scream sounds, and I don't know whether it comes from inside me or outside me, as the bullet lodges neatly into Helias' chest.

But...it's not a chest.

And it is not Helias.

"DENVER!" His name is a roar pulled from the depths of me, more a primal sound than a word, as I lurch toward him. Denver stumbles, hands grappling weakly for the wound in his back. The one he took to protect Helias.

No, no, no. The word pulses in time with my heart, and for a wild moment, I consider squeezing my eyes shut, shaking my head until the images clear. Surely this isn't real, only a nightmare pulled from my worst fears. Denver is still down in the city, still watching over his people. He isn't here, bleeding at my feet.

The Covinus snarls in rage as Denver stumbles forward, his open mouth gasping soundlessly before he falls to the ground. Mirren screams again, and tears toward her father. She can heal him before it's too late.

But when he meets her gaze, the same sparkling emerald as his, and shakes his head, I know for certain everything is lost.

Grief, more powerful than any crest of fire, crashes over me. The tether that's held me in place since I was twelve snaps, and I cannot bear it. *No, no, no,* I think again, a faithful chant, but no words sound from my mouth.

"I saw Jayan coming this way, and I had to protect you." His voice is an echo of what it once was, weak and pained, as his blood stains the flowers around him. Mirren shakes her head wildly, and tears spill down her cheeks as she steps toward him once more. Then he says softly, "Balance, Mirri."

Her eyes widen as she understands what he asks of her. What she will have to sacrifice in order to bring peace to the world—

The only family she has.

That which was taken must now be given.

Denver sacrificed his city but found his soul and saved his daughter. And now, we all must give it up in service of the curse.

"I—I love you." Denver whispers, before his head lilts and his eyes go blank. Dead.

Flame explodes in my chest, and races to every inch of my skin until I burn outwardly with the same fury currently tearing my heart to shreds. *You are made to destroy.* Destroy the man who's dared to take what's mine, who's underestimated the depths of my rage. I'll shred him apart inch by inch, flay the skin from his bones for stealing the only father I've ever loved. The man who taught me what it was to be light in a land filled with dark.

I'll make both of them regret taking the man who tethered me to my humanity. Make them understand who I am without it. With a sound somewhere between a scream and a roar, I lunge at the Covinus.

He pushes Jayan in front of him, and the councilmen screams as my body, my fire, collides with his and we both go tumbling to the ground. I'm already to my feet, tearing toward the Covinus when a wall of water rises between us. Its fury shoves me and Jayan backward, looping us both around the middle and pulling us toward the dais. I snarl, trying to claw my way through it, to burn or evaporate it.

But it's immovable, inundating me in an icy deluge and snuffing out my flame. Pushing me back, back, back; away from the man who's stolen everything from me. I panic, and my movements become desperate and frenzied as I furiously slam my fist into the water.

Burn. I will *burn* him, kill him. Tear him apart.

But it's no use as Mirren's power gives me one more powerful push and I stumble backward onto the dais. The wind whips around us as Avedis is thrown down beside me, powerless against the ropes of ice tethered around his body.

I'll kill him, too—the pain of Denver's loss wrenches so deeply in my chest, it doesn't matter that Avedis wasn't in control. I'll gladly watch the life leave his eyes as I burn him from the inside out.

But Mirren has always been far better than me. She steps onto the dais, the world around us now reduced to a swirl of water so deep, it feels like we're underwater. I can no longer see the Covinus at all, no longer see the lifeless emptiness in Denver's eyes.

Tears pouring down her cheeks, Helias gripped in her arms, Mirren drops the coin between us.

And the world disappears.

CHAPTER
FORTY-SIX

Calloway

Nadjaa burns.

Smoke obscures the light of the moon, and the air is tinged red. With fire, with blood.

My heart cries out as we regroup at the Council House for the guard's final stand. Aggie's sacrifice bought us enough time to escape the pass, but with so many lives already lost and the size of the Covinus' forces, we're forced to abandon the majority of the city's edges to protect those who cannot protect themselves.

Both the water-wielders are dead, and in Mirren's absence, the Covinus' ships have landed in the bay. More enemy forces stream up from the docks, destroying everything in their path. We've lost track of both Denver and Jayan in the fray, so Rocher, now bloodied and injured, has taken over orders.

Don't kill. It only adds to their forces.

It's an impossible feat—to best a beast that cannot die. That reforms to attack harder and harder, as we grow ever weaker. I feel the guards' morale lagging, as comrade after comrade falls beneath enemy swords. Drowns in their waters, chokes on their air.

My arm has long gone numb as I slice through soldier after soldier. My throat is hoarse and painful, my voice reduced to no more than a whisper from the strain of screaming. And still, they come.

A water-wielder steps before me, and I almost laugh as she winds a small bit of water around my nose and mouth. I hold my breath, whirling with my blade, but my muscles have nothing left, and I list sideways. My lungs shriek, demanding air as I trip on my own feet, and stumble to the ground.

I'm just about to give in, when suddenly, the water relents.

When I blink up at the sky, it's to see Harlan's golden gaze staring back, offering me a hand. I take it shakily, staring down at the now-dead water-wielder, and wondering vaguely if perhaps I *did* drown, and this is some sort of dream.

Harlan smiles, the gesture so soft and tender it belongs nowhere near the gruesomeness of war. It belongs with me, protected and safe. "Harlan, you'll lose your soul here," I whisper weakly. "You shouldn't have come. You're going to die here." A sob chokes me, even as the battle rages around us. "We both will."

But there is no fear on Harlan's face as he raises his blade, the same one I taught him to use all those months ago. "Then my pieces will go to the Darkness with yours. Exactly where they belong."

His eyes shine and there is so much I want to say. But time—time has run out on us both, so I settle for a meaningful look that says it all.

I love you.

And then, as we both dive back into the swarm of bodies and weapons, the sound of a siren echoes from the bay, the song threading deep into the city.

The sound of Siralene.

Harlan's eyes flash to mine, pride and hope shining there like a beacon in the night, as cries of happiness, of relief, ring out among the Nadjaans.

Shina came. Because of my hope, my mercy, the Siralenis came.

Unbidden, tears pour down my cheeks as I heft my sword into the air, and bellow, "Keep hope!"

The words ring out over the Nadjaan guard, and echo through the city. The citizens who still fight for a dream of a better world. The words trickle through the arts district, the market and the business districts. They spread through the Barrow and the Hithe, down to the Siralenis who fight in the bay. They travel through the forest, to the Xamani who fight to protect a home that isn't theirs, but a belief that is.

Hope travels faster than the fire ravaging our home, and for a moment, I believe in it's power.

CHAPTER
FORTY-SEVEN

Mirren

Together, we spiral down, down, down.

There is no more dais, no more flowers.

We have spilled into the moon itself, tumbling endlessly into its light.

There is no beginning and no end, only a swirl of ethereal colors I know no name for. Ones I can touch with my fingertips, taste on my tongue.

Anrai finds my hand, as he always does. The bond of our souls shines so brightly, even in the eternal light of this place, it is what I hold onto as we free fall into oblivion.

My *other* bursts from me, the ancient power both grounding me into my body and tugging me outside myself. It mingles with heart of flame, with the song of wind, with the body of the earth. I hold the ruthless beat of Anrai's heart; I touch the soft wanderlust of Avedis; I thread my fingers through the innocent love growing in Helias.

Our power tethers us together, interwoven into our own universe. Wonderful and terrifying, the threads of the world tie together, spooling from our chests and into the cosmos.

And it is so beautiful I feel like crying, though there are no tears in this space between worlds. Tears are power, and all of our power is fed to the center of the universe. The light grows stronger on our power, pulsing as it devours.

My eyes sting as I stare at its magnificence, but I cannot look away. To miss one moment of it would be death, for it is the most wondrous sight in all the world—this world and any that would exist beyond it.

The light grows and in turn, we dim. The beat of Anrai's heart slows. Avedis' song calms to a hushed whisper. The flowers of Helias' soul begin to wilt. But the power around us does not lessen, because now, the light pulls from our most ancient depths. The place where the sea roars, and the land is in a constant state of upheaval. Primal, raw power that has no place for humanity. The beginning of the world and the end of it.

The power that sustains us. That keeps us tethered to nature and to ourselves.

The light is luminous now, its sheen more beautiful than anything I've ever seen.

But love demands all of us. The light cannot break through the Darkness unless it takes everything.

I understand now.

Understand the lines of time, the call of the world that brought us all together. That brought me to this space. I needed Similis to have the Keys imprinted in my heart, Community before self. I needed the Dark World to understand love and loss and Darkness. Every wound, every triumph, carved me into the person I need to be at this moment.

With a smile, I tear my hands away from Anrai's.

I feel the shift of his desperation, his anger, as he grapples to keep hold of me.

I push away, and the light dims, but only momentarily.

Because I have spent my life fearing I am too much. But I am perfectly enough.

The others do not have to give everything in them to break the curse of Darkness, because for this, I am perfectly made.

The others fade away and I feed my grief for them, my gratitude, my unwavering love into the light.

I thank the dead gods for my *other*, for both the joy and horror it brought me. I thank them for the life that brought me to this place. And when the last piece of me is pulled into the light, I breathe a sigh of relief, and think, *I am enough.*

And though there is so much light, I have given everything up to it, so there is none left in me. I, alone, am swallowed by the dark.

CHAPTER
FORTY-EIGHT

Shaw

Waking up is like climbing from the depths of an underwater cave. For a moment, my body rejects air like its forgotten how to exist and I curl into myself, expecting the light to burn right through my skin. Vicious and consuming.

But when I finally manage to blink my eyes slowly open, there is no more blinding power. Only the calm light of the moon shining over the vibrant colors of the clearing. Helias lies next to me, blinking owlishly up at the night sky as if he, too, expects to be incinerated.

Jayan is dead, his body sprawled unceremoniously over the stairs to the dais, his cloak billowing in the water of the stream.

I hear Avedis stir from somewhere near my head, and a warm wind whips through the clearing to wrap around his trembling body.

And as my own flame rises, the familiar heat lapping at the edges of my mind, icy dread fills my heart.

We still have our power. Which means something is very wrong.

We didn't break the curse. Or—

Fear squeezes my ribs as I remember Mirren suspended in the place between the stars, luminous and beautiful. As I remember her pulling away from all of us, intent on giving everything herself.

I shove myself to sitting, and whirl around to see her unconscious beside me, her fingers splayed out mere inches from mine. My heart stumbles over itself, and flame spears to my skin of its own accord, as images from the past layer on top of one another. Mirren on the ground in Yen Girene, pale and unresponsive as she broke her soul to save mine. Mirren on the ground in the gods chamber, her beautiful heart silent and still.

I lunge for her, unbridled panic and terror surging up my throat.

No, no, no. Not again. You will not go where I can't follow.

Not a prayer. A godsdamn command. To Mirren, to the fucking universe.

And when I touch her skin and warmth blooms beneath my fingertips, I swear to the Darkness, it's because I've willed it so. A relieved breath shoots out of me as I gather her in my arms, but it isn't until I press her to my chest, until I feel the stubborn beat of her heart, that some of the ice coating my soul begins to melt.

Her dark lashes flutter against the flushed rose of her cheek. And when they flicker open, a sob rises in my throat. Because though they are the same emerald they've always been, they no longer churn like the waves of the sea. They are stagnant. Mortal.

"Mirren," I whisper. In horror. In gratitude.

She gazes up at me, the look on her face unreadable as

she searches mine. And then she says, "It's okay, Anrai. You always tell me not to diminish myself, not to be less. I finally listened. I finally understood."

I want to tell her how sorry I am that the world has taken one more thing from her. I want to tell her how much I love her, how beautiful and brave she is. Instead, I crush my lips to hers. Power or not, her taste is the same, driving into my skull, drilling into my lungs. And when she kisses me back, the last part of me that remained somewhere in the ether between worlds settles back beneath my skin.

I stand, helping Mirren to her feet, as Avedis heaves. Mirren rushes to him, placing a soothing hand over his shoulder. The wind-whisperer flinches violently, curling away from her and into himself as he retches again. And though a part of my heart breaks for him, for the pain he must feel right now, another part of me howls in victory.

Because in reversing the curse, Mirren's given Avedis his soul back. Every soul the Covinus stole for himself, now returned.

I pull Helias to me, and wrap the boy tightly in my arms, breathing in the scent of him. Alive. Whole.

Mirren kneels before Avedis, her face glowing with the pure will that has nothing to do with her power but is innate to her soul. She gently cups his face, runs her fingers over the stubble of his chin, and forces him to look at her even as he tries to shrug her off.

"Keep your distance, my lady." His voice cracks. "I've taken enough from you. And now your power—"

Mirren presses her lips together and digs her fingertips into Avedis jaw, refusing to let him to look away. "It was given, Avedis. Not taken." An odd look crosses her face as theBasic words Aggie spoke to me so long ago echo from her mouth. *Given. Not taken. Therein lies the difference.*

The moment passes, and Mirren relaxes into herself once more. "The curse is broken, but the Covinus and the militia remain. Don't break, Avedis. Not yet. Our fight isn't over, and we need you."

The assassin stares up at her, dark eyes split wide open like wounds in flesh. Every emotion he hasn't felt in the past weeks spill from them, a dam of blood and heartbreak. But no tears fall. And after a moment of heavy breathing, Avedis nods.

His gaze flashes to mine, the mask of the assassin he wears so well firmly back in place. "Shall we?"

I grin wickedly, as Mirren helps Avedis to his feet. He sways slightly beneath the weight of his soul. A muscle works in his jaw, but after another beat, he manages to steady himself as he pulls his sword.

Four bonded—through trauma and blood and loss and love—we've changed the world.

Together, we descend in the city to save it.

∽

When we step from the path and around Aggie's cabin, rage and heartbreak pulse through me in equal measure. Smoke billows over the skyline and the sound of gunfire ricochets between the trees, where Nadjaan, Siraleni and Xamani alike fight.

The Dark Militia is here. In the heart of my city.

The citizens gathered in the meadow have scattered, no doubt spooked by the approaching army. I only hope in their fear, they haven't run directly into them. There's no sign of Harlan or Asa, but I don't allow my worry to take hold. Instead, I burrow into the abyss and let fire scorch my veins. It burns away any hesitation, anything other than the cool strategy of Shaw. Assassin. Protector. Me.

"Find Cal and Max," I order Avedis. To Mirren, I nod to Aggie's cabin. "Can you keep Helias safe here?"

The rest of my words go unsaid. *Can you keep yourself safe so I can protect Nadjaa?*

I expect her vehement opposition, her insistence that we stay together. But Mirren isn't well trained enough to hold her own in combat, and without her power, the idea of her in the midst of the chaos is the one worry my abyss cannot alleviate, no matter the burn.

She pats her bandolier and nods. "We'll be here when you get back."

The words have barely left her mouth when I pull her to me and kiss her. She opens for me immediately, her breath my breath, and everything in me longs to drag her into that cabin. To give back some of what's been taken from her, to get down on my knees and worship the heart that beats strong enough to stave off the Darkness.

But I let her go, because if I'm ever to be worthy of being hers, I cannot hide from the world around us.

Avedis and I tear through the woods surrounding Aggie's clearing. The fresh scent of pine and damp earth has been overwhelmed by the sharp smell of gunpowder and the iron stink of blood. Shouts careen off the trunks, and then disappear into the smoke-filled air. Terrified people streak through the trees, some Nadjaan, but most soldiers from the Covinus' army who've been woken from their soullessness.

I allow those ones to retreat.

But the rest, the ones that still fight for Darkness in the face of light, I incinerate on sight. Avedis and I blow through the trees like our own storm. Where we go, soldiers fall. And they do not rise.

And though our souls no longer fracture with each kill, something in me still dims with each death. *There are so many ways to lose your soul,* Denver had said, and now, I understand. The violence of battle, even when it's to protect what you love, will always leave a stain, curse or not.

But now, I don't have to drown in it. There is hope, a chance, to climb from the abyss and into the light.

Mirren did that. And now, I fight to ensure her sacrifice wasn't in vain.

Avedis squeezes the air from a pair of Dark Militia soldiers, just as I shoot flame at three others pursuing two *ahtan*. Their red *legatus* liveries blaze, and they all go down in screams of agony.

And as we pass, making our way steadily through the forest, whispers follow us.

Fire-bringer. Scourge of the Continent. Heir returned.

But the words are not dark, the names not filled with fear.

They are awestruck. They're *grateful.*

Soon, they're no longer whispers at all, but full-fledged shouts of victory. *He's come back,* they shout. *Shaw's returned to save us all.*

The shouts grow in veracity, their call heartening the Nadjaans, who begin to fight back with newfound fervor. Their shouts echo into the city proper, where the people of my home answer with rallying cries. The heart of the city pulses with strength, as the light that lay dormant in every Ferusian now pours from them in waves. Light planted by Denver, with his ideas of peace and beauty. Light hard won by Mirren. Light I'll give everything to protect.

The city burns and explosions rock different sectors under the Dark Militia's attack, but as Avedis and I streak through the streets, I feel heartened. Because I understand the balance Denver spoke of, the one sung of in Asa's stories, woven in my power itself. It is in the bones of the city, in the souls of its people—it is both darkest night and lightest sun, the potential to choose what makes both so beautiful. Like the carvings of the moon dais, each entity enhancing the other.

"Our friends are at the Council House," Avedis says, perfunctorily snatching the air from an oncoming soldier. "A large force is gathered there to infiltrate."

My lip curls in disgust. A remnant of my father's war philosophy, fed by the emotionless power vacuum of the Covinus. Destroy the innocents and you destroy everything worth fighting for. It's what the Covinus did in Similis, what my father did in Argentum and so many other villages. I push my legs faster, the abyss burning through my muscles. It imbues them with strength, with wild, vengeful power.

And when the Council House comes into view, that wild power explodes out of me. Max, Cal, Harlan, and a hundred others have been backed up to the front doors. Guns sound and the clash of steel rings out over the cobblestones. Cal shoots off arrow after arrow into the crowd of soldiers below. Max whirls and stabs, her usual graceful movements now sloppy and sluggish. Harlan fights at her back, his untrained jabs wild, but powerful as he severs straight through the sword arm of a soldier intent for Max.

"High ground," I mutter to Avedis, and I don't need to repeat myself before I'm lifted off my feet and hurtled into the sky. My stomach flips up into my throat and stays there until my feet are solidly on the roof of the Council House.

From up here, the battle appears so distant, the smell of the gore far weaker and the sounds of violence dimmed.

Avedis joins me, and together, we move to the edge of the building. I stare down, poised on the precipice of dark and light.

I could burn them all, and it wouldn't even cost me my soul. Wipe the earth clean of their evil ways, their selfish whims.

But wound around my soul is the soul of another. The woman who was strong enough to love this world, even after it had taken everything from her. Who gave up her power to uplift the powerless, who spilled her heart to give every soul a second chance.

I meet Avedis' gaze, and he nods once.

Lifting my arms, I burst into flame. Frightened shouts sound from below as the flame pours from me, from my heart. They crackle down the Council House like a wave of magma, until they seep into a circle surrounding every member of the Dark Militia. But rather than burning them instantly, I speak.

"You serve a man who has lived his life in the light," I begin, as Avedis magnifies my voice on the wind. I speak to all in Nadjaa, to any on the continent who would ever again seek to destroy the free city. "The Covinus does not know the Darkness as we do, does not know the alluring tenor of its call, the addictive taste of its nectar."

The screams begin to die down, as everyone watches the man who burns above them. The man who has chosen not to smite them on sight.

"You serve a man who uses the Darkness for his own gain but does not understand it. He doesn't understand how you've had to fight for everything you have, lest it be stolen from you. He doesn't understand the way we have scraped, and clawed, and bled. He would keep you in the Darkness forever, buried beneath its thrall."

I feel the gaze of Max and Cal, as caught up in the hushed whisper as everyone else. In all the city, there is only the crackle of fire and the sound of my voice.

"You know me as the Heir of the Praeceptor. As the Bringer of destruction and fire. I know the song of the dark better than anyone. But the curse has been broken, and now, we all have a chance to choose something different."

"If you choose the Darkness' call, so be it. You choose to serve a man who has spent a millennium hiding behind a wall, who has never in his life crawled for what he loves. But know who I am and what I will do to you for threatening my home."

The air is entirely still, tension sparking like electricity.

"It only takes one choice to change your soul. Choose to kneel now, to lay down your weapons, and one day, you will feel the warmth of light."

For a moment, no one moves, like the city is suspended in time. And then, one by one, my father's militia kneels before me. Swords clatter to the ground as their heads bend in submission, line after line of men and women who were raised in the Darkness with me, finally given the chance at goodness.

And the ones who take up arms are immediately devoured by flame. Their screams echo as they burn with the heat of their own choices.

My soul does not shatter with their deaths. Instead, it thrums with the song of freedom, of the darkness and light needed to protect such a vulnerable thing. I have spent my life ashamed of my savage dark, but here, in the heart of Denver's city, with Cullen's army at my feet, I finally feel the perfect balance inside me.

"Well done, friend," Avedis whispers beside me, but as I scan the horizon, my victory is snuffed out as quickly as a solitary ember.

Because though I have his army in my hands, the Covinus is not here.

CHAPTER FORTY-NINE

Mirren

The air inside Aggie's cabin is stuffy and dark as I barricade the door behind us. The room, the temperature of which is normally akin to the inside of a tea kettle, has a frigid, abandoned air to it. The hearth is cold, and though the meadow outside was arid, frost covers the small windows.

I shiver, wondering where Aggie's gone as I wrap Helias in a thick quilt, before going to light the stove. I busy myself with making tea and try not to acknowledge the gaping wound in my chest. It bleeds as freely as if I've split open an artery, flayed apart by loss. Of Easton. Of my mother. My father.

My *other*.

I'd seen Anrai's heart break for me and erected a wall of bravery and resilience. He could not mourn what I'd given, not when I needed him to protect the city. To finish what Denver and I started.

But now, in the silence of the cabin, the enormity of the emptiness inside me threatens to consume me. Never again will I feel entirely at home in the edges of my body, each space exactly as it is meant to be. Never again will I dance in the power of the sea, in the power of my own heart.

Never again will I be entirely whole.

My hand shakes as I light a match, and for a moment, I stare at it and wonder what it would feel like to drop it. To feel something beside the acute ache of my soul.

"Mirri," Helias says behind me, his voice soft and tentative.

Hurriedly, I light the stove and blow out the match. "Yes, Helias?"

"You protected the quakes in my belly from that light." It's a statement more than a question, and one that settles beneath my ribs as I realize he means his power. As I look back at him and see the way his eyes shine, the hollow grief suddenly becomes more bearable.

Helias hasn't ever been protected the way he should. Parents gone, government corrupt, Helias was born to a path of darkness and desperation. But now, because of what I've given, he has a chance for something different. Something better.

Just as my father always dreamed for me.

I smile softly at him. "I'll always protect you, Helias."

For the first time, the little boy allows me to take him in my arms. I breathe in the scent of him, of freshly turned earth and damp leaves, and thank the dead gods for the emptiness—for what I was able to give.

"Have you still not learned, Ms. Ellis?" A cold voice says from the darkest corner of the cabin. My blood freezes in my veins, and my fingers dig into Helias' warm skin, as the Covinus rasps, "Love is death."

Still holding the little boy, I breathe one word into his hair.

"Run."

~

Helias and I tear from the cabin, stumbling down the rickety wooden steps and out into the open meadow. Those gathered here earlier have moved on, down into the city where the fighting is thickest, but smoke, from campfires and guns alike, still clings eerily to the air. "Run, Helias!" I shout desperately, shoving the boy in front of me. "Run and don't stop until you find Shaw! No matter what happens, don't stop!"

Helias' face has gone pale, and for a terrifying moment, I think he'll argue. Stay to protect me as he hadn't been able to protect his parents. But I don't get the chance to see if he listens, because the Covinus and three of his Boundary men catch up to me. Souls now intact, it isn't the curse that drives them to follow his orders. It's their own hearts, their own greed.

The first grabs at my hair, and my scalp stings as he yanks me back. I'm already driving my dagger upward. *Aim for the organs,* Shaw had told me. The soldier grunts as my blade sinks into his stomach, and we both go stumbling to the ground in a tangle of blades and limbs. Even as the pommel grows slick in my hand, both with blood and sweat, I don't let go, instead, driving it further in and twisting.

I snarl as one of my arms is wrenched behind me by another of the Boundary men. He drags me off his comrade, and I swing wide with the blade, only for my wrist to be caught in midair by the remaining guard.

Fingers dig painfully into my skin as I thrash wildly. I kick at knees, the sick crunch of bone beneath my boot satisfyingly loud. But together, their grip is ironclad as they haul me toward the Covinus. He stands on Aggie's porch, calmly watching as both blades are pried from my hands, and I'm shoved to my knees at the base of the stairs. Spitting hair and gore from my mouth, I gaze up him darkly.

I am enough to heal the soul of the world. A man too weak to stand in darkness of his own making will not be the end of me.

As the Covinus stares down at me, his eyes flash black. I broke the curse, and healed the souls once damned to the Darkness. But as I stare up at the man who's stolen everything from me, I realize I did not heal them all.

His shattered soul is still evident in the black of his gaze, lethal against the chalky white skin of his face. The prophecy did not repair the pieces thrown to the far edges of the continent by the curse.

And I have nothing left. No power with which to heal it, to force him to atone for the millennia of terror.

"Foolish girl. You gave away the power of the world and now you're on your knees and ready to die. And for what, Ms. Ellis?" he says calmly, taking a smooth step off the porch. "You'll never again see those you love. The world will move on, and your name will be lost to the wind, and still, *I will remain.*" He leans down toward me and his mouth twitches, the miniscule movement the only sign of malice he'll show. But I know what rages beneath his surface, even if the feel of it has been muted by the waves of time.

"The world has never seen fit to gift me with magic or money or influence, but you know what it did give me? The ability to adapt. To take what I deserve. To tear it out with my teeth and destroy any who would get in my way. So, while you will die on this field alone, I will remain. And I will make it my mission to bathe the world you think you've saved in blood."

I will remain.

The Covinus means to provoke fear, hopelessness. But his words only stoke a deep well inside me, one that has nothing to do with my *other*. It is mine alone, the part that drew my power to me in the first place. In it are endless depths of rage, of love, of hope, of grief. Things the Covinus sought to extinguish, to cut down and ban, because he is terrified of their power.

He has always known the strength of such things. Perhaps it is time I remind him.

The Covinus ambles down the steps, and I let him draw closer, until his face is nearly touching mine. He appears skeletal in the moonlight, as he whispers, "I shall start with your fire-bearer. I shall tear him apart piece by piece and rebuild him into something dark and twisted that breathes only for me. I will make him immortal so that you never meet him in the afterlife, so that he spends eternity in agony." He lets out a sharp laugh and it raises goosebumps on my skin. "And that is only the beginning, dear Mirren."

"You should have given up your power to me," he snarls savagely. "You should have given me the piece of *her* I never possessed. At least then, you'd live on in spirit."

I lunge forward, digging my fingers into the Covinus' face. He lets out a shout of surprise, and stumbles backward as the guards behind me bellow orders. They claw at my back, wallop me with their swords. My jaw cracks with the force, and my forehead splits open, and still, I hold on.

I dig my nails into the Covinus' skin, even as blood trickles down my face. And then I reach for the path between us. The one the Covinus forged when he tried to take what's mine, I barrel down it to what waits on the other side. The meadow fades away along with the shouts of the guards, as I plunge into the murky depths, enveloped in the fathomless dark.

It is ancient here and ice cold, like the depths of a glacial ocean. But there is no life as there is in the sea—there is only death. Twisted, malevolent. It searches and devours and destroys.

One more soul to heal, Mirren. The words are ageless and raw, the sound of both the old gods' song and their world before it.

I hurtle forward, clawing through the viscous malice. *I have nothing left to heal it with. It was taken from me to break the curse.*

The voice seems to smile, the light of it felt even in these horrored depths. *Given. Not taken. Therein lies the difference.*

There is beauty in the giving. In loving so purely, so fiercely, that nothing is held back for yourself. I've learned this in Anrai, in Max and Cal. In my parents' dream and sacrifice. There is redemption in the selflessness, in the unbreakable circle of love—because what is given back is precious.

In loving, I have been gifted so much more. Life and laughter and beauty and pain.

Given, not taken.

I gave everything to heal the world without expecting anything in return. I'd sacrificed my power because I loved life so fiercely, and somehow, never realized that in doing so, I'd be blessed with far more.

I plunge into the deepest well of myself, down to where Shaw and I fell last spring. It's no longer only a raging sea: there is the warmth of flame, the wild current of the wind, the deep abundance of the earth. It wreathes around my head, intertwines around my arms, and settles over my heart.

Until I *am* the elements. Water, Fire, Earth, Wind. All mine to command.

With a bellow of power, I push them all into the inky black night of the Covinus. The black evil thrashes beneath my grip, but holding on has always been my strength, for better or worse. I've held on when I should have let go, held on when the world around me tried to tear me away. But now, holding on is what keeps me from tumbling into the Darkness, even as I feel the pieces of the Covinus' soul begin to pull back together.

Dug from beneath the northern wastes of Argentum, from the trees of the Nemoran. They emerge from the depths of the Tyrilian sea, from beneath the Storven's waves. They come from the mines of Yen Girene and the leaves of Baak. They spiral up from between the peaks of the Shadiil mountains, and the barren snow of the Xamani camps.

The Covinus screams in agony as I knit the fragments together with iron stitches. He has spent so long empty; it's made him weak. Spent too long without carrying the weight of his sins, and it has made him brittle.

With one final push, the last piece is unearthed from beneath the red square of Similis.

Memories flash up and down the bridge between us, a jumble of mine and his. *Iara's smile. Anrai's smile.* So many people hurt in the name of his hunger. They weave together until they are indistinguishable, a maelstrom of emotion, the power of which yanks me from the murky depths of the Covinus. It tosses me off of him, into the nearby grass.

Limbs weak with exertion, my arms shake as I struggle to push myself up. Blades of grass stick to my cheeks, but I hardly feel them as I watch the Covinus scream and writhe a few feet away.

His hair has returned to its original color, a muted brown, and he yanks wildly at the strands. He claws at his skin, blood blooming beneath his nails as he wails, the sound rife with madness.

And I feel no victory in his agony, only justice.

I push myself upward, my knees wobbling and nearly giving out as I come to stand over the Covinus. His eyes are no longer black or gray—they are a clear shade of cerulean, shined by tears of agony. He doesn't see me as I stare down at him, his gaze lost in the haze of memory. His breaths come in wheezing gasps, each one weaker than the last. "It is...too...heavy..."

"It is only your own soul, Aurelius," I whisper to him softly. "You must have the strength to bear it."

As the words leave my lips, the Covinus is crushed entirely by the weight of his own soul, drowned in the depths of his actions over a millennium. Too much death, too much destruction.

And not enough love to help shoulder the heft.

With one last whistling gasp, the Covinus is no more.

CHAPTER
FIFTY

Shaw

Any who refused to kneel are met with the justice of flame; with Cal's arrow; with Max's blade; with Avedis' wind. There is no darkening of our souls as we deal with the few flanks of soldiers clinging to their search for power, and no room for mercy for those who have refused their second chance, who spit in the face of Mirren's sacrifice.

We sweep through the city, eliminating any remaining threat, and then up into the wood. And when the ramshackle slant of Aggie's roof comes into view, my heart tumbles over itself at what we witness. Some scream in terror at the power that pulses in the meadow, cower from its inhuman song.

Mirren stands above the Covinus, his crisp white robes now sullied as he writhes in agony. And I feel none of the others' fear, only pure awe as the ocean bursts from her heart and threads through us all.

And she is so beautiful wrapped once again in the power that belongs to her, but she is also so much more. Because now the water is accompanied by the heated lick of my flame. The wild wind of Avedis. The curling, searching vines of Helias.

Mirren is not just the ocean. She is *everything*.

The beginning and the end, the ancient light that threatened to consume us all, come to rest inside her heart.

Beside me, Dark Worlders drop to their knees in reverence.

Nadjaan, Xamani, Baakaan, Seraleni. Anyone who has chosen to live, to embrace the second chance of a pure soul, falls to the ground in worship of the woman who loved them all enough to save them. The good and the bad and everything in between, Mirren loved them enough to see the beauty in all of it.

I walk slowly toward her as two of the Covinus' Boundary men are incinerated into dust in the light of Mirren's power, their remains turning to ash and floating away into the dawn-stained sky above the Averitbas Mountains.

But even the light of the rising sun is dimmed by the radiance pouring from Mirren. And perhaps a more sensible man would be wary of the otherworldly power, but I've never had any claim to sensibility. Born in the depths of the darkness, honed by the abyss of violence and desperation— I have only ever had claim to her. And even now, I am drawn closer by the luminous bond of our souls, hers and mine, forever entwined.

I stop a few paces from where she stands staring at the place where the Covinus used to be and kneel before her. Her eyes snap to me, and I'm left breathless when I witness the way the emerald-green churns. Her gaze no longer holds only the power of the sea—it swirls with the power of the universe, of time, of *everything*.

But I do not shy away from it. I only bow my head.

In reverence. In gratitude. In love.

Only when I feel her fingers gently pulling my jaw upward do I look at her once more and realize she's come to kneel with me. Because only Mirren would hold the power of the world in her palms and be humble enough to ever get on her knees.

I put my forehead to hers, breathing her in, our lips barely brushing. "You did it," I whisper against them, suddenly desperate to crush her to me. To bury myself inside her and revel in the power and light she's created. Because somehow, we made it through. We're alive and the world is whole and if I'm going to face a new world, I only want to do it with *her*.

"We did it," she whispers back.

The rest of the gathered forces fade away as we fall together into the grass, her warmth tangled around mine. Her tongue sweeps the seam of my lips and I think I'll combust from the fullness of what presses against my skin.

Because we have fought our way through fire and blade, blood and Darkness, to have this. And I know without question, I would do it all over again if it meant I had only this moment. One moment of beauty, of peace. Of loving without shadows or chains.

Of being together in the light.

CHAPTER
FIFTY-ONE

Mirren

We honor my father and Aggie on the edge of the sea.

The whole of Nadjaa gathers around the manor, their mournful silence punctuated only by the crash of waves against the onyx cliffs. Anrai lights the memorial pyres with a soft wave of his hand, before stepping back and interlacing his fingers with mine. Together, we watch them turn to smoke and ash.

And though tears blur my vision, it is not a heavy grief that consumes me as now it is shared with the whole of Ferusa. A somber acknowledgement held aloft by the hearts of many: acknowledgement of the sacrifice it took to bring my father's dream of a better world to life.

Anrai, Cal, Max. Helias, Avedis, and Harlan. Asa and the Xamani tribes. Nadjaa and the remaining leaders of the surrounding territories. The Siraleni fleet bobbing on the waves in the distance. All come to honor my father for what he built in the midst of the Darkness. A place of hope. A spark in the night.

With the curse broken, my father and Aggie's souls are

no longer damned to the Darkness. Max says they go to the underworld of her people Reignhata, to dance and feast with the goddess of death. Asa says the Xamani of old believed our spirits return to the earth, to nurture the magic and balance of all life.

Wherever they are, I hope Denver is with my brother and mother. That he gets a taste of the love he built his whole world around.

And Aggie—I hope she becomes the magic she's worshipped; that she becomes the lines of time and the waves of the universe. She'd get a kick out of being able to mess with us from beyond the grave.

Though grief and anger still plague me, the unfairness of what had to be given in order to move on, it's been made easier by those who've stood by me in the days following the battle of Nadjaa. My friends who have loved me through the loss, the hurt, who haven't balked from the work of sorrow, from the messiness of figuring out how to begin again. They've allowed me the grace to fall apart and lent their strength to aid in piecing me back together.

They've made me laugh. They've held me while I cried.

Once, I thought my heart poisoned by abandonment and twisted by loneliness. But with each passing day of their companionship, it expands and grows, no longer cramped or crushed.

When the last of the pyres have burned to ash, Anrai sends flame catapulting high into the sky. Sparks burst above Nadjaa in a great show of light and beauty, their shimmer illuminating the purple dusk. I watch it and think, *your love lives on. Rest easy, now, Father.*

After, the crowd dwindles, slowly retreating to the city proper for tonight's lunar celebration. It was a tradition my father resurrected from the days of the old gods, meant to celebrate his people's dedication to magic, to freedom, and to each other, and one we intend to carry on in his memory. Because even in the depths of dark, there is always something to be grateful for. To celebrate and cherish.

Tonight, all of Ferusa is invited. Those who embraced second chances, who will toil in the heat of the light to rebuild our destroyed cities. To embrace both the good of the Keys and the Dark World; to ensure the freedom and equality of everyone. To fight for the betterment of all.

Asa lingers long after his tribe, most of them gone to begin the process of packing their lives into wagons. Tonight, they will celebrate beside us, but tomorrow, they'll begin the journey back to their homelands. The Kashan approaches us with a broad smile, clapping Anrai on the back and pulling him in for a hug. "*Zaabi*," he says warmly. "I will expect you when the rivers begin to melt and the *nookta* bloom, yes?"

Anrai nods, his eyes crinkling as he returns Asa's smile. Though he'll stay with me in Nadjaa, Asa still believes Anrai has the blood of a Kashan, and as such, should be trained in the stories. And while Anrai was initially hesitant to accept Asa's invitation, his love of words and tales eventually won out. "I expect we'll be busy here for a while," Anrai replies, motioning vaguely to the manor and the city beyond. "But we'll try to make it to visit by spring."

Asa nods happily. "I have much to do, but I will see you at tonight's celebration. I do hope our new Chancellor is not too busy to bring some of her eclairs." He gives me a wink, before turning to descend down the lantern lit path.

Calloway collapses dramatically, sprawling his long legs out over the manor stairs. "I'm beat," he announces, swiping the back of his hand over his forehead in a tiresome manner. "I don't think I even have the energy for dancing."

"And yet, I'm certain you'll manage to find enough for debauchery, as you always do," Harlan says with a quiet smile.

Cal grins devilishly, tugging a rose-flushed Harlan into his lap and nuzzling his nose into the crook of his neck. "Well, when the debauchery looks like you do, who can blame me?" Harlan turns, if possible, a darker shade of red, appearing simultaneously horrified and immensely pleased.

Max plops herself down beside them with an annoyed eye roll. "Thank the gods for you Avedis, because otherwise, I'd be stuck watching these four make eyes at each other by myself." She sticks out her tongue like she's tasted something particularly foul, which only makes Cal laugh harder.

The wind-wielder, who has been uncharacteristically reserved in the month since the return of his soul, smiles at Max sadly. "Regrettably Maxwell, I'm afraid I must leave you to weather their affection alone."

Anrai's jaw tightens, his eyes narrowing on the assassin. "What are you saying, Avedis?" he asks slowly.

Avedis meets his gaze, and though those dark eyes flicker with the song of the wind, there is something mournful about them. Lonely. A howling breeze above an abandoned moor. "While regaining your soul helped you find your way out of the dungeon, friend, it has locked me inside mine." His shoulders rise and fall with a slow breath. "I believe I need some time on my own...to learn the way out."

I take both Avedis' hands in mine and gaze up into his handsome face. His hair moves around his head like a playful halo, his skin pale and wan in the moonlight. The large scar tugs at his eyebrow, up his forehead, and disappears into his hair line. I imprint all of it to memory.

Because I understand I must let him go, just as I've had to with so many things. My friend through everything, who only ever believed in my strength and power. Avedis never once questioned me, only trusted that I knew what needed to be done. And now, I must do the same for him. Because as much as I want to clutch him to me, to never give him up, it wouldn't be fair. He is haunted by what he's done, by Nadjaa itself—by my face. And I need to grant him freedom from it. At least for now.

My throat grows thick, and tears sting my eyes. "Take as long as you need, Avedis. Travel as far as you have to. But know where your home is." The assassin looks away from me, tears clinging to his thick lashes. I press my hand to his heart fiercely. "Here. With us. Whenever you're lost, we'll always be your home."

The assassin nods once and swallows hard, before stepping smoothly out of my embrace.

"You aren't leaving before the party," Cal insists hotly, glaring at the wind-wielder as though he's suggested something sinister. "Or I will declare *you* the fun-killer. I'm going to be stuck in Similis for gods know how long...I demand a good time before I leave."

Though his words are indignant, Calloway's smile is the happiest I've ever seen it. Harlan, whose love for Similis has never waned, is determined to go back and help rebuild the Community. To lift up the good and reshape the bad. And Cal, whose home is wherever Harlan is, has decided to accompany him.

Avedis laughs softly. "I suppose I can stay for one more night, as every party is in sore need of my exquisite dancing and social repertoire." He bows dramatically. "I shall see you at the festival."

My heart grows heavy as I watch the shape of him slip

into the shadows of the manor path and then disappear. Something tells me we won't be seeing Avedis tonight. And that it'll be a long while before we do again.

Cal and Harlan are next to head down the manor path, arms wrapped around waists, heads nodded toward each other. They disappear in the direction of the city, where life awaits.

Max pulls both Anrai and I into a hug, squeezing the back of my dress tightly in the ball of her fist. "It was a beautiful ceremony," she says, her words tight even as she smiles. "He would have loved it."

I nod because even now, a month later, I have not been able to find the words. Words that encompass gratitude and grief in equal measure. But a nod is enough for Max, perhaps because she feels it, too. Denver's mistakes wrapped up in his final act of redemption. His dream come true when he isn't here to see it.

With one last hug, Max hollers for Cal and Harlan to wait up and chases them both down the path, leaving Anrai and I on the manor steps alone. He is as handsome as ever in a crisp white shirt and simple black pants, and my gaze snags on the glimpse of shimmering bronze skin left exposed by his open collar, now decorated with a whorling tattoo that trails from his collarbone, over his shoulder to rest on the scar above his heart. An acknowledgement and tribute of the things that have shaped him, the pain and the beauty.

The manor rises up behind him, the construction left half-done by Denver's death and the destruction of Nadjaa, but the contrast of it—the beauty layered atop ruin— frames Anrai perfectly.

We are all part beauty, part ruin.

He follows my gaze, before stepping toward me with a

soft smile. "Tell me, Lemming. Tell me what you want, and we'll make it so."

I almost laugh at the hopeful sentiment, but a different part of me feels like crying. Shaw was never a hopeful man, but it is easier now to allow it room without the suffocating weight of the Darkness. Now, time stretches out before us, endless and unencumbered.

Tilting my head, I shoot him a cheeky grin. "I thought you knew exactly what I want."

He watches my teeth dig into my lower lip, and his eyes spark at the challenge. "Oh, I do. But it's polite to pretend you know yourself better than I do." Anrai prowls toward me, his feline movements lighting an instant heat in my veins; his predatory gaze sparking fire in my chest. *Mine. His.*

He pretends to think as he slowly draws closer. "You want to stay in Nadjaa for the rest of the winter and help Evie."

The baker and councilwoman was voted in as Chancellor three days after the battle, and she's risen splendidly to the occasion. And though her new responsibilities would overwhelm most, Evie has still taken it upon herself to give Helias a new home. To love him like one of her own, without fear of his power or the pain he's endured.

It's been amazing to see the little boy begin to smile again, to run and laugh and jump like other children.

"You'll help her with the boring part of politics, and ensuring Nadjaa is stable. No one would dare cross a woman who holds the power of all four elements." Anrai laughs, with a wiggle of his dark brow. "And I'll spend my time keeping my promise to Helias to train him."

"*After* his school lessons, of course."

"Of course," Anrai agrees, stepping up so that he's one

stair below me. Even with the height advantage of the steps, I still have to look up to meet his gaze. "And during the day, I'll rebuild the manor."

My gaze snaps to his in question, and his smile grows wider, more wicked, as he steps up onto my stair, crowding me backward. My powers rise inside me like he's called them all to the surface, and the heady feeling threatens to send me into a dizzying oblivion. I still haven't gotten used to the pure intensity of it all, the way each element, so different at their base, somehow satiates the others.

Anrai runs a finger down the bare skin of my arm, watching intently as shivers rise to his touch. "We're going to travel the world, Lemming. We're going to climb mountains and eat a thousand different kinds of food and dance to every kind of music there is. We're going to see the sun set on foreign shores and swim in new oceans. But you want a home to come back to, and I'm going to make sure you have it."

I thread my arms up around his neck, tugging him closer. Pressing the hard ridges of his chest against the soft curves of mine. "And you? What do you want?"

The pale blue of his eyes turns silver in the moonlight, the flames like molten ore. "I have what I want," he replies, the low growl of his voice sparking beneath my skin. "You are my home. You are my balance. You are my light. I need nothing else."

He presses his lips softly to mine, and gods, I'll never get used to the desperate way he kisses me. Like I truly am the only thing he needs to survive. Everything about Anrai has always been wild and fierce, and as my mouth opens to him, I revel in the absolute freedom of it. Because balance is a delicate thing and though the curse has been broken, the fight doesn't end. There will always be those who threaten it in the name of more, always those who would exploit it.

But with Anrai by my side, there is nothing we can't face together.

I tangle my fingers in the thick waves of his hair, and his tongue sweeps along mine as he angles closer. For a moment, there is nothing but us—not the lunar celebration or the grief of loss. Just Mirren and Shaw, entangled.

Anrai pulls back, his breaths coming rapidly as he presses his forehead to mine. "Be mine forever, Mirren. I'll get you the arbor and the dress and the party later, but right now, marry me. I promise myself to you until the Darkness' final calling. My heart, my soul, my body, all of it is yours from now until the end of time."

I remember the first time I smiled at him, sopping wet and slippery in the middle of the cliff pond. It had felt wondrously light and beautiful, and I'd thought it was simply because it was new. But as I smile at Anrai now, happiness shining unrestrained, I realize how breathtaking each one is. Every smile, every laugh. How they edge the bitter parts of life to shine brighter.

"We were forever from the first stab wound, Anrai."

His laughter rings out in the sea air as he takes me in his arms and carries me into the manor. And I devour the sound of it greedily: the sonance of his happiness. Anrai deserves every moment of it, every soft thing he's been denied.

And I can't wait to live it with him.

We come together tenderly this time. Slow, languid worship of skin and curves. Dizzyingly deep kisses and long, unhurried strokes. And when I come apart around him, his eyes still on mine, he is there to hold the pieces. To cherish them.

And later, he holds me as we dance and drink and laugh and cry. Our family spins around us, as all of Ferusa celebrates the end of the curse. Music pulses and weaves through the night air, and laughter tinkles through the crowd.

We dance until the moon sets, and the sun begins to edge over the snow-capped peaks.

And when morning's rays spill over the city, we greet the light with hope.

The end.

PRONUNCIATION GUIDE

Mirren: *meer-inn*

Anrai/Anni: *on-rye/onn-ee*

Calloway: *cal-oh-way*

Avedis: *uh-vee-dis*

Gislan: *giz-lon*

Luwei: *loo-way*

Sura: *soo-ruh*

Asa: *ay-suh*

Evie: *ee-vee*

Akari Ilinka: *uh-carr-ee ill-inn-kuh*

PRONUNCIATION GUIDE

Covinus: *coh-vin-us*

Praeceptor: *pray-sept-or*

Legatus: *lay-got-us*

Xamani- *zah-mon-ee*

Similis/Similian: *sim-ill-iss/sim-ill-ee-an*

Nadjaa: *nod-juh*

Argentum: *are-gen-tum*

Castellium: *cass-tell-ee-um*

Siralene: *seer-uh-leen*

Dauphine: *doe-feen*

Ashlaa: *ahsh-luh*

Yen Girene: *yen geer-een*

Nemoran: *nem-orr-enn*

Yamardu: *yah-marr-doo*

Dahiitii: *dah-heet-ee*

Zaabi (Xamani word for friend): *zah-bee*

PRONUNCIATION GUIDE

Iara: eye-are-uh

Aurelius: or-rel-ee-us

Helias: hell-eye-us

ACKNOWLEDGMENTS

To every reader who's stuck with me this long—who fell in love alongside the characters, who let your hearts break with theirs—who took a chance on an unknown indie author: from the bottom of my heart, thank you. Every page read, every review, every message, every share...you've all kept me going on the days it felt too heavy.

And man, there were so many times I thought this book would swallow me whole. Shanner, thank you for keeping me from drowning in my own doubt. I talk a lot about souls in this series, and it's because mine has found its mirror in you.

Christin, my alpha reading, content hustling, book carrying, kick-me-in-the-ass hype woman, this one's for you. You entertain my nonsense, answer my endlessly repetitive questions about people that don't exist, and always tell me like it is, and I am so, so thankful for all of it. Olivia, I don't know what I would do without our unhinged driveway brainstorming sessions, and coffee writing dates. Thank you for all your feedback.

To Laura and Rebecca, thank you for your enthusiasm. The story wouldn't be what it is without your feedback and friendship. To every member of my street team—I couldn't do any of this without you all. Thank you so much for your time, excitement, and work. Thank you to Sarah at Okay Creations for another gorgeous cover. You blow me away every time.

Big thanks to my editor Tiarra Blandin. You always see through the mess to the true story beneath, and your eye for detail has made the trilogy what it is.

Mama, thank you for your kind heart. Dad, thank you for teaching me how to dream. Kiki, I love you. To my family and friends whose support has never wavered, thank you all.

Ez and Lu—you made writing this book a million times harder, and a million times more worth it. You're both the light of my life, and your fearlessness inspires me every day. I love you to the moon.

And to Jas, the reason any of this is possible. And not only because of the work you put in every day for our family, but because of how well you love me. Thanks for keeping me laughing, for never making me feel bad for fidgeting, for preventing me from dying of dehydration, and for how patiently you weather the ups and downs of living with a writer. You're my favorite.

About the Author

Amarah Calderini grew up in the Rocky Mountains, and spent her time imagining magic living in the shadows of the peaks. She writes fantasy imbued with equal parts magic, angst, and steam, featuring strong yet flawed heroines and the fierce-hearted men who love them. When not writing, she can be found soaking up the sun and singing along to the same dramatic songs she's listened to since high school. She currently lives in Colorado Springs, Colorado with her husband, two children, and their geriatric German Shepherd.

Check out my website for my newsletter and up-to-date info about what's next.

www.amarahcalderini.com

- facebook.com/authoramarahcalderini
- x.com/amarahcalderini
- instagram.com/amarahcalderiniauthor
- amazon.com/author/amarahcalderini
- goodreads.com/amarahcalderini
- tiktok.com/amarahcalderiniauthor

Also by Amarah Calderini

Want to learn more about Shaw and Max? Join Amarah's newsletter here and get their story, Storm of Iron, for free now.

https://dl.bookfunnel.com/ofwosd9p4i

Printed in Great Britain
by Amazon